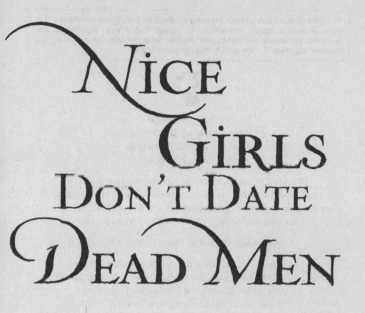

Nice Girls Don't Date Dead Men

MOLLY HARPER

Pocket **Star** Books
New York   London   Toronto   Sydney

The sale of this book without its cover is unauthorized. If you purchased this book without a cover, you should be aware that it was reported to the publisher as "unsold and destroyed." Neither the author nor the publisher has received payment for the sale of this "stripped book."

Pocket **STAR** Books
A Division of Simon & Schuster, Inc.
1230 Avenue of the Americas
New York, NY 10020

This book is a work of fiction. Names, characters, places, and incidents either are products of the author's imagination or are used fictitiously. Any resemblance to actual events or locales or persons, living or dead, is entirely coincidental.

Copyright © 2009 by Molly Harper White

All rights reserved, including the right to reproduce this book or portions thereof in any form whatsoever. For information address Pocket Books Subsidiary Rights Department, 1230 Avenue of the Americas, New York, NY 10020

First Pocket Star Books paperback edition September 2009

POCKET STAR BOOKS and colophon are registered trademarks of Simon & Schuster, Inc.

For information about special discounts for bulk purchases, please contact Simon & Schuster Special Sales at 1-866-506-1949 or business@simonandschuster.com

The Simon & Schuster Speakers Bureau can bring authors to your live event. For more information or to book an event contact the Simon & Schuster Speakers Bureau at 1-866-248-3049 or visit our website at www.simonspeakers.com.

Cover design by John Vairo Jr.; cover illustration by Gene Mollica

Manufactured in the United States of America

10 9 8 7 6 5 4

ISBN 978-1-4165-8943-3
ISBN 978-1-4391-6450-1 (ebook)

Critics adore Molly Harper's
NICE GIRLS DON'T HAVE FANGS

A *Romantic Times* TOP PICK for April 2009!

"An absolutely hilarious first book in what is sure to be an amazing new series. Jane is an everygirl with a wonderful sense of humor and quick sarcasm. Add in the mystery and romance and you have your next must-read novel!"

—*Romantic Times* (4½ stars)

"Hysterical laughs are the hallmark of this enchanting paranormal debut. . . . Harper's take on vampire lore will intrigue and entertain. . . . Jane's snarky first-person narrative is as charming as it is hilarious, retaining enough humanity to connect instantly with readers. Harper keeps the quips coming without overdoing the sarcasm."

—*Publishers Weekly* (starred review)

"Harper arrives on the scene with a chuckle-inducing, southern-fried version of Stephanie Plum's 'the Burg'. . . . Quirky characters, human and vampire alike."

—*Booklist*

. . . and these bestselling authors love it, too!

"Charming, sexy, and hilarious. . . . I laughed until I cried."

—Michele Bardsley, bestselling author of
Over My Dead Body

CALGARY PUBLIC LIBRARY

DEC 2015

"Wicked fun that had me laughing out loud . . . Molly Harper has a winner. . . . I read it all in one delicious sitting!"

—Candace Havens, bestselling author of
Dragons Prefer Blondes

"A hilarious new twist on vampire romance. . . . A brilliantly written adventure chock full of clever prose, hilarity, and hunky vampires!"

—Stephanie Rowe, national bestselling author of *Ice*

**Don't miss the first hilarious
Jane Jameson novel by Molly Harper**

NICE GIRLS DON'T HAVE FANGS

Available now from Pocket Star Books!

For David, who puts up with a lot.
Best. Husband. Ever.

Acknowledgments

Thanks go to my husband, David, who encouraged me when I needed it, listened to me dissect every little detail of the publishing process when I was excited, and, finally, told me to stop whining and start working when I was slacking.

My eternal gratitude to Michele Bardsley and her army of fellow paranormal romance authors, who taught me the secret art of book promotion. Long live the League of Reluctant Adults. To Brandi Bradley, for her endless patience and support. And to my new friend, Rachel Smith, always gracious, always snarky, always willing to drive twenty minutes for coffee. To my sister and personal archivist, Manda, thanks for putting up with so many phone calls. To Mom and Dad, thank you for everything that you do for me. To superagent Stephany Evans, my gratitude for sticking with me through so many drafts. You are some sort of copyediting saint. To Jennifer Heddle and Ayelet Gruensphect, who are always willing to answer silly questions and have made this process so much fun, please know how much I appreciate you.

With foot and paw planted in the human and animal worlds, were-creatures mix techniques from both cultures to secure relationships. This can lead to lifelong happiness or a very confused potential mate.

—*Mating Rituals and Love Customs of the Were*

"I can't do this."

"Jane."

"It's just wrong," I whimpered. "It defies the laws of nature, the thin line that separates good and evil."

Zeb rolled his eyes and snapped the bridal binder shut. "It's just a dress, Jane."

"It's a puce dress, Zeb."

"Jolene's getting it in peach." He grunted, clearly at his limit in dealing with whiny undead bridal-party members. "Why are you being so difficult?"

"Why is your fiancée insisting that I dress like Naomi from *Mama's Family*?"

"It's not that bad," Zeb insisted.

"Not that bad?" I opened the binder and pinned the offending picture with my finger. The model's defiantly blank expression could not mask her embarrassment at wearing this sateen nightmare. It was off the shoulder, with a wide ruffle of retina-burning color that gathered at the cleavage with a fabric cabbage rose. The traditional butt bow actually connected to what can only be described as a waist lapel.

Despite not having that many girlfriends, I had been a bridesmaid three times in ten years. Apparently, I was tall enough to "match" the rest of the bridal party for Marcy, my college roommate from freshman year. My sophomore roommate, Carrie, had a cousin who had the nerve to get pregnant, and I just happened to fit the cousin's abandoned bridesmaid dress. I'm pretty sure my junior roommate, Lindsay, only asked me because she wanted "plain" bridesmaids. She said something about not wanting to be outshone on her big day.

I was thankful to get a private room my senior year.

My sister, Jenny, never even considered making me a bridesmaid. Ironically, her reason for not asking me—not liking me—resulted in this inadvertent and certainly unintentional kindness.

I'd suffered butt bows. I'd carried those stupid matching shawls that never stayed on past the ceremony. I'd worn Mint Sorbet, Periwinkle Fizz, and Passionate Pomegranate—all of which translated into "hideous $175 dress with shoes dyed to match, neither of which you will wear again."

And now, Jolene McClaine, the betrothed of my best friend, wanted me to wear the ugliest dress of them all. Jolene and Zeb had met at the local chapter of the Friends and Family of the Undead, where Zeb had sought help after my new undead condition left him even twitchier than usual. It was your basic love story. Boy meets girl. Boy dates girl. Girl turns out to be a werewolf. Boy and girl get engaged and slowly drive me insane.

In a way, I brought the two of them together, which meant I had no one to blame for this hoop-skirted fiasco but myself. I knew the whole point of having bridesmaids was dressing them like circus folk so you would look better by comparison. But this was beyond the pale. I'd be lucky if angry villagers didn't pelt me with rotten produce.

"This is why I wanted to go shopping with you!" I cried, flopping back on the couch with the boneless petulance of a teenage orthodontia patient.

"Well, the Bridal Barn closes at about three hours before sunset, Jane. So unless you're willing to risk bursting into flame just to exercise your control issues over a stupid dress, I think we're out of options."

"Hmmph."

I hadn't been a vampire for very long, so sometimes I forgot about the limitations of my condition and the pains Zeb took to avoid throwing said limitations in my face. It didn't mean I was going to wear that monstrosity of a dress, but I would at least stop giving Zeb a hard time. I had developed a nasty habit of needling Zeb since he'd started planning his wedding. Zeb had been my best friend since . . . well, forever. I was used to having his undivided attention. Of course, he was used to me breathing and eating solid foods. We'd both had to make adjustments. He was just much better at them.

It seemed doubly cruel to pick on Zeb now. While

some members of Jolene's family were thrilled that she was marrying a nice guy with a stable income and his own home, there were several uncles who declared the union "clan shame,"the werewolf version of a *shandeh*.

Werewolves are the most highly evolved were species. They have the most regular change cycle and the most complete, dependable changes. Being natural pack animals in both forms, they also have the most stable social hierarchy. There is an alpha male mated to the female of his choice, who becomes the alpha female. While the lesser clan members have property rights and general free will, all major decisions must be filtered through the alpha couple, particularly the alpha male. Everything from mate selection to business management has to be deemed for the good of the pack.

Jolene's family was one of the first to settle in Half-Moon Hollow. Their farm was now home to the clan alpha couple, Lonnie and Mimi McClaine, their three children, eighteen aunts and uncles, and forty-nine cousins. Jolene was the last unmarried female in her generation, which is not to say she had been without proposals. She'd been courted by scions of several prominent werewolf clans. Her own cousin Vance—a tall fellow who reminded me of Jethro from the *Beverly Hillbillies,* only more broody— had made several failed bids for her paw since she'd turned seventeen. But it was my gangly, goofy, incurably human BFF who stole her heart away.

Lonnie had to tamp down Vance's open griping about Jolene's engagement with a visit to Vance's trailer. It was the werewolf equivalent of a trip to the woodshed. Vance responded by driving to Zeb's house and peeing in his yard. Apparently, you have to be a male or a wolf to understand what an insult this was. In a werewolf pack, you cannot interfere with the mate choice of a clan fellow. You cannot intentionally harm that werewolf's chosen mate. You are not, however, required to help that person should he find himself in a life-threatening situation. Somehow, Zeb had managed to stumble into several such situations in the few months since he'd been engaged to Jolene. He'd had several hunting "accidents" while visiting the McClaine farm, even though he didn't hunt. The brakes on his car had failed while he was driving home from the farm—twice. Also, a running chainsaw mysteriously fell on him from a hayloft.

He would never get that pinkie toe back.

Jolene insisted that her relatives were just being playful. I insisted that Zeb not venture out to the McClaine farm without a vampire escort, which certainly hadn't improved his stance with the future in-laws. Despite the grudging acceptance they offered Zeb, most of the clan was distrustful of vampires. Some, in fact, wore vampire fangs around their necks, next to the gold-plated charms that spelled out their names.

On the other side of the aisle were Zeb's parents, Ginger and Floyd, and they weren't exactly thrilled about the wedding, either. Mama Ginger had been planning my wedding to her son since we were kids. Apparently, the image of Zeb coming home to my pretend kitchen carrying a briefcase made of newspaper was permanently burned into her cortex. She figured that having known me since I was six and seen multiple examples of my being firmly planted under my own mama's thumb, I was the only acceptable candidate for a potential daughter-in-law. For my last living Christmas, she'd given me a Precious Moments wedding planner with my and Zeb's names already filled in.

Mama Ginger saw the world as it should be, according to Mama Ginger. And when something didn't conform to that vision, she went to drastic lengths to correct it. I didn't know what made her think she had the right. It may have had something to do with all the chemicals she inhaled at her not-quite-licensed kitchen beauty shop. Just to give you an example, Mama Ginger could not fathom that I would go to senior prom with anyone but Zeb, so she told several of the mothers at her salon that I was being treated for a suspicious rash. This fixed it so no boy at our high school would go anywhere near me with a corsage. With no other eleventh-hour options, Zeb and I ended up going together. Mama Ginger kept the pictures in a place of honor on her mantel.

As Mama Ginger couldn't have her say in choosing the bride, she'd decided to make planning the wedding as unpleasant as possible. She'd objected to the wedding date, saying it conflicted with her bingo night. Every plan Jolene had was dismissed as alternately "trashy" or "too highfalutin." Mama Ginger was also incredibly insulted when Jolene politely refused the Precious Moments bride-and-groom cake topper she'd saved for Zeb's wedding.

Precious Moments. *Gah.* I could rip a man's spinal column out through his nose, and I still found those things frightening.

Zeb's father, Floyd, had expressed little interest in the

wedding after he found out there wouldn't be a Velveeta fountain or a big screen showing the scheduled UK basketball game.

So, the reception was going to be fun. As much fun as one could have while dressed as Satan's tea cozy.

The Naomi Harper bridesmaids' dresses were a concession to the McClaine family tradition of renting formal wear from Jolene's aunt Vonnie's dress shop, the Bridal Barn. Vonnie made all of the dresses herself, using three patterns, all of which ended up looking like a circa 1982 pattern called "Ruffles and Dreams."

"I know, Janie, I know it's ugly," Zeb said, his big doe eyes all guileless and earnest. Dang it, I always buckled under the baby browns. "It is the world's ugliest dress. Of all the dresses you will ever wear, this is the one your body may reject like a faulty organ. As soon as I get back from the honeymoon, I will help you build the bonfire to burn this dress. But I'm asking you as my closest friend in the entire world, will you please just wear the stupid dress for one day? Without whining? Or describing it? Or making Jolene feel bad? Or pissing off Jolene's cousins?"

"Any more conditions?" I grumbled.

"I reserve the right to make addendums," he said, one sandy-blond brow arching its way up to curly hair of the same shade.

"What kind of kindergarten teacher talks like that?" I groused. Engagement had changed Zeb. He was more aggressive, more mature, partly from having to defend himself in life-threatening situations. Unfortunately, he was being more aggressive and mature with me, which sucked.

"What kind of children's librarian takes a job at an occult bookstore?" he countered.

"Vampire." I pointed to my chest. "And I'm not a librarian anymore. When they fire you, they kind of take the label, too."

Zeb's smile thinned as he blinked owlishly and pressed his fingers to his temples. He took a pill bottle out of his pocket.

"You OK?"

"Yeah." He sighed. "I've just been getting these headaches lately."

My pessimistic brain flashed on possibilities including clots and tumors. Batting down small flares of panic, I asked, "Have you seen a doctor?"

"Yeah. He said they're probably stress-related."

I poked a finger at the wedding binder. "I can't imagine."

"Wedding planning is stressful, even when you're not marrying into a family with mouths full of fangs and guts full of burning hatred, both of which are aimed at you," Zeb muttered as he dry-swallowed two Tylenol. "On a brighter note, where's your ghostly roommate?"

"Out," I said of my great-aunt Jettie, who had died about six months before I was turned and had been pleasantly haunting me ever since. "With my grandpa Fred again. They're becoming quite the hot and heavy couple."

"I didn't realize ghosts roamed around so much," he said. "Where do they go?"

"As long as it keeps me from seeing two deceased old people getting all touchy on my couch, I do not care."

He grinned. "That's so gross."

"Tell me about it." I grimaced. "I'm working extra shifts at the bookstore, unpaid, just to get out of the house. I keep walking into rooms and finding them . . . *guuuuh*. And speaking of the store, we need to table the dress negotiations for now. My shift starts in about an hour. We're expecting some ancient Babylonian scrolls that Mr. Wainwright found on eBay, so he's really excited. He thinks they may have been used in a summoning rite."

"So, you purchased ancient Babylonian texts, which may or may not call forth Gozer the Destroyer, on eBay?" Zeb asked. He cocked his head and gave a goofy grin. "You know, a year ago, I would have thought you were kidding."

I shrugged, pushing the dreaded bridesmaid's dress photo from my considerable field of vision. "And yet . . ."

I scooped up the ringing phone, knowing before I pressed it to my ear that it would be my mother. I didn't use my spiffy new mind-reading powers or anything. Mama called every night before my shift to make sure I was careful on the three-step walk from my car to the bookstore. She tended to "forget" that I now had superstrength and could twist any prospective mugger into a pretzel.

Mama had responded to my coming out as a vampire with the traditional stages of grief. She just got stuck at denial. She had decided to ignore it completely and pretend it away. She brought two frozen pot pies over to my house each week to "help me out with meals," which was handy, because I needed something around to feed the ever-ravenous Jolene. Mama dropped by during the day, then got upset when the vampire "sleepy-time" instinct kept me from chatting. It was as if she thought I could change my mind about being a vampire and give back my membership card.

"I have some bad news, honey," Mama said as I picked up the phone. She'd long since parted with the niceties of phone greetings. After a dramatic pause, she said, "Grandpa Bob passed last night."

"Awww," I moaned. "Another one?"

This may seem like a strange, even cold, reaction. But you have to understand my grandma Ruthie's marital history. She'd been widowed four times, via milk truck, anaphylactic shock, spider bite, and lightning strike (the lamented, aforementioned Grandpa Fred). I wrote a poem titled "Grandpa's in an Urn" in fifth grade. I had to spend a lot of time in the guidance counselor's office after that.

I loved Bob. Despite not being my actual grandpa or even a step-grandpa yet, Bob had always been nice to me. But he was engaged to Grandma Ruthie for five years and had chronic conditions of the heart, lungs, and liver. He had survived longer than expected.

"Your grandmother says there was some sort of mix-up with his medication." Mama sighed. I could practically hear the cap from her "nerve pills" rattling loose.

Knowing this would take a while, Zeb got out my blender to begin another batch of experimental "Jane shakes." He'd been using a combination of condiments and dessert toppings to make the synthetic blood a little bit more like the human food I missed so much. My current favorite was Faux Type O mixed with a little bit of cherry syrup and a lot of Hershey's new Blood Additive Chocolate Syrup: "The pleasant sensation of chocolate without the unpleasant un-dead side effects!" That was an excellent selling point con-sidering those side effects were the vomiting and agony that came with vampires trying to digest solid foods.

Mama's voice trembled under the weight of Grandma Ruthie's expectations. "I don't know what I'm going to do. Grandma seems to think we should be hosting the funeral as the next of kin. Bob's children are having a fit. She's already made a scene down at Whitlow's Funeral Home over the release of the body. And now she expects me to help her plan the visitation, the buffet, the service—"

"The full Ruthie Early-Lange-Bodeen-Floss-Whitaker special?" I asked.

"I wish you would stop calling it that," Mama huffed.

"She's held the same funeral service for four hus-bands. I'll call it what I want." I snorted.

"Jane, I'm really going to need your help with this," Mama said, the faintest wheedling tone creeping into her voice.

"Why can't Jenny help you with this?"

"Jenny's busy with the Charity League Follies, and she's serving as chairwoman of the Women's Club Winter Ball this year." Mama was in a full-blown whine now.

"But good old Jane doesn't have a life, right? Why not make her chairwoman of the funeral luncheon?"

"Don't start that, Jane," Mama warned. "If you would just talk to Jenny and work out this silly business, you could both help me."

"I think it ceased being silly business when I was de-posed," I told her.

Jenny had made good on her promise not to talk to me after I came out to my family. She had, however, sent me a lovely note through the law firm of Hapscombe and Schmidt, stating that Jenny wanted access to the family Bible. The Bible, which contained all of the Early genealogical information, had been willed to me through our great-aunt Jettie as part of the contents of our ancestral home, River Oaks. Jenny's lawyers had stated that as a vampire, I could not touch it and had no use for it. I'd had the local offices of the ACLU and the World Council for the Equal Treatment of the Undead send her a cease-and-desist letter stating that such statements were inflammatory and untrue. She'd responded by sending me a copy of the family tree she'd painstakingly calligraphed onto parchment, with my name burned out with a soldering iron. An ugly flurry of legal correspondence followed, and I ended up drinking Thanksgiving "dinner" with my parents after the rest of my family went home.

"Now, don't expect me to take sides," Mama said. "You girls are going to have to work this out yourselves."

"Most of the funeral stuff is going to be done during daylight hours," I said. "I'm not even going to be able to attend the burial. Humans get upset when vampires burst into flames right next to them."

"But you have all the time in the world to plan Zeb's wedding," Mama grumbled. She always got a little cranky when I brought up the "v word." "Where's the happy couple registered? The Dollar Store?"

"First of all . . . that was really funny," I whispered, glad that Zeb had ducked into the walk-in pantry and hadn't heard it. "But it was a mean thing to say. I'm the only one allowed to make mean jokes about Jolene's family, as I am the one wearing the ugliest dress in the history of bridesmaid-kind."

"What color is it?" Mama demanded. "It's not yellow, is it? Because you know yellow makes you look sallow."

"Mama, focus, please. I will help with the prep work for Bob's funeral as much as I can, during the evening, when I can fit it in around work hours. But I can't do much."

"That's all I'm asking for, honey, a little effort," she said, placated.

"As little as possible," I assured her. "How is Grandma doing?" I asked, trying not to let the resentment in my voice bubble through the phone line. "Should I stop by her house on the way to work?"

"Um, no," Mama said in a sad attempt to be vague. "There's going to be such a crowd there . . ."

"And it would be a shame for me to come by and make things awkward," I finished for her. The heavy silence on Mama's end said I was right, but Mama preferred not to put it into words.

I don't know why Grandma's rejection of me still stung. Elderly relatives were supposed to give you lipsticky kisses and ask intrusive questions about your love life. They were supposed to brag about your achievements to the point where nonrelatives wanted to gouge their eardrums at the mere mention of your name. They were not supposed to request at least one week's advance notice if you attended family gatherings or insist on wearing a cross the size of a hubcap whenever you walked into a room. My only consolation was that Grandma looked like Flavor Flav and usually tipped over under the weight of her bling.

Eager to get back to a subject she could control, Mama listed the dishes she expected me to prepare to perk up the usual funeral potluck offerings. Apparently, there was some sort of dessert involving Jell-O, cream cheese, and mandarin oranges in my future. While I saw it as completely unfair that someone who didn't eat should have to cook, these arguments failed to impress Mama. I promised to come by for my assigned shopping list after dark.

"How are things going with that Gabriel?" Mama asked. Mama was happy I was dating someone, particularly someone who literally came from one of the oldest families in town. But she was pretending that Gabriel wasn't, either. I could only expect so much. "Have you seen him lately?"

"Not for a week or so. He had to go to Nashville for business."

On the other end of the line, Mama sighed. Dang it. I had just extended the conversation by about twenty minutes. Ever since I'd established a semi-sort-of-relationship with Gabriel, Mama's favorite activity had been giving me relationship advice. I thought she saw it as a girlie bonding thing. "Honey, what have I always told you?"

Now, honestly, that could be any number of things, ranging from "Avoid contact with any surface in a public bathroom" to "Men don't buy the cow when you hand them the keys to the dairy." So I took a shot in the dark.

"Um, never trust a man with two first names," I guessed.

"Well, yes, but not what I had in mind."

"Never trust a man with a remote-control fireplace?" I suggested.

"No," she said, her patience audibly thinning.

"Never trust a—"

"Honey." I could almost hear Mama shaking her head in dismay at my lack of man-savvy. "Relationships are fifty-fifty, give and take. You have to make an effort. He's up there all by himself for a whole week. Why couldn't you go up to visit him?"

"I have to work. And isn't that kind of desperate?"

"There's nothing wrong with showing some interest. You could make a little more of an effort. I could have Sheila take a look at your hair—"

"Mama, I really need to get off the phone if I'm going to make it to work on time," I said. "And Zeb's over here, and we're trying to talk about bridesmaid stuff. I've really got to go."

"Don't let them put you in yellow. You know how washed-out you look in yellow!" Mama was saying as I put the receiver in its cradle.

"Someone has to lock my grandma up. She's single-handedly taking down the Greatest Generation," I moaned.

Zeb smirked at me as I slumped down and smacked my head against the counter. In a granite-muffled voice, I told him, "Shut it, or I'm calling your mama and telling her that your parents' names aren't on the invitations. That'll keep you tied up for months."

"That seems uncalled for," he muttered.

From were-weasels to werewolves, weres are territorial creatures. Once a pack has established a home, they will not leave that location for generations, until the local food sources have been depleted or they're burnt out by angry farmers.

—*Mating Rituals and Love Customs of the Were*

Half-Moon Hollow is a strange place for a vampire to spend her days. We don't have a performing-arts center or a museum, but we have had our own "Rowdy Rural Towns" episode of *COPS.* The program had never before featured the arrest of a naked guy stealing anhydrous ammonia.

The chamber of commerce had a hard time fitting that into the brochure.

Living in Kentucky is a mix of the ridiculous and the sublime. The same state that is home to top-shelf research hospitals, major manufacturers, and thoroughbred horse racing is a place where you can attend a schoolbus crash-up derby. (They do take the kids off the buses before they race them.) We have Opera Houses and

Opry Houses. We have cities that are home to hundreds of thousands and towns like the Hollow, where one day, if the right couple gets engaged, the entire population will be related by marriage.

News of my transformation was slowly making the rounds of the Hollow kitchen circuit thanks to my former boss, Mrs. Stubblefield, using my application for undead unemployment benefits as justification for firing me from my position as the library's director of juvenile services. Of course, she fired me hours before I was turned, but that didn't keep her from crowing, "I told you so!" She couldn't possibly let someone "like that" work around the public, much less as a children's librarian, she told anyone who would listen. Mrs. Woodley, whose five children I personally tutored in the library's Reading Remedy program, told her to shut her mouth or she'd toss Mrs. Stubblefield's lumpy butt out of the Half-Moon Hollow Ladies' Garden Club. I sent Mrs. Woodley a dozen frozen pot pies as a thank you.

Mrs. Stubblefield had recently "retired" (was asked to retire) after a band of roving teenagers —without my after-school tutoring program to keep them occupied— stuck pages from nudie magazines in all of the encyclopedias. And no one on the staff noticed. For a month. Plus, there was evidence that Mrs. Stubblefield shared her morning coffee with Jack Daniel's.

Mrs. Stubblefield's retirement meant that her stepdaughter, Posey, was the most senior member of the library staff. Posey, who was brought in to replace me, couldn't understand the Dewey Decimal System without "Sounds like . . ." clues and laughed the way it was written out: "Ha ha ha ha ha ha." I hated her on principle. And that principle was bitterness. Through Mama, I heard about Book Club nights, trumped-up late fines, and items being checked out of the (cannot possibly be replaced, never to leave the library) Special Collections room. Grant application deadlines had been missed. Federal funding fell through for Puppet Time Theater and the Adult Literacy Program.

Slowly but surely, my favorite library patrons were making their way over to the bad part of town to seek me out for their reading needs. It started when the Wednesday Night Book Club president, Anne Woodhouse, stopped by to talk to me about a selection. Anne had lost faith in Mrs. Stubblefield's suggestions after she recommended that the club read the sequel to *A Million Little Pieces*. Then Sally Dortch stopped by to ask about Newbery Medal selections for little Hannah's book report, but she saw Mr. Wainwright's display of fertility idols and bolted. To be fair, giant ceramic phalluses generally send me running for the nearest exit, too. Finally, Justine Marcum and Kitty Newsome, the same library board members who helped Mrs. Stubblefield give me the boot, put on trench coats and Jackie O sunglasses to sneak into the shop and magnanimously announce that the board was willing to overlook my vampire status and welcome me back to the staff.

I'm not going to say it wasn't tempting. It bothered me to see my library—a place that represented everything human and familiar to me—suffering, to see programs that had taken me years to cultivate crumbling. And I missed my kids. I missed their little faces, still and enraptured, during Story Time. I missed helping each one find just the right book to help spark a love of reading, introducing them to the books that I loved as a kid: Roald Dahl, Louisa May Alcott, Ann M. Martin. I missed bringing teenagers back to reading after they finally got through that horrible "I'm too cool to like anything" phase. But I had entered a new phase in my life, and as far I was concerned, I could still do the kind of work I did at the library at Specialty Books.

I had done my best to keep in touch with the human world, be a respectable undead citizen. Andrea Byrne, my new blood-surrogate friend, was helping me find classes and other constructive activities to fill the night hours. We had started taking yoga together. Sure, I didn't technically need breathing exercises anymore, but I was finally coordinated enough to balance on one foot. I had made a few friends there, several of whom switched to a different class after they realized I was a vampire. In further personal development, I'd started recycling everything in sight. Since I was going to be walking the earth a lot longer than originally forecast, I wanted it to last as long as possible. This, combined with the yoga, convinced my mother that I had joined a cult.

I was one of a few vampires in the Hollow who chose to maintain relationships with the living after being turned. Studies showed that most vampires who had turned since tax consultant/vampire Arnie Frink outed us with his right-to-work lawsuit dropped out of sight

and moved to big cities such as New York or New Orleans. They became assimilated into the large popula-
tions of vampires and learned how to adjust to their
new lifestyles . . . or they became addicted to chemically
enhanced blood, passed out in a gutter, and woke up as
the rising sun fried them to a crisp. At least, that's what
Mama told me when I mentioned that I might go to
St. Louis for a seminar called "Emerging Issues for the
Postmillennial Undead." Apparently, Oprah did a whole
show on "Vampires Led Astray."

And somehow, I'd made it onto the undead junk-mail
radar. I started receiving advertisements for Sans Solar
sun-blocking drapes and specialized vampire "sleeping
compartments," which were basically coffins. But at least
I'd stopped getting credit-card applications. After the gov-
ernment considers you dead, credit-card companies are
less likely to extend a credit line to you. It's the one dis-
criminatory attitude toward vampires that's fine by me.

But even the undead could appreciate the magical
air in the Hollow as Christmas approached. The early
December temperatures, always a crap shoot in western
Kentucky, were hovering in the mid-40s. As a human, I'd
been a summer person. But when "getting a little color
on your cheeks" could leave you with third-degree burns
and/or permanent death, you learn to appreciate the joys
of winter. The days were getting shorter, meaning that
I could get up and around earlier. The cold brought a
sharpness to the scents of the living, bright splashes of
scent against a misty gray.

The chill also gave me an excuse to wear the sleek new

black coat I'd bought on a rather disastrous shopping trip with Andrea. She took me on a tour of these nice underground shops (not literally) on the outskirts of Memphis. And I didn't buy a damn thing but the coat. But at least I no longer looked like I was walking around in a big puffy sleeping bag.

Christmas in the Hollow means spitting snow that never amounts to anything but still sends everyone running for bread and milk. It means exchanging decorative tins of cookies with acquaintances you don't like that much. It's mall Santas who arrive in fire trucks and challenging your neighborhood to a round of competitive outdoor decorating. Because you're not really celebrating the birth of Jesus unless your house can be spotted by passing aircraft.

I stamped the whopping half-inch of snow (mostly sleet and mud) from my boots as I neared the door of Specialty Books. The familiar smell of dust and crumbling paper greeted me as I called out to Mr. Wainwright. The shop was much cleaner than it had been that fateful night when I had wandered in and narrowly missed a shelf collapsing on top of me. Well, the mess was newer. We had at least lined up the bookshelves so that customers could navigate without climbing. The soft hum of fluorescent lighting flickered over piles of browning paperbacks and splitting leather bindings. Gilt titles, rubbed away by loving fingers, glinted dully from their piles. I slid my shoulder bag behind the counter and surveyed the damage Mr. Wainwright had wrought since I had left twelve hours before.

Trying to organize the shop was an uphill battle, and

I was making no progress. It wasn't that Mr. Wainwright ignored my efforts, but when he looked for something, he had this way of tearing through like a tornado. We had a system: I spent three days painstakingly arranging a subject section; he destroyed it in less than an hour. It was like working for a slightly dangerous three-year-old.

I was, however, proud of the fact that there were no longer dead spiders occupying an entire shelf in the reference section. They were now occupying a jar in Mr. Wainwright's office. He's a nice man. I try not to ask questions.

Our evening routine consisted of two hours of cleaning and boxing the online orders. Then, with no customers to speak of, he would make tea or warm bottled blood, and we would sit at the counter. He would tell me stories of his travels across the world seeking demon artifacts, vampire horde houses, and packs of rare werecreatures. He even spent five years in Manitoba searching for Sasquatch.

"Hello? Mr. Wainwright?" I called again. I would never get to a point where I could call him by his first name. A person who knows that there was more than one Brontë sister deserves to be addressed with respect.

"Back here, Jane," came a muffled voice from the rear of the shop.

I followed his voice to the stockroom, which we had only rediscovered the night before. Mr. Wainwright had "misplaced" the door behind a rack of old *Tales from the Crypt* comics sometime in the mid-1980s.

"Mr. Wainwright?" I saw two brown loafers sticking out

from under a carton in a horrible parody of *The Wizard of Oz*. Mr. Wainwright's about eighty years old and looks as if you could snap him like kindling. His being pinned under a giant box of heavy books was not going to keep my paltry part-time employment checks coming in.

"Are you all right?" I cried, lifting the box off him with little effort.

"Oh, thank you, Jane," he said, sitting up from his spot on the floor. He seemed to have made the best of his predicament. His ever-present lumpy gray cardigan was pillowed under his head. Clutched in one hand was an old dog-eared copy of Stephen King's *Nightmares and Dreamscapes*. "Fortunately, when the box fell on me, this bounced off my head. I haven't read it in years. You must admire the universal accessibility of Mr. King. He scares the bejesus out of me every time."

"And he's the reason I have clown issues," I said, shuddering at the thought of *It*. "How long have you been down here?"

He rolled his shoulders. "Oh, three or four hours at the most."

"Are you hurt?" I asked.

"I'm tougher than I look," he said as I lifted him up and set him on a dusty folding chair.

"I thought we agreed you weren't going to try to move things around without me here? After yesterday. When the other box fell on you," I said, struggling to keep a patient tone. I couldn't believe I was the practical one in this relationship.

"Well, yes, but I wasn't trying to move anything, I was

searching for the light switch, you see, and knocked the shelving unit over. I remembered a book I left in here that I thought you might be interested in," he said.

"You remembered a book you left in here twenty years ago?" I asked him. "What am I saying, of course you did. Why don't you tell me where it is, and I'll get it for you?"

"Yes, I think that would be best," he said. "Top shelf. In the box marked 'Bell Witch.'"

I spider-climbed nimbly up the wall and plucked the box from the top shelf. Mr. Wainwright was grinning like a kid with a new comic book. He always got excited when I manifested my vampire powers. I unfolded the top of the carton and then thought better of it.

"If I put my hand in this box, is there anything that will bite, sting, cut, burn, or turn me into dust?"

This is one of the problems with working in an occult store. The previous week, I nearly lost a digit to a diary whose lock clapped a silver trap around keyless fingers. Vampires are allergic to silver. Touching it feels like a combination of burning, itching, and being forced to lick dry ice. If Mr. Wainwright hadn't come along with the suspicious little lock-busting gizmo he carries in his pocket, I wouldn't be able to make all those shadow puppets I like so much.

Mr. Wainwright chewed his lip. "Just to be safe, I'll do the honors."

From the cobwebby, mouse-stained cardboard, Mr. Wainwright pulled a book titled *The Spectrum of Vampirism.* "Here we are," he said, handing it to me. "I thought you might find this useful. It's very good, written by a Harvard fellow named Milton Winstead in the 1920s."

"Harvard?"

"Well, they can't all be law scholars and presidential candidates." Mr. Wainwright shrugged.

"There are actual shades of vampirism?" I asked, reading over the table of contents and flipping to a chapter.

> *Vampires do not produce their own blood cells, which is why they must consume blood. The ingested blood is infused with the vampire's essence when metabolized, giving the vampire the ability to turn others. A vampire's power depends on the amount of vampire blood consumed during transformation. To make a childe, a vampire will feed on a victim until he or she reaches the point of death. The sire must be careful not to leave the initiate unconscious or unable to consume the blood needed to complete the transformation, usually two to three pints. The process is literally draining for the sire, meaning that a vampire will create only two or three children in his or her considerable lifetime.*
>
> *The stronger and older a vampire is at the point of creating a childe, the more likely that childe is to be a "healthy" vampire. A quick or careless turning can result in a*

sickly vampire, who may suffer from the
vampire's weaknesses—sensitivity to sunlight
and silver—but few of the strengths. Some
humans seek this level of vampirism to
achieve eternal youth and enhanced beauty.
Several devotees of the theatrical profession
have been rumored to have partaken in this
ritual over the years.

"Huh, I thought vampirism was pretty much a yea-or-nay proposition."

"Oh, no, no," Mr. Wainwright said. "There are many subtle levels of vampirism, of power and ability. You see, there is so much for you to learn. It's so exciting for me to be here with you for the journey from bloodthirsty neophyte to sophisticated veteran vampire."

"Happy to oblige," I said, shrugging amiably. "Although technically, I've never been what you'd call bloodthirsty."

"I didn't mean to hurt your feelings, dear," he said. "But don't you see how lucky you are? Vampires are among the few beings who trace their history as they live it. You can see the past, present, and future. You know who your great-great-grandparents, great-grandparents, and grandparents are. As your children or, in your case, nephews—now, don't make that face, dear—as your nephews have children and grandchildren and great-grandchildren, you'll be able to watch them grow and live and die, each generation, if you take care of yourself, for eternity."

Staggered by the depressing nature of that thought, I patted his hands. "But you can do that, too, just on a smaller scale. I mean, everybody around here knows who their great-grandparents are. And you have your nephew. You've been able to watch him grow up and have children."

"My nephew moved to Guatemala for mission work nearly five years ago, and I rarely hear from him. I don't see him having children, if there is a just and loving God." Mr. Wainwright shook his head fondly at the mention of Emery, his late sister's Bible-thumping, personality-free son. "And I don't know who my great-grandparents were, at least not any relatives in this area. My mother was from up north, upstate New York, and my father died when I was very young. I'm afraid their union wasn't a very happy one, and she didn't keep many of his things. He rarely spoke to her about his family. And it seemed to upset her to talk about him. It might have been nice to have relatives, but from what I can see, it's a sort of genetic crapshoot. You're not likely to end up related to people you like."

"Case in point, my grandma Ruthie. But then you have wonderful chromosomal coincidences like my aunt Jettie and my dad." He smiled. "How about I start clearing through these boxes and you can get back to the Internet orders?"

"Wonderful," he said. "And Jane, dear—"

"Don't throw anything away without showing it to you first," I repeated. "How was I supposed to know that was spirit writing? It looked like a bunch of doodles on a cocktail napkin."

By the time Mr. Wainwright brought me an ancient Limoges teacup filled with microwaved pig's blood, I was covered in a fine layer of dust but had cleared away most of the stock into "Keep," "Throw Away," and "Burn on Consecrated Ground" piles.

"Thanks," I said, accepting the cup with a grateful nonbeating heart.

"There's a young man asking for you up front, Jane," he said as I sipped. "I think he's one of your kind. He looks vaguely familiar, but I can't quite place him."

"Did he mention working for the council?" I asked. "Things tend to go badly for me when they drop by for a visit."

"I doubt it," Mr. Wainwright said. "He's wearing a T-shirt that says, 'One tequila, two tequila, three tequila, floor.' I don't think I've ever seen a vampire in a novelty T-shirt before. Extraordinary, really."

That could only be one vampire.

Richard Cheney, whom I delight in calling Dick, is an old friend of Gabriel's—about 150 years old. Buddies from the cradle, they split over a gambling debt in their early twenties. Dick was turned eleven years later, also over a gambling debt. Do you see a pattern here? Dick is the local center for not-quite-legitimate commerce. If you want something, just ask Dick. But don't ask where, how, or which international laws he broke while procuring it. Also, you'll want to pay in cash.

It wasn't as difficult as I'd expected to blend my one living friend into my new undead circle. Dick and Zeb got along famously. As Dick put it, Zeb "grows on you, like a stray, spazzy puppy that followed you home." And Zeb and Gabriel built a friendship on the shared experience of saving my ass from Missy, Dick's murderous ex. Even better, Zeb had somehow formed a bridge between Gabriel and Dick, former childhood friends who had turned eternal life into a prolonged male pissing contest. Thanks to the time they'd spent with Zeb, Gabriel and Dick had declared something of a ceasefire. And while they certainly weren't going to be getting matching tattoos anytime soon, at least Dick had stopped leaving silver shavings on Gabriel's furniture.

If I was the best maid, then Dick could be considered Zeb's man of honor. Dick secured his spot in the wedding party after spending several bonding-filled weeks on Zeb's couch after his trailer blew up. Gabriel might have been promoted above groomsman had he been in town more often lately . . . and not made fun of Zeb's extensive GI Joe collection.

Whether it's because he genuinely enjoys my company or enjoys irritating Gabriel, Dick and I had spent a lot of time together since I was turned. He became a regular visitor at River Oaks. In fact, he stayed on my couch for a few days after he wore out his welcome at Zeb's. Using his secret vampire wiles, Gabriel anonymously set Dick up at a nearby apartment because of Dick's tendency to make comments such as the following.

"Ah, the lovely Jane. I've always said you were a dirty girl," he said, swiping at the dust on my cheek. Dick could be considered attractive if you considered laughing sea-green eyes, razor-sharp cheekbones, and full pouting lips permanently twisted into a mocking, yet somehow seductive smirk attractive. Combine that with the constant barrage of sassy banter, and you got a "You'll regret me in the morning" charisma that had almost every female who crossed his path melting into little puddles of giggly goo at his feet. I was a rare exception and, as Dick often reminded me, his only strictly platonic friend who also happened to have breasts.

I had a soft spot for Dick Cheney. Technically, it was my fault that his trailer had been torched by Missy in an attempt to frame me for his murder. And in between the disturbing innuendos, there was normally a nugget of likability.

Buried deep, deep down.

"Wow, you are truly master of the single entendre." I rolled my eyes. "Do your lines work on anybody, ever?"

"I just wanted to check on you, Stretch," he said, patting my head, a gesture that he knew I hated. "Haven't seen you in a few days. I worry when I'm not called to save your cute little hind end at least once a week."

"I don't have a cute little hind end," I groused.

"I know, it's more medium to large, but I was trying to be kind," he replied, dodging the *Pocket Guide to Poltergeist Activity* I chucked at him. "Keep that up, and I'll go outside, take that rusty bucket you call a car, and drive it into a quarry. It would be a mercy killing."

I squealed. "She's here?"

I ran outside to find my old Ford station wagon, Big Bertha, parked in front of the store. Dick had used some of his not-quite-legal connections to barter for spare parts and repairs that I could not afford on a part-time shopgirl's salary. I just had to tutor some were-skunk mechanic's kids in English for the next semester.

"She's beautiful." I sighed, rubbing a loving hand over the dimpled hood.

"It looks exactly the same," Dick said. "Pathetic. It probably cost you as much in repairs as it would to put a down payment on a decent car that doesn't smoke when you turn the ignition."

"Big Bertha was my first car, my first love. Aunt Jettie taught me how to drive in this car. I'm just not ready to give her up yet."

Dick smiled, an indulgent patriarch tolerating my whims. "I figured, which is why I had Billy make some modifications."

My hands froze mid-stroke on Bertha's hood. "Dick, what did you do to my car?"

He grinned. "Well, let's just say Billy had some ideas for how to make Big Bertha a little more vamp-friendly. Tinted windows, SPF 500, thank you very much. Side-curtain sunshields you can pull down in an emergency. Emergency sun-protection packs tacked under the front seats. A little refrigerated cooler for traveling with blood—it's cooled through the AC. And the pièce de résistance." He opened the back hatch. There was a coffin-sized door in the floor of the rear compartment. "An emergency hidey-hole."

"This is great," I said. "This is just, wow . . ." He shook his head. "Would it be rude of me to question this sudden burst of generosity?"

"Well." Dick stretched a companionable arm around my shoulders and offered what I'm sure he thought was a guileless smile. "You could put in a good word with your friend Andrea."

This was the thousandth or so anvil-sized hint Dick had dropped on me to hook him up with my blood-surrogate friend. Most vampires are interested in Andrea Byrne's delicately flavored, extremely rare AB-negative blood. But Dick was far more interested in the fact that Andrea is also coolly, elegantly, irritatingly gorgeous. The two of them had a strange chemistry, like ammonia and bleach.

Dick and Andrea moved in very different vampire circles. Most of Andrea's undead clients had houses without wheels. In a deliciously karmic development, Andrea didn't want much to do with Dick—not because she was a snob but because he reminded her so much of Mattias Northon, a vampire college professor who had seduced her, introduced her to life as a blood surrogate, and dumped her like a bad habit. Smooth, effortless charm just pissed her off. I think being turned down by a woman for the first time in his long, long life fried something in Dick's brain, because he'd been obsessed since meeting her.

"Oh, you're pure evil." I led him back into the store. "You almost had me for a second there, pretending to be all sweet and vulnerable. Did you script this conversation out in your head before you came in here? Is your special vampire power flirty manipulation?"

Dick made a deep, distressed noise and covered it

with a cough. "Obviously not. Why won't she go out with me?"

"She knows your type," I said. "She's painfully familiar with your type, Mr. Love 'Em, Bite 'Em, and Leave 'Em."

"That seems . . . fair," he said dejectedly. "Could you talk to her—"

"No," I said, firmly enunciating each word very carefully. "I'm her friend, not her pimp. Put your big-boy pants on and deal with this yourself. Maybe you could ask her to Zeb and Jolene's wedding."

He chuckled. "Speaking of the Gormless Wonder, I got this in the mail today."

He took a cornflower-blue envelope out of his back pocket and slid it across the counter.

"Wow." I marveled at the Lavelle-McClaine wedding invitation. I'd been trimmed from the invite list when Zeb and Jolene realized I was honor-bound to attend most of the wedding events anyway, so we didn't need to bring engraved stationery into the deal. "I'd heard about them, but . . . there are no words."

Jolene and Zeb were having a *Titanic*-themed wedding. Personally, I think centering your nuptials around one of history's greatest maritime disasters is kind of creepy, but Jolene has a serious Kate-and-Leo complex. I guess I shouldn't judge. When I was a little girl, I dreamed I would get married in an ancient English castle and ride away in a horse-drawn carriage. And my sister would be tied up in the dungeon. Of course, I also thought I'd be marrying Mark-Paul Gosselaar from

Saved by the Bell, and we can all see how that turned out.

Jolene's theme was a mix of the morbidly histori-cal and old Hollywood glamour. Her wedding en-semble consisted of a rhinestone copy of the Heart of the Ocean and a slightly-too-flattering-to-be-true-to-period costume. Zeb just barely managed to talk her out of having decorative life preservers made up with their names and wedding date. She was, however, using a model of the *Titanic* to serve chips and salsa. The boat was split in two, the salsa in one side and the chips in the other. She ordered this monstrosity online, along with her wedding ensemble and the invitations with an embossed iceberg on the cover and the words "Struck by Love." If you looked closely enough at the crags in the pressed-relief iceberg, you could make out Jolene's and Zeb's initials.

Some people should not be allowed access to the In-ternet.

"What exactly are the rules for bringing dates to were-wolf weddings?" I asked. "I didn't get an invitation per se, so I can't exactly send back a response card with a 'plus one.' Then again, Gabriel is a groomsman, so I as-sume they know he's coming. You, on the other hand, got an invitation, but it's addressed to you alone. Are you allowed a 'plus one'?"

"I haven't been invited to a wedding in about ninety years," Dick admitted. "I'm still trying to figure out what those little pieces of tissue between the envelopes are for."

"Zeb said you guys are doing some sort of manly

bowling-drinking-bonding thing this weekend. Do I have to give you the 'Allow my friend to be hurt by one of your less-than-reputable acquaintances, and you'll wake up with my foot lodged in your nether regions' speech?"

"No," he said, grinning broadly.

"Good, because the title gives away the ending."

Dick muttered, "See if I help you escape certain death again."

"Well, do you have any other homicidal ex-girlfriends who might try to frame me for murder?"

He made a rude hand motion I choose not to describe here. It was enough to bring Mr. Wainwright out from the shelves to scold Dick for his lack of chivalry.

"In my day, gentlemen didn't make gestures like that at ladies," he said, drawing himself to his full height. All five feet and six inches of him. Osteoporosis had not been kind.

Dick grinned lazily, unashamed. "Once you spend more time with her, Gilbert, you'll understand."

Mr. Wainwright's eyes narrowed, staring. "Do I know you?"

"Yes," Dick said. He winked at me. "See you later, Stretch."

"Do you know him?" I asked after Dick left.

He shook his head. "I have no idea. I have a much better memory for books than for people."

"You're probably better off," I assured him.

"I couldn't help but overhear you talking about Zeb's upcoming nuptials, Jane. I think I have a book that might help you." He held up a soft-cover volume titled *Mating Rituals and Love Customs of the Were*.

I opened to a section titled "Human-Werewolf Relations" and read aloud: "The best way for a suitor to win over a female werewolf's father is to present him with a fresh carcass. The larger the game, the more impressive the suit. Deer and elk make a bold statement. Squirrels and rabbits will get you laughed out of the pack."

I kissed the top of his balding pate. "A book for every problem. I love you, Mr. Wainwright."

He flushed with pleasure, squeezing my hands. "The feeling is mutual, dear."

3

Because of their natural animalistic leanings, were-creatures are more connected to their sexual instincts than the average human. Because premarital relations are frowned upon in the were community, were honeymoons generally last three or four times as long as human honeymoons.

—*Mating Rituals and Love Customs of the Were*

Other than a new career, new hours, new diet, new friends, and a slightly unhealthy sire-childe relationship, not much had changed in the months since I'd been turned.

No, wait, I was going broke. That was new.

My part-time paychecks weren't enough to fund my "extravagant" lifestyle. Thanks to the wonders of vampirism, I'd been able to cut little extras such as food and medical insurance. But the taxes on River Oaks were coming due soon. The water heater was making weird noises, and there was a suspicious and expensive-looking sag in my roof just over Aunt Jettie's old room. I had a 200-pound dog to feed and an expensive dental regimen to maintain. And the payment people at Visa were start-ing to ask questions. The financial juggling was becom-ing a little more than I could keep up with.

Complicating matters was the delay in my "triumph settlement." Earlier that year, I'd fought Missy the Evil Realtor to the death after she'd framed me for a series of crimes, all in an effort to obtain River Oaks—or, rather, the property River Oaks stood on. My sprawling old fam-ily farm was the keystone plot in a tacky undead condo development she had planned. Frustrated by Aunt Jet-tie's refusal to sell, Missy had decided to use the World Council for the Equal Treatment of the Undead's laws governing vampire behavior to yank the property out from under me. So I didn't feel too bad about running her through with one of her own realty signs.

In the vampire world, if you kill another vampire in battle, you get all of his or her stuff. And since Missy had spent years amassing property and swindling vampires out of their homes, that amounted to quite a bit of stuff. But after months of red tape and delays, I wasn't holding my breath for the council to fulfill its promise to fork over Missy's holdings anytime soon. Of course, holding my breath wouldn't really matter one way or the other, but . . .

I hadn't told anyone about my financial woes, not even dearly departed Aunt Jettie. There was nothing I could do. I was stuck. I was too fond of Mr. Wainwright to leave Specialty Books. Even though I was basically an unglorified sales clerk with two advanced degrees, I'd gotten the distinct impression that Mr. Wainwright had come to depend on me. He was doing less and less at the shop, opening later, going to bed earlier in his little apartment over the store, and leaving me to close. I couldn't abandon him.

If I told my parents I was having money problems, Mama would, well, I don't think she would insist I move back in with them now. But I'm sure my life, liberty, and pursuit of healthy boundaries would be infringed upon in some way. And while Gabriel had made repeated offers to help me out financially, that just wasn't relationship baggage I wanted.

Most sire-childe relationships are not as complicated as ours. Gabriel is dark and intense, obsessive to the point of being just this side of creepy. Some guys bring you flowers and candy; others exact biblical revenge by pushing trees on top of the drunk hunter who fatally shot you. I'm more of a crunchy-granola-pacifist vampire, so I found this rather disturbing. OK, it was a tiny bit hot but mostly disturbing.

I knew Gabriel was not evil. For that matter, neither was I. Vampires have the same capacity for good and evil that humans do. To be fair, people can lose some notions of etiquette when they're no longer answering to the moral constraints of human society . . . and they thirst for human blood. The bottom line is that if you had evil leanings in life, you're probably going to embrace them wholeheartedly once you're undead. If you were a decent person, say a former librarian who loves America and puppies, you're probably going to be an upstanding, almost vegetarian vampire.

It took Gabriel and me weeks to work through the weird feelings that followed his murdering Bud Mc-Elray. As a human, I'd never been in love. I'd been in deep, abiding like with several of my boyfriends, but I'd never had that feeling, that "Wow, this is a person I could spend the rest of my life with" feeling. And even though Gabriel was one of the few people I could spend the rest of my long, long life with, I couldn't think of being with him as a permanent situation. He'd saved me. He'd killed for me. But I couldn't accept that someone like him could be interested in me.

Gabriel was everything I was not. Sophisticated and complicated and able to color-coordinate a room like you wouldn't believe. I craved him with a bone-deep lust I'd once reserved exclusively for Godiva truffles. I was fixated, not just in the physical sense—though that was an obvious, and occasionally distracting, bonus—but with what he thought, how he saw the world, how he saw me. It was addictive to see myself reflected in his liquid silver eyes as strong, beautiful, intelligent, interesting, though slightly exasperating. Even when we were together, all I could think about was the next time we could be together.

I needed order. I needed constancy. But being with Gabriel was like standing in the center of a swirling eddy, the dark water surrounding you, dizzying, powerful, and beautiful. But all the while, you can't help but feel those churning walls closing in, threatening to crash in on you and crush you under their weight.

I couldn't seem to find my footing in this relationship. It didn't help that Gabriel kept leaving town on business trips like this current one, the third excursion in as many months. Now that he wasn't keeping constant "Keep Jane alive and out of trouble" vigils, Gabriel was spending some time catching up with his various business interests. He was the proprietor of three radio stations in the Southeast, plus a hotel in Atlanta, a seafood restaurant in New Orleans, and a mini-golf course in Biloxi. And those were just the ventures in this country. I know it sounds like Tony Soprano's investment portfolio, but to be fair, he had more than 100 years to diversify. Older vampires are heavily invested in human real estate, medical research, music, publishing, and media. It's what has helped maintain our cover for two millennia. It's not a conspiracy or anything, we're just trying to keep you people from setting us on fire in our sleep. If we controlled everything, do you really think the *Lifetime* network would have had a vampire detective show?

So Gabriel floated in and out of my world, letting me think I could handle life without him, only to show up after a few weeks and make me crazy all over again. I was frequently left to wallow and wonder where he was and what he wasn't telling me. I excelled at wallowing and wondering. If I called, it went to his voice mail. If he called, it was always just before dawn, as I was falling asleep and didn't have the mental capacity to ask him much. This combined with a painfully active imagination led to scenarios that would have done that *Lifetime* show very proud.

And, of course, he had to come home from his latest trip on a Tuesday night to find me wearing my "housework" sweats and a dirty bandanna around my head.

"Have we discussed the 'Call first' rule?" I asked when I opened the door, suppressing a giddy smile.

Gabriel had been impossibly beautiful even in the harsh neon lights of Shenanigans that first night I met him. And now that I had sharp vampire vision, I could fully appreciate the leonine dreaminess that was my sire. There he stood, wearing his typical Johnny Cash full black, flowing dark locks curling at his collar. His full, soft lips quirked at my rude greeting, and a flicker of warmth reflected back at me in those clear, gray eyes. Despite our general resilience, he looked tired. There was the slightest hint of shadows under his eyes. And even for a vampire, he looked pretty pale.

"Hello, Gabriel, it's lovely to see you?" he responded in a feminine voice that, frankly, sounded nothing like me. "I missed you terribly. How was Nashville?"

"Hello, Gabriel, it's lovely to see you," I parroted in an explicitly pleasant tone. "How was Nashville? Have we discussed the 'Call first' rule?"

"Can I come in?" he asked, hefting a foam cooler with his hip. A girl couldn't help but appreciate the way those hips looked in black denim. I paused to give them the proper reverence.

I opened the door wider, then stopped him with a hand to the chest. "Wait. You have that 'We have to talk' look on your face, which usually means I'm going to be accused of something."

"For once, no." He advanced against my palm. I held him back. He pouted. "This is getting heavy."

"You have superstrength," I pointed out, grinning despite myself. "What's in the cooler?"

"A present." He opened the top and proudly displayed a dozen pint-sized plastic envelopes of blood packed in dry ice.

I cocked my head and studied him thoughtfully. "The next time you go shopping for me, take Andrea."

He carried his burden into the kitchen, where he carefully stored his repellent treasures in the empty vegetable crisper.

"This is prime Red Cross–grade human donation," he said. "Tested, screened, and cleared through a lab in the city."

"That's wonderful, but why did you bring it here?"

"Can't I do something nice?" he asked, clearly offended.

I stared at him. "You might have started with a card and maybe worked your way up to human blood."

"I worry about how you eat," he said as he sifted through the pathetic contents of my fridge. "I want you to drink a pint of this every day."

"I've told you that it makes me uncomfortable when you blur that daddy/boyfriend line, right?" I said. He held up half-empty bottles of Hershey's syrup and Bailey's Irish Cream. "That's just for flavor!"

"I'm afraid that you're becoming too accustomed to drinking synthetic blood, Jane," he said. "It's only a recent development, and production could stop with the turn of the political tide. And then where will you be?"

"On eBay, looking for remainders?" I guessed.

"What if you're too far away from a store to get a supply? What if the supply is tainted? You need to become more comfortable drinking human blood, feeding from live subjects." He hushed me when I opened my mouth to protest. "I know how you feel about feeding from humans, but I want you to have the skills you need to survive. Just in case. I want you to be able to hunt on your own."

"So, I'm like a domesticated bear, and you're working up to releasing me into the wild?"

"Yes, that's the worst possible way you could have taken this gesture, thank you," he muttered, setting the cooler aside.

"Thank you," I finally said. "I appreciate the fact that you thought of me while you were away."

"Every spare moment," he promised, moving in closer for a kiss.

I stopped him. "Are you sure I'm not accused of something? Feeding on senior citizens? Kicking toddlers? Stealing candy from babies?"

He was darkly cute when he was indignant. "It's not a bad omen *every* time I come to call."

"You're right," I conceded. "I'm being rude. To what do I owe the pleasure?"

In a very serious tone, he said, "I think we should have sex again."

"What?" I giggled. I couldn't help it. Gabriel and I hadn't been able to "date" per se. Dating a vampire is difficult, even if you *are* a vampire. I mean, it's not as if we can go out to dinner like a normal couple. We don't eat. On the rare occasion that we were both at one of our houses and sitting still, Zeb and Jolene or Andrea or Dick would show up, and our twosome became a group gathering. As much as I loved having a close group of diverse friends who understand my special needs, talk about a bunch of mood killers.

"I think we should have sex again," he repeated. "I think we've reestablished our rapport and friendship. I believe you're starting to trust me again. I know you want me."

"That's kind of presumptuous," I told him. He wasn't wrong, but it was still presumptuous.

Obviously irritated by my not jumping him right then and there, he added, "Also, the first time was rather rushed, and I don't feel that I was able to demonstrate my full range of, er, technique."

"So, you think we should have Naked Happy Fun Time because I didn't get to see all of your moves?" I said, barely able to contain a second giggle fit as he backed me against the counter. "You don't just say something like that. You have to take me out for dinner or something."

"Here." He reached into the fridge and pulled out a packet of A-negative. "Drink that."

I arched an eyebrow at him. "You really don't understand the concept of modern courtship, do you?"

"Drink it," he commanded. Humoring him, I popped the top and took a long drink of the smooth, lusciously nutty donated blood. Tasting genuine human blood after months of synthetic always left me a little woozy. Little pinpricks of sensation, nerves firing along my arms and throat, made me lean heavily against the counter to get my bearings.

Gabriel took the packet from my slightly trembling hand. "Now, kiss me."

"I'm not a light bulb, you can't just flip a switch and turn me—"

Gabriel gripped my cheeks between his palms and seized my lips, the last syllables of my sentence muffled into his mouth.

"I stand corrected," I admitted as we backed into the living room.

"Is your aunt here?" he asked, tugging at my T-shirt.

I shook my head. "Hot ghost date."

"I think—*gah!*" Distracted by the front closure on my bra, Gabriel had tripped over a footstool and knocked over a side table.

"It might be nice to have sex without breaking anything, what do you say?" I asked, peeking down at him over the edge of the table. Gabriel sat up, rubbing his forehead where my old hard-bound copy of *Sense and Sensibility* had conked him.

"Haven't you already read this a few dozen times?" he asked, flipping through the pages. "We're going to have to have a literary intervention for you."

"It's Jane Austen, so I'm going to pretend I didn't hear you say that," I said, settling next to him and taking the book from his hands. "You can never read Jane Austen too many times. And this is one of my favorites. She manages to pull a believable happy ending out of what could have been her saddest story. She could have left the Dashwood sisters alone, having learned their lessons from their respective traits. Marianne could have been left alone and ruined by her dramatic, impetuous behavior. Elinor could have taken her quiet dignity to a maiden's grave. But she gave them the men they wanted or, in Marianne's case, needed. Austen let both of them have a little bit more than they deserved."

"I love it when you talk about books," he murmured against my neck. "It gets you all excited. Quick, tell me your theories about *Jane Eyre* and sexual repression again."

My burst of laughter was silenced by the press of Gabriel's mouth.

It's amazing how much easier it is to be naked in front of another person when you have a little self-confidence. In order to attract prey, vampires are usually more attractive than they were in life. So I got the high-school bookworm's Golden Ticket. My skin was clearer. My hair had changed to an actually desirable color found in the brunette spectrum *and* did what it was supposed to on occasion. My eyes, formerly an unremarkable muddy hazel, were now a clear and compelling hazel. My teeth were whiter. And my chest was in the locked and upright position forevermore. I never had to worry about sagging. If Mama would admit to my being a vampire, even she would have to concede that it seemed to agree with me.

Mama probably wouldn't have mentioned the boob thing specifically, though.

Emboldened by my newfound confidence, I jumped over the couch and pounced on Gabriel, gleefully ripping at the buttons of his shirt. He was too busy slowly peeling off my socks to object. He grinned madly at my feet.

"What?" I asked, hoping that after all of this, I hadn't accidentally fallen for a foot fetishist.

"I just never know what color your toenails are going to be," he said, stroking my instep and kissing my ankle. "Will it be a prim pink? A contemplative cranberry? A playful plum?"

"My toes are like a mood ring. Good to know. Now, I believe you were kissing my ankle in a very pleasant manner. Feel free to continue," I commanded, wiggling my freshly painted carpals.

"What is that?" he asked, staring with horror at the virulent shade of pulpy peach on my toenails.

"I had to mix three different shades to find a peach that would match Jolene's bridesmaids' dresses. I did an experimental test run to see if my body would tolerate the color."

"Wow," Gabriel mouthed silently.

"Shut it," I said, tossing the remnants of his shirt into a wastebasket. He took advantage of this lapse of concentration to pull me onto his lap, wrapping my legs around his waist. I smirked down at him, tucking his hair behind his ears. "How about we try to make it to a bed this time?"

Gabriel didn't answer, as his mouth was occupied, scraping his fangs gently over the curve of my breast. I loved and hated it when he did that. Loved it because he was teasing me, toying with me, reminding me of every dark pleasure he could inflict on me. Hated it because it reduced my whole world to a square inch of responsive flesh, making me forget everything—pride, sense, the ability to refrain from bizarre birdcall noises. My only defense was winding my fingers through his ink-black hair, pulling his head back, and sucking on his bottom lip.

He groaned into my mouth. "Unfair."

"All's fair in—ummph." I grunted as he smothered my mouth with his and pushed me to my feet.

"You're wearing too much." His low voice vibrated across the skin of my throat. He refused to pull his lips away from my skin as he split my old 4-H camp T-shirt down the front and tossed it into the trash with his own shirt. I glared at him.

He shrugged, pulling the bandanna from my head and shaking my hair loose. "All's fair."

We were both grinning loopily as we stripped each other, tossing clothes carelessly across the room. Gabriel continued to put my sensitive nerves to good use as he stroked the line of my back with his long fingers.

I never stopped kissing him, deep, sweet, hot kisses that left me confused about where his lips started and mine ended.

One of the drawbacks of living in a Civil War home is knowing that no matter what you do there, it's already been done before. You're never the first. Well, I'm pretty sure I'm the first Early to do any of those things on the "grand staircase" once featured in the Half-Moon Hollow Historical Society's Spring Tour of Homes.

On an unrelated note, I was really glad I'd taken those yoga classes with Andrea.

Without them, I might not have had the strength and flexibility required to balance on the stairs with my arms while Gabriel raised my hips and sank deep inside me. I threw my head back, sighing, contented. How could I have forgotten how good that was? How complete and full he made me feel? I hardly noticed that with each thrust, I landed one step closer to the top of the stairs. I arched my back, grinding down until he nudged against that sensitive little bundle of nerves. I wrapped my arms around his neck on impulse, landing hard on my back without their support. The force knocked both of us down two steps, the impact of each bump sending shockwaves through my body. Gabriel groaned, the hum of his voice against my collarbone sending me over the edge. I clenched around him, crying out as red starbursts exploded behind my eyelids.

Seeing my face as I climaxed had some strange effect on Gabriel. Moaning softly in my ear, he begged me to open my eyes. I obeyed and found him watching me, memorizing every detail of my face. I turned my face into his cradling palm and bit down on the tender skin between his thumb and forefinger with my blunter teeth. He yowled, surprised, and grinned obscenely just before he shuddered over me. We slid down the stairs one at a time as he came.

We slithered to a stop on the third step. I sighed. "I missed you."

"That's what a man likes to hear," he said, pulling me onto his chest and nuzzling the curve of my throat.

I blew out an unnecessary breath. "This is just like our first time, without all the hitting and bleeding. I know we haven't addressed this, but I totally won that fight."

"I admire your competitive nature and optimism, but there's no way you would have beaten me in a fair fight."

I smirked. "Would it make you feel better if I went all traditional and asked what you're thinking in some soft, hesitant voice? Because right now, all I'm thinking is 'woo,' and if I might add, 'hoo.'"

"It saddens me that I don't know whether this is the stunning aftereffects of my technique or that you're spending more time with Dick.

"So . . . what are you thinking?" he asked in that faux feminine voice again, pressing little kisses along my wrist. "Because I doubt very much that 'woo' and 'hoo' is all that's going on in that massive, teeming brain of yours."

I propped my chin on his chest. "Do you really want to know? Because at any given moment, when I'm with you, I have about a million questions bouncing around in my head. Stuff that, frankly, I'm a little ashamed I don't know about you. For instance, why don't you have an accent? You and Dick grew up together. He has a respectable drawl. But you sound as if you're from the middle of nowhere, only with a slightly stuck-up British vernacular."

He pushed my hair back from my face. "Well, you know what they say, 'When in Rome . . .'"

"Attempt to sound nothing like the Romans?" I countered.

"No, I was actually in Rome, and I was saying, 'y'all,'" he said. "It was hard to blend into the crowd. While I was traveling, I did my best to get rid of my accent—and the use of 'y'all.' Happy now?"

"No, there's still stuff that I don't know about you, like what was your dog's name when you were a kid? What was the first book you can remember reading? What was your favorite food before you were turned? Did you like pancakes? What's your favorite movie made after 1970? Don't say *Scarface*. Please don't say *Scarface*."

"*Bridges of Madison County*."

"What?"

"Fine, that was a lie. I enjoyed *Edward Scissorhands*."

"Really, a loner with a dangerous condition that keeps him at arm's length from most people," I teased. "Don't see that at all."

"Would it have made you happier if I said *Rocky*?" he groused. "What's your favorite movie, oh, protector of cinematic integrity?"

"Whatever is readily available and has Gerard Butler in it," I told him. "Except for *P.S. I Love You*. Even I have standards. Well, the incompatible movie choices cinch it. Gabriel, as a couple, I'd say we're doomed." I shook my head sadly.

"I hope that's not true," he said, grinning. "I have long-term plans for you."

"Really?" I asked, and immediately cringed at the astonishment in my voice.

"Of course I do," he said, his eyes narrowed. "Don't you think of me when you imagine where you'll be in the next century or so? Don't I factor into your plans?"

I ducked my head and concentrated on the patterns in the rug. "Yeah, but it's different. I've never been a vampire without you. But you, you've been at this for so long. You know how vampire relationships play out. I don't. And you know how to get along without me. Sometimes I wonder . . ."

"Wonder what?"

"I wonder when you're going to get tired of me," I said. "I mean, this can't last forever, right? For me, nothing this good lasts forever. And we don't have any sort of . . . we haven't really talked about the long term . . . I'm going to stop talking now."

Gabriel opened his mouth to protest, then snapped it shut. After a few moments' consideration, he blurted out, "Is this because I haven't said that I love you?"

"No," I said, caught off guard enough to gape at him a little. "Are vampires even capable of love?"

"Jane, that hurts me," he said.

"It shouldn't. I honestly have no idea. I love my parents, I love Zeb. I love Aunt Jettie. But I had those emotions before I was turned. How do I know they aren't just residual echoes of what I felt when I was human? I was never in love with a man as a human. I'm not sure I would recognize the feeling. I really like you. Does that help?"

He made a face.

"Have you ever been close to getting married?" I asked. "Do you want to get married?"

He grinned down at me. "Is that a proposal?"

I ignored him. "Are we even able to get married? Legally?"

"No, not yet," he said. "If a vampire was married before being turned, and the spouse is still human, the marriage is still legal and valid. It took the council nearly two years of lobbying Congress to accomplish that. We're still working on establishing after-death rights for vampires. We are technically dead, so the hard-line conservatives insist that we don't have the right to life, liberty, and the pursuit of happiness. Marriage, adoption, voting—"

I gasped. "We can't vote?"

"You didn't notice that in November? During the election?"

"Of course I did, because I vote . . ." I protested. "OK, fine, I didn't even try to vote. I forgot. I'm a horrible person."

He shrugged, patting my head. "Well, you had to have flaws. You don't vote or have tact or have control over most of your gross motor functions—"

"OK, stop that," I said, pinching his arm. "And stop trying to get out of talking about your marriage feelings. Have you ever been close to getting married?"

"Yes," he said, rubbing his eyes. "Her name was Mary

Louise Early. Her parents were dear friends of my parents. My father wanted access to their pasture land. It was a good match."

"Wait, so you were engaged to one of my ancestors?" I scooched away from him. "Ew."

"This is why I don't tell you about my past! I'm not enigmatic and secretive. I'm trying to keep you from doing—ow!" he cried as I pinched him again. "That. We were not officially engaged at the time of my death. We were promised, that's all."

"Did you sleep with her? Because that would just be weird."

He seemed insulted that I was calling his before-death self a horndog. "Of course not! We were never left unchaperoned. She was wearing twelve layers of underwear at all times. And she had a laugh that made my ears bleed."

"Hmmph." I snorted.

Awkward silence.

"So how was Nashville?" I asked.

"The new manager is an idiot," Gabriel said of the radio station employee he'd traveled to Tennessee to "meet" (translation: yell at in a scary vampire voice). "He's a fan of Jethro Tull and wants to change the format to soft rock. I'm either going to fire him or make him believe he's a nine-year-old Girl Scout." He stroked my hair back from my face. "How's the wedding planning going?"

"I don't want to talk about it." I groaned.

"The dress is that bad?" he asked. He was trying to

look sympathetic, but vampire fangs tend to give away hidden smiles. "Well, if it makes you feel any better, at least you don't have to go to the bachelor party. Zeb said Dick has made arrangements for us to visit the Booby Hatch on 'Amateur Night.' " Gabriel grimaced at using the word "booby."

"You're telling your girlfriend that you're going to a strip club," I said, narrowing my eyes at him.

"Yes."

"Do you know what happens at strip clubs?" I asked.

He laughed. "I'm sure it will be fine. We'll have a few drinks, get him something to eat, and get him home."

"You honestly *don't* understand how strip clubs work, do you?"

Gabriel snorted. "So, how is Zeb's wedding driving you into the abyss of madness?"

"It's the whole thing," I grumbled. "It's not that I don't like Jolene. In fact, I'm pretty sure I like her much more than I would have liked anyone else who married Zeb. With the exception of her constantly eating in front of me, I like everything about her. She's nice and funny and obviously loves my friend. It's just that—"

"She drives you crazy," he offered.

"A tiny bit." I sighed.

"I think that you've gotten used to being the female influence in Zeb's life," Gabriel said, squeezing me. "There's nothing wrong with it. I think the friendship between you two is a beautiful thing. But he understood when you began spending time with me, and he's made it easy for me to become a part of your life. I would be very disappointed in you if you weren't able to do the same for him."

"Fine. I will take the mature route. Even if you have to check me into some sort of vampire mental institution immediately after the reception."

"Jane?" he said, winding his arms and legs around me.

"Letting it go." I nodded, playing with the curling ends of his hair. "Now that I have your attention, I think we should test that vampire endurance I hear so much about."

"To think you were this innocent little librarian when I met you." Gabriel heaved a mock sigh. "I've created a monster."

I grinned, my fangs extending over my lips. "In more ways than one."

Well, I finally got my revenge for all those times I'd walked in on Fred and Jettie. She came home to find me sprawled on the couch wearing nothing but Gabriel's shirt, sitting in a very naked man's lap.

I'd always been disappointed that River Oaks doesn't have a great ghost story attached to it. Of course, now it does. Aunt Jettie. Jettie was my own personal daytime security system. She woke me up when someone, such as grabby family antique enthusiasts Grandma Ruthie and Jenny, tried to get into the house. She also chased away door-to-door salesmen, meter readers, and evangelists with vague unease and spooky noises.

Unless you have some sort of psychic ability, ghosts decide when they want you to see them. Which is good, because I don't think I'd want to walk around seeing dead people on every corner. Just when Jettie had decided to let Gabriel see her, she was seeing a whole lot of him. Ever poised, he wrapped an afghan around his waist and held a perfectly civil conversation with her. The utter mortification forced me to block most of it from memory. I know she brought up the phrase "steam cleaning" a lot.

Gabriel promised to call and made himself scarce. There was practically a Gabriel-shaped hole in the door.

"Where have you been?" I asked her, hands on bare hips. "I haven't seen you for four days. And then you just waltz in without so much as a how do you do? Am I going to have to ground you to get you to spend time with me? It's that boy you've been seeing, isn't it?"

"I don't want to talk about it," Jettie huffed. "Your grandpa Fred is becoming an ass in his post-old age. We spent the last three days fighting. Do you know how difficult it is to win a conversation with a man who no longer fears death?"

I nodded. "As a matter of fact, yes, I do."

"If we're going to talk about boys, can we discuss the fact that Gabriel only wears pants on every other visit here?" Jettie asked.

"No. Instead, I will change the subject and announce to you that there is a new potential addition to Half-Moon Hollow's ghostly population. Grandpa Bob died on Tuesday. Grandma Ruthie said there was some sort of medication mix-up."

"The hell there was." Jettie cackled. "Fred says it's all

over the golf course. Bob Jessup died because he couldn't quite make out the dosage on his 'little blue tablets,' and he took too many. Apparently, it was their anniversary, and Bob wanted to rise to the occasion."

"Oh . . . oh, just, oh." I shuddered, clapping my hand over my lips. "I think I just threw up a little in my mouth. Is Bob still wandering around out there?"

"Oh, no, he's moved on. He just made a quick stop at his son's house to say good-bye. He happened to run into Sago Raines, who's been haunting the place for years. They talked for a bit before he went into the light. Sago was down at the golf course spreading the news faster than you can say 'erectile dysfunction.' "

"Lalalalalalala." I sang, pressing my hands over my ears, but even that couldn't keep me from hearing her.

"I just wish I could get to Ruthie long enough to tell her every dead soul in the Hollow knows her dearly departed had to have pharmaceutical help to—"

"Enough!" I cried. "First, you and Grandpa Fred, and now—just enough. I'd pierce my own eardrums, but they would just grow back."

"Ageist." Jettie sneered.

"Exhibitionist," I retorted.

"I don't think you can afford to throw any naked stones here, pumpkin."

I nodded. "Touché."

4

Because of the lifelong mating urge, werewolves do not adjust well to being widowed. In some cases, a surviving mate will die of mourning pains.

—*Mating Rituals and Love Customs of the Were*

Perhaps sensing that Bob's could be her last grand-dame funeral, Grandma Ruthie wanted to bury Bob in style. NATO summits were less tense than the planning of this shindig. Bob's adult children claimed that Bob, an avid fisherman, wanted to be cremated with half of his ashes spread into Lake Barkley and the other half interred with his late first wife. Grandma Ruthie, incensed that she might be upstaged, insisted that Bob's intact remains be buried adjacent to her "compound" of husbandly burial plots down at Oak View Cemetery. She made such a scene at the funeral home that Bob's shell-shocked offspring let her have her way, plus total control of the funeral program from the "Amazing Grace" opener to the "It Is Well with My Soul/Old Rugged Cross" closing medley.

There was only one place to host this weird-ass parody of grief: Whitlow's Funeral Home, where Grandma Ruthie had been mourning husbands since 1957. In fact, three generations of Whitlows had helped Grandma Ruthie bury her spouses. And apparently, none of them knew anything about decorating. Honestly, who finds dark wood paneling, blue velvet upholstery, and 3-D pictures of Jesus comforting?

With her "frequent flyer" status, Grandma Ruthie was treated like a queen from the moment she walked in the door. She never settled for the rattling Coke machine and sprung couch in the sadly worn family lounge. When the stress of public mourning became too much to bear, Grandma Ruthie retreated to the senior Mr. Whitlow's private office, where he stocked her favorite brand of butter cookies and an ample supply of bottled sweet tea. Membership has its privileges.

Visitations were held on the evening before the burial, giving the community the chance to offer condolences to the bereaved and give their real opinion of the deceased outside the bereaved's earshot. Grandma Ruthie was ensconced in the front row of the chapel, sending petulant looks at Bob's children. She was still pouting over their last-minute refusal to let her take over the memorial video or the photo board. Somehow, they seemed insulted that Grandma wanted to focus on the last five years of Bob's life, omitting his first marriage to their late mother and the existence of his children and grandchildren. She did get her vengeance by making a memorial *Wheel of Fortune* puzzle board spelling out "Ruthie Loves Bob" and putting it in the lid of his casket. Bob was a huge *Wheel* fan.

Based on the craftsmanship, I suspected my sister, Jenny, had a hand in this.

Grandma Ruthie simply did not understand why she was not being given the authority and respect due a widow. She claimed to have given Bob some of the happiest years of his life. The fact that Bob had been unconscious or hospitalized for most of that time seemed irrelevant.

Grandma Ruthie, and Jenny, for that matter, were a little miffed at Mama for her resolve that I be involved in the funeral. I would have been touched by Mama's insistence on my having the opportunity to mourn Bob, but I'm pretty sure she just wanted help policing the buffet at the visitation. I didn't eat, after all, so I wouldn't mind keeping the platters full. The main problem was that Grandma insisted on using her good silver serving pieces (from Wedding No. 2), which were mixed in with stainless-steel pieces from the funeral home. You'd think by now I'd be able to sniff out metal that causes me to burn and itch, but every time I moved a utensil, it was like Russian roulette. So I stuck with plates.

It is an unwritten law that a person could not be decently buried in the Hollow without the presence of deviled eggs and some form of homemade pimento cheese. My cousin Junie's hot-dog bake is also usually present. It's essentially diced hot dogs, Tater Tots, processed cheese food, and cream of mushroom soup baked until crusty. Still, it's preferable to homemade pimento cheese.

Of course, for humans, nourishment is needed to sustain them through the gauntlet of social interactions. If you met anyone in the deceased's family once, you are expected to bring a casserole for the bereaved and spend at least twenty-five minutes at the visitation. This meant that if I wanted to cross the room, I was going to have to talk to every person I had ever met in my entire life. And I had no idea how many of them might be packing stakes.

Not everybody in Half-Moon Hollow knew I'd been turned, but many of those who did looked at me with a combination of fear and revulsion. I'll admit that I spent much of my living time being annoyed at my human community, but being separated from them now was lonely and isolating. The only place I felt safe was at River Oaks, and then a group of high-school kids wrapped my entire porch in hanks of dried garlic. It was an incredibly lame and yet surprisingly effective way to make me afraid in my own home.

For this reason and so many more, I specifically asked Gabriel not to attend the funeral. I did not feel this was the appropriate occasion to introduce him to my family. When he asked which occasion would be appropriate and I stayed stonily silent, I think it hurt his feelings.

I could see now that I might have been better off with my sire nearby. After a few training sessions spent trying to hone my mind-reading talents, Gabriel and I determined that it only worked on humans. Most humans . . . some humans. Sometimes. It was pretty inconsistent. Still, after finding out how many people secretly disliked me inside their heads, not being able to see inside my fellow vampires' was kind of a comfort.

According to the swarms of thoughts and scents pecking at my cortex, some of those attending the funeral knew I was a vampire, but they were nice enough not to mention it. Or at least to mention it quietly behind their hands in a way that was not noticed by the other mourners. Such is the delicate social web of a small Southern town. I knew that they knew. My family knew that some of them knew. They knew I knew that they knew. But none of us said anything, because that would cause unpleasantness. And we are nothing if not pleasant . . . when other people are watching.

Zeb and Jolene were lurking among the crowd, earning attendance points for Zeb and his family but avoiding actual contact with anybody. Lucky bastard. Jolene did, however, bring a huge sandwich platter and a gallon of macaroni salad from her uncle's shop, the Three Little Pigs. I was ninety-nine-percent sure that meant Grandma Ruthie now liked her better than me. Mama Ginger was hovering over the mini-quiches and glowering in Jolene's general direction.

Fortunately, Mama Ginger had been "too ill" since Zeb's announcement to contribute anything to the funeral buffet—everything she made tasted like blue cheese and glue. You'd think she'd be thrilled that her son was marrying a good girl with a local family, who wouldn't ask her son to move far from hearth and home. Plus, with her flashing lupine eyes and auburn hair, Jolene was beautiful in that fierce "some people walk in the light" way that just seems unfair to those of us whose genes aligned in a less spectacular fashion. Instead, Zeb said that upon hearing his engagement announcement, Mama Ginger accused him of letting "little Zeb" do all of his thinking for him. Floyd had nodded in agreement, but it was in more of an envious, congratulatory way.

Much like the iceberg that doomed the "unsinkable" ship, the visible workings of the Lavelle-McClaine wedding plans were only the tiniest glimpse of passive-aggressive maneuverings below the surface. Being truly disliked for the first time in her life sent Jolene into some sort of prolonged panic state, where she did almost anything to try to get Mama Ginger to like her. This, of course, just irritated the hell out of Mama Ginger. She would not bond with Jolene. She simply refused to, just as she'd refused to shop for mother-of-the-bride dresses with the clingy bride. She would not meet Jolene for lunch to discuss floral arrangements or seating charts. She faked a gluten allergy to get out of tasting the wedding cake.

I hadn't seen Mama Ginger since I'd started keeping night hours. Henna-haired and built like a neurotic fire hydrant, Zeb's mother was wearing her "burying dress" of clingy black Lycra, Bedazzled with intricate patterns of tiny gold-tone studs and rhinestones. There was a matching hat, but Mama Ginger wouldn't dare cover her colored, curled, and coiled coiffure, which, as a hairdresser, she considered her own best advertisement. Mama Ginger, who never left the house without full pancake makeup and eyeliner, usually ambushed me with one of the fifteen nubbed lipsticks she kept in the bottom of her purse to "give me a little color."

Eager to avoid a scene in which I would be left with a linty coat of Risqué Red, I backed away. The movement caught Mama Ginger's attention, and before I knew it, I'd made inadvertent eye contact. *Bah!*

"Jane!" Mama Ginger squealed. "Oh, honey, come on over here and give me some sugar!"

Across the room, Zeb's eyes widened as Mama Ginger enveloped me in a hug that would usually have left me smelling of Jean Naté and Virginia Slims, except this time, the scent of lady-grade tobacco was dramatically understated. Zeb shot me an apologetic look and then turned his back and busied himself with some punch.

Coward.

"You're so skinny! You need to get over there and eat something. I worry about you, poor single girl, always on some crazy diet. You need someone to cook for, honey. That will put some meat on your bones." Mama Ginger mercilessly squeezed my cheeks with her carefully painted acrylic nails. "Now, how are you, baby doll? Tell me every little thing!"

"I'm fine. Mama Ginger, did you quit smoking?" I asked, sniffing her again.

"Yes, I did!" she cried. "How did you know?"

"Um . . ." *Don't say smell. Don't say smell.* I spotted a pack of nicotine gum in her purse and nodded to it.

Mama Ginger giggled. "You'll never believe this, but I went to that Madame Zelda over on Gaines Street."

"The 'mesmerist/tarot reader' who offers palm readings for five dollars from her den?"

"That's the one. She does a special course of 'Smoke-

Free Sessions.' It's five hypnosis sessions for two hundred and fifty dollars. Pricey, but it's done the trick."

Mama Ginger had left at least two packs of Revlon-stained cigarette butts in her wake every day since I'd known her. In fact, she once lit up in the middle of her annual physical, right after her doctor told her that she was at risk for seven kinds of cancer. People take bad news in different ways.

I could only guess that the faint cigarette smell still lingering on Mama Ginger was nicotine that had seeped into her DNA.

"I'm chewing this silly gum." She sighed, rolling up her sleeve to show me a nicotine patch on her arm. "And I only smoke after meals, but really, I'm feeling much better. I can walk all the way to the mailbox without a break."

I would be concerned, but honestly, the combination of occasional smoking, chewing, and, uh, patching probably equaled the amount of nicotine in Mama Ginger's system when she was smoking full-time.

"I never thought I'd quit, never wanted to." Mama Ginger said, ignoring common sense in her usual selective fashion. "But Mamaw Lavelle's doctor put her on an oxygen tank, and she screams that I'm trying to kill her if I light up anywhere near her. Hell, if I was going to kill the woman, I would have switched her heart pills for baby aspirin ten years ago."

I goggled at her. She blushed and gave a tinkling laugh. "Zeb says you have a new job. How do you like it?"

"Fine . . . Not that I'm not glad to see you, Mama Ginger, but I thought you were mad at me . . ." I looked in the direction of Hannah Jo, her favorite client and preferred daughter-in-law candidate, who was sulking in the corner with a plate of deviled eggs.

"Oh, Janie!" She smiled indulgently at me, fluffing my hair. "You know I could never stay mad at you, even though you did hurt my feelings. You're my little angel muffin."

I'd forgotten about the nicknames. How could I have forgotten the nicknames?

"Besides, I don't spend much time with Hannah Jo anymore, because . . . I didn't know"—Mama Ginger lowered her voice—"that she has a shoplifting problem. Every time we went to the flea market, she walked out with packages of socks under her jacket. Besides, do you know she has cut off her mama? Doesn't even talk to her anymore. Doesn't see her at Christmas or Mother's Day or send her birthday cards. Can you imagine, someone having such a hard heart that they cut off their mama?"

"Wow." I cringed as realization dawned. "So I guess that means you don't want her to marry Zeb anymore."

Mama Ginger sighed. "No, I only wanted Hannah Jo to get to know Zeb because she's so lonely, and I thought since Zeb's such a good friend to you, he could be a good friend to her, too. My boy is so generous and sweet and kind. He'd have to be to take up with that one." Mama Ginger shot a glare in Jolene's direction.

"Jolene's a very nice girl," I said. "She's very good to Zeb. He loves her very much. I just said 'very' three times, didn't I?"

"You're sweet to say nice things about someone who's taken what's rightfully yours." Mama Ginger pinched my cheeks again. "But it don't matter how perky their ass is, no one's gonna take your place in Zeb's heart. You're always going to be his first."

Ignoring the ass comment, I asked, "His first?"

"Love, silly, you're his first love. No one forgets his first love."

I had a vague vertigo sensation as Mama Ginger's maternal crosshairs focused on me again.

"I'll see you later, Mama Ginger. I need to get back to . . . I gotta go."

"We'll talk soon, baby doll," she called as I pivoted on my heel, made a grab for an empty iced-tea pitcher, and focused on the main stage, the front pew.

Grandma was resplendent in her traditional Casual Corner Petites black dress suit, but she had stepped up her game with a black picture hat and full veil. Long ago, she had figured out a secret combination of waterproof mascara and eyeliner that gave her a full Elizabeth Taylor lash that never ran. A black lace handkerchief was clutched to her lips as she stifled a sob.

Where do you even buy a black lace handkerchief? Widows R Us?

If she was this duded up for the visitation, I deeply regretted that I wouldn't get to see her burial ensemble.

As amusing as this was, the whole funeral process had put me in a bit of a philosophical funk. Despite Jenny's "offer" to give me a proper burial, there was very little chance that I would ever have a funeral. If by some chance (involving sunlight, stakes, or silver) I did die, the only remains left would be a little pile of dust. Unless someone was quick with the whisk broom, there would be nothing to put in a casket or urn. There would be no buffet, no packed chapel, and, unless Reverend Neel was feeling very charitable, no one praying over me. It was far more likely that I would watch all of my friends and family die. I would watch Zeb grow old and die. I would watch his children grow old and die. Nothing would change. Nothing would surprise me.

These dark, admittedly self-indulgent and depressing thoughts were not really putting me in the best frame of mind to deal with my grandma, who at the moment was sniffling into the black hankie and looking on old friends with baleful, glittering eyes.

"I'll be fine," she whimpered. "As long as I have friends and family around me, I'll be fine." She looked up and saw me standing nearby. "Jane, those coffee cups need washing."

Those were the first words she'd spoken to me since she found out that I'd been turned. And they were completely consistent with our BD (before death) relationship.

I thought back to the chapter in *Sense and Sensibility* when Mr. Dashwood has just died. Marianne and Mrs. Dashwood are overcome by grief. *They gave themselves up wholly to their sorrow, seeking increase of wretchedness in every reflection that could afford it, and resolved against ever admitting consolation in the future.* This leaves Elinor to deal with their grasping relatives. Elinor isn't given the chance to grieve because she's able to handle all of the grunt work.

I was definitely an Elinor, minus the quiet dignity . . . or the sense. But I was dependable, overly analytical, and unable to shirk excessive responsibilities. So I gathered the coffee cups and bit my tongue.

"I'll just take them into the kitchen," I muttered. "And join the other scullery maids."

I hefted the tray with one hand and nearly ran smack into my high-school crush, Adam Morrow, a blond, dimpled, and ridiculously clean-cut veterinarian.

"A-Adam!" I stuttered. "Hi!"

At least one thing had remained constant since my living days: I still couldn't find anything to say to Adam Morrow. While contemplating the back of his neck in sophomore English, I had daydreams where Adam suddenly realized how luminously beautiful I was, inside and out. He would finally realize that I was more than the brainy gal jocks wanted to be paired with on group projects. He'd ask me where I'd been all his life. There was also an imagined prom-night scenario that I won't go into. And now, all I could do was gawk at him and keep a death grip on a tray of dirty coffee cups.

"Hi, Jane," he said, smiling broadly. "It's nice to see you again. It's been a while."

"What are you doing here?" I blurted. Woo-hoo, a full, unstuttered sentence!

Adam was carrying a carefully Tupperwared seven-layer salad, though how anything involving hard-boiled eggs, bacon, mayonnaise, and sugar could be considered salad, I have no idea. "Mama sent me over with this. She had dental surgery this afternoon, and she's still laid up on the pain pills. She's sorry she couldn't make it."

"That was very thoughtful," I said, accepting the bowl with my free hand. "And heavy. How much bacon is in this thing?"

"Just enough." He laughed, bottomless cerulean eyes twinkling. "What about you? Are you doing something different with your hair?" he asked, staring at me closely. "Because you look different. Great but different."

He was staring at me again, as if I were a puzzle he was trying to solve. Apparently, word hadn't gotten around to Adam about my undead status. So, for reasons I didn't quite fathom yet, I lied through my pointy teeth.

"I've been working out," I told him, smiling brightly. His interest seemed to perk up even further at the display of teeth. "What have you been up to? How's the clinic?"

He shrugged those wide shoulders. "Oh, you know, patients who bite me and pee on themselves. It's a living. How about you?"

I grimaced. "Well, I'm sure you heard that I'm no longer working at the library."

His cheerfully blank face gave me the impression that he was too polite to acknowledge that I was being gossiped about behind my back. I continued, "I'm actually working at a bookstore over on Braxton Avenue now. I really like my new boss. I've never really done retail before, but I get to work around books again, so it's great. I've sort of moved on to another phase of my life. A phase that does not include Story Time and sock puppets."

Adam chuckled, winking his dimples at me. "You should keep your options open. You never know what might come up."

Like a bullet wound and an old guy willing to gnaw on my neck to save my life. That was a surprise. At the thought of Gabriel, I felt a little twinge of guilt. It felt very wrong to do anything even remotely resembling flirting. And even worse when Adam blurted, "It's been—I—I'd like to—would you like to meet up for coffee sometime?"

Well, there went a bigger twinge.

I did a bit of a double-take, sure I'd heard him wrong. "I'm sorry, could you repeat what you just said?"

"Coffee." He laughed. "Would you like to have a cup of coffee sometime? Catch up, talk about old times, share embarrassing memories, that sort of thing."

"You mean like when I used to follow you around at middle-school dances, trying to work up the nerve to ask you to slow dance to 'End of the Road'? Oh, crap. That was out loud. I have to stop doing that."

"Don't worry." Adam laughed. "It's kind of flattering."

I laughed, too, but more as a defense mechanism than out of actual amusement.

"So, coffee?" Adam asked pointedly. "Yes?"

There it was, everything I'd wanted as a human laid out on a platter before me. If you'd asked me when I was a teenager, "What would fulfill every romantic hope and dream in your obsessive adolescent heart?" Adam Morrow asking me out would do it. As much as I'd tried to embrace my vampire lifestyle, it was difficult to let that go. It actually pained me when I had to say, "I appreciate the offer, but I'm seeing someone."

Adam clearly wasn't used to being turned down. It took him just as long to process the fact that I'd said no as it did for me to realize that him asking me out wasn't an auditory hallucination.

He finally said, "Well, you can't blame a guy for trying. I'll see you around, Jane."

After watching a deflated Adam making his way through the funeral crowd, I busied myself gathering dirty plates and forks. I'd made it halfway to the kitchen when a sharp poke to my side made me squeal and fling cutlery. Panic and my vampire reflexes had me plucking the falling pieces out of the air.

"Fast hands," said my uncle Junior, the one who finds sneaking up behind me and startling me the height of hilarity.

"That just gets funnier and funnier every time you do it," I retorted, poking through his paunch at his ribs.

"Aw, honey, he doesn't know any better," Uncle Paul said, shaking his head. "Mama dropped him a lot when he was baby."

Paul and Junior were Dad's brothers. I liked both of them, but when I was growing up, they were always so busy with their big, strapping sons, Dwight and Oscar. And they actually managed to move a whopping forty-five minutes away from Half-Moon Hollow, so I didn't see them except around holidays.

"How's my shortcake?" Uncle Paul asked.

"You're seven feet tall, everyone's shorter than you," I said, kissing his cheek and following our usual "comedy" routine. "Just wait until old age catches up with you, we'll see who laughs last."

"Your mama told us you've had some health problems," said Uncle Junior, who hugged me hard enough to crack mortal ribs.

"I guess you could call it that," I said, suspicious thoughts beginning to churn in my brain.

"Those deer ticks are everywhere," Paul said, clucking and shaking his head. "That's why I duct-tape my pants legs around my socks when I go turkey hunting."

Had I accidentally walked into a French film? It was as if they were having a totally different conversation. "Yeah . . ."

"But there are treatments nowadays, aren't there?" Junior asked. "It's not supposed to affect your life span or anything, is it?"

"No, quite the opposite," I muttered.

"That's great, sweetie," he said, chucking me under the chin. "I'd hate to think of my niece keeling over from Lyme disease."

Lyme disease?

"Lyme disease?" I thought it bore repeating outside my head.

"You just let us know if you need anything," Uncle Junior said. "If those doctors don't treat you right, we'll kick their asses."

"You know, most of our conversations end that way," I noted.

"And we always mean it," Uncle Paul assured me. "Now we're going to say hi to your grandma and then give your dad a hard time."

I turned and zeroed in on a woman simultaneously serving coffee and simpering. Mama. "I'll see y'all later."

I stormed as quietly and subtly as possible across the room. Daddy saw "that" look on my face, caught my arm, and pulled me to a quiet corner. "Honey, whatever you're about to say to your mama, I'm sure she deserves it, but this is a funeral. Bob's family, at least, deserves our respect."

"Daddy, as the only sane member of my family, I love you and respect your opinion. That's why I'm going to address the situation quietly and calmly in a nice private corner, where I will not make a scene . . ." The eerily calm tone got Daddy to release my arm before he heard me say, "While I slowly choke the breath from her body."

By the time he called, "Jane!" in a warning tone, I had already grabbed Mama from a gaggle of tutting church ladies and dragged her into an alcove. "Lyme disease, Mama? Really?"

"What?" Mama asked, the picture of innocence.

"You told the uncles I have Lyme disease!"

"I told them you'd had some health issues," she spluttered. "They just assumed it was Lyme disease."

"No one *assumes* you have Lyme disease," I whispered. "How do you just assume Lyme disease? I know this hasn't been easy for you, Mama. I know you're embarrassed that I'm different. I know it took me months to work up the nerve to be around me without being afraid or ashamed."

"I'm not ashamed of you," Mama insisted. "It's just that everyone makes these assumptions about me and your daddy. I know it's not true, but it's so difficult knowing that people are looking at me and judging and whispering."

"But it's not even like this makes me the most scandalous member of the family. I'm bothered by the fact that Junie manages to pick up singles without using her hands while she performs at the Booby Hatch. But do I say anything? No."

It was at that moment that I realized that we were standing next to a podium. A podium with a mic on it. A mic that was on.

Crap.

We turned to find most of the bereaved watching us, horrified. And my cousin Junie didn't look thrilled with me, either.

5

Hostility toward human males marrying into were clans is to be expected and taken seriously. Potential sons-in-law may want to carry wolfsbane or silver items in their pockets. Weres find both substances to be extremely irritating.

—*Mating Rituals and Love Customs of the Were*

Despite Bob's being laid to rest on a cloudy day, I elected not to go to his burial. I thought it might build strange expectations for Mama. Aunt Jettie, who relished her role as my go-to daytime spy, reported that Bob's burial was much more entertaining than his visitation.

Grandma Ruthie had gone from grieving widow to seeing herself as some sort of postmodern, postmenopausal Juliet. She wore an even bigger veiled hat to the cemetery and a black crepe dress with a full, flowing skirt and trailing sleeves. I'm thinking she bought it from the *Gone with the Wind* Widows Collection. She wailed and screeched her way through the eulogy, screamed, "Why, Lord? Why?" through the final blessing, and tried to snatch Bob's service flag away from his son when it was presented by the honor guard. Also, she demanded front-row center seats for her and her male companion, Wilbur.

That's right. My grandma brought a date to her fiancé's burial. She's all class, that lady. Apparently, she'd met Wilbur at Whitlow's as he was heading into an old Army buddy's visitation. Sparks flew, time stood still, and Grandma Ruthie snagged another victim. On the upside, I think Wilbur's presence may have been the only thing that kept her from flinging herself into the grave on top of the casket.

But somehow, my outing cousin Junie as a day-shift dancer at the Booby Hatch made me an embarrassment to the family. At the burial, Grandma had declared that she wouldn't speak to me until I'd apologized to Junie. I would think this odd considering that Junie was a cousin on my dad's side of the family and Ruthie was my maternal grandmother. But Grandma Ruthie liked ninety-nine percent of the general population better than me, so why not cousins on the other side of the family?

During my shift that night, Aunt Jettie came into the shop to give me all of the details of the cemetery theatrics. She was in the middle of reenacting this declaration when a little woman in a double-knit pant suit came into the shop to claim a phone order. Aunt Jettie made herself scarce.

On the phone, Esther Barnes's voice had sounded deep and accented. In person, she was squat, with dyed jet-black hair, deep wrinkles at the edges of her eyes, and a smoky topaz cocktail ring the size of a door knocker. Her voice was reedy and thin as she asked whether I had the "Barnes order" ready yet. I pulled her reserved copies of *Mind over Matter: Maintaining Your Psychic Ability* and *The Search for the Inner Id* from under the counter and rang them up.

There was something off about Esther Barnes. Her eyes were too bright, too sharp. Her mouth was small, thin, pinched into a coral-painted, birdlike moue. From the way her gaze was sweeping across the shop, I would guess she was calculating the value of every item in the store.

"Are you new in town, Ms. Barnes?" I asked, my tone light and friendly, even as I watched her weigh a brittle amethyst ceremonial blade with her even more fragile-looking hands.

"No." She put the blade down, slapped her money on the counter, and stared at me. I would guess this stare had put many a shopgirl in her place over the years. But, well, I was bored, and she was there.

I smiled pleasantly. "Have family around here?"

Her eyes narrowed as what little politeness she offered drained out of her voice. "No."

I held up a newly printed Specialty Books brochure. "Would you like to be put on our mailing list?"

OK, at this point, I was just trying to be annoying.

Ms. Barnes narrowed her eyes at me. There was a buzzing sensation, like being slapped under the forehead.

Ow.

It was as if someone let loose a hive full of bees in my head, little stings and pricks on the edge of my brain. I gripped the counter as the room spun out of focus. My head dipped as if I were just a bit tipsy, then snapped back into place as I fought for focus. Annoyed, I closed my eyes and built up a wall around my mind. I focused on the little woman in front of me and attempted to slap back, but it was like grabbing at sand. I couldn't get a grip. The edges of her consciousness kept slipping through my fingers. I did well just to maintain control of my own psychic defenses and not pass out at her feet.

Exhausted by what was really just a moment's effort, I opened my eyes to find a smug smile stretched across Ms. Barnes's face. "Better luck next time, dear."

Did I just get psychically pimp-slapped by a little old lady?

After she sauntered out of the shop, I hustled back to the stacks and grabbed a copy of *Mind over Matter: Maintaining Your Psychic Ability.* "What the hell is in this book?"

I checked Mr. Wainwright's "records" for Ms. Barnes's contact information. And by records, I mean the stack of scrap paper he kept in the back of the cash-register drawer with scribbled customer names and addresses. She was nowhere to be found, which was not a surprise. He did, however, have the address for a man who lived in Possum Trot and called himself Nostradamus, which made a certain amount of sense.

I opened *Mind over Matter* and scanned a few pages, trying to find the section on how to use one's mental talents to smack people around. Nothing. Esther Barnes was clearly playing a deck stacked with a few extra cards.

How do you guard against someone who can reach into your skull and scramble stuff around?

"I'm going to have to make a tin-foil hat," I muttered as the phone rang.

It was then that I realized how wrong I was to think that being brain-assaulted was going to be the worst part of my day. It was my mother, calling to remind me that the annual Jameson family tree-trimming party was coming up that weekend and that I needed to wear my Frosty the Snowman sweater for the family Christmas-card picture. Mama always artfully arranged our "candid" family tree-trimming picture one week after Thanksgiving, so she was able to send the Christmas cards out by December 14, one week before her arch-enemy and best friend, Carol Ann Reilly.

"Um, I don't think Jenny and Grandma would be very happy about seeing me."

"But y'all got along so well at the visitation!" Mama cried.

"Being glad that someone will wash dishes and being happy that they were present are two different things."

"Now, you're just being silly, Jane. You're just going to have to learn to kiss and make up with Grandma and Jenny for the holidays. I won't stand for this. It was one thing for you to miss Thanksgiving, but this is getting ridiculous. Where else are you going to go?"

"Actually, I might have plans," I lied.

Mama gasped. "What do you mean, you have plans? It's not Christmas unless you're with family."

"Well, I have some new friends this year, and they

don't have family around here. I thought it would be nice to spend some time with them."

"New *vampire* friends," Mama said, just a hint of bitterness tingeing her tone.

"No, not all of them are vampires."

"Well, if you want to throw away years of tradition, that's your choice. If you really want to spend the first Christmas since we lost you with strangers, that's your decision to make."

"What do you mean, 'lost me'? I'm right here!"

"I can't keep talking about it, Jane."

"Talking about what? We don't talk about this. At all."

Mama sighed, the slightest edge of a sniffle curling at the end. "Will you at least come to the tree-trimming party so we can take the family picture? Not everyone has to know that you and Jenny have had a falling out."

"Can't you just Photoshop me in or something?" I asked.

"I don't even know what that means." Mama grunted. "Just show up on Saturday at six."

I hung up the phone and commenced thumping my head against the leaded-glass counter.

"If you keep doing that, it's going to leave a mark," a smooth, bemused voice said. "Even your healing powers have limits."

I looked up to find Andrea Byrne standing in front of me, smirking.

"You look perturbed. Well, more perturbed than usual," she said, examining the paling bruise on my forehead.

"What was your first clue?" I asked grumpily.

Andrea reminds one of what Grace Kelly might have looked like with red hair and a twisted backstory. Broke after her split with her (fickle bastard) undead ex and disowned by a firmly antivampire family, Andrea came to the Hollow years before to get a job in a boutique downtown. But her real income came from clients who enjoyed her blood in a mutually safe environment for a small fee. Andrea was the first—and last—human I fed from. It made for a rather awkward beginning to our friendship, but she was the one human I knew who truly understood the bizarre aspects of my new vampire lifestyle. She was sort of like my undead blankie, keeping me connected to the living world. Mama would have done the same thing but with more guilt and sunburns.

She hefted both *Mind over Matter* and *The Spectrum of Vampirism* off the counter and winced. "A little light reading?"

"Just researching my roots," I said, flipping *Spectrum* to the chapter titled "Global Origins." "Like this charming theory, for example: 'Gypsies believed that vampires returned from the dead to seek vengeance on those who may have contributed to their death or neglected to give them a proper burial. Graves were watched carefully for signs of being disturbed. Exhumed corpses that were bloated or had turned black would be staked, beheaded, and burned.' Well, why didn't they just blast the remains out of a cannon? Humans are stupid."

"I'm standing right here," Andrea griped.

"Oh, you're not really human. You're like one of us, only with a pulse."

"And Mr. Wainwright?"

"Same goes." I nodded. "You don't normally come in here. What's up?"

"I'm bored."

"Bored?" I asked.

She nodded. "Ever since Dick became interested in me, all but my most loyal clients have stopped calling. I don't know if they are in doubt of my taste or frightened of Dick, but either way, it's not good for business."

"Well, thanks for thinking of me." I grinned. "I'm off in a couple of hours. What did you want to do?"

"Oh, I know, why don't we go out for a nice girls' night, get into a bar fight, and then, just for kicks, one of us could end up suspected in a vampire murder. That could be fun," Andrea suggested brightly. "Oh, wait, we did that already."

"You think you're being funny, but you're not funny. When I tell the story, I don't tell people about you being knee-walking drunk, ergo unconscious, during the whole fight. I think I'm going to change that policy."

"You actually tell people that story?"

I nodded. "But when I tell it, Walter is six-foot-three and a trained cage fighter."

Andrea chuckled.

I grinned slyly. "Dick has been looking for you."

She grumbled. "He doesn't know the meaning of the word 'restraining order,' does he?"

"Technically, that's two words." I giggled. "Dick and Andrea sitting in a tree, B-I-T-I-N-G—ow!" I whined as she punched my shoulder. "You're just mad because secretly, underneath that sophisticated exterior, you're hot for Dickie."

"I am not hot for Dickie," Andrea spat.

"Me and my bruised shoulder say thou dost protest too much," I said dryly.

"He's practically stalking me. He just won't let it go. He's just being . . . he's being a jackass with a flaky jackass crust and a delicious jackass filling."

"So he's jackass pie?" I asked, making my "ew" face.

"There's no reason to be crass," Andrea mewed primly.

"You know, you're starting to talk like me. I find this more than a little troubling. Maybe we should spend less time together."

"I could come up with jackass pie on my own," she insisted, then mulled that statement over. "No. No, I couldn't."

"By the way, what are your plans for Christmas?" I asked.

"Pretending my parents haven't disowned me, watching *It's a Wonderful Life,* and drinking a few bottles of merlot. How about you?"

I chewed my lip. "I'm thinking of throwing together a little party for us disenfranchised monsters."

"You're using us as an excuse not to spend time with your family?"

"No, I'm choosing to spend time with my dearest friends," I retorted. "Fine, it's eighty percent spending time with you guys and twenty percent avoiding my family."

Andrea shot me her best doubtful glare.

"Seventy/thirty," I said as the doorbell tinkled. I was confronted with the sight of a weeping werewolf, clutching a bear trap in one hand and a wedding planner in the other.

There's something you don't see every day.

A curious Mr. Wainwright poked his head out of the office, illogically thrilled at the sight of a tearful werewolf in his shop. "This is the most traffic the shop has had in years," he said, smiling brightly. "Jane, would your friends like a cup of tea?"

"Why don't you put the kettle on?" I suggested in a voice as calm and soothing as I could muster. "Andrea Byrne, Jolene McClaine," I said, eyeing Jolene and the bear trap warily. "Jolene, honey, what's wrong?"

"Zeb!" she wailed plaintively.

"What about Zeb? Is he OK?" I demanded, sniffing the trap but finding no scent of blood.

"He's fine." Her deeply backwoods accent stretched the word out into "faaaaaaahhhnnnn" before she wailed, "He's called off the wedding!"

Visions of an unworn, unreturnable peach sateen bridesmaid's dress lurking in the back of my closet flashed before my eyes. I shuddered. "I thought we agreed that you guys weren't going to come to me anymore with your problems."

"But this time is different!" Jolene wailed. "This time *I* need help!"

"OK, OK." I took the trap out of her hands and wrapped my arms around her. She sniffled into my shirt, leaving a spreading wet stain on my shoulder. "Are you sure about that he called off the wedding, Jolene? Sometimes Zeb misspells stuff in e-mails, and it comes across badly."

"Of course I'm sure!" Jolene howled, drawing a sharp wince from Andrea, who was more accustomed to the slightly more sedate antics of vampires. "I'm not stupid!"

"OK," I said, scratching behind her ears. It may sound condescending, but sometimes that calmed her down.

"Do you have anythin' to eat?" Jolene asked, sniffing the air. "I can't talk like this on an empty stomach."

Jolene couldn't do anything on an empty stomach.

Mr. Wainwright helped me scavenge leftover pizza, canned stew, and some Chef Boyardee from his apartment and then made himself scarce. Even his fascination with were-creatures wasn't enough to keep him around a hysterical female. Note to self: Bring pot pies and bagged salad to the shop for Mr. Wainwright. This kind of diet could not be good for him.

"What happened?" I asked as she gorged herself on cold pepperoni. It was always oddly compelling to watch Jolene eat, with the stark contrast between the beautiful, trim girl and the huge amounts of food she shoveled into her face. If you didn't know about her werewolf metabolism, you'd wonder where she put it all.

I tried to reach out to her mind, but the jumble of images—confused, pained, and frenetic—made me dizzy.

"My cousins played a little joke on Zeb, and he got so upset," she said, gnawing on reheated crust. "I told him he was overreactin' and he should be glad that my cousins were tryin' to make him part of the pack. And then he said something about 'not wantin' to live on the farm with the Jerry Springer family' and how we were going to lose our house thanks to them. I asked what the hell he meant by that. He said he was sure I knew all about it. I told him he sounded like a paranoid jerk. He said that if I really felt that way, then he wasn't gonna to be able to marry me." Her eyes welled up again. "How could he do that? How could he just break it off without even looking upset about it? How could he just leave me?"

I waited for the yowl of "meeee" to end. "What kind of joke did your cousins play on Zeb?"

"They put a bear trap between his usual parkin' spot by the front door to Mama and Daddy's place. It was just a joke," Jolene insisted. "We do it to each other all the time."

"Wolves set bear traps for each other? Isn't that sort of, I don't know, culturally insensitive or something?"

Jolene seemed befuddled by the question. "No, it doesn't hurt that bad."

"You heal ten times faster than the average human," I told her. "That bear trap could have cost Zeb a foot. He's already lost a pinkie toe to your family's little jokes."

"They're just bein' playful."

"He lost an appendage, Jolene. That's not playful, that's wanton endangerment."

Jolene sniffed. "Don't! Don't use the 'talkin' down the crazy person' voice. And don't act like you're sad this happened. You probably set this whole thing up to get out of wearing the bridesmaid dress."

"What is wrong with you?" I asked. "Why would you say that?"

"I don't know!" Jolene cried. "He proposed to me! I was a normal person before this. He made me go crazy! I know my family is screwed up, OK? I know it's not normal for your cousin to want to marry you or for your parents to make you move in less than a hundred yards away from them.

"I know it's not normal to be so loud and in each other's business all the time. I know they're passive-aggressive and just plain aggressive and they pay no attention to boundaries. They know they could have hurt Zeb with these pranks, and that's half of the fun for them. But what am I supposed to do? This is my pack. This is thousands of years of breedin' and instinct. I can't stop that."

She sobbed and wiped at her eyes. "And that's what I told him. Then I said he wouldn't be so tense if maybe his parents were more supportive of us instead of torpedoin' the wedding every chance they got. He asked me what I meant by that, and I said that it was obvious his mama would be a lot happier if he was marrying you instead of me. And when he told me that was crazy, I told him to take his ring and shove it where the sun don't shine, and I stormed off, and now I'm sittin' here, miserable, and with no idea whether I'm gettin' married."

Andrea goggled. "That was a Jane-worthy tirade. Really, very impressive."

"Please don't help," I said, turning to Jolene. "And you,

you've got to draw a line somewhere. You're marrying Zeb. His safety and happiness have to be your priority, no matter what your family does. Stand up for him, if not to show your family that you're going to be the first McClaine to break this weird-ass cycle of human abuse, then to show Zeb that you're on his side.

"Apologize," I said. "And then go perform some physical favors for him that I never have to think about. And both of you have to stop coming to me when you have relationship problems. I barely have time for my own problems, and yours are, well, weird."

"You're a really good friend, Jane," she said, shoving the remains of pizza into her mouth.

I patted her arm. "I know. I was serious about that last part."

Gabriel's home on Silver Ridge Road would have been the crown jewel in any historical home tour . . . if anyone in town knew about it. Gabriel had worked for years to erase the house, with its white clapboard, big wraparound porch, and Corinthian columns, from public memory. The house was cozy and way less intimidating than you would expect inside. The rooms I'd seen were done in subtle, muted colors, soft fabrics, little knickknacks that spoke of Gabriel's years of travel, the kind of rooms where you wouldn't expect to find your boyfriend plying your best friend with liquor.

Poor Zeb looked absolutely miserable, splayed on the maroon leather couch with a glass in one hand and his head in the other.

When he looked up, I saw he was wearing an eye patch. This could not be good.

"OK, I heard about the bear trap. Did something happen to your eye?"

"No, I'm considering a career as a pirate," Zeb snarked as he gingerly adjusted the patch strap. He winced when it snapped back into place over his eye. The elastic had given him a quailish cowlick in the middle of his dark blond crown. "Some of the boys out at the farm were shooting off bottle rockets a few days ago. Jolene's cousin Vance wanted to show them how to use them to knock cans off the fence, and somehow one of the rockets went astray."

"You got hit in the eye with a bottle rocket?"

"No, I got hit in the eye with the bottle. Vance wasn't watching where he tossed it when they were running from the bottle rocket."

"So, that combined with bear trap is why you're doing the full-on Dean Martin routine?" I asked, looking at the bottle between them.

"I've been evicted," Zeb said, turning away two fingers of very nice bourbon.

Gabriel huffed and slugged it back himself. Considering the average vintage in his wine cellar, I wasn't surprised he wouldn't let it go to waste.

"This has not been your day, huh?"

"My landlord left me a notice today," Zeb said, making a face when Gabriel held up a bottle of vodka with a Cyrillic label. "I was supposed to renew my lease next week."

"He can't do that! Jolene worked so hard to leave

her mark on that place," I exclaimed. Gabriel gave me a cringing, questioning look. "With throw pillows and paint, I mean. Nothing gross."

"I went to sign the papers with Mr. Dugger, but he's decided to rent to another family," Zeb said, his pale face stretched in tight, miserable lines. "He said Jolene's fixed the place up so nicely he can charge more than we can afford. And somehow, Jolene's uncle Deke just happened to call today to remind her that her plot of land on the pack compound is still available. He even offered us a brand-newish trailer as a wedding gift." Zeb sighed, planting his face in his hands as Gabriel stood to pour him a scotch. "I don't know how they did it, but they got to Mr. Dugger."

"I think you might be giving them a little too much— yeah, you're probably right," I agreed, slipping an arm around his shoulders. "What are you going to do? Starting with, will you please pry the crying werewolf out of my shop? She's starting to disturb the customer. Emphasis on *customer;* we only have one."

"You saw Jolene?" Zeb grimaced. "She was crying?"

"Um, you kind of broke off your engagement. That can bring out the emotion in a gal."

"I know, I need to apologize," Zeb said. "But I'd like to have a home to offer her when I beg and plead." He took a sip of Gabriel's liquor, blanched, and coughed. "Seriously, that's what it tastes like?"

"Zeb can only drink stuff that tastes a little like alcohol and a lot like fruit punch," I told Gabriel.

"I'll start keeping some around," Gabriel said. "Until

then, try to finish the expensive single-malt I just poured for you. Peasant."

"I would insult you back, but you seem to own or know about all of the good rental properties around town." Zeb snorted.

Giving new meaning to the words "saved by the bell," Gabriel's cell phone began singing. His face when he saw the caller ID stopped me from making a joke about voice mail, which Gabriel didn't know how to use. Without a word, he left the room and said hello quietly into the receiver as he walked out onto the back porch.

For lack of something better to say, I told Zeb, "I wish I could help."

"Aw, I appreciate that," he said, leaning his head against mine. "But you're, you know, broke."

My jaw dropped. "You know about that?"

"I'm your best friend," he said. "And you haven't had a full-time job in months. I can do math above the kindergarten level. Besides, I would never take money from you. We've never mixed money into our friendship before."

"We never had money before," I pointed out.

"And so far, that's worked out for us," he said. "Besides, if we're not going to take that kind of 'help'—emphasis on the sarcastic invisible quotation marks—from Jolene's family, it would be hard to justify taking help from you."

"You have a well-thought-out and emotionally mature argument," I admitted. "Dang it. On an unrelated note, here's an interesting tidbit: Your mama kept trying to get me to eat at the funeral, which would have ended in my vomiting publicly. She does know that I've been turned, right? I assumed she has just refused to mention it because it interferes with her version of reality. But you did tell her, right?"

Zeb winced. "Every time I try, she repeats something stupid she hears on talk radio, like vampires should be rounded up and forced to live in communities far away from humans."

"Still, you're marrying into a werewolf clan, and you're worried about telling her there's a vampire bridesmaid? If anything, you could use me to take the heat off Jolene and Company." I gasped as realization slowly dawned. "She still doesn't know you're marrying into a werewolf clan, does she?"

"No," he admitted, covering his face with his hands. Whether it was from shame or to protect his eyes from my vampire death glare, I have no idea. "You know her. You know what she does with announcements like this. We're talking Valium and screaming, taking to her bed for weeks at a time. I knew there was no way she'd accept you, much less Jolene and her family. I'm just trying to get through the wedding without her making a scene. I saw what it did to Jolene when my parents threatened not to come. Can you imagine how she would handle Mama's werewolf meltdown? How much that would hurt her? Once we're married, Jolene will realize that she's better off with my family not liking her anyway."

"Don't you think your family will notice something's off when the bride's side mows through the buffet?" I asked.

"Oh, my family will be too drunk to notice," he said, rolling his eyes. "Why do you think we're having the open bar?"

"That's not—actually, that's brilliant."

"I've tried everything to get Mama to behave, to be decent to Jolene," Zeb said. "She says she'll straighten up and be nice, and then I get a phone call from Jolene, crying about whatever Mama's said now. I've told her to ignore Mama, but she just can't. She can't stand having someone not like her. And I'm exhausted. I'm tired of being the go-between. Why can't she just handle this stuff herself?"

I arched my brows at the angry, exasperated tone Zeb was using. He seemed to shake it off after a moment, rubbing his hands over his patch and then moving them to pinch the bridge of his nose.

"In a few months, this will all be over," he said.

"Because you will have succumbed to chronic stress headaches and bottle-rocket trauma?" I asked, taking one of his hands and gently pushing at the pressure point between his thumb and forefinger.

When he smiled, the skin around his visible eye crinkled. "Because in a few months, we'll be married. And we can enter the witness-protection program."

"Sounds like a plan," I said, quirking my lips as I stared at him.

"What?"

I shrugged. "It's just weird. Normally, I'd be the first person you'd call when something like this trailer deal comes up. But now it's Gabriel. I think you're entering

into a functional adult relationship with someone besides me. I guess the wedding is the final sign that we're
growing up."

"I don't know how I feel about it," Zeb said absently.
He was looking at me intently; his good eye seemed
glazed over, unfocused. This was not the way Zeb normally looked at me. This was the way Zeb looked at
mint-condition, still-in-the-package GI Joe Battle Force
dolls.

Since he was dealing with a traumatic injury, I was
willing to attribute this bizarre behavior to a concussion.
"It doesn't suck."

"It does a little bit." He cupped the back of my head in
his hand, bringing my face almost uncomfortably close
to his. For a weird moment, it felt as if he was going to
kiss me. Which, for our relationship, was highly unusual.
I leaned away, pulling his hands from my neck.

Gabriel came in and found the two of us staring at
each other, Zeb's hands in mine. Zeb dropped his hands
to his sides and looked vaguely guilty.

"If you weren't Jane's best friend and engaged to a
beautiful and violently monogamous woman, I might
find this upsetting," Gabriel commented dryly.

Werewolf fathers insist on preapproving proposals of marriage. In fact, it's rumored that the human tradition of "asking for a woman's hand" came from a human who failed to ask for betrothal permission and actually lost his hand.

—*Mating Rituals and Love Customs of the Were*

"Why did I try to make more friends?" I muttered, shielding my eyes from my reflection in the Bridal Barn's fitting-room mirror. "This is what comes of having girlfriends."

If the picture of Jolene's chosen bridesmaid's dress was bad, the live version was horrifying. Basted together, the putrefied peach piecework was not just unflattering, it was insulting. My hips looked wider than my shoulders; wider than the dressing-room door, in fact. My preternaturally pale skin looked cheesy and almost blue. I actually looked dead, which was a first. At no time had I ever wished harder that vampires couldn't see themselves in mirrors.

After much groveling on both sides, Zeb and Jolene

made up, which meant I was still trapped in bridesmaid-dress hell. I took cold comfort in the fact that I wasn't alone. I would be walking down the aisle with Jolene's legion of cousins. The McClaines went with a "lene" theme in naming this generation's females: Raylene, Lurlene, identical twins Charlene and Darlene, then trip-lets Arlene, Braylene, and Angelene. It was pronounced "Angel-lean," by the way. That's a mistake I didn't make twice. All of them were gorgeous, redhaired, and green-eyed, with ridiculously high cheekbones. And all of them pretty much hated me. First, I was an outsider, which could have been overlooked if I was not also a vampire. Compounded by the injustice of my position as best maid despite being a relatively new friend, this created another sense of clan shame among the cousins. The fact that Zeb and Jolene chose me to avoid a blood feud among Jolene's cousins escaped them.

Despite the snubbing of her firstborn, Lurlene, from the best-maid spot, Jolene's aunt Vonnie was finally persuaded to keep her shop open after dusk so I could come in for a fitting. I'm pretty sure the indignity of having to rework her schedule for a vampire is what put the burr up her butt.

Buying your first prom gown at the Bridal Barn is a rite of passage for every Half-Moon Hollow girl. Because it was the *only* place in town where you could buy a prom gown. Or a wedding gown. Or a bridesmaid gown. We had a formal-wear chain store called Mr. Monkeysuit in the early 1990s, but they mysteriously shut their doors after six months. Before I knew the Barn was owned by a werewolf, I figured that the lack of competition stemmed from the claustrophobic confines of Hollow commerce. Now I thought it may have been because Aunt Vonnie *ate* her competition.

Now that I knew how much time Aunt Vonnie spent in the nude, I found it deliciously ironic that she owned a dress shop. Werewolves don't like wearing clothes when they're in the home field. Clothing makes life awkward for werewolves, for whom the most comfortable state is to be in wolf form. In an environment where they're relaxed, sometimes they don't even realize they've changed. There's a subtle blending of light, and suddenly there's a full-grown wolf standing next to you. It's difficult to change form while dressed. At the same time, adult werewolves become conditioned to associate clothing with being out in public among humans. It's handy as a reminder to help keep the change in check.

Jolene says that modern weres have adopted the human habit of dressing for weddings since so many of them involve human guests, and a nude officiate can be terribly offputting. The weres figure if you have to be dressed, it might as well be the most elaborate, uncomfortable clothes possible, which led Vonnie to open her shop. The problem was that Vonnie's tastes hadn't quite evolved since the days of big shoulder pads and bigger hair. The dresses in the Bridal Barn only came in colors that cannot be found in nature. Also, I don't think any of the fabrics were manufactured after 1984. We're talking a lot of large-gauge sequins.

"Jane, are you comin' out?" Jolene called from outside the dressing room.

"No," I whispered, transfixed by the horrific reflection before me.

Wasn't there a Greek myth that ended like this?

From just outside the privacy curtain, Jolene said quietly, "Zeb says you're not thrilled with the dress."

"And that means I have to kill Zeb for telling you that," I said, poking my head out of the dressing room but keeping the curtain closed tight around my neck. "I hate it when couples make up. It means they repeat everything other people have told them in some sort of confessional fit."

"It can't be that bad—" Jolene ripped back the curtain. "Whoa."

"Yeah," I deadpanned.

"It will look different," Jolene promised. "After the rose and the ruffles and everything are put on. It'll look different."

"I don't think ruffles are going to improve the situation."

"I know," Jolene whispered. "I know it's horrible. I've worn that dress in six of my cousins' weddings, including my cousin Raylene, who chose black taffeta for a July ceremony. Nobody looks good in it. That's the whole point. Parade the bridesmaids out in this dress, make them look like cows—"

"Hey." I glared at her. "There's no need to agree with me quite so much."

She ignored me. "So that when you walk down the aisle, you seem gorgeous by comparison. That's the real tradition behind the dress."

"You're already gorgeous by comparison," I hissed.

"Thanks," she said, glowing briefly. "But it's the one concession I've made to the pack about the wedding. I'm not marryin' a were. I'm havin' a nighttime ceremony to accommodate the vampire guests. I'm not marryin' in the boneyard."

"Boneyard?"

She shook her head. "Don't ask. I went against almost every McClaine family tradition to marry Zeb. This is the one thing I agreed to." She paused when I arched an eyebrow. "That you have to wear. You can get me really, really drunk at my bachelorette party and take embarrassin' pictures," she promised.

"I was going to do that anyway," I snarked.

Aunt Vonnie bustled into the room with a bolt of lime-green chiffon. My lack of enthusiasm was clearly an affront to her craft.

"I haven't stayed open past six in thirty years of business," she reminded me.

"I really appreciate it, Miss Vonnie," I said with all the cheer I could rally dressed like an extra from *Footloose*. "And thank you for making the dresses. They're just . . . stunning."

Aunt Vonnie easily picked up on my shifting eyes and twitchy lips. Or maybe I was pushing it with the empty double thumbs-up.

I have got to learn how to lie.

"Every McClaine bride since 1984 has chosen the 'Ruffles and Dreams' for her bridesmaids." She sniffed, turning back to the sewing room. "It's very popular here in town. I've made this dress in thirty-two colors for more than one hundred weddings."

"Well, that certainly explains the Hollow's unusually high divorce rate," I muttered.

"I heard that!" Aunt Vonnie yelled from the back. I was going to have to watch myself around werewolves and their superhearing.

I turned to Jolene. "There will be pictures. Oh, yes, pictures and male strippers."

"I accept your terms," Jolene said solemnly.

"Get me out of this thing." I sighed, angling the ridiculously placed zipper toward her. "Can I at least see the wedding dress?"

"I ordered it special on the Internet!" she squealed as she ran into the back room.

"Still need help with the zipper!" I called after her. I turned and caught a look at myself in a mirror. *"Gah!"*

Seriously, how does a veteran seamstress sew a zipper so that you need Go-Go Gadget arms to reach it? I spun in circles like a dog chasing its tail. I heard shuffling and giggling as Jolene tried on her wedding dress.

She emerged from the dressing room a vision in an elaborately beaded white Edwardian gown. And despite the universal laws of wedding dress ordering, the standard size four actually fit her perfectly. The cut emphasized her tiny waist and gave her the ideal hourglass silhouette. Every move sent a burst of sparkles from the beading. Her skin seemed clearer, brighter, creamier, her eyes a truer green.

"I hate you. You're completely gorgeous, and I hate

you," I grumbled, feeling even more dumpy in my half-basted peach death shroud.

"Thanks." She sighed dreamily.

"Meanwhile, I'm still dressed like this and . . ." I sent a glance at my watch.

"The engagement party!" she cried. "I almost forgot!"

"Well, that's probably just your brain's protective response to the prospect of seeing Mama Ginger," I said as she dashed off.

"Hey, I'm still in this . . . thing!" I yelled after her.

You know that feeling you get when you walk into a room and you're completely underdressed? That feeling would have been welcome at the Lavelle-McClaine engagement fete.

Claiming that the McClaine family was hogging all of the prewedding revelry, Mama Ginger threw together a last-minute "celebration" of Zeb and Jolene's engagement. Engagement parties are a rarity in the Hollow, generally thrown by swankier families at the Half-Moon Hollow Country Club and Catfish Farm. Mama Ginger pulled a fast one when she listed the venue address on the invitations. Since few of us spent a lot of time at Eddie Mac's, where local rednecks went to find their future former spouses, we were not familiar with the exact street number. Floyd and Mama Ginger had special access to the back room there as members of the pool league.

It was a surprise party, as in "Surprise! You're wearing three-inch heels, but your party's being held at a place where the table linens come from wall-mounted dispensers."

I should have suspected something when the invitations encouraged us to "dress up." This may have been a counterattack following the Great Wedding Date Change. A week after the wedding invitations were sent out, Mama Ginger decided that her allotted 100 were not enough. Apparently, her open distaste for the bride didn't preclude Mama Ginger's right to invite every person she'd ever met to her only son's wedding. She convinced a neighbor who sold stationery out of the back of her dad's gas station to help Mama Ginger design her own version of the invitation, featuring a Precious Moments bride and groom. Mama Ginger sent it out to another 150 distant relatives and passing acquaintances, so that instead of assuming the risk of inviting 100 carefully selected strangers to their farm, the McClaines now risked exposing their secret to 250 people even Mama Ginger might not recognize face-to-face or sober.

When Mimi and Jolene got wind of this maneuver, their only logical defense seemed to be moving the wedding up a week without planning to tell Mama Ginger until the last minute. And it would have worked, if Misty Kilgore, whose husband was shooting the wedding photos, had kept her mouth shut in line at the Piggly Wiggly.

Mama Ginger responded with a world-class hissy fit, further exacerbated when she was told that anyone who was not on the original mailing list would be turned away at the McClaines' gate by large male cousins. This steely-

spined response by Mimi McClaine forever secured my
loyalty and devotion. Mama Ginger's countermove was to
tell Misty Kilgore that the wedding was off, prompting Mr.
Kilgore to rip up the contract and schedule another wedding that weekend. Since there were no local photogra-
phers available, it was decided that Jolene's cousin Scooter,
who had a lazy eye *and* astigmatism, would be taking the
pictures. It was safe to say at this point that Jolene had lost
all control of the wedding-planning process.

So I guess I shouldn't have been surprised to be
standing under a guttering neon Budweiser sign wearing a strapless black dress and hair that took an alarming amount of time and pins. Vampires don't fare well in
redneck establishments. There tend to be a lot of easily
breakable wooden objects and, well, rednecks. And Eddie
Mac's just happened to be the county's main supplier of
T-shirts showing a cartoon vampire being stomped on
by the Statue of Liberty.

"Oh, hello, Jane, honey!" Mama Ginger cried, rushing past Jolene and the recently de-eye-patched Zeb. She
wrapped her arms around me in an inescapable viselike
grip and swung me around in time to the jukebox's blar-
ing "Islands in the Stream." "There's my girl! How are
you?"

"Fine," I said, smiling politely, even as Jolene's face
fell at this blatant display of favoritism. Behind her back,
Mimi sent Mama Ginger a poisonous glare.

"Mr. Lavelle," I said, smiling politely at Zeb's father.
Floyd Lavelle hadn't had a civil word for me since I refused to fetch him a beer at a Labor Day barbecue. I was

seven, and even then, I didn't know my place. He grunted in what passed for a greeting and headed for the bar.

"Now, I made my special pimento cheese balls because I remember how much you like them," Mama Ginger said, pinching my cheek. "You're so skinny."

"OK, that hurts," I said, prying her carmine-tipped pincers from my face. "This is Gabriel. He's a friend of mine and Zeb's, oh, and a groomsman."

Mama Ginger caught sight of our joined hands. Her sharp brown eyes narrowed at Gabriel. She mumbled, "How nice," and turned on her heels.

Mama Ginger continued to greet her guests, most of whom were bar regulars. Jolene might as well have been furniture for all the attention she was paid. For example, the little banner Mama Ginger had hung simply said, "Congratulations, Zeb," leaving room for possibilities. To add insult to gastronomical injury, the bar's "special event package" provided a crock pot of beer weenies, a grocery-store sheet cake, and lots of beer on tap. That was it. For fifty people. Fortunately, Mimi McClaine saw this coming and called in werewolf reinforcements.

Constantly thinking and talking about food is what makes werewolves some of the world's greatest chefs and restaurateurs. For example, Jolene's uncle Clay owned one of the best lunch places in town. His personal food philosophy was "Meat, meat, and more meat," which might explain the shop's specialty: a sandwich piled high with two pork tenderloins, Black Forest ham, and bacon. Within a half hour, several aunties and uncles arrived

with huge platters of cold cuts, barbecue, salads, cup-
cakes, and cookies, which the bar crowd fell on like hy-
enas on a fresh zebra carcass.

I sidled up to Mimi, who was watching the proceedings from a very dark corner. Her irises were constricted
in a distinctly nonhuman manner. I slipped an arm
around her waist, stroking a soothing hand along her
spine. "Will you adopt me?"

"Will it piss off Ginger?" she muttered.

I nodded. "Probably."

"I'm trying to be as patient as possible, but if that
witch doesn't ease up on my baby, I may not be held ac-
countable for my actions."

We watched as the buffet was moved off Pool Table 3
so Herb Baker's Friday-night group could proceed with
their usual game.

I whispered, "I'll help you hide the body."

Mimi winked at me and snuffled my cheek. "You're a
good girl."

It was at this point, after her third rum and Coke,
that Mama Ginger decided to make a toast. Ish. She
tinkled a napkin dispenser against the side of her glass
to get our attention, which, given the noise level, only
worked for those of us with superhearing. Finally, she
asked that someone unplug the jukebox. Actually, she
told Dick to "unplug that damn thing before I put a
foot through it."

"Now, settle down, you all. Settle down. I have something to say." She sighed, letting loose what appeared
to be a silent belch. "Well, none of us thought this day

would come." She put her arm around Floyd, who was propped up next to her on a bar stool, just this side of pleasantly buzzed, just south of the hostile-outburst zone. "And if anything, we always thought, well, hoped, that Zeb would be marrying Jane."

The entire room fell silent. Hell, the world stopped spinning. Mimi shot me a mortified look. Jolene turned a sort of pale blue-gray. Zeb seemed oblivious to the fact that his future wife had just been insulted. In fact, he smiled at me and winked, which seemed to make Jolene's uncles' faces contort into sock-puppet shapes.

"You know, those two have been friends since they were in preschool. They were always together, always so close. We worried about him being best friends with a girl. I mean, his daddy nearly died when he caught them playing with Cabbage Patch dolls. And Jane never dated anybody for very long. Anybody."

Dick snorted, earning him an elbow to the ribs from me. Mama Ginger flinched at the sudden movement and wobbled a little against the bar. "We all just assumed she'd give up on other guys and come back to Zeb. Jane wore the prettiest blue dress to the prom. I still have the boutonnière she gave Zeb, pressed in my Bible. I just always thought that Jane would give me the most beautiful grandbabies. They say sometimes it skips a generation . . ."

Mama Ginger warbled, "We all just love Jane so much. We've always said she was the daughter we always wanted. She's always been a part of the family—"

"But now, we're just so happy to be welcoming Jolene into that family," I said in a loud, explicitly cheerful voice.

"Oh, yeah, Joanne," Mama Ginger said, sobering enough to glance in Jolene's direction but not, apparently, to get her name right. "She seems like a nice enough girl."

Jolene watched her future mother-in-law expectantly, waiting for some semblance of a welcome, a compliment. Instead, Mama Ginger smiled brightly and announced, "Well, let's eat, everybody!"

Jolene's face fell. I tried to make eye contact, tried to make some sort of connection to show her I was on her side, that being Mama Ginger's favorite was about as desirable as being the prettiest pig at the fair. But her own mother had wrapped a protective arm around her and ushered her into a quiet corner. I fought against my instincts to soothe and smooth ruffled feathers and backed out of sight toward the back door.

I slammed the door against the chatter and the smoke. I sank against the building, ignoring my natural aversion to touching whatever was growing on the peeled aluminum siding. I cringed as Gabriel poked his head out the door. His look of concern melted into an absurd smile. "This is just—"

"Yeah." I laughed. He wrapped his arms around me, rubbing my bare arms to ward off the chill. The brisk motion took on a slow circling pattern as I wrapped my fingers around his collar and pulled him toward me. His mouth was so cool and clean and soft on mine, reminding me that there were normal places and people in the world. Normal, at least, by my standards. It was every great kiss you'd ever imagined, only we were surrounded by junker cars and leaning against a molding air-conditioning unit.

I leaned my forehead against his. "I will repay you in unspeakable physical favors if you can erase any trace of this party from my memory."

"I am intrigued by your offer. Can we discuss a down payment?" He grinned as his fingers danced along my spine, deftly manipulating the zipper. This was a matter of some concern, considering that (a) this wasn't the kind of dress that allowed foundation garments, and (b) we were sort of out in the open. Released from their chiffon prison, my breasts spilled into his waiting hands.

"Do I look like the kind of girl who would do this sort of thing in a parking lot?" I asked, entering the battle for control of my zipper.

"Dick said you've gotten down and dirty in a parking lot." Gabriel smirked.

"What happened to ignoring and disdaining Dick? Can we go back to that?" I whispered as he pressed me against the wall, pinning me with exquisite pressure. I could hear the ping of hairpins on the pavement as his fingers slid into my carefully arranged updo. Gabriel slipped his free hand under my skirt to tug at my panties. Unable to support me and strip me at the same time, he finally ripped them off my hips.

"You owe me a pair of good black panties," I told him in mock dismay. My fangs extended, nipping at his bottom lip. He grinned at me, even as the pin drop of blood welled at his mouth. Maybe I am the kind of girl who will get down and dirty in a parking lot.

"I'll just hold on to these, then," he said, tucking them into his jacket pocket.

"When can we leave?" I murmured against his lips. "When can I take you home and—"

We both froze as the door swung open and our sensitive eyes were assaulted with light.

"Oh, my!" We turned to see Mama Ginger framed in the doorway, eyes wide with shock. And I was pinned against the wall. And the wreckage of my panties hung from Gabriel's pocket like a frayed handkerchief.

"Mama Ginger!"

Gabriel set me down on my feet and held out his jacket to hide my efforts to pull up my dress. I burst into helpless giggles as I lost my grip on the bodice and the dress fell—no jokes about having nothing to hold it up, thank you—puddling at my waist.

"This isn't funny," Mama Ginger scolded.

"Maybe if I bash my head against something enough times, it will be." I grunted as I once again secured my chest under my dress.

"Jane, I am ashamed of you!" Mama Ginger cried, pulling me into the doorway. She turned on Gabriel. "And you, I can't believe you! If you weren't in the wedding party, I would send you home. Now, you get in there and sit with the rest of the groomsmen."

Gabriel was truly flustered. "Now see here—"

"I don't want to see you near Jane for the rest of the night. When I was a girl, nice young men did not paw at young ladies in dirty alleys."

When she was a young lady, Mama Ginger got cited

for mooning a busload of tourists in town for the annual lace-tatting convention. But Gabriel didn't know that, so he looked appropriately chagrined.

"Yes, ma'am," he said, slinking back into the bar.

"And Jane, you just go on over to the bride's table and sit down. But first, fix your lipstick. You look like a tramp." My jaw dropped. "You heard me. Now, scoot!"

When I emerged from the bathroom, feeling far less clean than when I went in, Jolene, Zeb, my vampire friends, and some of Jolene's uncles were doing shots at the bar. This included Uncle Zane, who sounded a lot like Boomhauer from *King of the Hill*. The only words you could understand were his curse words. And he cursed a lot. His twin brother, Dane, made a point not to curse, instead using elementary-grade curse substitutes. When I made my preshot toast, "Here's to heavy security at the wedding," Zane said something along the lines of "Like that will do any damned good." Dane told Zane to watch his effing mouth in front of the effing ladies, and I couldn't help but laugh.

"Oh, come on, just say the words," Jolene drawled, patting Dane on the back. "We all know what you're trying to say, just go ahead, be a man and go for the guessto."

I chuckled. "Either you've had too much punch or I think you mean gusto."

Zeb snorted as he took another drink. "Well, Jolene's not exactly a rocket scientist. She also says 'foo pas' instead of faux pas and 'lie-berry' instead of library."

Jolene recoiled as if Zeb had slapped her. Zane and Dane looked at Zeb as if they were sure they'd heard him wrong, then abandoned their drinks, returned to the werewolf side of the room, and glared at their nephew-to-be. Even Dick and Gabriel seemed uncomfortable.

Despite the disturbing pallor that had sapped her cheeks, Jolene gave a forced, tinkly little laugh. "It's a good thing I have smart friends. I think I'll just get some more punch."

Zeb rolled his eyes and punched Gabriel's shoulder. "It's a good thing she's got such a pretty face, because there's not much going on behind it."

I sent a significant look toward Zeb. He had that hazy, befuddled look on his face again, like someone coming out of anesthesia. He seemed to shake it off, his eyes blinking as he tried to follow Jolene's path across the room. A brief flash of remorse crossed his features. Then it was replaced by some empty macho smirk. "You might want to go apologize to her."

Zeb took another drink and crushed the cup in his hand before tossing it over his shoulder. "You're right. Otherwise, I'll be paying for it later. Am I right?"

Zeb slapped me on the butt and wandered away. My jaw dropped. Gabriel's eyes narrowed, but from the look on his face, I don't think he was able to process whether Zeb had just besmirched my honor or butt-slapping was something we did when I was still human. Trust me, it was not. But I wasn't about to goad my drunk vampire boyfriend in this tense atmosphere.

"What was that about?" asked Dick, who was watching Zeb with a mix of irritation and concern. "Zeb's not usually such a—"

"Ash-hole?" Gabriel slurred, and swayed slightly.

Eager to change the direction of the conversation, I stared into Gabriel's dilated pupils. "How did you get drunk so quickly? I thought our vampire constitutions kept us from being cheap drunks."

"I'm not drunk!" Gabriel cried, indignant. "All I've had to drink was this punch Jolene's cousins gave me. It's delicious. It tastes like pineapple."

"You were completely sober when I left you a few minutes ago." I sniffed the cup and turned to watch as the bartenders poured two gallon jugs of grain alcohol into a galvanized metal tub with Kool-Aid, sliced apples, pineapple, and pears.

Like many a college freshman before him, Gabriel had fallen into the hooch trap.

Hooch is liquid evil. It's about forty-proof, but the Kool-Aid and fruit cover the taste of the alcohol. So before you know you're drunk, you've had about four Solo cups' worth.

"Well, it's a good thing you can't eat the fruit," I muttered.

"I think I'm going to enjoy this." Dick chuckled, watching as Gabriel squinted at the neon bar lights. "Gabriel couldn't hold his liquor when we were kids, either. He ruined the last good carpet at my house sicking up my daddy's best bourbon. You should have seen how green his face got—"

Gabriel slapped a clumsy hand over Dick's mouth. "Shh. Jane shouldn't have to hear that story. It's not a nice story, you can tell by looking at her face. I love Jane's face. She makes the sweetest little face when I take her—hey!" He pouted when I slid his hooch out of reach.

"I think I'd like to hear this," Dick said, his expression serious.

"You, go outside and sober up," I told Gabriel, shoving him toward the door. I turned on a smirking Dick. "You, stop thinking about my sex faces."

Dick grinned. "I'll just follow Gabriel outside to see if he throws up."

"Worst. Party. Ever," I grumbled as I searched for the bride-to-be.

Jolene was drowning her sorrows in beer weenies. I would tell her that she was going to eat her way out of a size 4, but she had that hypermetabolism going for her. Plus, you just don't want to interrupt someone with superstrength when they're stress-eating. So I sort of nudged a plate of chicken wings at her without making eye contact. I saw a biologist do it once on a tiger special, something about submissive gestures and keeping all of your digits intact.

Jolene tore into the wings with a sort of glum sniffle, but I could tell her heart wasn't in her munching.

"I'm sorry Zeb said that," I told her.

"Oh, he didn't mean it." She sniffed. "I know he's just under a lot of stress right now, with the wedding and my family and everything. I mean, the poor thing's been getting those headaches, and they make him cranky. It would help if his mama would ease up a little bit and stop being so . . ." Jolene paused, tears shimmering at the corners of her eyes. "Why doesn't she like me?"

"Oh, honey," I said, wrapping an arm around her. "She doesn't like anybody. She doesn't even really like me. She just likes to feel she has some control over the situation. She's planned for me to marry Zeb for years, and she accepts change about as well as my mama. You just have to give her a few months. She'll come around. Maybe a few years. Give her a few years."

Jolene stuffed a nacho into her mouth and didn't respond.

"Zeb loves you," I offered.

She sniffed but was not cheered.

"Mama Ginger just caught me in a compromising position with Gabriel out back, half-topless and fully commando. That's got to add a few points back in your column."

Jolene brightened, stuffing three meatballs in her cheek. "Thanks. That helps."

"What are friends for?"

Humans may mistake the wooing techniques of werewolves, particularly males, as predatory. Studies show that 10 percent of human-werewolf relationships begin with the male being maced.

—Mating Rituals and Love Customs of the Were

After the shipwreck that was the engagement party—*gah,* even I'm doing the *Titanic* thing now—I had to establish some special phone rules for Jolene.

For example, calling me several times during my midday sleepy time because someone is bleeding, unconscious, or on fire is acceptable. Calling me several times during my midday sleepy time because Mama Ginger tried to persuade the county clerk that Jolene and Zeb were actually first cousins and ineligible for a marriage license? Not so much.

Mama Ginger was well on her way to the Mother of the Groom Hall of Shame. Convinced that the Invitation Debacle hadn't sent a clear enough message, she started making demands. She wanted her friend, Eula, who had never baked more than a bundt, to handle the blue-and-white nautical-themed wedding cake for 200. She wanted Jolene to announce at the reception that the wedding coincided with Uncle Ace's fifty-fourth birthday and to arrange for the DJ to play "Friends in Low Places" in his honor.

Mama Ginger also had very firm ideas about what she did not want for the wedding. For instance, Jolene's aunt Lola runs a florist shop and had generously offered to make the floral arrangements. Mama Ginger claimed that she was allergic to pollen and insisted on silk flowers. She even went to the local floral outlet and bought out their supplies of silk daisies in magenta and yellow, nowhere near the delicate white lily arrangements Jolene wanted.

Mama Ginger had also eschewed the tradition of hosting the rehearsal dinner after Jolene's mother declined another evening at Eddie Mac's. Instead, Mimi offered to hold the dinner at the farm, since that's where the rehearsal would be and it was rather remote. Mama Ginger said, "Hell, just plan the whole thing," and decided to take no part in it.

When Mama Ginger tried to change the theme of the wedding from *Titanic* to "North and South," I had to turn my phone off.

I had never seen Mama Ginger this fired up. Well, there was that time Zeb got cut from the Academic Team in high school and she slipped ipecac into the team advisor's coffee. Poor Mrs. Russell was throwing up for three days and missed the state Governor's Cup meet. The scary thing, then and now, was that Mama Ginger honestly thought she was doing what was best for Zeb. Much like that cheerleader's mom in Texas.

Zeb had problems of his own with Jolene's far-too-affectionate cousin. Like most predators, Vance sensed a weakness. For all their grudged acceptance of Zeb, the pack did not appreciate Mama Ginger's lack of affection for Jolene or her clear favoritism toward me. Vance was exploiting that, grumbling here and there among the relations that Zeb's family didn't appreciate the jewel they were getting. Oh, and that I was not to be trusted, because "no man can just be 'friends' with a woman, especially a vampire woman."

If I'd had my phone on, I might have gotten a warning that Mama Ginger was planning to show up at my house early one evening "for a chat." Translation: to pick apart my relationship and zero in on my soft emotional underbelly. The woman was like Hannibal Lecter in polyester pants.

Wearing my flannel reindeer pajamas and sipping my morning cup of Chock Full o' Platelets, I was not prepared for company or the toxic apple cobbler she was carting into my house. I could only pray that Aunt Jettie didn't decide to pop in at home. The first (and only) time Mama Ginger had visited River Oaks was for Jenny's first baby shower. She lit up in the parlor and put the cigarette butt in a decorative urn that was on the mantel . . . which contained my beloved Great-Grandma Early's ashes. Jettie, who was corporeal at the time, tossed Mama Ginger out on her ear and threw her straw handbag after her, telling her never to darken the door again. In retaliation, Mama Ginger started a rumor that

Aunt Jettie was secretly a vegetarian. It wasn't nearly as damaging as she'd anticipated.

Faced with a noxious dessert and no available escape routes, I took Mama Ginger into the kitchen and shooed Fitz out the back door. While lovable, Fitz, a pound-adopted product of indiscriminate breeding among several species, was neither handsome nor smart. Also, his proclivity for rolling around in dead things left him vulnerable to accidentally consuming Mama Ginger's cobbler. I scooped up two pungent helpings and offered Mama Ginger some coffee, which I needed myself if I were going to socialize at the vampire equivalent of five A.M.

"Well, isn't this nice?" Mama Ginger sighed as we pulled stools up to my island countertop. She tucked her fork into the gooey concoction. "We didn't really get a chance to talk at the engagement party. And I miss our talks, Jane. So, tell me all about this Gabriel. Tell me all about the man who stole you away from my Zeb."

I spluttered my coffee a little while I tried to come up with a palatable explanation of my relationship with Gabriel. "I met him last year, right after I left the library. He's a very . . . interesting man. He's good to me, very protective. He's helped me make a lot of big changes in my life . . ."

I have to learn to speak with fewer ellipses.

"But what's he like?" Mama Ginger pressed.

"He's lived around here his whole life. He likes Zeb a lot, and he's comfortable with my having a male best friend. We're a great fit for each other. We practically finish each other's sentences."

Because I'm usually interrupting him.

"Well, if he's lived here all of his life, why haven't I ever met him?" Mama Ginger demanded. "Who are his people? What does he do for a living? How serious is he about the two of you?"

"Wow, that's a lot of questions," I said.

"I'm just worried about you, Jane." Mama Ginger *tsk*ed, patting my hands. "I don't want you to settle for some no-good loser with a good line because you're desperate."

"I'm not desperate!" I exclaimed.

"You're thirty—"

"Twenty-eight!" I corrected.

"And at this point, you'll grab on to anything." Mama Ginger shrugged.

I grumbled, "That is not completely accurate."

Mama Ginger demanded, "Then where is Gabriel right now? Why isn't he here with you?"

This was a pertinent question, but I wasn't about to admit that to Mama Ginger. The truth was, I hadn't seen Gabriel since the engagement party. He was in Lisbon this week, discussing the sale of some residential buildings he owned there. At least, I thought that was what he said in the voice mail he left me the day after the party. He hadn't picked up his cell phone when I'd called, oh, twenty or so times over the last few days to try to get a better explanation. I even went so far as to call the hotel where he was supposed to be staying, but they didn't have a Gabriel Nightengale registered. I was clinging to the hope that he'd either changed his plans or registered under some assumed name, such as Mr. I. M. Deceased.

"Gabriel spends a lot of time traveling for work," I said, choosing my words carefully. "He owns a lot of different businesses, and he has to look in on them from time to time—"

Mama Ginger sighed, rolling her heavily shaded eyes at my naiveté. "Oh, honey, my cousin Pam said the same thing about her husband, Claude, and his plumbing-supply business, and then she found out that he had another family over in Butler County. He even gave their sons the same names so he wouldn't mess up and call the wrong kids to supper."

"I don't think that's something I need to worry about. And we don't have the kind of relationship where we have to see each other every day."

"Well, why not? Why doesn't he want to see you every day?" she demanded. "Aren't you worth that kind of commitment? Where is he going with this? Have you two even talked about marriage?"

"No!" I laughed. "We haven't talked about getting married."

Because state law prohibits it.

"Well, why not? Tick-tock, tick-tock, Jane. I can hear your biological clock ticking. You don't have time to waste on some silly little fling that's not going to go anywhere. If you want to have babies, you have to speed things along."

Dang it.

The finality of vampirism had kept me from thinking about motherhood, or my inability thereof, for a while. Realizing that little Andy and Bradley were to be her only grandchildren, Mama had stopped inquiring after my stalled uterus and devoted her energy to her "grand-dog," Fitz. And since I'd been avoiding the church ladies who normally inquired after my reproductive plans, I was no longer thinking defensively. My usual list of responses to "When are you having kids?"—including "When they come with a return policy"—had long since vacated the tip of my tongue.

So, faced with the age-old kids question for the first time in months, all I could do was stutter, "Wh-Who said anything about having kids?"

"I always just assumed you wanted them. You were so good with the kids down at the library. They loved you. And Zeb always talked about how much his students liked it when you came in for Fairy Tale Time. I've always thought you were built to be a mom. You know, you have those good roomy breeding hips anyway. Might as well put them to good use."

The cracking of my unhinged jaw echoed in the empty kitchen as Mama Ginger resumed munching her dessert. She shrugged and chewed. "I mean, if you don't have children, what's the point of being a woman?"

I think I deserve some sort of karmic reward for not using my vampire strength to pull Mama Ginger's lip over her head. Obviously, kids weren't an option. That door closed the moment I swallowed vampire blood. In general, vampires do not make great parents. Our night hours are incompatible with healthy human sleep patterns. It's hard to discipline a child when they can just run out into the daylight to escape you. And then there's the whole "never aging and outliving your children by hundreds of years" thing.

Parents who have been turned while their children are still minors have to fight fang and nail to retain custody, even when there's a living parent in the home. And the last legislator who brought an undead adoption-rights bill before Congress was literally laughed out of office.

Gripping the countertop in a way that left moon-shaped dents in the surface, I counted to ten and said, "That's just—"

Mama Ginger dropped her fork dramatically and cut me off, "Honey, I just can't stand it. I have to tell you. A mother's heart can't bear to see her son in such pain."

"Zeb's in pain?"

"Well, sweetie, isn't it obvious? He only went after Jolene when you hooked up with this Gabriel character. He said he doesn't see you nearly as often since you met Gabriel, and I know it's just breaking his heart. Jolene's just his rebound girl. He's not in love with her. He's trying to get back at you."

"For what?"

"For not loving him back!" Mama Ginger cried.

"Zeb doesn't love me. He loves Jolene," I said in a slow, deliberate tone one might use with someone who was very dim or slightly drunk. Or both.

"But you're the perfect match, you always have been. You have such a long history together. You can't just throw that away. Hot pants and hormones do not make a marriage. Believe me, honey, I should know. I married for lust, and look what happened to me: a husband who doesn't talk and in-laws who talk too damn much. What you have, friendship and companionship, that's what makes a solid, lasting marriage. That's what is going to make my boy happy."

"Please, God, let that be the last time you ever say 'hot pants' in front of me."

"It's always been you and Zeb, in my head." Mama Ginger paused to press her fingers to her temples, as if she were about to peer into a future where I was somehow living and bearing her lots and lots of little Lavelles. "Whenever I pictured Zeb's wedding, it was always you walking down that aisle."

"You're just not making sense right now," I told her. "If you'd just get to know Jolene, you'd see why Zeb loves her so much."

"She's not you! When you and Zeb are married, we'll be the perfect, big happy family. You and Zeb can come over for dinner every other night. We'll go to flea markets on the weekends. And I'm sure Mamaw or Daddy Lavelle would be dead by the time you and Zeb started having babies, so you could move right into one of the trailers behind the house."

I think I might have sprained something trying to keep a straight face in response to that. "But if you really want a mother-in-law/daughter-in-law relationship like that, Jolene would be more than willing to do all of those things with you. She *wants* to be close to you."

"But it won't be the same. That's not the way I pictured it."

"But it would be the way Zeb pictures it. I don't want

Zeb. And he doesn't want me. He wants Jolene. Isn't it important to let him have some say in choosing his wife?"

"Oh, he's a man, he doesn't know what he wants." She snorted. "If I didn't help him figure out what's best for him, what kind of mother would I be?"

The kind of mother whose son doesn't dodge her calls?

"You're going to see things my way soon enough," Mama Ginger insisted.

"What does that mean?"

"I just want to help you and Zeb figure some things out, honey," Mama Ginger said, standing up and hitching her bag over her shoulder. "Well, this was fun, but I'll just let myself out. I have to go meet with Jolene's mama over at the Bridal Barn to talk about dresses for the wedding, like I need fashion advice from that dowdy thing. Vonnie's making some big deal about keeping the shop open late."

I stared after her as she toddled toward the back door. She smiled beatifically at me. "If you ever want to talk, give me a call."

I sat at the counter, staring at the untouched oozy layers of pastry on my plate, my head spinning. Aunt Jettie appeared next to the sink, her lips quirked into a sneer.

"What is that?" she asked, pointing at the remains of Mama Ginger's cobbler. "It's like an autopsy with fruit."

"Mama Ginger came calling, to set the alarm on my biological clock. Oh, and to remind me that there's no point to me being a woman if I never have children."

"Well, if that's true, I wasted a hell of a lot of money on panty hose and lipstick." Jettie snorted.

"I don't know where this is coming from. Why would she say something like that? And why am I letting it bother me? It's not like I can just decide to turn my lady parts back on."

"Oh, honey, don't you think I heard the same thing my whole life?" she said, stroking her cold, insubstantial fingers down my back. Her voice pitched up two octaves. " *Don't you know you're wasting your life? You're going to end up alone with no one to take care of you when you get old. What makes you think you're too good to get married and have babies like you're supposed to?'* Most of that was just your grandma Ruthie. You have to ignore them."

"But don't you ever regret it?" I asked. "Not having children of your own?"

"I didn't need to have children of my own." She grinned. "I had you. I cared for you, taught you, learned from you. I may not have carried you in my womb, but I always carried you in my heart."

"If I wasn't thinking about your womb right now, that would have been such a sweet sentiment," I said, leaning my forehead against her ghostly noggin.

"Do you feel better now?" she asked.

"Eh." I waffled my hand. "I'd feel better if I could eat about a gallon of Ben and Jerry's without vomiting."

When Gabriel finally called three days later to let me know he was back in town, I decided it was time for me to take some initiative. With my ever-present fear of being a needy childe, I usually waited around for him to call. But I figured a little manufactured romance was just the thing to get me out of my Mama Ginger-induced funk. I slipped into a silky red T-shirt and jeans and marched out the door to see him. Or at least I would have, had I not opened the door to find Adam Morrow standing on my porch. And because I had a bit of momentum going, I ran smack into him and, in my panic, lifted him by the armpits to move him out of my way.

"Adam!" I shrieked.

He made a gurgling sound as I dropped a limp pile of veterinarian onto my porch.

"Adam, I'm so sorry," I said, picking him up and settling him back on his feet.

"It's OK," he said, clutching a squashed box, which I could now smell was flowers. "It was kind of cool."

"What are you doing all the way out here?"

"I wanted to see you," he said, uncrumpling the box and straightening the shiny red bow attached. "And I see now that surprising a vampire is not a good idea."

I stared at him, my mouth open, gaping like a suffocating goldfish.

"Yeah, I figured out the vampire thing," he said, a sheepish blush coloring his cheeks. Oh, man, even in the dark, that just made him cuter. "At the visitation that night, I didn't see you eat anything. And, well, no one sees you during the day anymore. You don't have to worry. I won't tell anyone. I just wanted to—I just wanted to see you. I've been thinking about you a lot lately. And I've never known a real vampire before."

I laughed. "I'm so glad I could be the first."

"These are for you," he said, offering me the mangled box. "It's jasmine. I thought you might like it. It's night-blooming."

"That was thoughtful," I told him.

Adam Morrow brought me flowers. On the checklist of "Teenage Daydreams That Will Probably Never Happen to Me," that was number one. Now, all I had to do was make out with one of the straight members of 'N Sync and star in a movie with Hugh Grant.

Unsure what to do with the box, I opened the door. A boulder of fur flew at us, giving me a full-on tongue bath. After deeming me sufficiently licked, Fitz turned his attentions to Adam, a strange man in dark clothes standing on our porch. Fitz is adorable in his own hideous way, but as a security system, he's pretty much useless.

"Hey, boy." Adam grinned, rubbing Fitz's muzzle as I led them into the living room. "You're just a whole bunch of breeds, aren't you?"

Adam was not my vet, because the idea of spazzing out in front of him every time Fitz needed a checkup was not a happy one. Fitz proved to be a fascinating Mendelian model for him. I guess Adam had never seen a dog with eyes and ears that were each a different color. Fitz leaned into the scratching and let his tongue loll out to full length, useless and prideless.

"So, you're not weirded out at all by this?" I asked, drawing my lips back from my fangs.

"No," he insisted. "Like I said, it's really interesting. You've changed a lot since high school."

I snorted. "That's an understatement."

Aunt Jettie appeared behind Adam and gave me a big thumbs-up. With Adam concentrating on Fitz, I mouthed, "I know!" and shooed her away. Jettie grinned and vanished.

"What's it like? What's it like to be a vampire?" he asked.

"Weird," I said, looking at him. "Powerful, exciting, and occasionally humiliating, confusing, and painful. It's sort of like going through puberty all over again. Nothing about my life is the same. But there are some good things. Awesome night vision, for one. I'm still trying to balance things out. I mean, when we were taking those aptitude tests on Career Day, vampirism was not something that came up. I never could have predicted my life turning out this way, but I'll have the best story at our class reunion."

Adam looked up and blurted, "I was wondering if you might want to go to dinner sometime?"

"I don't really eat," I said.

"Oh, right," he said, slapping his forehead. "Well, what about coffee? Or we can stay in and watch a movie if you're more comfortable with that. I'm up for anything. Just—I would like to spend time with you. What are you doing tonight?"

"I was actually heading out to see my friend. The friend I mentioned at the funeral. The . . . man friend."

Adam's face fell a little bit. "You're not making this easy for me, are you, Jane?"

"I don't think I'm supposed to make it easy for you," I said. "In fact, when I was a teenager, my mother gave me several lectures on why I shouldn't make this easy for you."

He laughed. "Well, you can't blame me for trying. Anytime you want to hang out, even if it's just as friends. I mean, I don't want to be just friends with you, but I'll take what I can—I'm not saying this right." He backed away from me, negotiating the steps without even looking down. "Just call me sometime, please."

Giddy little butterflies danced around my belly. I brushed my cheeks with my fingertips and found a big silly grin stretched across my face.

"Adam Morrow wants to date me," I told Aunt Jettie, who stood next to me as I watched him drive away. "That's weird."

"That's one very sweet boy." Jettie nodded. "Respectful, thoughtful, and kind. His mama raised him right."

"I know." I sighed, taking the flowers into the kitchen and putting them into one of Jettie's favorite pressed-glass vases.

Jettie nodded. "Nice ass, too."

"Gross." I shuddered.

She smirked. "I'm dead, not blind, honey."

"And still, I say, ew." I grabbed my purse and slipped into my coat. On a whim, I grabbed Jettie's old wicker picnic hamper out of the front closet. "I don't have time for this. I need to go be confused by the man I'm actually dating."

As it turned out, Gabriel was the one confused.

"What's wrong?" he asked as he opened his front door before I could even knock.

It was more than the weary tone that had little alarm

bells going off in my head. Gabriel's face was drawn and pinched. His eyes were a dull slate color and lacked the spark I'd come to expect. He looked almost ill. This was more than just traveler's stress. Something was wrong. But I could tell by his guarded expression that asking would leave me without answers and alone on a perfectly good date night.

"Nothing," I said, smiling to hide my worries. "Absolutely nothing."

"You never come to see me unless you're angry or something has gone wrong."

I gasped, feigning hurt. "That's not true."

"The first time you were here, you came storming up my front steps because I'd sent Andrea over to your house. The last time you were here, it was because Zeb and Jolene were on the verge of collapse. We never spend time here. I'm always at your place."

"You know, you're right. I'm so sorry. I'm terrible at the relationship thing."

He shrugged. "You just like to be comfortable." He sniffed slightly, then ran the tip of his nose down my hairline. I took this as a sweet, intimate gesture, until he asked, "Why do you smell like a German shepherd?"

I stared at him, thinking maybe this was some sort of bizarre riddle, when I realized Adam's eau de canine had probably rubbed on me when I'd plowed into him. I blew out a startled laugh. "Oh, I ran into an old friend from high school, Adam Morrow. He's a vet, and he must have had some leftover dog residue on him."

"You ran into him on the drive over here?" Gabriel asked.

"No, he dropped by the house to say hi, just as I was walking out the door," I said, the suspicion in his voice setting off my "babble" response. "It's no big deal. It's really kind of funny. It's this boy I used to have this huge crush on when were kids, but he never looked twice at me. I was this gawky band geek, and he was the most popular boy in our class. But now that I've been turned, and grown out of my braces, I guess he's interested in me. I told him I was seeing someone. And it's too little, too late, obviously. I mean, I'm a grown woman, and it was just a silly schoolgirl fantasy crush thing. I'm over him. Completely. Totally. Completely and totally over him."

Gabriel grimaced, his features radiating doubt and discomfort. Maybe that second "completely and totally" was overselling it.

"So, take me on the tour," I suggested, changing the subject far too enthusiastically. "I've only seen two rooms of your house. The parlor and your bedroom."

"That wasn't my bedroom," he said. "That was a guest room."

"You left your fledgling vampire childe to rise in your guest room?"

His lips twitched, and I could see him slowly coming out of his bad humor. "Where would you put a fledgling vampire childe to rise?"

I paused to think about it. "I don't know. So, show me your bedroom. And I mean that in a perfectly respectable home-tour kind of way."

Gabriel's bedroom was surprising. I'd expected something lavish and baroque. Sort of Henry VIII meets Rudolph Valentino. But the walls were bare, a pale blue edging toward purple, the color of the sky just after dawn. The bed was wide and soft but plain, something you'd order from Ikea and then immediately regret. A thick navy tapestry curtain was pulled back, revealing a broad cushioned window seat, the only seating in the room. And his bathroom featured a shower big enough for six. He specifically mentioned that, which, frankly, worried me.

I ducked my head into his closet. Black as far as the eye could see. Black T-shirts, black sweaters, black button-down shirts, black slacks, broken up only by occasional splashes of slate gray.

"You ever thought about wearing a print?" I asked. "Maybe even a jewel tone? One of the less intense colors. Blue. Green. How about red? We know you like that one. Wait, are you color-blind?"

"I don't wear jewel tones," Gabriel muttered, leading me back out into the bedroom. "Or prints."

There were no pictures, no mirrors, nothing on the walls save for a print of Edvard Munch's *Vampire*, an ambiguous portrait of a seminude redheaded woman with her arms around and head bent over a dark-haired man. I stood, studying the image with a tilted head. Is he the vampire? Is she? Is he simply a lover seeking comfort at his redhead's breast? Or are they two humans cowered in the shadow of the dark form looming behind them?

"What do you think of it?" he asked.

"It's beautiful and sad and vague," I said.

"You know, the original title of the painting was *Love and Pain*," he said. "An art critic picked up on the underlying vampiric theme, and the name stuck. Munch experts were and are horrified, but you can't deny the subconscious imagery."

"You know, his ears are sort of shaped like yours," I commented, looking from the slightly pointed painted ovals to Gabriel's own lobes.

Gabriel grinned. "The artist found the back of my head to be quite compelling."

"So, this is an altar to your vanity?" I asked, teasing.

"I enjoy the irony. A man interpreting me as a vampire but being told it's impossible. What brought you rushing to my front door if it wasn't bad news?" he asked as I pulled him back down the stairs toward the surprise I'd brought for him. He offered more than a little resistance as I pulled him farther and farther from the bedroom.

"I thought we might actually leave the house for a date. I figured we've covered the couch date. You are master of the corner lean and the casual backrub that might lead to something. I thought you might like to up the degree of difficulty. It's time to leave the comfort of the make-out couch, Gabriel. Let's go out to see a movie."

He arched his eyebrows at me as I pulled him to the foyer.

"Moving images projected onto a screen in front of a darkened room full of people." He shot me a withering look. "And since I don't think even your broad horizons are quite ready for the Hollow Cineplex, I thought we would visit the dollar theater."

"The dollar theater?"

"The old two-screen place downtown. They show old movies for a dollar a ticket. It's sort of a gamble. Sometimes you see the ending, sometimes the film melts. But the seats are cushy, and there's a lot of ambience."

"You mean the Palladium?"

I chewed my lip. "I think that's what the sputtering neon sign says."

"The Palladium used to be the premier moving-picture palace in this end of the state. I saw my first film there, *Casablanca*."

"You waited until the 1940s to see your first movie?"

He shrugged. "I had things to do."

"Well, now the Palladium is the place where you can buy a bucket of beer with some very stale popcorn."

"But . . . all those humans."

"We're vampires. If someone talks during the movie, we tear their throats out. Come on, I wore my cute date shoes and everything."

He peered down at the strappy black pumps peeking out from my jeans. "You know I can't resist you when your toes are exposed," he grumped.

"Good, that means wearing open-toed shoes in winter is well worth it. And since we can't exactly swing by for a pizza on our way into town, I brought you this." I pulled a very nice bottle of donated Type B-positive, which I knew Gabriel favored, from the picnic basket.

"Very nice," he commented, appraising the label. "Your palate is improving."

"Thank you. Now let's go."

"What about drinking this?"

"I have a whole thing planned. Just relax that ramrod spine of yours and come with me."

I took Gabriel to Memorial Park, a tiny patch of grass in the middle of downtown. It was home to a gazebo flanked by blackened cement statues of famous Civil War veterans from the Hollow, including Waco Marchand, who now served on the local commission for the Council for the Equal Treatment of the Undead. High-school kids posed for pictures in their prom-night finery at the gazebo each spring. But tonight it was abandoned, empty save for the fairy lights strung from the carefully preserved gingerbread eaves. I winked at Gabriel and began unpacking the picnic basket on one of the gazebo's little wrought-iron benches.

"It's December," Gabriel said, staring at me and tucking his coat tighter around his body.

"We stay at room temperature," I reminded him, patting the bench. "Besides, we have twinkly Christmas lights, only available at this time of year. We have a lovely bottle of oaky B-positive. We have grapes and cheese, which, I'll admit, I bought on the way over to your house strictly because I've seen people pack them for fancy wine picnics in movies. We have romance and atmosphere out the ying-yang."

He gave me a smile that assured me that he was working hard to humor my girlie romanticism.

"I'm wearing the date shoes," I reminded him.

"Curse your sassy toes," he huffed. "Let me open that. You don't want to cork it."

"Are you implying that a little old thing like me can't operate something as complicated as a corkscrew?" He grinned at my indignant tone. "OK, you're right. But that's not because I'm a woman. It's because most of the stuff I drank when I was alive involved screw tops."

"I've always enjoyed your little quirks." He grunted at the faint pop of the cork coming loose. He carefully poured into the plastic wine glasses that came with the picnic set. "What do we drink to?"

"World peace?" I suggested. He grimaced. "To doing things that normal couples do?"

He cleared his throat and raised his glass. "To Mrs. Mavis Stubblefield, without whom we would not be here together tonight."

I laughed. "That's kind of twisted."

He nodded while he sipped. "But true."

"To Mavis Stubblefield, without whom I wouldn't have been fired, publicly drunk, mistaken for a deer, shot, and turned into a vampire by you," I conceded, and took a deep drink. Despite my pacifist leanings, I enjoyed the sizzle of human red cells as they zipped through my system. "Maybe I should send her a thank-you note."

"We both know that's not going to happen."

"Also true," I admitted, snuggling my head into the crook of his neck.

"What are you doing?"

"Enjoying the moment." I sighed.

"You are, without a doubt, the most interesting girl I've ever shared a gazebo with," he murmured, kissing my forehead.

"Interesting. There's your favorite word again."

"I think we've established how interested I am in you." He chuckled, kissing me. He sighed when he released me. "I feel as if we haven't been able to spend much time together lately. I'm sorry business has taken so much of my time."

My lips parted, and I could feel the rush of questions gathering. Why wasn't he answering his phone? Why was he being so uncharacteristically vague about his travels? Where had he been, really? But the evening was so perfect, so relaxed. Again, passages from *Sense and Sensibility* popped into my head. Elinor almost loses her Edward because she doesn't speak up and tell him how she feels. She might have ended up alone, but Lucy Steele lets Edward off the hook by eloping with his brother. Would Edward stay in love with Elinor if she pitched a tantrum when he left her at Norland without confirming his feelings? Would making demands and ultimatums confirm that Edward made the right choice in Lucy?

I was an Elinor, not a Marianne. I didn't want to waste precious, uninterrupted time together with outbursts or questions that might provoke an argument. So I feinted for a safer topic.

"It has helped that I've been all about wedding, wedding, and more wedding lately." I sighed. "Tell me how it's possible that this shindig has taken complete control of my life and I'm not even the one getting married? I'm just a lowly bridesmaid, and yet I'm the one doing cocktail-napkin comparisons and in-law interventions."

He mulled that over for a moment. "Oh, I saw this in one of those ladies' magazines you leave scattered around at your house. I think the term is 'Bridezilla'?"

"I don't know if I would use the word 'Bridezilla.' It's not that Jolene's being all that demanding or . . . yeah, were-bride just about covers it," I admitted. "I don't know what to do. I just keep getting pulled in. Dress fittings, engagement parties from hell, favor-making parties. It's not that I don't have the time, I'm just getting worn out, you know? But I don't think any of her cousins will do any of this stuff with her."

"And her fiancé has made vague yet disturbing advances toward you and is treating her badly, so you feel incredibly guilty."

"No!" I insisted. I looked down into my glass and grumbled, "Yes."

"You're a very good friend."

I waited for the sage advice he normally dished out in these situations. And got nothing. "And?"

"That's all the platitudes I have," he said. "Generally, people don't invite vampires to their weddings, much less make them their undead bridal handmaidens. This is a situation I have never had to deal with."

"In more than a century?" He gave me an apologetic look. "Well, that's disappointing," I said, looking down at my watch. "We'd better get going, or we're going to miss the previews."

"I thought the theater only showed movies that are at

least twenty years old. That means the previews are for movies that are twenty years old."

I drained the last of my blood. "There's a principle at stake here, Gabriel."

Since we were sticking to strict dating principles, Gabriel insisted on paying the two-dollar admission. He was a little put off when he saw our options listed on the old-fashioned marquee: *Pillow Talk* or the 1932 version of *Dracula* starring Bela Lugosi.

"Isn't that sort of obvious?" he asked.

"Oh, we'll go see *Pillow Talk* if you really want to. We're talking singing, Tony Randall, lots of pastels . . ."

Gabriel shuddered. "*Dracula* it is."

It was oddly fitting that our first "real date" involved *Dracula,* considering that our first couch date featured Francis Ford Coppola's version, which Gabriel still insisted is a comedic spoof on the tale. We took two slightly sprung seats near the rear of the theater and settled in. Seeing the dilapidated state of the theater obviously bothered Gabriel. The gold leaf had worn away from the plaster angels guarding the screen long ago. The red velvet curtain was motheaten and dirty. The balcony railing was studded with generations of grayed chewing gum.

I narrowed my eyes at him as he squirmed uncomfortably in his seat. "You're going to buy this place, aren't you?"

"I'm thinking about it," he confessed, wiping at a mysterious sticky substance that had transferred itself from the armrest to his hand. "This is criminal."

"Well, if it would keep you in town for a while, I'm all for it. How many of us are in here?" I asked as he scanned the crowd. "Can you tell?"

"A few," he admitted. "This version of *Dracula* is one of the few movie adaptations that vampires find generally palatable. The main character is powerful yet somewhat sympathetic."

Gabriel looked nervous as he continued to scan the crowd.

"You OK?" I asked.

"Fine." He smiled. "So, what is the procedure for a movie date?"

"Well, we sit here, not touching until the lights go out. Eventually, we'll bump knees or fight for elbow-rest dominance. If we ate popcorn, we might pay an incredibly exorbitant amount of money for a bucket to keep between us so our hands could occasionally brush against each other as we reached for bites. If you were a total pervert, you'd cut a hole in the bottom of the bucket . . . never mind." He shot me a questioning glance. "There's also the yawn maneuver, which we've covered in previous sessions."

"Excuse me for a minute."

Gabriel walked out of the theater, leaving me to look over the crowd. Most of them were older couples, people who might have seen the original theater run when they were children. There were a few teenagers in goth regalia, some of whom I recognized as skateboarders I'd had to chase away from the shop. If there were vampires here, I couldn't spot them. Gabriel came back carrying an obscenely large tub of popcorn.

"Did you know that butter comes in a liquid chemical form?" he asked, grinning over the oil-slicked kernels.

"But we can't eat it." I giggled as he set the tub between us.

"You said this is what people do on dates. I wanted to do this right."

I grabbed his face between my palms and kissed him good. This was the Gabriel I'd fallen for. I could put up with the uncertainty, the brain-wracking questions, for just a little taste of this kind of happiness.

"Are we skipping the popcorn hand-brushing thing?" he asked, between nips on my lips.

"Hey! Go get a room!" bellowed a loud male voice behind us. Gabriel glared over my head at the elderly hall monitor. I giggled as he stood up and headed in the guy's direction.

"Sit down," I told him.

Gabriel glared at the loudmouth. "But that was very rude."

"It's all part of the experience."

Gabriel mastered the yawn move and the knee squeeze and was well on his way to the around-the-shoulder chest grab by the time the credits rolled. As we left the theater, he talked animatedly about seeing Bela Lugosi play Dracula in the original Broadway play.

"But I must admit that his screen performance was even more compelling. It's fascinating that they managed to film his eyes as ours appear, as if lit from within."

"He had help. The cinematographer shone little pinpoint spotlights into his eyes during filming. It was the cheapest, most effective way to get the effect. Did you know that there was a Spanish-language version of the movie shot at night on the same set with different actors?"

"No, but it makes sense that you do."

"So, what did you think of dating outside our homes?"

"It reminded me of my youth. Being close to a beautiful woman I wanted desperately to touch and not being able to," he said, winding his arms around me as he led me to his car.

I chewed my lip and made a pouty face. "Was there a good-looking woman sitting next to us?"

"Are you ever going to just take a compliment and not turn it into a joke?"

I considered for a moment and shook my head. "Not likely, no."

We had a few blocks to walk before reaching the car. It was a beautiful night, and I was enjoying strolling down a downtown sidewalk arm in arm with a handsome man. The downtown area was an odd mix of beautifully refurbished buildings and abandoned storefronts. One of those lovingly restored buldings contained the Coffee Spot, a Hollow institution known for bad java and unbelievable pecan pie. My father and I used to make up errands on Saturday mornings, then hide out at the Coffee Spot and eat cheese fries. From across the street, I peered through the window, smiling at the memory of Mama demanding to know how Daddy had gotten melted Velveeta on his shirt during a trip to the hardware store. I was about to seize an opportunity to share a nondisturbing experience from my human years with Gabriel, when I recognized two faces in a front booth. It was Mama Ginger and my synapse-slapping senior friend, Esther Barnes.

"What the?"

I couldn't step closer to the window for fear of Mama Ginger's internal Jane-tracking device going off. Instead, I ducked behind a nearby car and squinted at them. Really hard.

"Jane?" Gabriel grinned, staring down at me. "What are you—"

"Shhh!" I hissed, pulling at his coat and making him crouch next to me.

"This seems unnecessary," Gabriel grumbled, frowning as I shushed him again. "We will discuss the shushing later."

Framed by the coffee shop's logo in the window, Mama Ginger and Esther seemed to be arguing. Knowing Mama Ginger, this was not unexpected. She'd once started a fistfight at a Relay for Life meeting over whether her card club's booth should be luau- or casino-themed.

I couldn't hear through the glass, but both Esther and Mama Ginger talked with their hands. Esther was pointing one of her long, bony fingers at Mama Ginger and then made a gesture that meant "More money" or "I need moisturizer." Mama Ginger was shaking her head and seemed to be saying, "I need it sooner."

I tried to zero in on Mama Ginger's thoughts but heard only white noise. I looked up to Gabriel, who was sticking a finger in his ear and seemed to be trying to pop some pressure loose.

"You, too?" I asked, narrowing my gaze at the septuagenarian psychic. Maybe Esther's psychic presence acted like some sort of scrambler, keeping both of us from reading the people around her. I clutched a fist and shook it at her. "Esther Barnes."

I watched their conversation for a few more minutes, culminating in Esther's threatening to get up and leave. Mama Ginger made placating gestures and finally broke out her wallet. She slid some cash across the table, which Esther counted. Twice.

I waited for either of them to get up and leave. Maybe if I could get Mama Ginger alone, I could ask her a few questions about Esther. But they wouldn't budge. They both seemed determined to win some sort of impromptu pie-eating contest.

Sighing in exasperation at my own suspicious nature, I stood up, turned my back on the scene, and brushed off my coat. More than likely, all I was witnessing was some sort of illegal transaction involving unlicensed Precious Moments figurines.

"Can we stop skulking now?" Gabriel asked.

I nodded and quickly led him away before Mama Ginger could spot us.

"Is everything OK?" he asked.

"I don't know. That woman that Mama Ginger's talking to, she walked into the shop the other night and . . . well, she smacked my brain around in a psychic sense. I don't like that she and Mama Ginger are talking. The two of them joining forces cannot possibly be good for Zeb . . . or mankind, in general."

Gabriel nodded solemnly. "Agreed."

I put my arm through Gabriel's and tried to resuscitate our date night as we walked away. "Did I ever tell you that my dad and I used to go to that coffee shop every weekend?"

Werewolves look for three key components in a mate: ability to hunt, viable genes, and a sense of humor.
—*Mating Rituals and Love Customs of the Were*

I shouldn't have told Mama to Photoshop me into the family Christmas picture. She'd found some photo kiosk at the mall and cropped in a picture from three Christmases ago, taken just after I'd had minor dental surgery. With eyes both red and bleary, I was wobbling near the rear of the tree attempting to hang an angel ornament in midair. Everyone else in the family is smiling and looking at the camera (with this year's hair), and I was copied and pasted into a corner as if my top half was springing out of the tree. Mama sent it to 120 of our nearest and dearest, including Zeb.

"It looks like *Christmas Night of the Living Dead*!" he hooted.

"That's incredibly culturally insensitive," I muttered. "See if I invite you to my Christmas party."

"Aw, sweetie, you know it's not Christmas without us watching *A Christmas Story* until one of us passes out."

Zeb and I usually spent Christmas Eve together. He could only handle so much of his parents and used me as a reason to get away. We would hoard as much peanut-butter fudge and sausage balls as possible, then hide out at Zeb's place to watch Christmas movies. Gifts were exchanged, relatives were avoided. God bless us every one.

But this year, we were having "A Holly Jolly Undead Christmas" at River Oaks. Gabriel had promised to be there, which was fortunate, because I'd found the perfect present for him. Zeb was bringing Jolene, as Mama Ginger had made it clear that she was not welcome at the Lavelle family Christmas. Andrea was coming, which meant Dick would be there, even though he said he had plans that night. Fred and Jettie would try to fit us into their busy holiday schedule. Of course, Mr. Wainwright would be there. He was eager to question Jolene about her family.

River Oaks hadn't been opened for a big party since the Great Depression, when Great-great-great-grandpa Early lost a good portion of the family fortune in oil speculation in Florida. It was the first adult party I'd ever hosted, with real hors d'oeuvres and fancy clothes. I'd put up a real spruce tree and brought out all of the old glass ornaments. I hung fairy lights from every stationary object in the house. I lit a couple dozen good vanilla-scented candles and then blew half of them out. Having a lot of open flames around highly flammable guests was surely the mark of an inconsiderate hostess.

Jolene promised to handle the human food, which was fortunate, since I think my stove had atrophied from disuse. Jolene said it just didn't seem fair to make me cook stuff I couldn't eat. I asked if she could put that in writing and send it to my mama.

Jolene was also providing a crock pot full of cow's blood from her farm, for the undead guests. I thought about adding spices to make it sort of a mulled-wine thing, but Mr. Wainwright advised strongly against it. He even gave me a book titled *Elegant Undead Entertaining*. Based on the "Foods That Vampires Can Prepare without Becoming Nauseated" menu, I was providing crackers and cheese, fancy cookies, and sparkling cider and thanked the ever-patient, ever-generous officials of the Visa corporation, for providing the groceries.

With the tree, the candles, and the scent of blood warming in the crock pot, the house smelled wonderfully of home and hearth. (My standards have changed a bit.) All that was left was for me to run around like a crazy person double- and triple-checking everything.

Pretty decorations? Check. Good food? Check. Not telling Mama about it? Check. It was the recipe for the perfect party.

And what else would a vampire wear to a Christmas party but a blood-red cocktail dress?

It was perfect, fabulous even, maybe the most flattering dress I'd ever worn. Cinched at the waist with a scarlet sash and a rhinestone poinsettia brooch, the luscious, floaty material fell in a perfect bell around my knees. I even broke the Curse of Bridesmaid Shoe Past, finally finding a use for those sassy pomegranate-dyed pumps.

Believe it or not, I found the dress in Aunt Jettie's

closet. Jettie wasn't always a sweatsuit fanatic. She was quite the sharp dresser before she declared open rebellion against foundation garments. And fortunately, we were both tall, "athletically" built girls. And it smelled nothing like mothballs, so double points for me.

"Everything looks wonderful, honey," Jettie said as I changed the CD in the stereo for the fourteenth time. I have no centralized music taste. I listen to an alarming amount of Sarah McLachlan, the DefTones, and the Red Hot Chili Peppers. Musically, I kind of got stuck in the 1990s. Gabriel called my CD collection "pedantic." I think he forgot he was dealing with someone who knew what "pedantic" means.

Unfortunately, my pedantic collection did not include any Christmas music, so we had a choice between celebrating the birth of baby Christ with "Suck My Kiss" or a Lilith Fair concert recording. Neither felt appropriate, so I settled for the regional NPR station's broadcast of Handel's *Messiah*.

"Maybe I should rearrange the—" I turned toward the candles.

"Don't!" Jettie cried. "Honey, they're perfect. And it's not good for you to handle candles too much." I relented, and she stepped back, motioning for me to raise my arms. "Now, let me see you. That dress never looked that good on me."

"Fibber." I rolled my eyes.

"I don't know any one-word insults for false modesty, but I'll come up with one," she said. "In the meantime, sit, catch your breath, er, relax. Enjoy this quiet time when the house looks perfect and you look beautiful and no one is frazzled or complaining that they can't eat anything because of their lactose intolerance."

"That's lovely," I said. "Which shelter magazine did you get that from?"

She grinned. "Original material. Now, I'm going to go stare at the cheese and crackers and long for days gone by."

"You and me both," I muttered as someone or something battered at my kitchen door. Jolene, werewolf strength abounding, threw open the door with her hip and lugged a Coleman chest cooler into my kitchen.

"Either that's a lot of food or you're planning a really cheap funeral in my backyard," I said, eyeing the man-sized cooler.

Zeb hefted a tray of mini-quiches onto my counter. "Given your luck this year, do you think you should be joking about that?"

"Duly noted," I said as Jolene unpacked a ham, mashed potatoes, stuffing, rolls, and what looked like a twenty-pound deep-fried turkey. "How many people are you planning to feed?"

"Me, Zeb, Mr. Wainwright, your friend Andrea . . ." she said, ticking off on her fingers. "Do you think I brought enough?"

I held up a two-gallon Tupperware container of yams. "Well, if nothing else, I have some pot pies in my freezer."

"You have more pot pies?" Jolene cried, looking at the freezer with longing.

"Now you went and ruined her Christmas present." Zeb grinned.

Gabriel came to the door looking almost festive. He was wearing a dark blue scarf, which may have been the only time I'd ever seen him wear an actual color. He was also carrying a load of packages, several bottles, and a bright pink bakery box.

"You're all coiffed," he said, clearly shocked.

"I am capable of cleaning up nice," I said grumpily.

"Very nice." He nodded and gave me a friendly peck.

"That was just sad," a voice behind us drawled. We turned to see Dick, radiant in a holly-green T-shirt that said, "Join me on the naughty list," carrying presents, a bottle of Boone's Farm, and a sprig of mistletoe. "I've seen old people kiss better than that. Aunt Jettie is kissing Fred better than that right now."

In honor of the occasion, Jettie and Fred had agreed to let all of the guests see them. I turned to my living room to find that Grandpa Fred had materialized and was, indeed, kissing Aunt Jettie like a character in an old World War II movie.

"Well, that's just embarrassing," I said, pushing Gabriel's packages into Dick's hands and laying a hell of a smooch on my special vampire fella. "Happy now?"

"Blech, no." Dick grimaced. "It's like watching your parents make out."

Gabriel set his jaw and advanced on Dick.

"OK, River Oaks is neutral ground, you both promised," I said, standing between the two of them. "Gabriel, please go inside. Help Jolene unpack her movable feast."

I turned on Dick. "I thought you had plans," I said, leaning against the door and smirking at him.

"Yeah, well, they fell through. I figured, why not throw you a bone?"

"I'm just not responding to that imagery," I said as I accepted what could only be termed wine in the strictest sense of the word. "But I'm glad you're here. Merry Christmas, Dick. You have just enough time to go inside and look cool and unaffected when Andrea comes in."

Dick perked up.

"But first, a few ground rules. No 'ho, ho, ho' jokes. That shirt is the only 'naughty' reference you're allowed tonight. And keep the mistletoe where I can see it," I said.

"Well, tie my hands, why don't you?" he grumbled, then scrambled to get inside when he saw Andrea's car pull onto my drive.

Andrea had volunteered to drive Mr. Wainwright, whose night vision was not what it once was. Neither was his day vision, for that matter. It took Gabriel and me to help him up the steps, but he was determined to carry his own presents and the jar of potpourri he had brought as a hostess gift.

At least, I hoped it was potpourri.

Oddly enough, the first person he greeted when he walked into the living room was my Aunt Jettie, who was confused but flattered. "He can see me?"

"You can see her?" I asked. "I thought vampires were the only ones who could see you; when you decided to grace us with your presence, that is."

Mr. Wainwright chuckled. "Well of course, I can see her, she's standing right there. She's a bit transparent but still visible to those who have a . . . broader personal perspective."

"Jettie Early, meet my boss, Gilbert Wainwright," I said. "Mr. Wainwright, my late great-aunt Jettie."

"Charmed," he said. I noticed he didn't offer to shake her hand, an effort to avoid calling attention to the fact that she was noncorporeal.

"Jane's told me so much about you," Jettie said, smiling sweetly. "I'm so glad she's found such a wonderfully interesting person to work for."

"Well, she is a pleasure to have at the store," he assured her. "She has revolutionized our filing system."

"She said you didn't have a filing system before she was hired," Jettie pointed out. My gaze shifted from my aunt to my employer. Did Aunt Jettie just giggle in a coquettish manner, drawing a suspicious look from my dead step-grandpa? Mr. Wainwright chuckled again and adjusted his suspenders.

My dead aunt was flirting with my boss. My dead aunt who was practically engaged to my dead step-grandfather. And my boss appeared to be flirting back. This could go nowhere good.

They started talking and realized they'd gone to high school together. They were in the last class to graduate from the original Half-Moon Hollow High before Milton "Firebug" Chambers burned it to the ground. They reminisced about Mr. Allan, the math teacher who spoke in the third person; the design of the first-ever Half-

Moon Howler mascot costume; and Milton's multiple failed attempts at burning the school down before he got it right. Mr. Wainwright asked Aunt Jettie about her demise and how the "tunnel of light" appeared to her. Jettie laughed uproariously and told him it was more like a tornado. Eager to catch every detail, he asked Jettie to meet him at his office sometime, where he could interview her properly.

Grandpa Fred was not pleased. Fortunately, he couldn't solve this problem as he did when Grandma Ruthie drove him crazy during his living Christmases: drinking buttered rum until he was near comatose, forcing my dad and I to cart him, Barcalounger and all, out to the car.

It's awkward introducing two groups of friends. It's even more awkward when one of those groups decides not to like the other. While Mr. Wainwright was thrilled to be acquainted or reacquainted with the supernatural beings, Jolene had taken an instant dislike to Andrea. A few minutes after the two of them gingerly shook hands, Jolene pulled me into the kitchen to whisper at a decibel far below human hearing that she didn't trust her.

"I trust Andrea," I said. "She's been a really good friend to me. You're just used to being the prettiest girl in the room, and having someone who remotely rivals your blinding hotness is throwing you off your game. And we don't have to whisper. Andrea's perfectly normal hearing is not going to pick up this conversation."

"I'm just sayin' one girl to another, I think you need to

watch her around Gabriel," Jolene said, grabbing a hunk of cheddar and chowing down. Around the cheese, she said, "A lot of girls, especially wounded human girls, go for the whole mysterious, dark-haired guy with the full lips, piercing soulful eyes, cheekbones you could slice a ham with—"

"Maybe I should watch *you* around Gabriel," I said, eyeing her warily. "I think we should get back into the living room with your lovely canapés before everybody else figures out that we're talking about one of them."

"You're right, I'm bein' silly," Jolene said, watching Zeb try one of Mr. Wainwright's cigars, then get pounded on the back when he started to choke. "I just want everybody to be as happy as Zeb and me."

"Lovebirds on amphetamines couldn't be happier than you two," I said, linking arms with her.

She sighed, leaning her head against mine. "I know."

I lingered and watched the party from the kitchen doorway. Someone, mercifully, had dug up a Nat King Cole CD. Even over the bluesy cheer, I could hear Andrea and Zeb chatting about the merits of being the only "normals" in the room. They didn't consider Mr. Wainwright to be normal. Jolene swept in and marked her territory by kissing Zeb's cheek and pulling him away from Andrea. Gabriel and Mr. Wainwright discussed Gabriel's library and its shocking lack of information on freshwater sea monsters, until Dick distracted Gabriel by mentioning all of the parties they used to attend at River Oaks. Gabriel sent a furtive look my way. I think he offered Dick money not to reminisce further. Mr. Wainwright then engaged Dick in adamant conversation regarding the sales of were-pelts on the black market. Dick was smiling at him in a way I didn't normally see. It was almost tender. And it was weirding me out.

"Please, in the name of Christmas, don't let Dick try to sell him anything," I asked, looking skyward.

Fortunately, Andrea passed by in her slinky black party dress, and Dick's attention shifted gears. Mr. Wainwright grinned as Dick trailed after her. He made eye contact with Aunt Jettie, rolled his eyes, and muttered, "Young people." Aunt Jettie gave a girlish giggle, which got Grandpa Fred's back up.

Andrea heard Mr. Wainwright's side of the conversation and tapped me on the shoulder.

"Is Mr. Wainwright talking to himself again?" she asked.

"Nope. Aunt Jettie. I think he might have a little bit of a crush going. This is going to be a big shock for Grandpa Fred. This may be the love triangle that undoes the fabric of our universe."

She cringed. Gabriel sauntered my way, offering me a punch cup of an imported dessert blood called Sangre.

"You throw a great party," Gabriel said, nodding at the happy crowd.

"God bless us everyone," I said, grinning. "This may actually be the best Christmas ever. People I love. No pressure. No drunk cousins fistfighting on the lawn."

"Well, I'm sure that's an interesting story that I'll ask about later." He cringed before calling across the room, "While we're on the subject of families, Zeb, can you tell me why your mother has been leaving me increasingly threatening voice-mail messages? She plans to put her foot, among other things, up several orifices."

"I honestly don't know," Zeb said. "It's possible she just dialed a random number. Sometimes she leaves those messages for strangers."

"I think I know," I said, sighing. "Zeb's mama seems to think you're the only obstacle standing between me and Zeb, true love, and some sort of Precious Moments wedding extravaganza."

Zeb seemed stunned but not nearly as disturbed by this as I was. He smiled at me with that weird, glazed-over stare, which was becoming way too familiar. I moved closer to Gabriel, twining my fingers through his. "You might want to keep your doors locked during the day, Gabriel. Also, cover your butt, because what she has planned would sting a little."

"I don't think Mama would actually do anything," Zeb assured me, his voice low and soft.

"Easy for you to say," I told Zeb. "It's not your orifices at stake."

"And on that lovely Yuletide note, I have something for you," Gabriel said, leading me closer to the lights of the Christmas tree before handing me a small silver-wrapped package. With visions of jewelry dancing in my head, I opened it to find a little canister with a plastic trigger. "Mace?"

"Nope, silver in aerosol form," he said proudly. "To prevent further parking-lot fights. Just don't stand downwind when you use it."

"Oh, how thoughtful," I said, lifting it carefully from the box. With all the enthusiasm I could scrape together, I told him, "It's really, really great."

"It's a gag gift," he said crossly. "Zeb said you'd find this kind of thing funny. Lift up the tissue."

"Zeb has spent most of his adult years playing Game-Boy alone on Friday nights," I said, rooting to the bottom of the box. "Don't take relationship advice from Zeb."

In the bottom of the box was a tissue-wrapped bundle. It was a little silver unicorn on a fine chain.

"Andrea said that paying homage to a little quirk in your personality, the closet unicorn obsession, would show that I care," he said.

"It really does," I told him. "Can I touch it?"

"It would be a good first step toward wearing it."

"But it's silver," I said, hooking a tissue-protected finger around the clasp.

"No, it's white gold," he said as he looped the chain around my neck. "Perfectly safe for vampires."

"All of the beauty of silver without the burning and itching," I cooed, running my fingers over the curves of the unicorn's tiny legs.

"Does that mean 'thank you' in your language?" he asked, tilting his head.

"Thank you, it's very sweet," I said, kissing him. "This is a wonderful coincidence, because I have this for you."

Across the room, Zeb was making a sour face. Jolene jostled his arm, attempting to tease the scowl from him, but he shook her off, stalking toward the kitchen and out of sight. She stared after him, her face twisted into confused, hurt lines. Dick saw this and asked some random question about his responsibilities as "the man of honor" and how it related to cummerbund color, teasing her into a smile.

I handed Gabriel a square package. "I was sorting through some old family photos with Aunt Jettie. We found this."

Jettie and I spent hours looking through old boxes of River Oaks tintypes when I was a little girl. We would study the sepia-toned photos of Earlys from the 1870s and comment on the clothes, the hairstyles, who looked like toothless Uncle Vernon. (Somehow, we always voted for Grandma Ruthie.) Jettie would tell me stories about my ancestors, such as Great-great-great-grandma Lula, who set fire to the Hollow's only cathouse after finding her husband, the Reverend James Early, "proselytizing" there. The fire took out the cathouse, a nearby saloon, and the general store, where the owner sold dirty French pictures from the back room. She did more good in forty-five minutes with an oil lamp than Reverend Early did in thirty-five years of preaching.

We're a proud family.

On a recent trip down Disturbing Genealogical Memory Lane, Jettie and I found portraits from Clarissa and Stewart Early's wedding in 1877. In one smaller photo, two young Early cousins, Leah and Mariah, were shown smiling up at two strapping fellows in silk coats. I had seen this photo a hundred times before I was turned. Until now, I hadn't recognized the young men being adored by my simpering foremothers: Dick and Gabriel, grinning like mad at the camera. They were so young. And Dick actually had his arm around Gabriel's shoulders, laughing as if he had just told some raunchy joke.

I'd taken the photos to a camera shop to have copies of the print made. I'd framed one for Gabriel and one for Dick. It was not a manipulative *Parent Trap* ploy; I honestly couldn't think of anything else to get them.

"I remember this day," Gabriel said, grinning. "This was right before Dick persuaded your cousins to go skinnydip—" He caught sight of my raised eyebrows. "Um, never mind."

Dick came to peer over Gabriel's shoulder. "Leah and Mariah, twins in every sense of the word."

"Did you leave any of my cousins untouched?" I cried, remembering Dick's "fondness" for my ancestor, cousin Cessie.

Dick guffawed. "Hey, Gabriel's the one who—" Gabriel narrowed his eyes at Dick. "Never mind."

"Horrifying revelations and the confirmation that some of my relatives are/were publicly nude. You know, suddenly, this has become like Christmas with my family. Thanks," I said, patting them on the back.

Gabriel's cell phone sounded. OK, so it wasn't the most mature thing to do, but I snuck a look at the caller ID. It read "Jeanine." I didn't know any Jeanine. Gabriel had never mentioned a Jeanine. Who the hell was Jeanine?

I practically chewed through my tongue to keep from

commenting. He took the call outside. And, I'm ashamed to say, I sort of lurked around the door to try to overhear. But he stepped off the porch, out of my range of hearing through the glass.

Defeated, I turned to the eating crowd. "Who's ready for dinner?"

Jolene wasn't the only one who could plan a tablescape. I had clear glass bowls of various sizes filled with vanilla candles and cranberries, Great-grandma Early's wedding tablecloth, and the good china with the delicate silver ivy pattern. I was going for a *Good Housekeeping* look, which tends to be less angry than *Martha Stewart Living*. I used gloves to set out silver place settings for the humans.

"You spent six hours setting a table for food you can't eat," Zeb marveled. He took it upon himself to "escort" me to the table, since Gabriel was otherwise occupied.

"It's my first vampire Christmas," I said. "I still want to enjoy dinner."

Gabriel appeared at my right, ready to seat me, and seemed a little put off when Zeb did not relinquish my hand or take the seat I'd assigned him across from Jolene. He seemed intent on sitting next to me, forcing Gabriel to sit next to a confused werewolf bride-to-be.

"I'm surprised you didn't mix eggnog in your blood," snorted Dick.

"Jane's firmly antinog in all its forms," Zeb told him, pulling out my chair.

Caught off-guard by Zeb's clueless move, I made a quick comment along the lines of "Eggs, milk, and rum should not be mixed unless it's in cake batter," and asked Mr. Wainwright to pour the blood.

Gabriel's contribution turned out to be pastry shells filled with a jiggly pink mousse. I might have suffered from dessert envy, but the filling smelled vaguely of cat food. Gabriel told Jolene he'd gotten them from a bakery downtown that she was familiar with. She was clearly delighted, eating three of them before Zeb could take a tentative bite.

Zeb made a gagging sound he hadn't uttered since his dad made him try chitterlings, then spat the pastry in his napkin.

"What exactly is this?" he asked.

"Heart mousse tarts," Jolene said, moaning the way I used to over cheesecake.

"Beef heart, to be exact," Gabriel said cheerfully, watching Jolene devour her fourth.

"They're a real delicacy," Jolene told Zeb. "We only get these at Christmas."

Zeb wiped his tongue with his napkin and smiled wanly at Jolene. "I'll finish mine later."

**Werewolves are also territorial about holiday time.
It would be unwise for a human to underestimate
her werewolf mother-in-law's desire to see her son
on Thanksgiving and Christmas Day.**

—*Mating Rituals and Love Customs of the Were*

I didn't invite Gabriel to Christmas with my family. Because I don't do that to people I like.

Grandma Ruthie spent every Christmas Eve neck-deep in nog, feeling at liberty to tell me exactly what she thought was wrong with my life and which of my poor choices had led me there. One particularly memorable holiday, in 2004, she offered to pay for plastic surgery, a total tune-up, including boobs, nose, teeth, and a little reconstruction to "soften my mannish features." While generous, this offer kept me from coming to Christmas 2005.

And just as on Christmas 2005, Mama had not responded well to my skipping out on this year's family festivities. Thanksgiving was spent with Mama's extended family. I was allowed to skip it this year because the family preferred to eat lunch together, and an afternoon of watching other people eat just wasn't worth the risk of spontaneous combustion. Mama made some lame excuse to the uncles about my needing to get the bookstore ready for the Black Friday shopping rush, which seemed to satisfy everybody.

Christmas, however, belonged to Mama. There was the prolonged Christmas Eve gathering in which Mama, Daddy, myself, Jenny, and her spawn, plus Grandma and that year's grandpa exchanged presents. We then enjoyed the traditional Jameson meal of turkey, stuffing, and a piping-hot side dish of guilt-stuffed manipulation. Unmarried and childless (read: pathetic, with no place to go), I usually slept at my parents' house and spent Christmas morning with them. I was one step away from wearing footie pajamas.

Jenny and her boys, loaded up with sugar and obnoxiously noisy toys, usually arrived at around 6 P.M., and we were stuck together in family harmony until Mama decided to warm up leftovers for dinner and parole us until next year.

I had already violated the sanctity of Christmas Eve by spending it with people who actually liked me, so avoiding my family on Christmas night this year was not an option. I showed up at sundown and gave myself a forty-five-minute window to duck out before anyone arrived for the warmed-over feast. Mama got her usual bottle of Windsong, which she asked for every year. I gave Daddy a book on the haunted battlefields of Kentucky, which Mr. Wainwright recommended. I got slipper socks and a copy of *The Seven Habits of Highly Effective People*.

The house seemed even more quiet than usual, the gaps

in conversation echoing just how much my estrangement from Jenny was putting a strain on my parents' holiday. Mama did, however, manage to mention how much everybody missed me on Christmas Eve and that it would be so much easier if I just stayed for dinner. About twenty times.

By easier, I'm pretty sure Mama meant easier for her. It was easier for her not to have to address my issues with my sister, such as the fact that Jenny had helped Missy the psychotic real estate agent by (albeit unwittingly) feeding her information about my schedule, River Oaks, and all manner of things that helped her harass me and frame me for murder. Oh, and the lawsuit she filed against me.

That sort of discussion can put a real damper on Baby Jesus' birthday.

While Mama started preparations for re-dinner, I think I lost track of time talking to my dad about the possibility of tracing Mr. Wainwright's family. Normally, I can sense my grandma's approaching presence, like Bambi's mom sensing when Man has entered the forest. I was caught off-guard in both senses, when Grandma Ruthie arrived with her newest catch, the aforementioned Wilbur.

They say the mourning period for a relationship is at least one-half of the time that was spent in the relationship. Grandma had reduced it to her shortest time ever, one-twenty-seventh of the relationship.

I smelled Wilbur long before I saw him. This went well beyond your typical old-man aroma. This was rot, decay, mold, black stinky gingivitis, and bad cheese. On top of that, he looked like a cheap Halloween mask come to life, all papery wrinkles and saggy, yellowed eyelids.

Sadly, he was still better-looking than former grandpa Tom.

"Oh, Jane, I didn't know you were going to be here." Grandma Ruthie sniffed as Mama took her coat, the unspoken but clear sentiment being that she wouldn't have come if she'd known I was going to be there.

Mama hustled their coats out of the room. Daddy, obviously determined not to get caught up in whatever was about to transpire, kept his eyes glued to the television and relentlessly changed the channel. Wilbur looked from me to Grandma to me again. I crossed my arms and grinned at Grandma, happy not to be the rude, socially backward one for once.

Finally, Grandma sighed and said, "Jane, this is my fiancé, Wilbur. Wilbur, this is my, this is Jane."

"So nice to meet you," he said. "Your grandma has told me so much about you."

"I doubt that very much," I said, smiling sweetly. I didn't flash my fangs. I'd leave it to Grandma to send senior men into mysterious cardiac-arrest episodes.

Wait, did she say fiancé? I zeroed in on Grandma's left hand, where a tasteful diamond engagement ring twinkled.

"You're engaged?" I gasped. "Again?"

Sensing the shift in the room, Mama poked her head into the living room. "Jane, honey, can I see you for a minute?"

Jaw unhinged, I followed Mama into the kitchen, where a wealth of Tupperware was carefully laid out in the traditional Jameson post-Christmas smorgasbord formation on the countertop. I clamped my hand over my nose when confronted with Mama's reheated "fancy" cheese grits, made with gouda and bacon and an obscene amount of garlic.

"Is she crazy?" I demanded around my hand. "Is *he* crazy?"

Mama shrugged. "Well, I will admit that the mourning period was a little short."

"She brought a date to the burial," I hissed, removing my hand from my face and concentrating on talking instead of smelling. (Stupid instinctual breathing!)

"At the time, he was just a friend, trying to help her through a difficult time," Mama said in what could only be described as her "denial" voice. I simply watched her, expressionless, prompting Mama to say, "Your grandma isn't like you, Jane. She's from a different time. She's the kind of woman who needs a man in her life."

"For a brief time, before her evil curse kills them in a terribly ironic way," I said, which made Mama's face pucker. "You know, this never would have happened if you had taken my advice and put up those 'Warning— Black Widow—Do Not Marry' posters with Grandma's picture down at the senior center."

"Honey, you know I don't like it when you talk that way."

"I don't like having a grandma with a four-volume wedding album. We all have our burdens to bear."

The tiniest eye twinkle under the veneer of annoyance told me Mama was trying not to laugh.

"When's the wedding?" I asked.

"They haven't set a date yet," Mama said. "But you

know how she likes to get married in the fall—" Mama caught herself. "See? Now you have me doing it."

I pressed my lips together to suppress the smirk.

"Wilbur seems like a very nice man," Mama told me in her "Don't argue" voice. "He treats Grandma how gentlemen used to treat ladies. He opens doors for her. He carries heavy bags. He orders for her in restaurants."

"So he's like a concierge," I said.

Mama was not amused.

"Mama, she's going to kill another one!" I moaned. "This has got to stop. Hasn't she had all the husbands she needs?"

"Shh, they're going to hear you," Mama said, sending furtive looks at the door.

"Oh, they can't hear anything." I rolled my eyes.

In an obvious ploy to redirect the conversation, Mama looked furtively toward the door and said, "I've been meaning to ask you, but I didn't want to in front of your daddy. How are things going with your Gabriel?"

"Fine." I jerked my shoulders.

"Fine?" she asked. "Just fine?"

I nodded, my lips pressed tightly together, narrowing my gaze as Mama shot me a canary-devouring feline smile. She said, "You'll never guess who was asking about you at prayer meeting the other night."

"You're right. I won't."

"Adam Morrow, you remember, you used to have such a big crush on him in high school. I used to find his name doodled all over your notebooks. Adam Morrow. Mrs. Adam Morrow. Jane Jameson-Morrow, Jane E. Morrow. Jane and Adam Morr—"

"I got it. I remember."

She smiled. "Well, he has been asking about you at church. And I thought, why not ask him over for dinner sometime? A poor single boy who works as hard as he does knows how to appreciate a good home-cooked meal."

"Mama, please don't."

Mama pursed her lips, turning back to the steaming contents of her stove. She stirred. She salted. She tasted. Finally, she turned back to me with a dreamy expression of the generous mother-goddess that, frankly, scared me. She cleared her throat and used her special "imparting motherly wisdom from the mountaintop" voice. "When your daddy and I were dating, he planned on going fishing with some friends over Homecoming weekend. This was back in high school. We'd only been dating a little while, and I think he didn't want me to think I could plan things out for him."

"Clearly, he didn't know you very well," I said.

"Mmm-hmm," she said, stirring the potatoes. "I told him it was perfectly fine if he wanted to go fishing with his buddies, because Eddie Carroll had offered to take me to the dance."

"Mr. Carroll? My math teacher? Ew."

"You should have seen him in high school. With a full head of hair, he was quite the man about town. If things hadn't worked out with your father—"

"Stop," I told her, laughing. "I do not want to hear that I could have been a Carroll."

Mama giggled. "You know, he still tells me on occasion that I have lovely ankles."

"They are lovely. But back to the story, please," I said, shuddering at the thought of Mr. Carroll ogling my mother at Parent-Teacher Night.

"Well, the moment your father heard that, he called his buddies and canceled the fishing trip," she said, preening. "He was pinning that corsage on my dress faster than you could say 'dog in the manger.' And every dance or party after that, your father knew that he would be going with me, because I might have other offers. Sometimes men need a little competition to realize what they have. It's healthy for a relationship."

"Did Mr. Carroll really ask you to the dance?" I asked. A Cheshire-cat smile spread across her face. I laughed. "You know, Mama, sometimes I completely underestimate you."

"You're probably right. So, if I ask a question, will you bite my head off?" she asked.

"You know I won't actually bite you, right?"

"You know what I mean," she said, tasting the gravy. She offered me a spoonful, but I declined, as its bouquet reminded me of that smell refrigerators get after long vacations. "Why not just call Adam, honey? You were crazy about him in high school. And he's such a nice boy."

"I think I'm at the point in my life where I need more than a nice boy. I need a nice man."

Mama *tsk*ed and patted my cheek. "Is Gabriel a nice man?"

Recalling the unfortunate Bud McElray incident, I

hesitated. "Not particularly. That may be what I deserve, though."

Mama sighed and stirred. "Well, I don't really follow you. I can tell you that when Eddie Carroll tried to cut in at the Homecoming Dance, Daddy broke his nose."

"Tempting, but Gabriel might not stop at the nose."

"Let things with Gabriel take their course," she intoned. "And in the meantime, see where things go with Adam. In the end, knowing they have a little competition may speed things along."

"Speed what things along to what?" I asked.

Mama shushed me and handed me a tray of eggnog and slightly damaged leftover Santa cookies. "Now, just take this out to them, and mind your manners. Behave yourself with your grandma."

"I will if she will," I hissed back.

When I walked back into the den, Daddy was still mindlessly changing the channels, ignoring Grandma's very presence. Wilbur and Grandma were snuggled up on the couch. Grandma was trying to tempt Wilbur with a candy cane, swiping it sensuously along his lips. Wilbur was smiling fondly at her as he reminded her about his diabetes. I guessed chronic disease precluded her need to seduce him with seasonal candy.

Repulsed, I turned on my heels and headed back to the kitchen, but Daddy called, "Jane?" Desperate for someone to share his suffering, he demanded, "Is that eggnog? With liquor?" I winked at him and gave him a double helping.

"It's so nice to see you helping your mama for a

change," Grandma said, nodding imperiously toward the tray. I ignored the bait.

"Would you like some?" I asked Wilbur.

Wilbur was about to answer when Grandma patted his hand fondly and simpered, "Oh, Wilbur is lactose-intolerant. His stomach is just so sensitive. He can't have salt because of the high blood pressure or sugar because of his diabetes. Or fats. Or nuts. Or meat. He usually sticks to Ensure or these macrobiotic shakes."

Grandma pulled a canned shake out of her enormous Aigner purse. Wilbur took it out of her hand and stuck it back into her purse before I could get a good look at the label.

"So, how did you two meet?" I asked. "*When* did you two meet?"

"Oh, it's the sweetest story." Grandma sighed. "I was on my way into Whitlow's to plan Bob's service, and Wilbur was there in the hallway, waiting for a friend's visitation to start. He saw how upset I was and offered me his hankie. It was so romantic and chivalrous, I just had to invite him for a cup of coffee in Mr. Whitlow's office."

I stared at Wilbur, reaching out, trying to touch his mind. Nothing. It was like scraping my knuckles on a brick wall. Stupid inconsistent vampire powers.

"Mr. Goosen—"

"You can just call me Grandpa," he said, smiling.

One would think that at this point in my life, with as many grandpas as I've had, one more wouldn't bother me. But something, possibly step-grandparent weariness or allegiance to Bob, made me say, "I don't think so."

Grandma sighed and sent me a wounded look. Wilbur took a deep breath and sat forward, his hands in a steepled, grandfatherly stance. "Now, Janie, honey, I know it's been a rough couple of weeks. But everyone else seems to be happy for your grandma and me. Ruthie said that you don't deal with change well."

"You don't know me well enough—"

He interrupted me again, which was not doing much to warm my heart toward him. "I understand that you love your grandma and you're concerned for her well-being. I think that's admirable, Jane."

How horrible was it that I wanted to tell him he had it totally wrong?

He reached out to pat my hand. His own was clammy and damp enough to make me want to pull away. "I just want you to know that I love your grandma and I'm going to take care of her."

"It's not her I'm worried about."

Mama popped her head into the doorway again. "Jane, could I see you in the kitchen for a minute?"

Daddy sent me a frantic look. Clearly, the idea of more alone time with the geriatric lovebirds had him panicked. Slinking out of the room, I muttered, "Everybody stops interrupting me, or I'll publish a newsletter featuring your secret thoughts of the day."

Mama had heated all of the food. She'd also rolled the plastic picnic ware into paper napkins and filled all of the cups with ice. She was now organizing and reorganizing the Tupperware lids, first putting them on the containers, then tucking them under the containers. She was doing pointless busywork. Thinking back, I realized Mama rarely came out of the kitchen for the leftover Christmas dinners.

"You're hiding in here," I accused. "You don't want to be in there any more than I do. You've been hiding in here for years."

"I have not!" Mama cried, not meeting my gaze.

"Oh, it's over now. I've seen the man behind the curtain," I whispered. "I take no holiday guff from you, from now on. Ever."

Mama ignored me while she fiddled with the defrost feature on the microwave.

"Look, as much fun as it is trying to send secret warning messages to Dead Grandpa Walking, I need to go." I looked at the clock. "It's getting close to six, and I would like to avoid further awkwardness with Jenny."

"You're already here. Why don't you just stay?" Mama wheedled. "The boys haven't seen you—"

"Since the funeral home, last week," I said. "And they were too busy destroying the telephone-shaped 'Jesus Called Him Home' floral arrangement to talk to me. I don't think my absence will scar them for life."

The pounding arrival of the boys at the front door told me that I was too late.

"Grandma! Grandma! We got Blood Spatter Carjacker Mayhem Four!" Andrew shouted, waving the gore-soaked video game case at my mother. "Can we play it now? Please?"

"Oh, honey, you know Grandma doesn't have a game system—" Jenny said, coming into the kitchen. She skidded to a stop when she saw me.

"Everything here is boring." Andrew sighed as he and Bradley slinked into the living room. If he had paid attention to the look on his mother's face, he would know that if he stuck around, it might get interesting. Or at least blood-spattery.

My brother-in-law, Kent, the chiropractor whom I've rarely heard speak, followed at Jenny's heels. The moment he saw me, he pivoted and trailed after the boys.

"I didn't know you'd be here," Jenny said, sending a reproachful look Mama's way. "Mama, I agreed to see her at Bob's visitation, but that's it. You can't let her come over and not tell me. It upsets the boys to see her."

I rolled my eyes. "The boys didn't even notice I was in the room. And if they did and you actually told them their aunt was a vampire, they'd probably think I was the coolest thing since Blood Spatter Carjacker Mayhem Four. And don't blame Mama. I didn't mean to stay so long, but I got caught up talking. I'm leaving now."

"Oh, but you can't go!" Mama cried. "This is the first time we've all been in the house together since you . . ."

"Died?" I finished for her. "You can say it. I died."

"Shh!" Jenny shushed me, looking toward the den.

"Please, can't you both just put this all aside for the holiday?" Mama begged. "For the family?"

"No!" Jenny and I chorused.

Mama switched tactics just by dropping her voice an octave. "Now, girls, this is just silly. We're family. And it's Christmas. If you can't forgive your family around the holidays, what—"

"Stop," I told her. The way she stretched the word into

"faaaaaamily" when she wanted something always set my teeth on edge.

"The time of year doesn't change anything. I don't want her around my family," Jenny ground out.

I shot her a look that could have dropped a more observant woman. So, it was *her* family. As far as she was concerned, I wasn't part of it anymore. Frankly, she was welcome to it. "I'm going."

"Now, Jenny, be a good sister," Mama told Jenny. "We have to have the whole family together for Christmas. The good Christian thing to do would be to—"

"She's dead!" Jenny cried. "The good Christian thing to do would be to give her a decent burial."

"Now, Jenny, you know you don't mean that," Mama said through clenched teeth.

"Burial talk is my cue to go," I said, grabbing my jacket. "I think I'll be leaving the country for New Year's, so please don't call."

I stuck my head into the den to give Daddy a quick good-bye, which he couldn't hear over the screeching and beeping of the boys' new radio controlled-monster trucks.

From the kitchen, I heard Mama whine, "Tell Jane it just won't be Christmas without her."

"You have me, Kent, the boys here, why—" I closed the front door on Jenny's wounded response.

I looked back through the window. Wilbur looked absolutely miserable. I was sympathetic, but when it came to the Jameson family Christmas, it was every man, woman, and vampire for themselves.

Adult werewolf children are expected to stay within the confines of pack territory. Those who move more than a five-minute run from pack headquarters are either disowned or hosts to frequent weekend guests.

—*Mating Rituals and Love Customs of the Were*

From the dawn of time, women have formed friendships for one purpose only: to make sure they'll have someone to provide unpaid serf labor for their weddings. And we all just go along with it, spurred by fear that if we don't submit to the bridal demands, there will be no one to slave over our own weddings.

That's why, six months before the actual wedding, I was spending an evening measuring and cutting exactly fourteen inches of cornflower-blue ribbon over and over and over and . . . over. These ribbons would be sent to a printing company to be stamped with "HMS *Titanic*" on one side and "Zeb and Jolene—Struck by Love" on the other. They would then be tied around old-fashioned hurricane lamps as part of Jolene's carefully planned tablescape.

Each table was going to be named for famous (read: deceased) *Titanic* passengers, such as John Jacob Astor and Molly Brown, then decorated with hurricane lamps and fake ice. Of course, no one would pay attention to a seating plan, which is another Southern wedding tradition.

Jolene had the gall to call this gathering a "work party," in the style of Amish people who get together to make a quilt or build a barn. I didn't think Amish women typically had a Camel hanging from the corner of their lips while they worked, like Jolene's aunt Lulu. Also, the Amish employed more lenient leaders than Jolene, who had the tendency to become a little bossy when it came to her nuptials.

"It has to be at least fourteen inches to make sure each bow has about three inches of hanging ribbon on each side," Jolene told us. I would have questioned whether Jolene was serious, but she didn't respond well when I laughed at her "All bridesmaids must cut their hair to exactly three inches below the shoulder by March" edict.

Pointing out that the printing company would have cut these ribbons for an additional $250 would have resulted in huffy eye rolls from Jolene's battalion of cranky cousins. Besides, Aunt Vonnie, who had somehow heard my full opinion of the bridesmaids' dresses, was already giving me the dagger eyes.

The McClaine clan alpha couple—known to Jolene as Mom and Dad—lived in the main house on the compound, a quaint little yellow farmhouse, with white shutters and a porch swing, surrounded by a series of increasingly dilapidated trailers. Inside, the walls were decorated with Thomas Kinkade prints and silk floral arrangements saved from funeral services. Everything was neat and clean and protected by doilies. And everybody was naked. Which explained the doilies.

Jolene and her cousins whipped their clothes off the moment they got in the door, the way most people kick off their shoes.

"Does this bother you?" she'd asked the first time I stumbled into her mother's house.

"I just don't know where to look," I said, settling for a strange orange silk-flower arrangement mounted on the wall. The truth was, as the only clothed person there, I felt weird. I felt more naked than Jolene.

The only cousin who was remotely friendly was Charlene, who had asked for my home and e-mail addresses twice in the four hours since meeting me. She wanted to be my best friend. Seriously. My *best* friend. You cannot be nice to people like Charlene. It's like feeding a stray cat. The cat just keeps coming back until you have to move. So I was being overtly rude to her, which wasn't really helping my standing with the rest of the family.

Fortunately, among werewolf women, the word "bitch" is not offensive. I was having a lot of fun with that.

"Hey there, bitches!" I called as I came through the door. "What are my favorite bitches up to today?"

The only response was a chorus of unenthusiastic, drawled "Hi's" and "Heys."

"I know what you're doin'," Jolene muttered as she hugged me. "And it's not funny."

"See, that's where you're wrong," I said, tucking wavy

crimson hair behind her ears. She scowled at me. "I'll try to keep it to a minimum."

Jolene was clearly the Golden Child in her clan. Her mother, Mimi, and all of the aunts fawned over her, telling and retelling cute stories from when she was a cub. Any accomplishment or news from the other cousins was matched with something about Jolene. Jolene was the only one of her cousins to attend community college. Jolene could skin a rabbit in two bites. Jolene was Miss Half-Moon Hollow 1998. Jolene and Zeb would be the first couple in her family to plan an actual honeymoon—to Gatlinburg, Tennessee, which was where you went when you couldn't afford to go to Florida but wanted to be far enough away that your parents couldn't "drop in" on the wedding night.

"Jolene works at Uncle Clay's sandwich shop," Aunt Lola said, beaming beatifically at Jolene. "He says all the customers just love her. She's so helpful, so sweet. She just makes everybody she meets so happy."

Raylene, Angelene, Lurlene, and Company let loose a collective sigh and synchronized eye roll. Sensing that the mob might be turning ugly, Jolene asked, "How's the new job, Raylene?"

"Fine," Raylene said, her voice flat as she concentrated on cutting the ribbon without fraying it.

"Just fine?" Jolene asked. "I mean, it's got to be fun, right?"

Raylene shrugged. "Sure."

"Well, you seen one, you seen 'em all, right, Raylene?" Angelene asked slyly.

"Angelene," Mimi growled. (Yes, literally.)

"I just started as a cake decorator at the Sweet Tooth," Raylene explained. "I specialize in adult cakes."

"Like Black Forest?" I asked. "That always seemed pretty grown-up to me."

I really missed Black Forest cake, or any kind of cake. I missed chocolate. *Bah!* I still can't believe the last food I ate was potato skins.

"No, Raylene makes cakes that look like"——Aunt Tammy looked around as if there were spies lurking behind the lace curtains—"sex parts."

Raylene sighed. "I make penis cakes."

Well, at least I knew what we were serving at the bachelorette party.

"How does one get into the penis-cake field?" I asked. "Where do you buy the cake pans for that?"

Raylene stared at me, unsure whether I was teasing her or honestly interested. Sensing a lull in the conversation, Aunt Lola—Raylene's own mother—changed the subject back to Jolene.

"We're all just so excited about Jolene's wedding." Lola sighed. "We've all waited for this, for just years now. And Zeb's such an . . . he's a sweet boy. Tell us again how he popped the question?"

Arlene muttered, "'Cause we haven't heard this story in almost an hour now."

Jolene obviously heard her cousin but ignored her. To be fair, I had heard the story a few times myself.

"Zeb had this big plan with a restaurant and hidin' the ring in a soufflé," Jolene said, smiling dreamily. "And then I stepped out my front door, he saw me all dressed up, and he blurted out 'Willyoumarryme?' and shoved the ring at me. It was so cute!" Jolene cooed, looking down at the little diamond ring for which Zeb had plunked down two months of his teaching salary. "He almost shouted at me when he proposed. He was supposed to have the waiters at Julian's sing this cute little 'Will You Marry Me?' song. Most of them are in the high-school swing chorus, and when we got to the restaurant and they found out we were already engaged, they were so mad they had missed their chance to perform! After that, Zeb was afraid to order the soufflé. Who knows what they might have done to it?"

"Did he cry?" Lurlene asked. "I heard that human males cry at the drop of a hat."

The amazing thing about werewolves, who spend half their lives behind a human mask, is that they have terrible poker faces. It's part of that canine earnestness thing. For a brief second, a look of pure annoyance flashed over Jolene's perfect features. Lurlene smirked.

"How's it goin' with Roy?" Jolene asked. "Isn't he the one who drives the ice cream truck?"

There was that annoyed flash again, only on Lurlene's face.

"That was Ray," Lurlene said, glaring. "Roy and I aren't dating anymore."

"Wait, didn't I see his name in the paper for somethin'?" Jolene said.

"Oh, he got busted for trying to sneak a brisket out of the Super Saver in his jacket," Tammy said in the most helpful tone I'd heard in a while. "He would have gotten away with it if he hadn't dropped the brisket."

"Oh! Is he the one who yelled, 'Who threw this meat at me?' and then tried to run out of the store?" I giggled. "Didn't it take three Taser shots to get him down? Knowing that he's a werewolf now, well, that makes a lot more sense . . . I'm not helping, am I?"

I ducked my head and pretended that measuring ribbons exactly was the most important thing in the world.

"So, Jolene, tell us all about your dress," Aunt DeeDee squealed. "I haven't seen it yet, but Vonnie said it's just gorgeous."

Cue another eye roll from the cousins.

"It is," I volunteered. "Really gorgeous."

Cue another eye roll. Sensing the shift in the tide, Jolene generously switched subjects to Braylene's son. "Mama finished Jake's little captain's outfit."

At my questioning eyebrow, she said, "Jake's going to be our ring bearer. We found a pattern for an authentic period captain's suit. I just hope he can get down the aisle without stripping it off."

"Have you found a figurehead yet?" Aunt Tammy asked.

"No, I'm thinking about having Uncle Deke carve one," Jolene pouted.

"*Titanic* didn't have a figurehead."

Three guesses who said that. They all turned to me, the person who had dared to disagree with Jolene.

"I know." Jolene shrugged. "But it's just so nautical and romantic."

"Actually, most figureheads on ships featured bare breasts because sailors believed that the best way to keep storms and misfortunes at bay was to have a woman sacrifice her dignity to the gods. Flash a little boob, get smooth sailing. It's not so much romantic as *Clash of the Titans* meets *Girls Gone Wild*."

And if they weren't staring before, they certainly were now. "I'm the only person in the room who knew that, aren't I?"

Jolene wrapped an arm around me. "I love it when you pretend to be normal."

"Even when I was human, I wasn't normal," I admitted. I lowered my voice as the pack returned to their handiwork. "So, what's Mama Ginger been up to lately?"

"Nothin'," she muttered. "That has me worried. It's been too quiet. Zeb said she's been distracted by hatin' your boyfriend, which is kind of nice. I know it can't last long, but I'm enjoying it while it lasts."

"I think that's about as healthy as you can expect to be," I assured her.

Mollified for a moment, Jolene measured out several lengths of ribbon, rolled it back on the spool, measured it again, rolled it back. Grunting, she yanked the entire length of ribbon off the spool in a heap of blue sateen. When she picked up the scissors, I gently took the ribbon out of her hand. "Jolene, I may be going out on a limb here, but is something else bothering you?"

"Have you noticed anything odd about Zeb?" she asked. "I know this wedding stuff has him all stressed out, but he's just been so distant, like he doesn't even want to talk to me. And he's been kind of mean. Some of the things he's been saying are just hurtful."

When I gave her an intentionally blank look, she said, "Like that joke about me not being very smart. And I don't think he realizes how much he talks about you. We'll be out to eat, and he'll talk about what sort of food you used to like. We'll watch a movie, and he'll say, 'I've already seen this with Jane.' It's just hard, you know? It's like you're an ex-girlfriend, but you never really broke up with him."

"I never really dated him, either," I told her.

"I know that," she said, nudging me with her arm. "It's just hard to live up to you, Jane."

"No, it's not. You've already got me beat hands down on looks."

"I know," she said, grinning.

"Agree with me a little slower, please," I said, smacking her arm. "And you can go out during the day, have kids, eat, tan, grow old with him. And Zeb loves you. He's just going through a weird phase. Just watch him at the wedding. He'll be the happiest groom ever."

Jolene didn't look quite convinced but mumbled, "OK."

The conversations became even more awkward as my night wore on.

"This is just beyond the pale," Gabriel grumbled as I opened my door for him.

I'd been halfheartedly Googling Wilbur's name, hoping I could find some relatives I could warn about Grandma Ruthie's marital record before it was too late. Unused to Google failure, I was thrilled to have a distraction, even if that distraction was my agitated sire waving what looked like a ransom note at me.

"I found this in my mailbox tonight," he said, holding a slip of bright yellow paper with letters cut out of magazines and newspapers—the standard font for crazies.

" 'Your bustin' up a happy home. Brake it off with Jane or else,' " I read aloud as he stormed inside. "Mama Ginger's spelling is atrocious."

"If you're to write harassing letters in upsetting type, you should at least have the courtesy to proofread," he muttered, stretching across my couch.

"Some people," I said, rolling my eyes.

"She did, however, ruin her anonymity by enclosing this," he said, handing me a check for $352.67 from the account of Ginger and Floyd Lavelle. "I think she's trying to pay me to stay away from you."

"What gave it away?" I asked, holding up the check with a finger on the memo section, where Mama Ginger had scribbled, "To stay away from Jane."

"Well, that is a lot of money," I said. "It was good while it lasted."

Gabriel barked out a laugh. "I'm glad to see you," he said before leaning across the cushions and kissing me.

I gave him a bemused smile and blithely ignored the fact that it had been almost a week since he'd called or visited. Or that I'd been going crazy wondering where he was and what he was doing, but I didn't want to be "that girlfriend" and call his cell phone constantly. Instead, I said, "I'm always right here."

Gabriel opened his mouth to respond but was interrupted by a knock at the door.

"Maybe we shouldn't answer it," I said. "It could be Mama Ginger. She might try to throw remaindered sausage products into the deal."

"I'm not going to hide from a middle-aged woman who cannot spell," Gabriel insisted darkly, advancing on the front door. I held him back with a hand against his chest.

"Well, let me answer the door, at least. She's much less likely to douse me in battery acid."

It was not a pleasant surprise to find Ophelia Lambert, the scary forever-adolescent head of the local panel for the World Council for Equal Treatment of the Undead, at my front door wearing a man's shirt and tie with a skirt that might have been originally marketed as a headband.

Ophelia oversaw my failed prosecution for several random killings and fires the previous year and ultimately decided that I was justified in dusting Missy the Realtor with one of her own yard signs. Despite her being reasonably civil to me and electing not to set me on fire, I still found 300 years' worth of predatory grace wrapped up in a fifteen-year-old's body to be extremely offputting. On her part, I think she found my convulsive antics charming, but she was afraid to admit it.

"I didn't do it," I blurted out after opening the door.

"Do what?" she asked, her brow arched.

"Whatever," I said. "Whatever big suspicious badness brought you to my door."

She smirked, her carefully painted coral lips quirking

into a bow. "Some people believe that the best way to avoid suspicion is not to declare their innocence before they're accused of anything."

"Well, I played it your way last time, and we see where that got me," I said, waving her inside.

"As I understand it, it got you a very nice triumph settlement," she said, slinking into the living room and perching on the nearest settee. She nodded in cool greeting to my sire.

"So I keep hearing," I muttered. "I'll believe it when I see a black balance on my bank statement."

Ophelia grinned, her fangs glinting from the low-burning firelight, and offered me a slip of paper. It was my bank statement, and the balance was black. Very, very black. Apparently, Missy's holdings had been transferred into my checking account. And her holdings were a little more extensive than I'd estimated. But it made sense, considering how many vampires she duped, cheated, and murdered to get their property. Plus, she did charge a healthy commission on her sales.

I'd been raised to think of discussing money as vulgar and rude. So I'll just say that I would not have to worry about money. Ever. I could live the rest of my unnaturally long life, sitting on a sofa stuffed with twenty-dollar bills, sipping dessert blood, and avoiding any form of effort, and I would still have a little left over to make sure my alma mater named a parking lot after me.

"I guess the council decided that I've learned my lesson about being a good little vampire and staying out of trouble?" I said.

"Something like that," Ophelia said, smirking again.

"The council couldn't legally hold on to the money any longer without charging me with something?" I suggested.

"Something exactly like that." Ophelia grinned, delighted by my grasp of the situation. "What do you plan to do with the money?"

"I'm still in the 'Yay, I won't lose my house' phase of processing this information," I told her. "Give me some time."

"That's very normal," she said, shifting uncomfortably in her seat. Given the brevity of her skirt, it wasn't exactly comfortable for any of us. Out of deference to me and continued indifference to Ophelia, Gabriel made a comprehensive study of the window treatments.

"We will be getting back to a long discussion of how exactly you came by my account information, by the way," I said, avoiding eye contact with her lack of skirt. "Can I ask why you brought me this news in person? This sounds like the sort of thing that should be delivered by registered mail. I thought you were supposed to be a disinterested third party."

"You interest me," she said nonchalantly. "You're very entertaining."

"Like a dancing monkey," I muttered.

Ophelia smiled nastily, her bone-white fangs fully extended as she threw her head back and laughed. When she was done, she wiped at her eyes and smirked at Gabriel. "Actually, I needed to see Gabriel as well. As much as I'd love to let you and your charming paramour return to . . . whatever it was that you were doing, there is something I need to discuss with you."

Silence.

I looked from the ancient teenager to my sire. Gabriel stared at Ophelia, who returned his silver gaze, unmoved and unimpressed. Clearly, whatever it was, Ophelia was not going to talk about it in front of me. And neither of them seemed willing to ask me to leave. Apparently, that would be rude. Pretending I didn't exist, however, was totally OK.

"I'll just go check on . . . something," I said, scurrying into the kitchen with as much dignity as possible.

"All the way outside, Jane," Ophelia called after me.

Well, there goes that.

I would like to say that I stood on the porch and enjoyed the pleasant evening air, contemplated the fullness of the moon and my place in the universe, giving not one thought to what was being said in my own house and how it might affect me. But I crept around to the front door and used my vampire hearing to eavesdrop.

I'm a deeply flawed person.

It should come as no surprise that I am not good with stealth. Ophelia and Gabriel obviously knew I was doing it because they spoke in hushed tones that I strained to hear. All I could make out were furious whispers and Ophelia saying the words "unhinged," "nightmare," and "Jeanine."

There was that name again. Who the hell was Jeanine? I stepped closer to the door, catching the wrong porch board and sending an ear-splitting creak directly into their ears. They were now more than aware that I was

standing outside listening. Ophelia snickered and said in
a louder voice, "This is your problem to deal with, Gabriel. But if you cannot handle the situation, the council
would be happy to step in."

I could hear Gabriel's insistent, almost desperate whis-
per in return, but I could not understand his response.
I think he was speaking Chinese. I could only speak bad
high-school Spanish. Ophelia, clearly exasperated at
his pretense, responded with a rather impressive tirade
that I could not understand. But then again, everything
sounds sort of angry in Mandarin.

Realizing that further listening was pointless, I spent
the next few minutes tossing a beloved but much-abused
tennis ball to Fitz. He was in hyper-doggie heaven, running at me and making playful nips at my jeans. I heard
the front door open and watched with dread as the ec-
static "New person!" expression flashed in Fitz's eyes. I
could hear myself yelling "Nooooo!" in slow motion as
Fitz ran at Ophelia. My brain had just enough time to
calculate exactly how much time I would be spending
in the council clink if Fitz ruined one of Ophelia's inde-
cently expensive outfits or, worse yet, if Ophelia would
leave Fitz with all of his appendages intact.

Instead of the canine carnage I foresaw, I was shocked as
Ophelia smiled warmly at my loping mutt. She held up one
finger and said something soft in German. Fitz skidded to
a halt directly in front of her and plopped obediently on
his butt. She smiled again and gave another command. Fitz
held up his paw, and she deigned to shake it, scratching
him behind the ears with an expression of . . . well, it was

the first genuine expression I'd ever seen on Ophelia's face, so I can only describe it as "young." For a moment, the centuries fell away, and she was just a beautiful girl standing on my lawn, petting my dog.

I'm pretty sure my jaw was resting on my chest, because when Ophelia looked up at me, all traces of the young human faded like smoke. Her face hardened into more familiar lines. She narrowed her eyes at me. I raised my hands in defense.

"I didn't see a thing," I promised her.

She arched her eyebrow, gave Fitz one last pat on the head, but said nothing. Gabriel came out the front door, leaning against the porch post as Ophelia made her way toward her sporty red Corvette. I'm sure the act of driving that down Main Street made her an object of obsession and envy, but frankly, I found it rather obvious in terms of jail-bait appeal.

Ophelia opened the door, tilted her head, and considered me for a moment, her piercing blue eyes glowing at me through the shadows. "I am very glad that Missy's money has landed in your hands. I think you're going to do far more fascinating things with it than some tawdry housing development."

"So, now isn't the time to tell you about the Dracula theme park I have planned for the back fifty acres?" I asked brightly. Gabriel snickered but covered it by a hearty clearing of the throat.

"For both of our sakes, I'm going to assume that was a joke," she muttered, climbing into her car and giving us one last flash of thighs.

Ophelia departed, leaving my head spinning with the possibilities of Missy's money. I would never have to worry about paying the property taxes. I would be able to keep the house up for centuries to come. The Early family legacy, such as it was, was secure.

I could travel. I could finally see all of the places I'd dreamed of seeing all my life. Edinburgh. Tahiti. Beijing. Granted, I would see them at night, but still, I could go. I would just have to talk to Gabriel about safety precautions and passport issues for the undead.

I could adopt one of those orphans on TV who make you feel so guilty. Hell, I could adopt a whole family. I would donate a catalogue full of children's and young adult books to the library. I could secure funding for Half-Moon Hollow High School's computer lab. (The students were still using Commodores.)

I would have to do all of this anonymously. You wouldn't believe how quickly relatives come out of the woodwork when money comes into play. Lottery wins bring out kin you never knew existed, and they all have inventions to invest in, trailer payments to be made. My cousin Glory (who was, sadly, male) won a $10,000 scratch-off once, and within twelve hours, our great-uncle Stuart had moved his camper onto Glory's driveway.

Of course, if my family found out I had money, I'm pretty sure I would die in a mysterious window-treatment accident, and Jenny would immediately claim it as my next of kin. And given my last couple of months, death by Venetian blinds was becoming more likely.

Note to self: Write a will. Leave everything to Zeb.

I squealed and hopped into Gabriel's arms, wrapping my legs around his waist. Fortunately, he did not drop me. "You are now dating a very well-off woman. And I know it would be against your gentlemanly principles to ask just how well off. And it's even further against my own good character to tell you. But let me put it this way, if you ever run into financial trouble, you don't have to worry."

"That's sweet but unnecessary," he said, pulling me against him.

"Maybe I'll let you be my cabana boy." I sighed.

"I will not dignify that with a response."

He chuckled but held me to his chest with a sort of quiet desperation, pulling me so close that breathing would have been an issue if I needed oxygen. Obviously, his conversation with Ophelia had upset him more than he was letting on. Was this Jeanine an old girlfriend? A current girlfriend? What sort of "situation" would require the council to step in and interfere?

As Gabriel clung to me, I stroked his hair, knowing that no matter what I said or asked, it wouldn't make either of us feel better. So I let him hold me and pretended that everything was fine. It was the loneliest I'd ever felt in his presence.

Over the past 100 years, female weres have embraced certain human mating rituals. Werewolf males who neglect to present their mates with meat or floral offerings on a birthday or anniversary can expect to sleep in an actual doghouse.

—*Mating Rituals and Love Customs of the Were*

I was a little nervous about what vampires get each other for Valentine's Day, because, as far as I knew, it could involve actual hearts.

So, when I found a white box on my doorstep, tied with a huge red bow, I went into full-on spastic girlie-girlie mode. There was squealing. A lot of squealing. For just a minute, the inside of my head was like a living Lisa Frank poster.

The contents were . . . unexpected. For one thing, I didn't know whether Gabriel was actually going to be in town on Valentine's Day. And second, I'm usually a white cotton panties kind of girl, occasionally a black cotton panties kind of girl. But if Gabriel was game for the red satin bustier thing, I could give it a try.

Yes, giving your girlfriend naughty lingerie for Valentine's Day is tired and cliché, and I'd spent years railing against the commercialism and crassness of a holiday designed by corporate America to compel men to buy their way into a lady's affections and make single women feel pathetic and alone. Of course, at the time, I was pathetic and alone, so pardon me for taking the opportunity to feel smug for a day.

Gabriel's gift was a modern twist on the classic Victorian corset, buttery soft satin in a perfect Valentine's red, stretched over whalebone. It was some sort of miracle underwear, cinching my waist into a tiny point and giving me anatomically improbable cleavage, all without cracking my ribs. The hem of the bustier just barely skirted a pair of satin briefs, which were connected to a pair of lacy black stockings with the thinnest of red silk ties. I struck a languorous pose in the mirror and—despite looking pretty damned hot, if I do say so myself—felt a little ridiculous. I looked like a cover model for the romance paperbacks my mother read. All I needed was a title like *The Tempestuous Schoolmarm* spelled out over my head in an overcurlicued font.

Still, I slinked around the house and lit the vanilla candles. I wanted to build some ambience for Gabriel to appreciate before I jumped him. My home was considerably more welcoming than it had been the last time he visited. I hadn't had disposable income in a while, so after months of scrimping and saving and buying generic market-brand blood, I went into a sort of online shopping fit. I bought blackout curtains for every window in the house, a new comfy couch, a bigger fridge. I even booked a prefab contractor to come out and attach the garage to the house with a covered walkway. It was like babyproofing for someone with fangs.

I was feeling adored and very in touch with my inner sex kitten when he showed up at my door later that night.

"Someone earned himself a very nice Valentine's Day 'dinner,'" I purred, leaning against the door frame. "In case you didn't notice, 'dinner' was in special naughty secret-meaning quotation marks."

Gabriel stared at me, his expression blank. I liked to think it was the barely there black dress I was wearing over the lingerie hindering his neurological processes, but . . . no.

"The lingerie . . . the red satin thing with little garters . . ." I watched his face go from blank to thunderous. "Judging from that expression, you have no idea what I'm talking about, do you?" My stomach seemed to ripple as I squirmed in the suddenly icky red undergarments. "Oh, not good."

I started toward the stairs, then turned on him, hands on hips. "Wait, what did you send me for Valentine's Day?"

His face was set in grimmer lines but for a totally different reason.

"Valentine's Day, commemorating the martyrdom of Saint Valentine, patron saint of beekeeping, epileptics, and greeting-card manufacturers?" I said. There was a beat of silence where I was smacked in the head with a clue-by-four. "You didn't get me anything for Valentine's Day, did you?"

Gabriel cleared his throat. "Valentine's Day was not something we recognized in my day."

I poked him in the chest. "First of all, yes, it was. Lacy cards and love tokens were widely exchanged even in Victorian times. By now, you should know better than to screw with me on historical trivia. Also, you've had one-hundred-forty-something years to adjust. Get with the program. You didn't notice the giant hearts and paper cupids hanging off every stationary object?"

"I've never dated a modern woman before."

I poked him again. "You can only use that as an excuse so many times. And don't offer to give me 'awesome sex' as a present, because I think we've established that given the right circumstances, I can hurt you."

"I wasn't going to—" I narrowed my eyes at him. Instead of finishing that ill-fated protest, he said, "Let's focus on the creepy anonymous gifts."

"You don't say 'creepy.' Don't try to get in good with me by talking like me. I just don't understand how some-one could select a pitch-perfect girlfriend Christmas gift and then completely ignore Valentine's Day."

"Well, what did you get me?"

"You will never, ever know," I promised him. And he wouldn't. Because now that I'd made such a big deal about it, boxer shorts with little glow-in-the-dark vam-pire lips and fangs all over them didn't seem that great.

"Let me see the gifts you did get," he said. "You were going to show me."

I crossed my arms over my chest. "Not now I'm not."

"Jane."

"Fine." I slid the straps off my shoulders and let the dress pool at my feet. Gabriel's eyes went wide as he scanned me from head to toe. "Gabriel?"

"Give me a moment. All of the blood just drained out of my head."

"I find this whole thing to be incredibly gross now that I know I'm wearing some stranger's undies." I shuddered and shrugged out of the suddenly disturbing get-up.

And now I was naked and embarrassed, which was a sensation I was much more familiar with. The phone rang.

"Saved by the bell," he muttered.

"If we had time, I'd tell you about that figure of speech's origins in connection to gravedigging, but I'm not going to," I said, picking up the phone. "No gift means no trivia."

"And yet somehow I think I'll survive," Gabriel groused.

I gave him a meaningful look as I barked a greeting into the phone. A sly female voice asked, "Did you like the presents?"

"Who is this?"

"It's Andrea." The voice on the other end of the line sounded hurt.

"Hi. I don't—I can't talk right now," I whispered. Gabriel's eyes narrowed at the stress in my voice, and language that, after I thought about it, sounded awfully suspicious. "I'll call you later."

"What's wrong?" she asked.

I turned away from Gabriel and tried to lower my voice even further, but let's face it, my boyfriend had superhearing.

"I can't really explain. Let's just say the words 'Happy Valentine's Day' are probably going to make my eye spontaneously twitch for years to come," I grumbled as Gabriel stared at me, his expression annoyed and somehow helpless.

"What happened?" Andrea cried.

"I don't want to talk now," I told her through gritted fangs as Gabriel took a subtle but deliberate step toward me, his ear cocked toward the phone. I shot him a venomous look and started into the next room.

"But I left that package on your front porch to help things along. Seriously, that outfit was flawless, practically a foolproof recipe for the perfect first Valentine's Day as a couple. How could you screw this up?" Andrea cried, using that tone my mama used when I'd butchered a recipe.

"That was you?" I demanded, keeping my voice low. "What—why? Wh—you and I are going to have to have a serious discussion about boundaries. What the hell were you thinking?"

Her voice lowered to a slightly more contrite level. "Well, I've known Gabriel for a while, and he's just not the type of guy who puts a lot of stock in relationship milestones like a first Valentine's Day. I knew you would freak out and read a lot into it if it looked as if he forgot. And I knew he wouldn't ask for help or accept advice on what to get you, so I thought I'd help you out. I thought he'd be so thunderstruck at the sight of you in simply stunning underwear that you wouldn't have time to talk about where it came from."

If she wasn't so depressingly right, it would really piss me off that Andrea had managed to figure out my relationship before I did. No, wait, I was pissed anyway.

"We have got to get you dating again, because you clearly have too much time on your hands," I told her. "This is not normal behavior."

"It's very normal behavior to want your friend to have a nice Valentine's Day. What's not normal is you somehow turning this into some Jane disaster. Hell, even your grandma Ruthie knows to buy lingerie on Valentine's Day. I saw her at Victoria's Secret the other night. She said she was getting something special for her fiancé. I thought her fiancé died."

"Oh, my God, why are you making this worse?" I cried. I didn't know whom I felt more sorry for at that point, myself or poor, unsuspecting Wilbur. "I do not need that image in my head. And as much as I appreciate your intentions, don't ever do this again. It's weird. Wait, wait, if you thought we would be all naked and blissful by now, why are you calling?" I asked, ignoring the way Gabriel's eyebrows shot up at that comment.

"Well, even vampires have a recovery period."

I scrunched my nose. "Ew. That's a conversation ender. I'll call you later." I hung up the phone and turned on Gabriel. "I'm going to take a shower. Maybe you shouldn't be here when I get out."

Leaving a trail of discarded lingerie in my wake, I stomped toward the bathroom. I turned the water to the white-hot range, slid into the shower, and fought back tears. Oh, how was I mortified? Let me count the ways. One, I put on strange underwear collected from my doorstep without knowing whom it was from or what they could have done to it. Two, my boyfriend blew off Valentine's Day. Three, my girlfriend was so sure this might happen (and rightly so) that she provided me with a pity present to get me laid. Four, I had images of a teddy-clad Grandma Ruthie doing some sort of fan dance in my head. And five, my boyfriend blew off Valentine's Day.

I thought that bore repeating.

I soaped my hair, deliberately avoiding the almond-scented antifrizz shampoo Gabriel liked in favor of plain old Pantene. I heard the bathroom door open. Gabriel came in and sat on the bathroom counter.

"Jane, we've talked about this," he said softly. "I'm your sire and your lover. My bond to you is very strong. I won't share you with another man, even if he does have impeccable taste in lingerie."

That was sort of a confession of love, right?

I snapped the shower curtain open, glaring at him through the soap bubbles slipping down my face. "Why is it that your first assumption is that it's another man? What about me makes you think I would cheat on you?" Then I snapped the curtain closed.

Somehow, his voice lowered even further, his tone worn thin. "I don't know if I can make you happy, Jane.

That makes me sick inside. I see the regrets you have. I see the longing in your eyes when you talk about your life before, the things you miss. I don't know if I'm good for you. There are times when I wonder if you're really happy as a vampire, whether you wish I'd never met you that night. If some part of you would be happier as a human."

This time, I slung the curtain so hard the rings popped off the curtain rod. "Well, of course, some part of me would be happier as a human, you *dumbass*!" I yelled. "For one thing, I wouldn't spontaneously combust when I wanted to, say, take a walk before sunset. I wouldn't have to put up with my mother's undead denial issues. I wouldn't have to worry about people shrinking away every time I walk into a room. And I'd be able to eat. I haven't eaten in months, do you realize that? No carbs, no fats, no chocolate. Nothing! I mean, do you know what it's like for someone like me, not being able to get chocolate?"

Gabriel was obviously unprepared for the level of anger (or volume) in this wet, naked outburst. Looking slightly dazed, he closed what was left of the curtain. He was barely audible over the sound of the shower spray. "I'm sorry. I didn't realize you were so miserable."

"I'm not. I'm not miserable. But I'm not completely happy as a vampire. And it's not fair for you to expect me to be. If you want a real, honest relationship, I can't put on a happy fanged face for you. Were you thrilled with your new life after you were turned?"

"No, but my family did tie me naked to a tree to wait

for the sunrise," he pointed out calmly. "We're straying from the point."

I stuck my head under the rapidly cooling spray. "Which is?"

"That another man is sending you underwear."

I could let him keep wondering, I mused, rolling my eyes. I could let Gabriel think I had a secret admirer, make him jealous. After weeks of wondering where he was, what he was doing, whom he was with, he deserved it. But I'd never been that girl, the game player, the girlfriend who played by asinine "rules" laid out in the self-help book of the week. And even though it would probably make me feel better, I don't think Gabriel pushing a tree on top of some poor guy he suspected of being my suitor would help our relationship.

"It wasn't another man," I huffed. "It was Andrea."

There was a heavy silence on the other side of the curtain. "Er . . . that wasn't something I was prepared for. I thought maybe it was Zeb."

"Ew!" I cried.

"Well, he's been acting so strange lately," Gabriel protested. "And I don't see how Andrea giving you sexy underthings is any less disturbing. I don't think anyone should be buying you sexy underthings but me."

"Well, you didn't." I cut the water off and snapped the curtain open. I pushed past him and snatched a towel. He grabbed my hand and pulled me to eye level with him. "Andrea felt the need to step in for you. Instead of assuming the worst, you could just talk to me, Gabriel," I said as he followed me into my bedroom. I yanked open a dresser drawer and pulled out my flannel cow pajamas.

"Not the cow pajamas, Jane, please, there's no reason to let this ruin our evening," he groaned. "I'm sorry."

"Beg pardon?" I asked, cupping my hand around my ear. "What was that?"

"You heard me," he grumbled. "With our hearing, it's impossible for you not to have heard me."

"No, I don't believe I did," I said. "Because I'm sure the Master of Poise could not possibly have just apologized to little old me."

"Smugness is not attractive on you, Jane."

"Smugness is one of my best features," I retorted, backing him against the footboard of my bed. "I'm really, really good at it."

"I've noticed," he muttered, nuzzling his nose along my jawline. Laughing, he slipped his hand through my hair and kissed my temple.

I shrugged him off. "Hey, I'm still mad at you, Valentine's Day skipper. You are going to be punished. And not in the fun way."

"I acquiesce to your demands," he said solemnly. He nodded at my bovine sleepwear. "Now, I think you should take this off."

I snorted. "Not going to happen, my friend."

And it didn't. Instead of hot Valentine's Day sex, I made Gabriel paint my toes lavender (he has incredibly steady hands) while we watched the most dreaded of all chick flicks, *Sleepless in Seattle*. I would say he learned his lesson, but I caught him wiping at his eyes toward the end.

"Are you crying?" I asked.

"No!" he exclaimed. I snickered and patted his shoulder. "It's just, it was so unlikely, the two of them showing up at the Empire State Building at the same time after missing each other so often. And—"

"Do you want to sleep over?" I asked suddenly.

"Will I have to sleep on the couch?"

"No, you can sleep in the guest room," I said sweetly as I secured the blackout curtains.

"I'd rather make a run for my house," he muttered.

I pulled back the comforter for him. "Fine."

He grinned and stripped down to his slacks. As a habit, Gabriel didn't wear underwear. I guess he wasn't feeling secure enough in my good humor to sleep in the nude. He fluffed the pillows on both sides of the bed and flopped down in giddy anticipation.

"What's with you?"

"I'm just excited," he said, grinning.

I rolled my eyes as I reached for the bedside lamp. "Just for the record, this is my first coed sleepover since Zeb and I were in fifth grade. And even then, Mama made Zeb sleep on a different floor of the house. I am the spoonee, by the way. You are the spooner."

"I don't spoon," Gabriel said.

"Well, you do now," I told him, wrapping his arms around my waist. "You don't snore, do you?"

"I don't breathe."

"Good point."

It was nice to know that our bodies still fit together perfectly outside the sexual arena. Gabriel rested his head on my shoulder, drawing my back against his chest and his knees under my knees. We lay in silence, and I burst out laughing.

"What?" Gabriel asked. "Am I not doing the spooning right?"

"No, it's great." I giggled. "But sunrise is not for another four hours. We're basically going to bed at the equivalent of two P.M. We've officially become the least interesting people we know. And considering that we drink blood and burst into flame when we tan, that's sort of sad."

"You're saying the magic's gone," Gabriel said.

"Yep."

"Well, it was nice while it lasted." Gabriel released me and started climbing out of bed. "I'll be going now."

"OK, well, keep in touch." I clasped his hand. "It was nice knowing you."

"Thanks. You, too."

I yanked his hand, forcing him back into the bed and rolling over me. He kissed me to show me exactly how boring we were.

"I'm sorry I ruined your Valentine's Day," he murmured against my neck, his voice soft on my skin. "I didn't know it was so important to you."

"Well, you do now. You've been put on notice."

"I'm glad we're sleeping together," he said.

"Of course you are," I snorted. "You have a Y chromosome."

"I mean sleeping, as in resting," he said, pulling me flush against him. "It's very intimate."

"I never should have let you watch *Sleepless in Seattle*," I moaned. "I've ruined you."

Gabriel did not snore. Nor did he squirm around or steal covers, which made him a far more considerate bedmate than Fitz. At dusk, I could feel the sun fading as I rolled against the contours of his side. It was sweet to wake up next to him, to see his face relaxed and his mouth hanging open. Everything was still, quiet.

I slipped my hand around his back and snuggled my face into his neck. It was oddly cool. I inhaled deeply, trying to memorize the scent of sleep on his skin, soft and clean and sweet.

I closed my eyes and swallowed against the rising sensation in my chest, a mixture of happiness that I'd finally arrived at this place in my life and fear that it would be over soon. I was even less experienced at long-term relationships than I was at decent sex. And what did I really know about either? Pledging your eternal love took on a whole new meaning when you actually lived forever.

What if Gabriel got bored with me? What if he woke up in both senses of the word and realized that I was really the same boring librarian under the fancy new fangs? What if Jeanine was the last vampire girl he'd cast off? Or worse yet, the vampire girl he was planning to be with once he'd cast me off?

These were heavy thoughts to have at vampire dawn. The noise of the gears turning in my head must have jarred Gabriel awake, because he stirred next to me, pulling on the front of my cow pajamas until I was flush against his chest.

"Morning," he rumbled.

"Morning," I whispered into his neck. "You sleep with your mouth open."

"I learn something new from you every day," he murmured, kissing my temple and stroking my back. He pulled me under him. I felt boneless, liquid, more relaxed than I'd been in weeks. I belonged here. I was wanted. I didn't even worry about morning breath when Gabriel pressed his lips to mine, because, technically, neither of us had breath at any time of day.

The remnants of my unhappy thoughts still haunting me, I took the time to run my fingertips along his long, sinewy limbs, his smooth, pale skin. I cupped my palms around his cheeks, lazily tracing the line of his bottom lip with my thumb. I was almost beyond caring when Gabriel peeled my pajama top over my head.

"I hate these pajamas," he muttered, tossing them over the edge of the bed. "The pajamas must go."

"The pajamas stay," I told him. He arched his eyebrows, making me giggle. "Well, not at the moment, obviously."

He snickered, pushing the bottoms down to my ankles with his feet. He tucked his fingers between my hips and the waistband of my panties and tugged. The cotton buckled and tore, landing in a frayed heap next to my pajamas.

"What do you have against my panties?" I moaned, mourning the loss of yet another pair.

He smirked, casting a glance to where he was brushing against my wet, willing flesh. "Well, I think that should have been fairly obvious."

I was still laughing when he slipped inside me. I stretched my arms above my head, gripping the head-board as he trailed kisses down my chest, increasing his pace. The deeper he drove, the tighter I held on, until I ripped the wood spokes out of the frame. I gasped, horrified at what I'd done to a family heirloom. And then I just gasped, lost in the waves of sensation that threatened to drag me under.

When I came to, I still had the hunks of wood clutched in my hands. Gabriel looked vaguely guilty.

"We made it to a bed," he offered meekly.

"And then we destroyed it," I moaned. "But it was worth it."

He pulled me onto his chest, pushing my hair out of my face before pulling me close.

"It's kind of weird to see Mr. Big Bad Vampire being all cuddly." I chuckled. "It kind of destroys your mystique."

"I haven't had a lot of good, soft things in my life," he said against my forehead. "Not since my family sent me away. Apart from being your sire and feeling that pull to you, it's that goodness, that softness and warmth, along with the resolve and strength in you, that I love. Being turned hasn't taken that from you. If someone were going to design the perfect mate for me, it would be you. Even when you infuriate me with your pigheaded stubbornness and your temper and incredible lack of anything resembling self-preservation—"

"Stop describing me, please."

"You're the most fascinating, maddening, adorable creature I've ever met," he said, sighing and pushing my hair out of my eyes. "So, when I seem possessive or I'm raving like a lunatic, it's just that part of me is still very afraid that I'll lose that—that I'll lose you. I love you."

"That's such a normal boyfriend thing to say. I'm so proud and yet a little freaked out."

"Stop joking and listen to me," he said. "I'm being serious."

"So am I," I objected. "That was a very normal thing for a boyfriend to say."

He grinned down at me. "Does that mean I'm your boyfriend?"

"Oh, my Lord, this is such a juvenile conversation to have with a hundred-and-fifty-year-old man," I groaned. "Yes, Gabriel, I would like you to be my boyfriend. I think we should go steady. I don't want to be with any other vampire but you. I love you. Idiot."

"We need new nicknames for each other," he said. When I shoved at his shoulders, he grinned. "I haven't loved anyone in a long time. And I'm glad it's you. I'm glad I met you on the worst day of your life."

"Well, you certainly made it more memorable."

12

Bachelorette parties are less about celebrating the bride's acquisition of a husband and more about making the female relatives feel vindication after the wedding planning process.

—*Mating Rituals and Love Customs of the Were*

When we were kids, Zeb and I used to spend post-sleepover mornings eating Cap'n Crunch and watching the Smurfs. Somehow, I didn't think Gabriel would appreciate the same routine.

I padded into the kitchen, still clad in flannel cows, and warmed up a healthy breakfast of donated Type A. Gabriel let Fitz out to snag the evening edition of the *Half-Moon Herald* from the end of the driveway. Unfortunately, Gabriel overestimated Fitz's capabilities and had to get the paper himself. We climbed onto the porch swing to sip blood and read the happenings in the *Herald* while Fitz gamboled around the yard chasing his own tail.

It was strangely domestic, with the exception of finding another package on my doorstep. We were both relieved that it was just the genealogical information Daddy had found on Mr. Wainwright's family. Despite my library background, my strength tends toward data-base research, whereas Daddy excels with the dusty-old-book route. After Mr. Wainwright lamented his lack of family history, I'd asked Daddy to use his mojo.

Gabriel left for some council meeting, and I ripped into the research without bothering to change out of my pajamas. Daddy had done an impressive job. He found copies of Mr. Wainwright's old school pictures from Half-Moon Hollow Public School archives and an old newspaper clipping announcing Gilbert Wain-wright's engagement to Brigid Brannagan, a girl he met while traveling in County Cork. Daddy found Mr. Wainwright's parents' marriage certificate and both of their obituaries. Searching through old records kept in the courthouse basement—records Daddy accessed through a school chum named Deeter who worked there as a night janitor—Daddy found the origins of the Wainwright family. Gilbert Wainwright's father, Gordon Wainwright, was the son of Albert Wainwright, son of Eugenia Wainwright, a laundry woman who had worked on the Cheney family farm. She had Albert in 1879 but drowned a short time later during the town's inaugural Fourth of July picnic down at the riverfront.

Eugenia was unmarried, and there was no father listed on the birth certificate for young Albert. Albert was sent to an orphanage and raised there until he ran away at age ten. According to a book Daddy found in the library's special collections, called *The Hollow Frontier*,

Albert worked at the railway station and eventually took a job on a barge traveling the Ohio River, before returning home to the Hollow in the 1920s. He was known for opening one of the first successful saloons in the Hollow, the one my great-grandmother burned. While water-stained and crumbling, the book contained a copy of a tintype of Albert.

"Oh, man," I breathed, startled by Albert's face. I flipped to Daddy's research on Eugenia, whom one of the groundskeepers at the Cheney farm described as a "big buxom piece of woman."

I flipped back to the picture of Albert, who bore a striking resemblance to Dick. The same light, laughing eyes, the same devilish smile, the same long, patrician nose. But Albert looked to be at least fifteen years older than Dick had been when he was turned. I checked the date on the photo and did some quick math in my head, then groaned. "Dang it."

I sat at Specialty Books' counter, drumming my fingers compulsively against the glass. Mr. Wainwright was puttering in the back, tossing his way through the reference section I'd just spent the better part of two days cataloguing. Knowing that my nephew Andrew had a birthday coming up, he insisted that a tome entitled *A Pop-Up Dictionary of Demons* would be a perfect gift. I was inclined to agree with him, because it might make Jenny swallow her tongue.

In a rare show of discretion, I didn't mention my discovery to Mr. Wainwright. I wanted to surprise him somehow, and I didn't think blurting it out as soon as I opened the door would fit the occasion.

The front doorbell tinkled, and I turned to find Mr. Wainwright's long-lost great-granddaddy standing at the counter with a scowl on his face.

"Well, Jane, you crook your little finger, and I come running," Dick said, clearly in a very grumpy mood. "Seems I'm always running after women who aren't interested."

"Andrea turned you down again, huh?"

He made a sour face. The more I stared at him, the more I saw a resemblance to Albert—and, for that matter, to Mr. Wainwright. My employer had a smaller build and more delicate features but the same tilting smile, the same green, twinkling eyes. I was a little ashamed that I had missed it.

"Well, we could reminisce about the girl who didn't get away," I offered. "Dick, do you remember a woman named Eugenia? She used to work at your house?"

"Yes," he said. His lips quirked at a memory I wouldn't touch with a ten-foot pole, then locked into a completely un-Dick-like grimace.

"Did you know that she left your employ because she got pregnant out of wedlock? And that she drowned about six months after giving birth to the——" He refused to meet my gaze, looking to the left.

"You already know, don't you?" I said. "You know about the baby, about Albert. You know."

"What are you—who told you—how—" he spluttered.

"Which question do you want me to answer first?" I asked, cringing.

"Jane, you need to stay out of this," he whispered darkly. "Just forget you ever found any of this. Don't say a word to Gilbert."

"But why?" I asked. "Why not just tell him? I think he would be thrilled to know he had a family. I love him, but I'm not related to him. He loves talking to you. I saw you together at the Christmas party."

"Stop," Dick said, grabbing my shoulders and covering my mouth with his hand as he cast panicked glances at the rear of the shop. "You're meddling in something you have no part in. Whatever good deed you think you're doing here, just stop. This is none of your business."

"But—"

"Just butt out, Jane." The bell clattered to the floor as he slammed the door behind him. Mr. Wainwright, disturbing pop-up book in hand, hobbled up to the counter. "Was Dick here? I thought I heard his voice."

I shook my head. "Just some guy who insisted that we were, in fact, the adult video store next door. He was very upset by our limited selection."

Mr. Wainwright laughed, handing me the book. "Maybe we should think about getting a new sign."

Generally, it's considered a faux pas for the bride's family to host a prewedding party for her. Fortunately, on the Great Invisible Scroll of Southern Wedding Etiquette, there's a loophole stating that if most of the guests are in the bride's family, it's acceptable. And werewolf women are very into prenuptial events. Jolene's festivities alone included two showers, a pounding, a mate-fasting, and something called a bloodening. The pounding is far less violent than it sounds, a party where family and friends give the happy couple a pound of some staple—sugar, flour—and items to set up their household. A bloodening, on the other hand . . . well, we'll talk about that later.

Tonight's agenda included kidnapping the bride to get her sloppy drunk and treating her to a parade of half-naked man flesh, which was some sort of McClaine female tradition. But since Jolene's cousins hadn't quite taken the initiative in planning, Jolene had to take matters into her own hands. She suggested we break into her trailer with a provided key to "surprise" her. It just happened to be on the night Jolene had reserved a table for eight at the Meat Market, the only all-male, nearly nude revue in the tristate area. Because nothing says "celebration of connubial bliss" like men who spend a suspicious amount of time at the gym thrusting their spandex-covered man parts at desperate dollar-waving soccer moms.

And because I was the best maid, I got the "honor" of writing Raylene a check for the genitalia-shaped cake that would be gracing our table. I was also expected to foot the bar tab and serve as designated driver. I ended up driving Mimi's twelve-passenger van, which was necessary to haul the half-lit bridesmaids and gift bags containing penis-shaped note pads, refrigerator magnets, coasters, and ice-cube trays.

When the hell am I going to want penis-shaped ice cubes?

Our party was seated in the dark, humid, but surprisingly clean club, as Marcus the Matador completed his last twirl about the stage. Jolene was sporting a veil with little foam penises sewn on the hem and a T-shirt covered in Lifesavers that offered a "Suck for a Buck," both of which were provided by her cousins, along with the penile party favors. Though the cousins' attention was currently focused on the butt-cheek bacchanalia, Jolene just seemed happy they showed up.

She looked so content, sitting there in her obscene veil, oblivious to the improbably dressed fireman shaking it to "Hot Stuff." Her expression was dreamy, extremely out of place considering the setting. It was just like the night she and Zeb announced their engagement, happiness bordering on a coma—the announcement that I responded to by questioning their brain functions for getting married after such a short time. Zeb had to cart me outside before I further hurt Jolene's feelings. And when he told me she was a werewolf, I freaked out even more and accused Zeb of losing his mind.

Dang it. Dick had a point. I was a meddler.

"Do you think I'm intrusive?" I shouted over a remix of "It's Raining Men."

She started and turned her lazy gaze at me. "Hmm?"

"Am I intrusive?"

"Yes," she said, nodding. "But in a good way."

"How can you possibly be a good kind of intrusive?"

She set her drink down, barely noticing when the verdant liquid splashed onto the already sticky table. "Well, you can be bossy and suspicious and quick to judge. Sometimes your mouth writes a check your butt can't cash."

"We've discussed that you could agree with me less emphatically, yes?"

She giggled. "But you do it 'cause you need to protect the people you love. And that's not such a bad thing."

"I know that I can be sort of—" I paused and then settled for "overbearing, when it comes to Zeb, his happiness and safety and hygiene. But I would like to say that I'm really glad that he's marrying you."

She sniffed and threw her arms around me. There's nothing quite like an armful of drunk werewolf to help you find some perspective.

"I love you, Jane," Jolene slurred. "I love Zeb. I really love Zeb. He's the first man to ever see me as more than a pretty face and hot body."

"It's nice that you're so modest."

"He treats me special, not because of who my parents are or because I'm pretty but because, just because that's his way," she rambled. "He's gentle and sweet and he loves me. And I love him."

"I know."

"And you love Zeb." She giggled, the alcohol in her having clearly convinced her that this was a revelation.

"Yep."

"But not in a love-love way," she said suspiciously.

"Nope. I have a boyfriend. A boyfriend who engages in mind-blowing sex with me and then doesn't return my calls for two days, but a boyfriend all the same."

"Good. 'Cause otherwise"—she heaved a drunken sigh and then giggled—"I'd have to kick your ass."

"I'm aware."

The cousins turned around to see us hugging and collectively rolled their eyes. We straightened up and focused on the show.

"Speaking of your groom-to-be, where has he been lately?" I asked. "I haven't seen him in almost a week. Please don't take this as a gripe against him being in a grown-up relationship, but normally he comes by the house every once in a while."

Jolene rolled her eyes and sipped her drink. "Mama Ginger's been runnin' him ragged doin' chores around their place. She said she's afraid that after he's married, *I'm* goin' to run him ragged, and he's not goin' to have time to take care of 'his poor agin' parents' anymore."

"But Zeb has never done chores at his parents' place. *They* don't do chores at their place. Instead of raking their leaves, they just set fire to their whole yard every fall."

"I think he's just doin' it to keep her off my back, poor thing," Jolene said. "The more he does, the less she complains about him 'abandonin' his family.' Of course, she still complains about me, but that's different . . ."

A shadow seemed to pass over Jolene's face. Her lip trembled, and I was afraid the drinks had caught up with her. I reached for her hand, but she straightened and took a deep breath. She stretched a too-wide smile over her face and turned her attention back to the stage.

"I wonder how much he spends on body waxin'?" she mused.

I smirked. "It's probably a tax deduction. It's a necessary item. I mean, it takes a little hair and a lot of confidence to dance around in that get-up."

We tapped glasses. Jolene snorted. "Confidence and a couple of gym socks."

After pouring several drunken lady werewolves into bed, I drove the McClaine van to River Oaks, taking a shortcut through a sketchier part of town. It was two streets over from where the shop is located. As I passed the Silver Bullet, a bar known for less-than-savory vampire traffic, I saw my grandma Ruthie's new beau walking out of the place, carrying a case of canned drinks. I managed to stop the van, no small feat for someone unaccustomed to piloting a land yacht, and pulled into a dark corner of the adjacent parking lot.

Without enhanced night vision, I wouldn't have been able to make out the labels on the cans, which read, "Silver Sun Senior Health Shakes." It was the same kind of can Grandma Ruthie was toting around for Wilbur in her purse.

"Maybe it's just a coincidence that he's walking out of a vampire bar at four A.M. carrying mysterious beverages," I murmured to myself as Wilbur hefted the case into his car. He looked around to make sure that no one was looking and popped the top of one can. He drained it in a few gulps, tossed it into a nearby Dumpster, and drove off.

"Well, at least he doesn't litter," I muttered.

Unfortunately, I found that Wilbur hadn't tossed the

can into an easy-to-find spot in the Dumpster when I inevitably climbed in to retrieve it.

"I can't believe I'm doing this." I grunted, sifting through endless beer bottles and newspapers drenched in a substance I dared not consider. "This is not normal, rational behavior, sifting through three days' worth of extremely pungent bar garbage to find your future step-grandpa's recyclables. There's probably a perfectly reasonable, rational explanation for Wilbur being here. This is probably just some black-market health shake with ingredients that aren't approved by the FD—oh, dear *gah*!" I squealed as something squirmed beneath my feet. I grabbed the can, leaped out of the Dumpster, and did the freaked-out girl dance for a few beats.

There was no list of ingredients on the side of the can. I held my "prize" to my supersensitive nose and sniffed. I sensed herbs, vitamins, some supplements for joint health (OK, that part was touted on the label), and beneath the slightly chalky bouquet, there was blood. Cold, dead pig's blood.

"OK, maybe there's *not* a reasonable explanation."

I drove myself crazy over the next few days making complicated but ultimately useless "Explanations for Wilbur's Drinking Pig's Blood" line charts on legal pads.

This near-Oliver-Stone-level conspiracy theorizing kept me absorbed right up until the process server arrived on my doorstep. Jenny's lawyers were demanding that a forensic accountant look through all of my financial records to determine whether I'd sold precious Early family heirlooms to pad my personal bank accounts during the course of her lawsuit. Against my better judgment, I had told Mama about the settlement, to assure her that I was financially secure for eternity and would never, ever need to move in with her, so please stop asking. And despite my dire warnings against doing so, Mama had mentioned my windfall to Jenny. And because Jenny does not believe I'm capable of improving my own situation without screwing her over, she concluded that I was up to no good in the Hollow's vast antique black market. Basically, my sister was having me audited. Lovely.

Grumpy and frustrated beyond belief, I took advantage of my night off, turned off the phone, and, despite the siren's call of *Sense and Sensibility,* I read a few more chapters of *Mating Rituals and Love Customs of the Were.* I finally found what a bloodening was. The women of the clan get naked under the new moon and track down a deer, killing it as a pack and bringing it home for a shared meal. It was supposed to be held during the week of the wedding to assure the bride symbolically that she was still part of the clan and that she would always be welcome to share its food but also reminding her that she was responsible to continue the clan's traditions. It was a warm, though blood-soaked, sentiment. It was a special privilege for an outsider to be invited to witness a bloodening, much less run with the pack—which, as you might have guessed, as best maid, I was expected to do. I was going to need some sturdy running shoes and a really good sports bra.

I do not run naked.

My lolling about on the porch swing in the cold, making no effort to leave the house, seemed to disturb Aunt Jettie. "Is this sudden lean toward shiftlessness linked to all the time you've been spending with Dick?" Aunt Jettie said, in a tone that sounded eerily like Grandma Ruthie.

"Actually, Dick hasn't wanted to spend much time with me lately, Aunt Jettie. We had an argument and he's pretty irritated with me."

"Is that why he's coming up the drive?" She pointed to the driveway, where a battered El Camino was cutting through the dust. Dick climbed out of the car without making eye contact. He slinked up the porch steps and took a seat beside me. I closed my book and waited.

"Am I supposed to talk first?"

"Give me a minute." He cut me off with a slicing gesture.

We sat in silence, with me staring into the distance, wondering what to do with my hands. Finally, he said, "I've been scared to say anything to Gilbert because I didn't want him to be afraid of me or to turn away from me. It's one thing to read about vampires and ghosts, it's another to find out that you're related to one."

He studied the creases on his jeans. Unsure of my place in this exchange, I sat and waited.

"I knew Eugenia had the baby. My parents paid to keep her away while she was pregnant. When she had him, most of the town whispered about him being mine, but I didn't do anything about it. I knew my parents were sending her money every month, and I figured that was all she needed from me. Don't make that face at me, Jane.

I was young and mortal . . . and stupid. I was sent away to handle some contrived piece of family business, and by the time I came back, my parents had sent the baby to an orphanage over in Murphy. They wouldn't hear of bringing him to our home. The scandal, they said, the shame—even though I know for a fact my Daddy had several scandals of his own growing up around town. And then my parents died, and I lost the house to the jackass—"

"Gabriel," I corrected.

"Right," he said. "I told myself Albert was better off living at the orphanage, in a safe place, instead of bouncing around with me, living off card games, sleeping in a fine hotel one night and a ditch the next. That was just an excuse, of course. I didn't know anything about kids. I wouldn't have known what to do with him if I'd had him. I was a terrible father but a fun uncle. I'd visit Albert, give him penny candy and whatever money I could scrape together. But as soon as it came to real problems, the kid getting sick, getting into trouble at school, I was out of there."

He grimaced. "When I got turned, I realized I shouldn't be around him. It would be too confusing for him, a mysterious uncle who never aged and only visited at night. I was a piss-poor role model, anyway. And the people I did business with, they wouldn't have minded roughing up a little boy to make a point. I stopped showing up for visits, and he ran away a couple of months later."

"What did you do?" I asked.

"Part of me was almost relieved," he admitted. "I didn't have to worry. I didn't have to bother. And then he came back, full-grown and the spitting image of me, especially in some of his less legal habits. And it was . . . nice. It was nice to be able to watch him, to see him running his business, being a man. I couldn't always agree with some of his decisions, but at that point, I was supposed to be about sixty years old and still looked thirty-something. I couldn't exactly come back to give him a spanking and fatherly advice. He married, had a son. His son married, had a son. And I watched over them, all of them, watched them live their lives, enjoy their successes, make their mistakes. And most of their mistakes were a lot like mine. It's sort of the Cheney family curse."

"Good with women, bad with money?" I suggested.

He shrugged and smiled. "I never made contact," he said. "I was still hanging around with the same type of people, and the less likely they were to connect me to the family, the better. I couldn't stand it if any of them got hurt because of me. I thought I'd gotten rid of the paper trail when I set the fire in the courthouse."

"Why do you tell me these things?" I huffed. "You know I have a Girl Scout complex."

"I never made contact with them," he said, ignoring me. "Not until Gilbert."

"Why Gilbert?"

"He was the first in our family who looked like he might amount to something. He was such a good boy, and in a sincere way. He honestly cared about his mother, his little sister, his classmates at school, his country. He was one of the first boys in the Hollow to sign up for the Army after Pearl Harbor. He was the first man in our family to start college, much less finish it." Dick smiled proudly. "And his sister was a sweet girl, just a little, well, stupid. But she was the first girl born to the family in about five generations, so she was special, too.

"When their father died and his mother was having trouble making ends meet, I came forward. Just knocked on the door one night. I didn't tell her who I was exactly, just a distant cousin who was interested in making sure the family was well taken care of. I think she knew there was something not quite right about me, especially when I told her I didn't want to meet the kids or tell them I was helping them. But she was too happy to accept my money to say anything."

"I always got the impression that you were lucky to take care of yourself. How'd you support a family?" I asked.

"I have ways of making extra money when I need it," he said, slightly offended. "When Gilbert needed money for graduate school, I sold a kidney on the black market for tuition."

"We can grow those back?" I asked.

"It wasn't my kidney."

"And now we're back to the disturbing territory I'm comfortable with." I snorted. "So, you're a family man, a loving patriarch. In essence, you're a total fraud."

He looked chastened. "Don't tell anybody."

"Are you going to tell him? I think it would mean a lot to Mr. Wainwright to know he has some family left."

"What am I supposed to do? Come barreling into the store and shout, 'Hey, pal, wanna go outside and play catch with Grandpa?'"

I shrugged. "Well, you might want to work your way up to catch. He does have that bad hip. You should at least think about telling him. What have you got to lose?"

Dick tucked his canines over his bottom lip. All pretense, all of the smug self-assurance, fell away as he said, "What if he's ashamed of me?"

"You're a vampire. You're the coolest grandpa on the block. He'll be thrilled."

"I'll think about it," Dick said. Suddenly, he raised his voice and poked me in the shoulder. "Let me work through this. Don't try to nudge the situation along. Don't drop hints or make conversational segues or—"

"I got it, I got it," I told him, raising my hands in self-defense. "I wasn't even thinking about it."

Dick looked down his nose at me and arched his eyebrow.

"OK, I was thinking about it a little bit."

**Humans who prove unfaithful to their were-spouses
are rarely heard from again.**

—*Mating Rituals and Love Customs of the Were*

My future step-grandpa was an enigma wrapped in a riddle stored in a Rubik's Cube, which I always had to resort to rearranging the stickers to solve. I won't pretend my interest was rooted in concern for my grandmother, just a general weakness in my character that would not allow me to leave a question unanswered.

For the record, four cans of Starbucks Double Shot Dark Blend Blood and Espresso is just enough to yank a vampire out of bed before sunset. Zeb wisely armed himself with caffeine before entering my daytime lair and enlisted Jettie's help in shoving me into an ice-cold shower (in my pajamas) to complete the wake-up process.

Some older vamps can venture out in the day under controlled circumstances with no problem. I blister and smell like burnt popcorn, which stays with you for days. So I slathered myself in Solar Shield SPF 500 sunscreen and donned huge Jackie O sunglasses and a wide-brimmed hat before venturing out to my newly sun-safe car. OK, fine. Zeb had the motor running, and I dove through the open door, unbelievably exhilarated by my not bursting into flames.

As he turned the key in the ignition, Zeb asked, "Remind me again why we're risking you bursting into flame to drive seventy miles to visit some old folks' home?" Clearly, he didn't appreciate the Mama-caliber guilt tactics I'd used to get him to accompany me on this little excursion.

"Because when I snuck a look into Wilbur's wallet, this was the address on his ID."

Zeb was aghast. "You snuck a look at his wallet? When?"

"Christmas," I said, looking down to avoid his glare.

"Why would you do that?" he demanded.

"He left it right there in his coat pocket, come on."

"You're not allowed to hang out with Dick anymore," he told me as he turned the ignition. "So, why couldn't we do this after dark?"

"I called the front desk pretending to be a potential resident's daughter. The nurse said dinner was served at three-thirty. And I'm guessing the people we'd want to talk to will be asleep by four."

"You're a scary woman, Jane Jameson."

I shrugged, pulling my hood over my face and leaning my seat back to a snoozing position. "I do what I can."

I jolted awake when Zeb cut Big Bertha's engine outside the Sunnyside Village Retirement Community. With one eye squinched shut, I wiped the drool off my cheek and looked around. The building seemed innocuous enough. Overtly cheerful yellow siding on a cracker-box building, glowing in the orange light of the fading sun. Newly painted white shutters framing windows with the shades drawn tight.

I pulled out my sunblock for safety touch-up. I'd decided against gloves, as it was a typically mild early spring day, and full-length opera gloves would probably attract attention. The thick, white SPF 500 lotion took a while to absorb into my neck, chin, and hands. I pulled the hat over my eyes.

"How do I look?" I asked, turning to him.

"Well, if we were going to a performance of Kabuki Mugger Theater, this look would be perfect," he snorted, gesturing to my smudged jawline. "You might want to blend some more."

"Dang it," I grumbled, swiping at my cheeks.

After a few more minutes of sunblocking, I carefully opened the door and stepped out. I gasped, enveloped in the sun for the first time since my turning. Even though it was weak late-afternoon light, I was overwhelmed by the warmth that swirled over my skin like a caress. The colors made me want to weep. I hadn't realized how monotonous the night sky could be. I'd missed the burnt golds, the blushing pinks giving way to deep purple as the sun faded over the horizon. I smiled, stretching out my hands and basking in heat like a cat. And then *ow. Ow. Owowowowowow.*

I'd forgotten to sunscreen the delicate webs between

my fingers. *Ow!* It felt as if I'd dipped my hands in acid. I stared in horror, transfixed as the skin sizzled and smoked.

"Put your hands in your pockets, Jane!" Zeb cried.

"Oh, right!" I stuck my shaking hands into my jacket and turned my back to the light, doubling over, waiting for the pain to subside. After a few moments, I felt the tissue in my fingers knit itself together again, a new and unpleasant stinging sensation unto itself. I took a deep breath and straightened, flexing my fingers gingerly. Zeb was staring at me over Big Bertha's hood.

"I don't think you want to go in there with smoking hands that smell of blackened Jiffy Pop," he said.

"I think I'll just stay in the car," I said meekly.

"Probably for the best," Zeb said, nodding and pressing his lips together in a resigned line.

I stayed huddled behind the heavily screened windows, napping, while Zeb ventured inside. I was tired, drained, all of my being focused on my raw, healing skin. When your mortality is taken out of the equation of life, you tend to take certain things, such as paralyzing agony, for granted. Is that what it would feel like to go out during the day? I imagined it was only a fraction of the pain an unprotected vampire would suffer in full sun. And even that small portion was torture. Of the few ways vampires could die, death by suntan was definitely at the bottom of the list.

A short time later, my partner in crime startled me awake with a sharp knock on the window.

"I just barely convinced them that I was the great-grandson of the oldest guy there, whose name I did not know. I had to keep calling him Pappy."

"What did he say?" I asked, rubbing my tired eyes. "Had he heard of Wilbur Goosen?"

"No, he was far more interested in a rerun of *Matlock* than talking to me. And then some other guy heard me say Wilbur's name, and he made the weirdest, wrinkliest face I'd ever seen. Then he cursed at me in Lithuanian and whacked me with his cane," Zeb said, rubbing his arm gingerly. "He then switched to English and suggested I perform various sexual acts on myself."

"If you could do that by yourself, we would never see you," I said, despite the glare Zeb sent my way. "How did you know it was Lithuanian?"

He seemed offended. "Like you're the only smart one around here."

"Sorry I put you through all of that for nothing."

"No, on the way out—while I was dodging the cane— a much nicer lady stopped me. She apparently had her hearing aids turned all the way up and heard our conversation. She was an old flame of Wilbur's."

"Say what now?"

"When Wilbur Goosen lived at Sunnyside, he was quite the Don Juan. Ila Faye Pogue, the lady in question, was one heart torn asunder in the swath he cut across the Shuffleboard Circuit. At one point, there was a catfight in the rec room among three of his interests. Wigs and walkers and glass eyes flying everywhere . . ."

"I don't need to think about that."

"Mrs. Pogue had photos in her album. The administration was on the verge of asking Wilbur to leave when he just passed away in his sleep. It was very sudden."

"He died? Are we sure she had the right Wilbur Goosen?"

"How many Wilbur Goosens could there be?" he pointed out. I nodded. "Besides, she had pictures of the two of them. Kissing."

He showed me a sample photo. I winced. "Bleh. Don't I have enough randy geriatrics in my life? And she was sure he died?"

"Well, they buried him," he said, starting the car. "So, what would that make him? A vampire? A zombie?"

"This isn't really my area of expertise," I said. "But it explains the health shakes."

"Well, have you ever seen him during the day?"

"I don't see anybody during the day."

"Aren't there some vampire tests we can do? We can make him touch silver, put him under a sun lamp. Oh, we can force-feed him garlic bread."

"I like your enthusiasm. But why don't we just ask him?" I suggested.

"Well, where's the fun in that?" Zeb pouted. "Besides, what are you going to say, 'Hi, I know you want to marry my grandma, who I'm not on great terms with, but I was hoping you could tell me whether you're, you know, an undead gigolo hell-bent on killing her and taking the family fortune'? I'm sure that would improve your relationship with Ruthie. Come on, let's sprinkle silver shavings in his pants.

"Well, what are you going to do?" he said when I ignored his proposal. "Find his lair? Do your best Peter Cushing imitation?"

I shot him the Arched Eyebrow of Bewilderment. He responded by wrapping his fingers around a pretend stake and made stabbing motions. At least, I hoped it was a pretend stake and stabbing motions, because otherwise our relationship just took an upsetting and inappropriate turn.

"Why would I do that?" I asked.

"Because he's evil!"

I gaped at him. "Because he's probably not one hundred percent human, we should assume he's an evil monster?" Zeb's face sagged into "oops" lines. "Yeah, how's that foot taste?"

"Sorry," he said. "Sometimes I forget that you're not one hundred percent human."

"Hmph."

On the drive back to town, I tried to work up the nerve to bring up Zeb's odd behavior, the unexplained absences and "chores" at his mama's house. Was Zeb thinking about leaving Jolene at the altar? Was that even possible when you were mated to a werewolf?

Zeb avoided the fully exposed highways in favor of the more shaded backroads, where we were treated to fantastic scenery. Weeds almost high enough to hide the junked cars and defunct riding mowers. Trailers with rotting underpinning flapping in the wind. And there was a school bus parked next to almost every house, most of which did not appear able to run. I kept telling myself I would just blurt out the first question at the next trailer we saw, and the next, and the next. But I couldn't bring myself to do it. I wasn't sure if I wanted to know if Zeb was capable of jilting Jolene. I didn't want know if he was capable of hurting someone that way, of that level of deceit. These aren't thoughts you want to have about your best friend.

We were halfway back to the Hollow when I started feeling a little dizzy. I ignored it until the sensation turned into full-on vertigo. My throat was so dry. I looked at the clock. Crap.

"What's wrong?" Zeb asked. "You look pale . . . er."

I covered my mouth with my hand and shook my head as a hot iron fist closed around my belly.

"Remember when we were nine and we rode the Tilt-A-Nator until you threw up cotton candy in my lap?" he asked. "You looked better then."

I braced myself against the dashboard, palms against the worn, warm faux leather. "It's just that I—I'm getting a little, um, hungry."

"I thought you had a special little fridge in here for blood. Didn't you bring anything with you?"

"I didn't think a bag lunch would be required," I said. "I ate right before we left, but being out during the day—I didn't realize it would be so draining."

"What about a store? Can we stop somewhere?"

I doubled over as another cramp clenched my belly. I wheezed, "The closest store is Bubba's Beer and Bait, and that's about ten miles away. I don't think he carries bottled blood. In fact, Bubba has a little sign on his door that says, 'No Shoes, No Pulse, No Service.'"

Zeb mulled that over. "They used to use the milk of young coconuts for a plasma substitute because of its high iron content. I saw it on the Discovery Channel."

"Well, that will be really handy to know if we're ever stranded on a desert island." I smacked him. "If I can't get blood, how the hell am I going to get a young coconut?"

"I know! I'm sorry! I'm panicking!" he cried.

"Just keep driving." I panted. "Talk to me. Keep me thinking about something else."

"What do you want me to talk about?"

"Anything! Your kindergartners, wedding stuff, anything!" I exclaimed, wincing at the empty churning in my stomach. "You've been talking my ear off for years, Zeb. Don't tell me you've run out of things to say."

After a long silent moment, Zeb's voice came deep and clear. "You could feed from me."

"Don't you think that would be weird?" I said, thinking about the first feeding with Andrea. I hadn't fed from a human since that cringe-inducing attempt. And it was a good while before I was completely comfortable around her again.

"I love you, Jane," he said, parking the car on the shoulder. "I want to help. This is our last big stupid adventure. Let's go out with a bang."

"I don't think it would be—"

"Jane."

I sighed. "I'm not biting your neck. Too intimate." I made an icked-out face at him, prompting him to offer his wrist. "Are you sure?"

"Do it before I change my mind!" he snapped, then

yowled when my fangs pierced his skin. He tensed, then forced himself to relax, leaning back in the seat, avoiding contact beyond my mouth on his wrist. I focused on the mechanics of feeding, fangs into skin, sealing the lips around the wound to gently pull the blood to the surface. I thought fondly of Funyuns and Cokes sipped through uncapped Twizzlers, the sort of cuisine we enjoyed on afternoon trips to Hickman Lake after Zeb got his driver's license.

When he stroked a hand across my back, I shrugged it away. More insistent, his hand curled around my jaw, caressing my cheek as I fed. I did not want to think about the pseudo-Freudian aspects of penetration and oral fixation. This was lunch. This was take-out. At least, that's what I told myself until Zeb moaned a little, throwing his head back against the seat. This sly, creepy voice in my head whispered, *You could take it all. Snuff out his life like a sputtering candle, turn him, keep him with you. A few more sips, he's enjoying it—*

"Stop," I said, pulling away. A sleepy, almost sensual expression had settled on Zeb's features, and he leaned back in the seat and stretched. He grinned conspiratorially at me as he rubbed his wrist.

"You OK?" he asked, his eyes glazed over and hazy again. He seemed barely able to focus on me.

"Fine," I promised, shaking away the guilt-inducing voice in my head. "Does it hurt?"

"No," he said, massaging his wrist, where a dark purple mark was forming. The wound was already closing up, but he would have the bruise for a while.

"Here." I dragged my fingertip across a fang and made a tiny cut. I squeezed it over Zeb's wrist, letting a few drops of blood fall into the closing wound. The skin immediately healed, and the bruising vanished.

"Thanks." Zeb smiled fondly at me, stroking the tendrils of hair back away from my face. His voice sounded so far away, as if he was repeating lines he'd heard in a movie. But it was the eyes that were unnerving. They were so vacant; there seemed to be no trace of Zeb in them.

His lips parted, and his breath quickened as he leaned toward me. A zing of panic slipped up my spine as his mouth drew closer to my own. I struck out, popping Zeb on the nose with my half-closed fist. It was sort of a cross between a punch and a slap, right in the middle of his face. "What are you doing?"

"Ow!" he cried, now fully undazed and clutching his bleeding nostrils. "What did you do that for?"

"You do *not* kiss me, you got it?" I shouted.

"What do you mean, I don't kiss you?" he cried, tilting his head back against my seat as I shoved a tissue at him.

"I mean, *you don't kiss me.*"

"I wasn't going to kiss you," he insisted.

"Zeb, it's been a while, but I'm pretty sure I recognize the ninety-five percent lean-in when I see it."

"The last thing I remember is your fangs breaking my skin," he said, dabbing at his nose and checking it in the rearview mirror.

"You honestly don't remember leaning toward me with your mouth half-open?"

"No!"

I stared at Zeb for a long time, debating whether I should look inside his mind and determine whether he was lying. Ultimately, I chickened out. Looking into his head at the moment seemed so intrusive . . . and scary. Honestly, I wasn't sure if I wanted to know what the hell he was thinking. Or if he was thinking. What if the reason he seemed so unsatisfied with Jolene lately was that he was having feelings for me? How could he do that to either of us? How could he change the rules of our friendship that way without even telling me? How was I going to tell him that the two of us would never, ever be more than what we were?

What if I lost my best friend?

"Just take me home," I said finally, slumping against the seat. We spent the rest of the drive in silence, with me staring out the window, trying to ignore the nervous bundle of BFF at the wheel. As soon as he pulled Big Bertha into my driveway, I threw a solar blanket over my head, yelped, "Good night!" and dashed for the door.

"Jane, we need to talk!" Zeb called after me.

"Good night!" I yelled as I struggled to fit the key into the front door and keep the protective blanket in place.

I slammed the door behind me and threw the deadbolt in place, just in time to hear Zeb say, "All right, then."

I closed my eyes, praying he wouldn't come to the door and try to talk about what just happened. I leaned my head back against the glass, listening for the sound of Zeb's car starting up and driving away. I caught sight of my reflection in the pier glass in the foyer, the oddly beautiful, pale woman in the mirror, her face flooded with relief at the sound of a Datsun's engine revving.

I glared at the image. "You are a coward."

My reflection was decidedly unhelpful.

**Any male who marries more than two mates is
ostracized from the pack. Most females would
consider him a jinx at that point, anyway.**

—*Mating Rituals and Love Customs of the Were*

In order to avoid thinking about Zeb and inappropriate
touching, I threw myself into ferreting out more information on my future step-grandpa. I figured of the two
problems, Wilbur's past was far less likely to come back
and bite me on the butt.

Gabriel found me up to my elbows in cyberspace,
searching through a not-quite-legal connection to the
state's vital-statistics database. The library was granted
access for archive purposes, and Mrs. Stubblefield hadn't
bothered to change our password since I was fired. Honestly, what was she thinking?

I had access to birth certificates, marriage licenses,
and death certificates, the only problem being that they
were in abstract form, giving the barest essentials of
names and dates.

After I gave only a cursory grunt for a greeting, Gabriel cautiously climbed onto the couch next to me and watched as my fingers flew over the keyboard.

"I'm fine, thank you, dear. How are you?" he said pointedly.

I made a kissing noise in his general direction but continued my search.

"I didn't mean to interrupt," he grumped. When I finally looked at Gabriel, I saw that he was wearing a well-cut black suit with a blue silk tie. I'd never seen him in his "business" attire before. He would have been mouthwatering, if not for the anxious lines between his brows, the nervous glint in his eyes. "What are you doing?"

"Stalking my future grampy via an obscenely fast wireless connection," I said, tapping away at the keys.

He blinked at the wildly scrolling screen. "Is that slang or a Jane-ism?"

"A little of both," I said. While the search engine compiled marriage records for Goosens between 1960 and 2007, I kissed his chin and rubbed my eyes. "I'm looking up old Mr. Goosen in the state archives. So far, all I've found is his birth certificate, which is normal. And his death certificate, which is, considering that he's walking around, not normal."

He stroked a hand across my shoulders. "You know, I've never seen this aggressively intellectual side of you before. It's rather disturbing and yet somehow a little sexy."

"Which is pretty much how we define our relationship," I said, turning back to the screen.

I heard his delicate intake of breath beside me. "Was

Zeb just here? His scent seems particularly strong in this room."

"Please stop sniffing me for evidence of other people," I groaned, cutting off my contrived, indignant response. Instead, I quietly said, "I had to feed from him."

"Why are you making that face?" he asked, tucking his thumb under my chin. "There's no reason you shouldn't feed from Zeb."

"I sort of vowed not to feed from humans, remember?" I said. "I was doing great, six months clean and passive . . . and then Zeb tried to kiss me, and it all just went to hell from there."

"I'm sorry." Gabriel shook his head, laughing. "For a minute, I thought you just said that Zeb tried to kiss you." I gave him a look that was part wince but mostly cringe. "Oh."

"I know," I groaned. "I don't know what's going on. It's like the whole world's just gone cockeyed. And while I was feeding, I had all these weird thoughts. And they were . . . dark and hungry and sly. And they kept telling me to drink more, take more, turn him, keep him with me. Does that mean this is my fault? Did I accidentally put some of my subconscious thoughts in his head because I'm afraid of what's going to happen to our relationship when he and Jolene get married? Is that why he tried to kiss me? Did I do this with my evil vampire temptress powers?"

Gabriel leveled me with his serious, paternal gaze. "Jane, do you want to have sex with Zeb?"

My eyes widened to the size of dinner plates. "Lord, no."

"So, this couldn't be your fault. The voice in your head? That's just a blood thought." Gabriel laughed and cupped my face between his palms. "It's the vampire brain's response to live fresh blood, a physiological attempt to keep the vampire as well fed as possible for as long as possible. We never know when our next meal will be. So the receptors in your brain that interpret pleasure all start firing at once. You get overloaded with endorphins, and you start having thoughts . . . well, thoughts I'd rather you didn't describe to me. But it's perfectly natural, particularly for those who rarely feed on live blood. Your brain was just overcompensating for time lost."

"So I don't really have dark, hungry feelings for Zeb?"

"In a universe that is decent and good, no." He shook his head.

"Thank you," I breathed, leaning against him. "I thought I was having some sort of bizarre psychic reaction to the wedding. Or maybe an aneurysm. I was hoping for aneurysm."

Gabriel's voice tightened. "That does, however, mean that I must have a talk with Zeb about appropriate behavior for engaged men, particularly engaged men who expect to continue to spend time with you and retain the use of their limbs."

I snorted. "And if that doesn't work, what's next? A paid chaperone?"

"If necessary. I'm sure Dick could use some extra cash," Gabriel muttered, tensing when I shot him a warning look. "I am very fond of Zeb. He's a fine young man, and I enjoy spending time with him. But if he thinks he can make advances toward you because of a misguided case of cold feet, he is sorely mistaken."

"I'm pretty sure I got that point across when I made his nose bleed," I told him.

"You hit him?" he asked, grinning. "That's my girl."

"I don't think he even realized he was doing it. He had this odd, glazed-over look in his eyes, and he just leaned in. We were both pretty mortified once we got his nose mopped up. Is it possible his brain was just overreacting to being bitten? I mean, Andrea's reaction when I fed from her was sort of . . . happy. But she didn't try to make out with me."

"It's possible," he conceded. When he saw the relief flood my face, he groaned. "This is one of those issues you're going to insist on handling yourself, isn't it?" I nodded. "If he does it again—"

"If he does it again, you have my permission to break his legs and arms *and* make him believe he's a rodeo clown from Walla Walla," I promised. "We can make him call himself Slappy the Wonder Clown."

"Fine. On to less disturbing subjects; can I see what you've found so far?"

I turned my laptop to show Gabriel the sad little "No records found" screen. "I can't find him registered in the state's database of the undead. According to this, he died almost fifteen years ago, so why wouldn't he register? He's an old vampire, hardly threatening. What's he afraid of?"

"Maybe he's not a vampire," Gabriel said.

"But what else could he be?"

"I honestly don't know," he admitted.

"Well, you're no help," I grumbled. "I've tried reading his thoughts, but he must be one of those people I can't get through to. Because I got nothing."

"You can't just go around thumbing through people's brains when it suits you, Jane."

"Oh, you've wiped my parents' memories like Windex, and now suddenly there's a boundary?"

Gabriel gently pried the laptop out of my hands and put it on the coffee table. "I can only guess that Wilbur is a lonely being, either natural or supernatural, and he genuinely enjoys your grandmother's company."

"No, that can't be it," I muttered, grabbing the laptop and clicking into another search engine. I typed in Wilbur's name. "Does this seem like a lot of results in the wedding license section?"

I scanned the folder. The name Wilbur, Will, Bernie, or Gus Goosen showed up six times over the last fifteen years. "Each wife died within a year of their marriage."

"Can you tell what they died of?" he asked, intrigued.

"I'm going to do something slightly illegal, so you might want to turn your head," I told him. Gabriel, unfazed, merely smirked. I gave an exaggerated sigh. "You have been warned."

I clicked on an online database that was supposed to be limited to licensed medical examiners. It said so right at the top of the screen, in big red letters. I entered a valid user name and password, prompting Gabriel's jaw to drop. I explained, "Jolene has a cousin working in the county coroner's office. He can be bought with summer sausage."

Gabriel sighed. "Well, of course she does."

"OK, first up, first wife, Dulcie, had a stroke in 1991, age seventy, nothing suspicious," I said, poring over the digitized paperwork. "Here's a death certificate for Wilbur, dated 1993. Cause of death listed as natural."

"Natural what?" Gabriel asked.

I clicked and scanned. "Just 'natural.' There was no autopsy. The coroner wrote that the death was unremarkable and likely connected to the deceased's chronic heart condition."

Gabriel scrunched his nose. "So, the cause of death was 'he was old'?"

"According to this, his body was released to Aaronson's Funeral Home a day later. Next of kin listed as Jerry Goosen, Wilbur's son, a resident of Ashton, Oklahoma. I can only hope that Jerry chose the cheapest funeral home in the state because he picked the first one he saw in the yellow pages. Is it normal for vampires to get a death certificate?"

Gabriel, fully vested in my little Nancy Drew investigation now, nodded. "It can happen if a just-turned fledgling is found by humans before he or she can rise. Since autopsies and embalming involve removing organs and most of the blood from the body, vampires don't tend to fare well. They turn out wrong somehow, weaker, diluted. When was his next marriage certificate dated?"

I chewed my lip, switching back to the vital-statistics database. "In 1994, a Bernie Goosen married Ms. Ethel Brown. She died a year later as the result of anaphylactic shock from multiple bee stings. She'd been gardening. Coroner ruled it accidental. Then in 1996, a Will Goosen to Mrs. DeeDee Wilkins-Reed. Her death certificate is dated six months later. Cause of death: blunt trauma to the head. A leg of the shower stool she was sitting on collapsed, and she was thrown to the floor, hitting her head on the tile. Coroner ruled it accidental. In 1998, Gus Goosen married Mrs. Judy Wooten. She choked on a piece of peanut brittle. Coroner ruled it, all together now—"

"Accidental."

I sifted through the online files. "I'll grant you that the first one was natural, and maybe even the second one was an accident, but after that, I think Wilbur figured out how much fun marriage for profit could be. What are the odds that Wilbur isn't bumping his wives off Bluebeard style?"

"It could just be a coincidence, you know." I stared at him. He jerked his shoulders. "It's not likely, but it could be a coincidence."

"I think my grandma may have finally met her match," I marveled.

"You are very good at this," he said, adding, "Stay away from my tax records."

"Too late," I told him absently. He jumped, but that was probably because I suddenly started waving my hands. "Wait, wait, wait."

"Is that an 'I'm thinking' gesture or an 'I have a head-ache' gesture?" he asked.

"Thinking. Weakened old vampire. Diluted. I read something like this."

I ran upstairs and snatched my copy of *Spectrum of Vampirism* off my nightstand. As I sprinted down the steps, I called out, "Normally, it doesn't take me this long to finish a book. This thing reads like stereo assembly instructions, in Korean. But listen to this:

" 'Of the many shades of vampirism, the most weakened and diluted state is that of so-called ghouls, vampires who have been embalmed. Because some vampire fledglings are believed to have been murdered or attacked by animals, they are embalmed and treated for burial. Despite the blood being drained, the vampire will survive the process if the heart and brain are left intact, which sometimes happens with lazy or inept embalmers.

" 'Reports of this phenomenon can be found as early as ancient Egypt. The nightmare of cursed mummies rising from their sarcophagi was born of priests skipping steps in the mummification process on newborn vampires. Embalmed vampires rise on the third day, deprived of the vampiric blood that turned them. They are able to withstand serious injuries, though they heal more slowly than full-fledged vampires. They also lack the strength and agility of vampires. They can withstand weak sunlight and require only small amounts of blood to survive.' "

I looked at him expectantly. He shrugged.

"He's a ghoul. I knew it!" I yelled.

Gabriel laughed. "No, you didn't."

I grunted in frustration. "I know. What should I worry about first? Him hurting her as a human or biting her and trying to turn her? Because I do not want to think about an eternity with Grandma Ruthie in it."

"Actually, ghouls aren't that dangerous," Gabriel said. "They're only interested in dead blood. It's the only thing they can digest. So they don't go around biting people.

And they can't turn a human into a vampire. They can only create other ghouls. The question is, what do you do with this information?"

"I don't know. I mean, I could warn her," I said. "Or I could let it play out for my own personal amusement."

Gabriel *tsk*ed and lifted my chin. "The Jane I know and love wouldn't let her grandmother suffer for her own personal amusement."

"Oh, baby doll." I snickered and kissed the tip of his nose. "I don't think you know me as well as you think you do. So, what are we up to this evening? You want to go see another movie? Or we could just hang out here."

Gabriel's face tensed, all of the breezy charm of the last few minutes melted away. "Actually, I can't stay. I should have mentioned I was just dropping by on my way to the airport. There's a quarterly staff meeting at my hotel that I can't afford to miss again. I like to put in an appearance every couple of months; it tends to keep the humans honest. I'm flying out to Atlanta tonight. It's just for a few days. I'm sorry I forgot to mention it."

"I could come with you," I offered. "I love Atlanta. Well, I've never been there, but I'm a big fan. You know, *Gone with the Wind*, the Braves, the Turner Broadcasting System."

I was really grasping with that last one.

"It wouldn't be any fun for you, Jane. I'll be in meetings all night. I'd hate for you to wander around alone. Who knows what sort of trouble you could get into?" He meant for it to be a joke, but there was a brittle, too-bright quality to his voice.

"I really don't mind," I said, acting oblivious to his hasty refusal. "I'd like to see the hotel. I feel I only know the Hollow version of Gabriel. I'd like to see what you're doing when you're out in the world."

Gabriel seemed to grasp the double meaning. We stared at each other for a long time. I was practically daring him to make another lame excuse, another lie. I was done letting him off the hook. He could keep making up stupid stories if he wanted to, but I wasn't going to make it easy for him. Gabriel's mouth set in a thin, cool smile.

"Not this time, Jane," he said, standing abruptly and kissing me on the temple. "I'll see you when I get home."

He was halfway to the door when I finally worked up the nerve to say, "You know, eventually, you're going to run out of excuses. You're going to have to tell me the truth."

His smile was quick, effortless, but it didn't reach his eyes. "Is that another Jane-ism? Your version of 'Have a nice trip'?"

I glared at him, refusing to be charmed.

"I'll see you soon," he said quietly, and walked out.

The click of the door closing behind him seemed to echo in my ears, a harsh, metallic scraping that bounced off the sudden emptiness of the house. Alone again, I continued to tap at the computer keys, afraid of what I might do without something to occupy my shaking hands.

15

Offspring are considered the purpose of marriage, so newlywed weres should expect heavy pressure for babies early on. Many couples receive layette sets as wedding gifts.

—*Mating Rituals and Love Customs of the Were*

When I heard the baby crying on my front porch, I thought I was having a nightmare. Still in bed, I stuck a finger in my ear and wiggled it, hoping to pop loose whatever might be causing that godawful noise. But it persisted. I sat up. There was weak sunlight peeking around the edges of my blackout curtains. Judging by the *why why why*? reaction radiating from my internal clock, I guessed it was around five P.M.

I'd managed to race into bed before dawn the morning before. About an hour after Gabriel left my house, I Googled directions to his hotel and decided that I was going to drive down there to see what he was up to myself. I'd crossed into Tennessee by the time I realized that I was behaving like a crazy person. I pulled Big Bertha off onto the shoulder just outside Union City and leaned my head against the steering wheel. What was I *doing*? What was my plan? Was I going to follow Gabriel around with a pair of binoculars and spy on him? Break into his hotel room and tell him I just couldn't resist surprising him? Gabriel had told me he didn't want me there. At best, I would find nothing was amiss and look like an annoying, clingy psycho who didn't respect boundaries. At worst, I would go to Atlanta and find him shacked up with some other woman or find that he wasn't in Atlanta at all. And what could I do then? I would have a meltdown in the middle of a strange city with no connections, no friends, nothing. I would probably wander the streets in a daze until the sun came up and I was a little pile of Jane ashes on the sidewalk.

This was definitely a Marianne move, and not in the good way.

I drove back to the Hollow and pulled into the driveway just as the sun was rising over the roof of River Oaks. I dashed into the house and pulled the covers over my head, falling into a fitful sleep. Nightmares about crying babies fit right into that.

The baby's squalling was soon joined by pounding on my front door. I stumbled down the stairs, calling for Aunt Jettie in a voice that couldn't be heard by my visitor. No response. My dead aunt picked a fine time to become a social butterfly.

Careful to stay in the cool, dark recess of the foyer, I opened the door to find Mama Ginger standing on my front porch, holding a squirming bundle of pink blankets.

"What—what the—this had better be a hallucination," I stammered.

"Jane!" Mama Ginger squealed. "I'm so glad you're home! This is Neveah. We call her Nevie for short."

"Neveah?" I repeated as she bustled into the house, trailing blankies and diaper bags.

"It's 'heaven' spelled backwards, isn't that clever?" Mama Ginger trilled, putting the baby into some sort of collapsible bouncy thing she pulled out of her bag.

"Way to sentence a kid to a lifetime spent popping out of cakes," I muttered. I felt an immediate flash of guilt when the baby opened her heavily lashed blue eyes and focused on my face. I patted her tuft of dark hair gently. "I didn't mean that."

OK, I totally meant that.

Mama Ginger popped a pacifier into the baby's mouth, which temporarily stopped the ear-splitting wails. "I was supposed to babysit little Nevie tonight, but poor Floyd is having an emergency down at the Goose Lodge and needs my help."

Floyd frequently had emergencies down at the Goose Lodge, most of them involving injuries sustained while fistfighting the pinball machine.

"So I figured you wouldn't mind watching her while I just popped over to the emergency room," she said, hoisting her purse onto her shoulder.

"Wait, what? No!" I cried. Mama Ginger was startled as I cut her off at the door, trying to comprehend how I'd managed to beat her there. "I don't know how to take care of a baby!"

"Oh, don't be silly, she's only four months old. What's to know? Besides, you used to babysit all the time."

"Yes, small children and preteens," I insisted as Nevie bubbled a yellowish goo from her nose. "People who were potty-trained and didn't ooze weird substances."

"You'll be fine," Mama Ginger insisted, and dashed out the door into the setting sunlight, where I could not follow.

"Gah! Persuasian voice. Why can't I ever remember to do that damn persuasion voice?" I cried, prompting a mewling cry from Neveah. "OK, now," I said, scooping the baby awkwardly out of the bouncie and balancing her on my arm. "Let's be reasonable. I don't know you, and you don't know me. We don't have to start the evening off by annoying each other."

The baby, who didn't know the meaning of the word "reasonable," wailed even louder.

"Mind if I cry, too?" I asked as the weight of the situation settled on my shoulder. I didn't even know who her parents were. Of course, I wasn't sure I wanted to know someone who would name their daughter Neveah. But for all I knew, Mama Ginger was trying to set me up on a kidnapping charge. My house wasn't baby-proofed. I didn't have any emergency contact numbers or a first-aid kit. I could only pray there was formula and diapers in that bag, because otherwise, this kid might have to make do with Diet Coke and paper towels.

I rocked the baby gently, making a swishing noise until she quieted. She stared at me under heavy, half-closed lids, her little rosebud mouth slack. Of course, this was just a precursor to her projectile vomiting on me.

I shrieked, swiping at the milky ick dripping from my chin. This startled Nevie, who commenced with more crying. I joined in with her again as I tried to remove the chin goo with the wipes I found in her diaper bag.

"What is it?" I asked desperately. "Are you sleepy? Grumpy? Just name a dwarf, and I'll do what I can. Are you hungry? I can fix hungry."

I carried the baby and the bag into the kitchen, where I fished out a bottle with a small amount of white powder. I sincerely hoped it was formula and not part of some elaborate drug-smuggling operation. The problem was, I didn't know how much water to add to the mix and ended up reenacting Goldilocks and the Three Bears. The first bottle was too thin. The next bottle was so thick Nevie couldn't get anything out. I finally aimed for middle ground and shook it into something she could tolerate.

The act of drinking apparently filled the baby with an inhuman amount of gas, because she belched like a long-haul trucker. The noise was enough to make her soil herself and then spit up again. This upset milady's delicate sensibilities, and she started screaming full-blast. At a loss about where I would even start addressing these issues, I started crying, too.

Seeing a grown woman cry seemed to have a soothing effect on the baby. She calmed down enough to let me pull off her little pink outfit and open her diaper. I don't want to go into details, but I have a hard time believing that much of such a disgusting material could come out of someone so small. I changed Nevie into a clean "Little Diva" onesie and laid her in the bouncie seat long enough to take the diaper out back and bury it.

When I came back into the house, she was dozing. I crept quietly up the first stair so I could get to a non-vomit-y shirt. The baby sensed this and let out a hoarse cry. I rushed back to her, searching the couch cushions for her pacifier. This calmed her down until I tried for the stairs again. In fact, every time I tried to get near clean clothes or left the ten-foot baby perimeter, Neveah made her dissatisfaction known. And they say babies aren't aware of their surroundings.

This sleeping/crying/holding-my-clean-shirt-hostage cycle continued for an hour or so. Then a tentative knock sounded at the front door.

"Thank God you're back," I said as I opened it, carefully balancing the baby on my hip. "Don't you ever do this again, Mama Ginger, do you under—Adam?"

Adam was standing on my porch, looking tousled and tanned in a blue pullover that brought out the violet undertones in his eyes. He was carrying two carry-out cups of coffee.

"Hey, Jane. I thought that since we haven't been able to get together for coffee, I would bring coffee to you." He smiled broadly, and I felt warm. It was like standing in sunlight, only without the spontaneous combustion. He took one look at my desperate, frazzled state and put the coffee down on the porch. "Who have you got there?" he asked in a typical male "jabbering at babies" tone.

"This is Nevie. Ginger Lavelle dropped her off a while ago, and I thought it was her at the door, ready to pick her up. She's got to come back for her soon, right?" I babbled as I checked the clock. Mama Ginger had left four hours ago. Where could she be? What if Mama Ginger left her until morning, when I was basically inanimate and unable to hear the cries of a hungry, uncomfortable baby?

"Oh, my Lord, what if she doesn't come back?" I cried. "I can't take care of a baby! I'm terrible at this. She's been crying off and on for hours, and no matter what I do, she won't let me put her down long enough to get a clean shirt, and I don't know what to do!"

"Oh, it's OK, Jane," he said in a calm, soothing tone, which I assumed was as much for my benefit as the baby's. He took her from me, and she gurgled and cooed at him as she settled into his arms, obviously preferring him over me after just a few moments. The little traitor. "Why don't do you go upstairs and clean up? I'll look after her for a few minutes."

"Are you sure?" I asked, though I already had one foot on the bottom stair. He nodded, and without further hesitation, I raced up the stairs to de-goo myself.

Within ten minutes, Adam had Nevie fed, burped, cleaned up, and asleep on his shoulder. Wearing fresh clothes and carrying my soiled shirt at arm's length, I found him bouncing her gently in his arms, with her little head tucked under his chin. The low lights danced over the dark gold of his hair as he swayed Nevie back and forth. The sight of Adam with a baby in his arms made my silent heart do a little flip. In my best daydreams, that was what I imagined it would be like to be married and have a family—a good, steady man standing in my house with a sleeping child cradled quietly against him. This was the price I had paid for dodging death. Though the previous hours had taught me that I certainly wasn't ready for a baby, and likely never would be, I couldn't help but feel a tiny pang of regret for an opportunity lost.

Seeing me standing there, staring at him, Adam winked and pressed a finger to his lips. He carefully placed Nevie in her little bouncie seat and went outside to retrieve his carry-out coffee.

"How did you do that?" I whispered as we tiptoed into the kitchen.

"Practice," he said, setting the coffee cup in front of me on the breakfast bar. He slid onto the stool next to me as if this were a long-held routine.

"I thought you were an only child."

Adam looked sheepish. "Well, taking care of a baby isn't that different from taking care of a puppy or a calf. They have the same basic needs and give the same sort of cues for hunger, discomfort, being sleepy. And they make almost the same amount of mess. So I've picked up a lot of fathering experience down at the clinic."

I snorted.

"That came out wrong," he acknowledged, chuckling. He took a sip of his coffee and smiled that warm, crooked smile.

I waited for my nerves to kick in, to start spewing nonsense words and fidgeting. But it seemed that all of the embarrassment and shyness I'd felt before in Adam's presence had melted away.

Sitting there with Adam was . . . quiet, restful. There was no dire emergency looming on the horizon. I didn't have to monitor every expression, every word, carefully to keep from upsetting him. And I didn't feel tempted to look inside his head, because his feelings were pinned right on his sleeve.

"It was nice of you to drop by with this . . . now luke-warm coffee." I chuckled while I sipped.

His dimples flashed. "Well, I do what I can. Other than panic attacks stemming from spit-up, how have you been?"

"It's . . . complicated."

"Vampire stuff?" he asked.

I considered. Of all of the things I was dealing with— a distant and secretive boyfriend, my potentially murderous step-grandpa, the possible mental breakdown of my best friend, his mother's attempted jumpstarting of my defunct biological clock—none of it had much to do with me being a vampire. "Not really."

"But I could see how being a vampire would be, you know, complicated. I mean, where do you get your blood?" he asked. "And what time do you wake up every night? Is it difficult for you to be around people without wanting to feed on them?"

"Are you writing some sort of book report?" I asked, making him flash that mile-wide grin.

"I'm just curious," he said. "You never know whether what you read in the news about vampires is true. But it seems you have to make so many adjustments, just to function."

"It's not that big of a deal," I told him. "OK, yeah, it is, but it's worth it, especially if it means I can stay here, in my home."

"But you could do anything, go anywhere."

"This is where I want to be."

Nonplussed, Adam asked, "How did this start? How were you turned?"

"It's not a story I tell most people," I said.

Adam seemed offended that I considered him "most people." "Why not?"

"If there was a very special episode of *I Love Lucy*, where Lucy was turned into a vampire, she'd probably use my story. Let's just say I didn't have any choice. It was either death or this. I'm fortunate that my sire happened to be there."

"This sire, is that the guy you're seeing?" he asked.

I nodded. It was so weird to discuss this with him, the touch of jealousy tainting his otherwise clear tenor.

"Is it serious?" he asked.

I stared down at my coffee cup, ashamed that I was unable to answer. I didn't know where I stood with Gabriel right now. Was it unfair that I didn't want to give Adam the impression that I was totally unavailable? Was I just using his unabashed interest as a convenient excuse to look for a way out of an uncomfortable, uncertain situation with my sire? Why did I feel so guilty for thinking that way when Gabriel's actions were so suspicious?

Why couldn't I be a Marianne instead of an Elinor?

Just live in the moment and take what I wanted from life? Why did I have to think everything through? Elinor is a pushover. She lets everyone else act any way they please, leaving her to clean up their messes without complaint. Marianne may be misguided and silly, but at least she has some fun every once in a while.

Adam took advantage of my silence. "If you can't answer, that probably means something."

I nodded, still unable to add anything to the exchange.

"Well, if something changes or you decide that you're . . . I just want you to know that if you ever need someone to talk to, I'd like that person to be me. Damn it, that made no sense. I'm sorry, you just make me a little nervous," he admitted. His blush brought a flood of deep, healthy pink to his cheeks.

"I make you nervous?" I was strangely pleased by that. After all, he'd made me stutter and drool for most of my adolescence. Turnabout was fair play.

The blush that had subsided only a few seconds before rushed back into his cheeks. "Well, yeah. I like spending time with you. I'm grateful that I'm getting to know you again. I don't want to screw this up."

I was able to tamp down my instinct to squeal. I had some cool, flirty speech prepared about Adam playing his cards right, but he suddenly stood up, took my face in his hands, and brushed a quick kiss across my cheek, leaving a tingling path where his lips had touched my skin. He was so warm, vital, full of life. He smelled like sun-dried cotton and peppermint, though I imagined that last part was probably just doggie shampoo. The pattern of his hands seemed burned into my cheeks, branding me. How could I have forgotten how warm human men were? It was like sliding into a bone-softening hot bath at the end of a long, blustery day, comforting and sweet. He pulled away from me and smiled. I sat stunned, watching him cross to the kitchen door.

"Just think about what I said, Jane," he said as he stepped outside. "Give me a call sometime, even if it's just to talk. I want to see you again."

"I will," I promised before I had a chance to filter my response. I seemed to be channeling the teenage Jane, who had no impulse control or loyalty to Gabriel.

Adam took care to close the door quietly, but somehow that tiny *snick* woke Nevie up and had her squalling.

I sighed and thumped my head against the counter.

By the time Mama Ginger saw fit to return, I'd changed six more diapers and spent an hour cleaning substances I'd rather not describe out of my carpet. There were suspiciously permanent-looking stains on my new couch. I was not a happy camper.

"Are you crazy?" I demanded as Mama Ginger opened my door. "What is wrong with you?"

"What?" she asked, peering into the bouncie, where Neveah dozed peacefully. "She's fine. I knew she would be."

"What if she'd gotten sick?" I hissed. "What if something went wrong? I didn't know how to get in touch with you. I am covered in baby spit-up. My house smells like compost!"

"But honey, doesn't she make you want one of your own?" Mama Ginger held up the baby like a prize cut of meat on display.

"If anything, you've confirmed for me that I don't need to have children," I said, and from the bottom of my heart, I knew it was true.

"But Janie, I only did this to show you that you need to stop playing around. Stop with this silly singles lifestyle. A different man every night. Working in some adult bookstore. You need to settle down. Stop pretending you're happy, and just tell Zeb how you feel."

"I'm not pretending," I said.

"Well, I think I need to have a talk with this Gabriel character and tell him what he's doing. He has to know he's standing in your way," Mama Ginger insisted. "He has to know he's keeping you from your one true love. If it wasn't for this boy, this Gabriel, you and Zeb would be free to be together."

"But Zeb is in love with Jolene."

"I don't want to hear that, Jane. I know what's best!" she cried, gathering the baby's stuff and making a dash for the front steps. "You'll see."

"Mama Ginger, stop," I said in the most powerful persuasion voice I could muster. "Stop it right now. You will stop this campaign against Jolene, and you will accept her into the family. You will make her feel welcome. You will never again mention the idea of Zeb and me as anything but friends."

Mama Ginger swiped at her ear as if there were annoying insects buzzing there. I guess vampire powers were nothing against the determination of an angry mother-in-law-to-be.

"And I don't work at an adult bookstore," I shouted out the door as she bustled Nevie off the porch. "I work at an occult bookstore. There just happens to be an adult video store next door."

I watched as Mama Ginger's taillights disappeared into the darkness.

"This is not good."

16

Werewolves express many emotions through physical contact—joy, rage, a need for comfort. Prepare to be hugged, snuffled, snuggled, or possibly licked.

—*Mating Rituals and Love Customs of the Were*

"Hello?" I called, propping a delivery box against the counter long enough to get the door shut. It had been locked, which was unusual. And Mr. Wainwright never left deliveries out front. There was too much crime in the neighborhood.

"Mr. Wainwright?" I called. Technically, it was my night off. I wasn't supposed to come by the shop, but Gabriel had called me from the Nashville airport to let me know that he'd be returning to town that night and wanted to talk. I didn't want to be home waiting for him. Despite my protests to the contrary, I didn't want to have whatever conversation Gabriel had planned. As unhappy as I was with his evasiveness, I knew the truth would hurt worse. So I was using work as a defensive shield.

The shop was empty, eerily so. I cast my senses out and found nothing; no vampire presence, no humans.

Around the corner of the counter, I could see a pair of brown loafers poking out from a pile of seventeenth-century manuscripts on vampire feeding patterns.

"I thought we agreed that you wouldn't try to move anything by yourself," I said to the feet as I set the box down.

The silence seemed to buzz in my ears, slowing my ability to hear, to respond.

"Mr. Wainwright?" My boss lay prostrate on the floor, the books covering him like a crazy quilt. His eyes were closed, his face serene, as if he'd just lain down for a nap on the floor.

"Nononononononono," I murmured, my numbed fingers searching for a pulse under his cold parchment skin. "Please, no."

I wailed, my hot tears blinding me. "Mr. Wainwright! Please wake up! Please!"

Using what little I could remember from first-aid class in Girl Scouts, I shoved several books away and tilted Mr. Wainwright's head back. I wiped my running nose and breathed through the sobs. I blew into his mouth. I pushed down on his sternum with both hands and shrieked when I heard something snap. I'd broken something, probably one of his ribs. I continued to pump his chest, praying to bring something back.

"Please!" I screamed again, burying my face in his shirt.

"Jane, dear, it's time to stop that. As much as I appreciate it, it's too late."

I looked up and locked eyes with the former Mr.

Wainwright. He was wearing the same gray cardigan and brown corduroy ensemble as the body lying on the floor, only more transparent. He smiled gently.

"Mr. Wainwright?" I whimpered. "What's going on?"

"To a young woman of your intelligence, Jane, I would hope it would be obvious." I shook my head, still sniffling. "I'm a ghost, Jane, have been for, oh, six or seven hours now."

He held up his hand, examining the way the light filtered through it. "Look at that."

"What happened to you?" I asked.

"Well, you were right about my not moving boxes by myself. I knew there was something wrong the moment I picked it up. I had all of the classic signs—shooting pains in the left arm, crushing sensation in the chest, shortness of breath. I just keeled over."

"I'm so sorry. I should have been here."

"Don't," he said. "Don't blame yourself. I was an old man, and I lived a good, long life. And you made me very happy during my last months. You've become very dear to me, Jane. I hope you know that. I was never meant to have children. But I like to think that if I had a daughter, or a granddaughter, she would be like you. Good Lord, is that really what my hair looks like?"

"Focus, please, Mr. Wainwright. Why are you still here? Do you have unfinished business or something?" I asked.

"No, no, I'm just not ready to cross over. There's too much happening in the world right now. And my friendship with you, it's so exciting. I want to see what happens next."

"But don't you want to see what's, you know, on the other side?"

"I'm not afraid of crossing over," he said. "I'm just not ready to go. As soon as I am, I will. As a wise man once said, 'To the highly organized mind, death is just another adventure.'"

"That's from *Harry Potter*," I said. "Dumbledore said it in the first book."

"Trust you to know." He smiled. "Everything's going to be fine, Jane. Don't you worry."

"But what's going to happen?"

"Who knows?" He shrugged, grinning wildly. "That's the best part."

"But what about—"

"Jane, I think you'd better call nine-one-one, dear, to pick up my body," he suggested.

I nodded. "I'm going to miss you."

"Not for a while yet," he promised.

I thought about calling Dick, but I knew the mix of Dick and the authorities—human or otherwise—was not a good thing. Even though Mr. Wainwright's death was natural, the 911 dispatcher apparently went to church with my mama and notified the responding paramedics that I was a vampire. And I guess they asked for a police escort. Also, when vampires cry, the tiniest bit of blood streaks through in their tears, so when the police arrived, my face was covered in red stains. Needless to say, questioning took a while.

"How long have you worked here, Miss Jameson?" Sergeant Rusty Bardwell asked as he scribbled in his little notebook. A tall, dark-haired fellow with a no-nonsense set to his jaw, Rusty did not trust me. In fact, he kept a free hand on his gun for most of his visit. Pointing out that using it on me would be useless didn't seem wise.

"Rusty, we've known each other since third grade. You threw up on me on the field trip to Mammoth Cave. Just call me Jane," I said irritably as I sniffled into a tissue.

Rusty's level gaze didn't waver. "How long have you worked here, Miss Jameson?"

"About six months," I said, my voice flat and annoyed.

"And how long have you known the deceased?"

"About six months," I said.

Mr. Wainwright watched as the paramedics loaded his mortal coil into a body bag, then waved cheerfully as he was packed into the ambulance. I shook my head at him.

"And you were recently promoted to manager."

"No." I frowned.

"The deceased left a note on his desk," Sergeant Rusty insisted, digging into an evidence envelope. *"Note to Self: Have 'Jane Jameson, Manager' plaque engraved for Jane."*

"Aw, Mr. Wainwright."

Mr. Wainwright ducked his head. "You deserve it, Jane. You're going to be running the store now, anyway."

Annoyed at my lack of attention, Rusty cleared his throat. "And you found the body?"

"Yes. I told the dispatcher that when I called nine-one-one."

"And you performed CPR?"

"I did, but I think he'd been gone for a while at that point."

"I thought vampires couldn't breathe," he said, narrowing his eyes at me.

"I don't have to, but it doesn't mean I can't," I told him. "Do I need to call a council representative? I'm allowed to under the Undead Civil Rights Act of 2002."

"We'll let you know," Rusty said. "For right now, let's just say that you'll probably be hearing from us again."

Rusty cleared out of the shop as if his polyester pants were on fire. The ambulance crew drove away with the body—I couldn't think of it as Mr. Wainwright. I was alone. And it was suddenly so quiet. Numb, I sank into a chair behind the counter and stared at a ledger next to the register. I could make out Mr. Wainwright's chicken scratch, a reminder for me to reorder a book called *Life on Loch Ness*. I ran my fingers over his indented scrawl, leaned my head against the counter, and cried.

I'm not sure how long I sat there. The next thing I remembered was Gabriel striding through the shop door, calling for me. I couldn't seem to look up, to put together the words to respond. The smallest movement took too much effort.

"I've been calling you all evening," he said, coming behind the counter to check me over for obvious contusions and stab wounds. "Normally, there's a reason for your ignoring me. What's going on?"

"Mr. Wainwright's dead," I said, tongue slow and heavy. I held myself together for a total of two seconds before bursting into hysterical tears again. Gabriel wrapped his long arms around me, and I suddenly didn't care where he'd been or what he'd done. The important thing was that he was there, at that moment, when I needed him.

"Was it one of us?" he asked.

"Oh, no, completely natural. It was a heart attack," I said, my eyes welling up again. "He was an old man. He said he lived a good life . . ."

Gabriel pressed me to his chest and let me sob there, until the front of his shirt was soaked. "Better?" he asked.

"No," I said, wiping at my nose. "I must look a mess, which is really the least of my concerns right now. I'm not one of those women who are beautiful when they cry."

"No, you're not," Gabriel agreed.

"So rude." I smacked him.

"See, you feel better now that you've hit something."

"I don't know why I'm crying so much." I sniffled. "It's not as if I lost him. I mean, he's happy as a clam, staring through his hands. He's thrilled that he's dead. Why do I feel this way?"

"If I suggest a theory, will you get angry?"

"Well, you've pretty much guaranteed that I will now." I blew my nose.

"So much about your life has been unstable. You lost your aunt Jettie, your job, your life as you knew it. Mr. Wainwright and his shop became a touchstone of normalcy. It was somewhere you could go and know what to expect when you walked through the door. Now you can't hold on to even the smallest shred of your former life or the shaky sense of security you've developed."

I stared at him. Having someone inside your head is offputting.

"No, that's not it," I said. "Not it at all. I hereby revoke your license to play armchair psychologist."

"What can I do to make you feel better?" he asked. I shrugged. "Happy Naked Fun Time?"

I laughed, a rusty sound that made my throat hurt. "You know, sometimes I forget that at the heart of things, you're still a guy."

"Well, let me remind you."

"We need to call Dick."

"I think we should leave Dick out of this."

"Because—oh, God, it hardly matters now. Dick is Mr. Wainwright's great-grandfather."

Gabriel sank onto the couch. "Dick had children?"

"A son, that we know of. His name was Albert. He was Mr. Wainwright's grandfather."

"Dick had a child?"

I stared at him. "Did I break your brain?"

"It's just, I gave up the idea of being able to have children long ago, for obvious reasons. I mourned, but I made my peace with it. I'd never even considered that Dick could . . . though it makes sense that he did. He always sort of played fast and loose with his, er, companions. How long have you known?"

"A month or so. I'm sorry I didn't tell you. Dick asked me not to say anything."

"Jane?" Dick came rushing through the door with

Zeb on his heels. He skidded to a halt as he saw my tear-tracked face, then whirled on Gabriel. "Why is she crying? If you made her cry, I'm going to kick your—"

"Why are you here?" Gabriel asked Dick.

"The clerk at the video store next door saw an ambulance over here and called me," Dick said.

Zeb made a face. "The porn-store guy has your home number?"

I ignored this disturbing tidbit and wrapped my arms around Dick's neck. "Dick, I'm so sorry. It's Mr. Wainwright. He's gone."

Dick's bravado melted away. "From where?"

"The earthly plane," I said. "He died earlier tonight."

His face contorted in pain. "I've been spending time at the shop—"

"No, no," I said, clutching Dick's hands. "Nobody 'got to him.' It was just a plain old heart attack."

"I didn't get to tell him," Dick said. "I didn't get to say good-bye."

"Actually, he plans on sticking around for a while, so you could tell him right now."

"Tell him what, exactly?" Mr. Wainwright asked, his transparent form sliding through the door.

It's embarrassing to be surprised when you have vampire senses, particularly when the person who snuck up behind you is older than dirt. Also dead.

"What?" Mr. Wainwright asked, the gray tufts of his brows rising on his transparent forehead. "What's wrong?"

"This seems like a private conversation. We should

probably leave," Gabriel whispered to Zeb, though both of them stayed rooted to their spots.

"OK, you two, out," I told them.

"But, but, but—" Zeb spluttered pitifully as I shoved the pair of them into the office and closed the door behind us.

I waited while I heard Dick quietly explaining the situation. When Mr. Wainright didn't respond, I poked my head into the room to make sure he was still there. There was an expression of relief around Dick's eyes as Mr. Wainwright stumbled forward and hugged Dick in an insubstantial manner.

This was so strange, an ancient man calling this thirty-something fellow Grandpa; in a world where logic lived, the roles would be reversed. But years melted off Mr. Wainwright's face as he studied Dick's features.

"You have my nose," Dick said sheepishly. "Sorry about that."

"It's a good nose," Mr. Wainwright said. "Why didn't you ever say anything?"

"Thought you'd be better off," Dick said.

"But I wasn't," Mr. Wainwright said. "If you'd been around, if I'd known that vampires were real, I wouldn't have felt so lonely. It's no wonder my mother hated my interest in the paranormal. Every time I picked up a book on vampires, she was afraid I was going to turn out like you."

Dick seemed ashamed, which was something I'd never seen before. "I never told your mother. I think she guessed, but she never asked, and I always figured it was better left unsaid. I'm sorry."

"I have so much I want to ask you. About your life, about my father, and his father, and your son."

"I can give you some answers," Dick said. "The rest you may not want to know."

"I'm not frightened," Mr. Wainwright promised.

"This reunion is really touching," I said, backing toward the office door. "But if I see one of you cry, I may actually implode. So I'm going to go elsewhere."

How did I end up going to so many funerals in one year?

There was no one else to plan Mr. Wainwright's service, which I found very sad. His nephew, Emery, sent a telegram from Guatemala saying that he wouldn't be able to make it to town for weeks. Emery advised us to proceed without him. Seriously, he used those words. Real sentimental guy.

The nighttime service was held three days later, after the police finally released the body. Mr. Wainwright had a hand in the planning, which definitely helped me cope with the grief. He was in attendance at the memorial, of course, though very few others were. It was just me, Dick, Andrea, Gabriel, Jettie, Jolene, and Zeb. Daddy came, though we neglected to tell him that we couldn't speak ill of the dead, not out of respect but because the dead was standing right there.

Mr. Wainwright didn't belong to a church, so there was no one to give a eulogy. In fact, he'd left specific instructions that he did not want to be buried. He wanted his ashes spread into the Ohio River, where they would "float downstream to the Gulf of Mexico and out into the oceans, circulating around the world."

There was no visitation, no pimento cheese, no irritating relatives circling like vultures.

In other words, it was the best funeral I'd ever been to.

The riverfront in Half-Moon Hollow was a series of half-finished cement docks and inlets. The county commission had started dredging to build a channel for a riverboat in the 1970s, hedging against the chances that riverboat gambling would be legalized in Kentucky. When the state referendum failed and the outraged populace voted the commission out of their seats, the project was abandoned, leaving a gap in the Hollow's watery smile. Which, in a way, was fitting.

The one project that was completed and used was the public restrooms. I tried not to think about that.

The water, smelling of old pennies and new fish, lapped gently against the cement embankment. The moon was only half-full and half-mast, lending a soft, kind light to the proceedings. Mr. Wainwright asked that we avoid the traditional black in favor of cheerful colors, forgetting, of course, that Gabriel didn't own anything in cheerful colors. Dick's plain white T-shirt, *sans* sarcasm, lent an appropriate sense of solemnity to the proceedings.

The earthly remains of Gilbert Wainwright were stored in a hollowed-out copy of *For Whom the Bell Tolls* that Dick had purchased from a novelty store. Mr. Wainwright thought it was hilariously funny. I held the book in my hands and stood at the edge of the dock, shaking a little from the wind and the nerves.

"We're gathered here today to say good-bye to the mortal body of Gilbert Wainwright. He was a good man and a good friend. I didn't know him until late in his life. But he became very special to me in that time. He was a man with an endless thirst for knowledge. He asked the questions that other people are afraid of and never doubted that the answers were out there, waiting to be discovered. I'm going to miss you, Mr. Wainwright. You were kind to me when you didn't have to be. You gave me a place to belong when I was adrift. Thank you."

"You will always have a place there, my dear," he said, chucking my chin with his clammy invisible hand.

I handed the book to Dick. "It's only right," I said, smiling despite the surreality of the situation. "He was your family."

"Quite right," Mr. Wainwright told Dick. "I'd be honored."

"This is the weirdest funeral I've ever been to," Zeb whispered.

"Shh," I said as Dick stepped forward.

Dick cleared his throat. "It's not right for a man to bury his children, so to speak. But this is the path we chose. It's a vampire's lot in life to watch those around him age and die. Gilbert, I'm sorry we didn't get to know each other better." In a low voice, out of my father's earshot, he murmured, "But I hope you stick around for a while, so we can make up for that."

Gabriel was looking at Dick with a strange expression. The whole "Dick reproduced" thing had definitely thrown him for a loop. I slipped my hand in his and gave him an encouraging nudge. Gabriel stepped beside Dick and with a stiff arm patted Dick's back as he sprinkled the ashes into the churning water.

"Good-bye, cruel world," Mr. Wainwright wailed in a fading mock cry.

Everyone but Andrea, Zeb, and Daddy turned to stare at him. He grinned. "Too melodramatic?"

"Why is everyone laughing?" Daddy asked.

"It's a vampire thing. We laugh at death," I told Daddy, who nodded sagely.

Mr. Wainwright insisted on a reading of his will right after the memorial. The funeral party, without Daddy, met Mr. Wainwright's lawyer, Mr. Mayhew, the only male Hollow resident over seventy whom my grandmother had never dated, at the shop. He greeted us warmly and told us what nice things Mr. Wainwright had to say about us all.

"I've known Gilbert Wainwright for forty years. In that time, he spoke of two things ad nauseam: the supernatural and you. He enjoyed spending time with you, very much," he assured me. "You made the last year of his life very comfortable and happy."

"Is he here now?" Mr. Mayhew asked.

I looked from Mr. Wainwright's apparition to Mr. Mayhew's wry smile. "Yeah. How did you know?"

"He always said he would make appearances after death. I thought it was part of his wild 'creatures of the night' talk. Then, after the Coming Out, we found out that creatures of the night actually exist, so my mind opened a little bit."

"Is it open enough to handle vampire wills?" I asked. "Because I've got some grabby relatives."

He handed me his card. "Give me a call."

"So, how do we go about this?" I asked. "I wasn't allowed to attend any of my step-grandpas' will readings."

"Well, I need y'all to sit down and have a listen. I think you should know that Gilbert changed his will quite recently. When an elderly man changes his will to include a group of recently acquainted young people, it can be of some concern for someone in my profession. But Gilbert spoke very highly of you, and he wasn't the type to gush." He cleared his throat and used an official voice. "The will goes something like this. 'I, Gilbert Richard Wainwright, being of sound mind and body as defined by the commonwealth of Kentucky'—a lot of legalese y'all are more than welcome to look over later, so we can skip to the good part—'do bequeath the following items to my loved ones:

" 'To Zeb Lavelle, I leave a copy of *Mating Rituals and Love Customs of the Were*, plus the entire stock of self-help guides related to inter-were-species marriage.' "

"That was thoughtful," Zeb said.

"That stock includes several illustrated antique marital guides which you will find in a locked box in the storeroom," Mr. Wainwright whispered to me.

"Oh, ew." I shuddered.

"He just made a joke, didn't he?" Mr. Mayhew asked.

"Why don't you just let him see you?" I asked Mr. Wainwright.

Mr. Wainwright chuckled. "It's more fun this way."

" 'To Jolene McClaine, I leave the rosewood box in my bedroom. It contains a collection of best-loved recipes I have collected from werewolf friends all over the world.' "

"That's very sweet." Jolene sniffed.

"I thought you could put it to the best use," Mr. Wainwright said.

" 'To Andrea Byrne, I leave my silver claddagh ring.' "

"Oh, thank you," Andrea whispered.

"It should have been included in my personal effects when my remains were collected," Mr. Wainwright said.

"Actually"—I reached under the counter and grabbed the velvet pouch where I'd stashed the ring—"I didn't think it was smart to send you to the funeral home wearing it."

"This belonged to a lady who was very special to me," Mr. Wainwright said as Andrea slipped it on. "Her name was Brigid, and she was special and beautiful, like you. And I loved her very much."

Knowing that Andrea couldn't hear him, I said, "That belonged to the love of his life."

Andrea smiled.

"You're going to want to be careful how you handle that around us," Dick told her. "Might as well be wearing barbed wire around your finger."

"Well, that has possibilities," Andrea said, wiggling her finger at him. Not the rude one.

Dick muttered something I couldn't quite make out.

" 'To Gabriel Nightengale, the selection of his choice from my personal literary collection. To Dick Cheney, my personal spirits collection, including the wine and brandy.' "

Dick and Gabriel smiled.

" 'To Jane Jameson, I leave the Specialty Books shop located at 933 Braxton Avenue and all of its contents, including the apartment upstairs and my personal effects contained therein. I trust you to allow my nephew, Emery, to look over my personal effects and select what he would like to keep as mementos.' "

My jaw dropped. I had expected a few books. Maybe a memento or Mr. Wainwright's personal collection of Ouija boards. I had not expected him to leave me anything as important as the shop.

My eyes stung as I smiled shakily at Mr. Wainwright. I really didn't want to start crying again. I'd just managed to stop. "This is too much. I didn't do anything to deserve this. And I don't know anything about running a store. Look, with your nephew coming soon, I think maybe we should consider—"

"No one will care about the shop the way you will," Mr. Wainwright insisted. "No one will take care of the books, take care of the customers, such as they are." He turned to Dick. "If I had known about you, I would have planned differently—"

"Not your fault," Dick interrupted. "And you left me the booze, so it shows how well you knew me, even before you knew we were related."

"And anything you want from the personal effects is yours," I told Dick. "The store stock will be available at a twenty-percent bereaved-ancestor discount."

Mr. Wainwright guffawed. "See, you've got the makings of a brilliant entrepreneur."

I protested, "I don't know anything about running a business."

"Then sell it. Do whatever you think is best. I trust you."

Those words, combined with Mr. Wainwright's earnest, ghostly gaze, left a weird, heavy feeling in the pit of my stomach.

When an undesirable suitor is unwilling to accept a werewolf female's refusal, her family is likely to step in to help communicate her feelings more clearly. It can take said suitor six to eight weeks to heal up from the clan's communication skills.

—*Mating Rituals and Love Customs of the Were*

We all adjusted to our grief in different ways.

On this particular Tuesday, Jolene and Zeb were doing a family thing with the McClaines. I think it involved wrestling Jolene's father. Andrea had a standing appointment with a client who was not afraid of Dick. Gabriel was in London. I didn't bother asking why. This left me with Dick.

No pun intended.

Dick seemed lonely, spending nights at the shop, talking to the ever-more-sprightly ghost of Mr. Wainwright, and helping me sort through boxes. We had a running bet about when Emery would show up. I had two weeks; Dick had six weeks and four days. Mr. Wainwright, who lovingly referred to his nephew as "a bit mealy-mouthed and milquetoast," had twenty dollars on an even month, though how we were going to collect it from him, we had no idea.

I'd dropped my investigation into Wilbur's background for the time being. I told myself that it would help me to step away, get a fresh perspective, but the truth was, I was getting nowhere. Instead, I worked from sunset to the wee hours of the morning cleaning areas that Mr. Wainwright had never let me touch: a rear storeroom, the area behind the counter, his office. For his part, Mr. Wainwright entertained himself by moving various objects around, walking through walls, and making videos float at the adult store next door, scaring several locals off porn forever.

Despite my recently developed fear of Realtors, I'd had one come by and appraise the shop. He suggested burning it to the ground and going for the insurance money. While my destructive urge was just as healthy as the next girl's, I didn't consider that a viable option. I was going to have to close.

It felt like packing up Aunt Jettie's room after she died. Something important had ended, and I was left to pick up the pieces. Fortunately, Dick and Andrea seemed to pick up on this and somehow ended up at the shop every night to help me. On this particular evening, Dick was boarding over windows and putting a "For Sale by Owner" sign in the window. With Andrea quietly boxing up books, I went upstairs to Mr. Wainwright's apartment, something I hadn't been able to do since the funeral.

The air was dry and smelled of cinnamon and Lipton tea. As one would expect, the place was a wreck. Good antiques were covered in Mad Hatter–style stacks of books. Almost every surface not occupied by books held picture frames. There were photos of Mr. Wainwright's mother, his sister, his nephew, Emery. There was a framed photo of a beautiful redhaired woman, who I assumed was Mr. Wainwright's lost love, Brigid. There was a picture of a very young Mr. Wainwright in his Army uniform, one of him in a pith helmet exploring what looked to be an Egyptian tomb, and pictures of him bundled up against Canadian cold during his endless search for Sasquatch.

The latest addition seemed to be a picture of our Christmas party. Zeb had set up the camera timer to take a shot of the whole group. My eyes were closed, of course, but everyone looked so happy. Jolene had turned that million-watt smile on Zeb. Gabriel had his arm around me. There were two little white orbs where Aunt Jettie and Grandpa Fred had stood. Andrea was wedged between Mr. Wainwright and Dick, who had his arm flung around both of them. Mr. Wainwright had placed it on the nightstand next to his low-slung single bed. It was the only photo from the last ten years in the apartment.

I felt him materialize behind me.

"It was the best time I could remember in a long time," I heard him say as I put the frame back in its place. "You were a family to me, one I sincerely wish I'd had more time with."

I smiled at him, even when he asked, "How's the packing going? I saw that Dick has put up the 'For Sale' sign."

I felt tears bubbling up, threatening to spill. I wiped at my nose as I focused on staring at the Christmas photo.

"Oh, no, dear. Don't cry."

"I can't help but feel that I'm failing you," I told him. "You didn't leave me the shop to close it down. But I don't know anything about running a business. I'm sorry. I got fired from the only real job I've ever had. I don't know how to do taxes or handle staff issues. I'm just afraid I would screw it up."

"You're not failing, Jane," he said, his clammy hands stroking down my arms. "Having the shop, having a purpose, gave me a reason to get up every morning. I knew the shop wasn't making much money, just enough to keep me afloat. You're just making decisions I couldn't bring myself to make." Mr. Wainwright squeezed my shoulder, sending shivers down my sensitive spine. "Everything has to come to an end, Jane. Except for you, of course." With that, he winked at me and faded away, leaving me to my thoughts.

I went to the stairs and stared down into the store, chewing my lip and sulking. The shop could have been something. With renovation, new stock, a new business plan, I could turn it around. If anything, the slow migration of library patrons showed that people would come to the shop if they really needed to.

Besides investment capital, the main problem was organization. Even people who knew what they were looking for couldn't find it. Hell, I worked there, and I could rarely find what I needed. If I overhauled the selections, emphasized self-help and family dynamics, aimed for people who were newly turned or whose families were newly turned, tried to help them find the resources to deal with the changes, it might work. I could even offer the Friends and Family of the Undead a place to meet, since their usual spot, a health-food restaurant called the Nomad's Bowl, was on the verge of closing—again. I could put a comfy meeting area in the back, especially if I bought out the adult-video store next door and expanded through the wall.

If I added a fancy coffee bar and got a license to carry blood, people would come to the store and actually stay. And then they would buy.

It would mean selling off some of Missy's properties. And hiring a cleaning crew. A very committed cleaning crew.

Maybe I could actually hire some staff. Would I hire living people or vampires? Maybe Andrea needed a night job.

Newly resolved, I marched downstairs and told Dick and Andrea to stop boxing up.

"I'm not closing," I told them. "I'm going to keep the store open."

Dick grinned broadly and whipped the sign out of the window. "I'll just take this out to the trash."

"Dick's been weird all night," Andrea said as we heard the sign clang into the Dumpster in the alley. "He's barely propositioned me or anything. Is this what happens when you agree to date him? He loses interest before you even go out?"

"I still can't believe you agreed to a date," I said. "I thought you were getting some sort of sick, retaliatory pleasure from repeatedly rejecting him. I was getting sick, retaliatory pleasure out of your repeatedly rejecting him. Can't we keep playing?"

"I don't know," Andrea said, laughing. "He just kind of grows on you, like . . ."

"Like fungus," I suggested.

"Oh, hush. You like him, you know you do. And I do, too. I guess I was just looking for an excuse to like him." She smiled to herself. "Beneath all his bull and his charm, Dick's a good guy."

We turned to the door as the bell jingled. It was Adam, still wearing his soft blue scrubs from the Half-Moon Hollow Veterinary Clinic. I smiled up at him, and he responded with a dazzling grin.

"Wow, so this is where you work?" he marveled, taking in the disheveled surroundings. "This is great, Jane. Really, really great."

"Well, actually, it's my shop now. My boss just passed away, and he left it to me," I said, crossing to him and leaving a confused Andrea standing at the counter.

"That's great," he said.

I'd never noticed before how much Adam used the word "great." Instead of offering him a thesaurus, I said, "This is my friend Andrea."

Adam didn't even acknowledge her presence. He was totally focused on me, looking at me the way I'm sure I looked at him all those times in math class. As if he were trying to memorize every word and gesture, so he could replay it in his head later. Now that it was turned around on me, I had to say it was unnerving.

"What brings you down here, Adam?" I asked.

He shrugged and stepped closer to me. "I just wanted to see you again."

Giving me a confused look, Andrea made quietly for the office door. Whether it was emotional fatigue from Mr. Wainwright's death or his being in the store where my friends could see him, it seemed wrong for Adam to be there. I couldn't really be angry with Gabriel for sneaking around and not being honest with me when I hadn't been exactly upfront about Adam. I could lie to myself and say I didn't know what Adam was hoping for. But even I could recognize the signals he'd been sending out. And I'd done nothing to discourage him. Out in the open like this, the fairy-tale, adolescent-fantasy haze seemed to be stripped away, and I saw exactly how wrong I'd been. Some instinct had me backing away with every step he took closer to me.

"Have you recovered from your babysitting adventure?" he asked, that warm, familiar smile dimpling his cheeks.

"Yeah. Nevie may never be the same, but every kid needs something to talk about in therapy. So I feel I've served some purpose." I tried to keep my tone even and friendly, even as I was cornered against the counter.

He laughed, but his expression turned serious as he asked, "Have you given any more thought to us spending more time together?"

My heart sank a little. I'd really hoped to avoid this. "I'm still seeing Gabriel."

Adam huffed, "But I thought we talked about that!"

I chose my words deliberately, in that even voice that seemed to soothe Fitz when he was riled. I ended up sounding like a mother talking her toddler down from a tantrum. "You said if my situation ever changed, I should come talk to you. My situation hasn't changed. I'm still with Gabriel."

"But I thought you were going to change that. I thought you were going to leave him so we . . . I thought we were building on something, Jane, this tension between the two of us. We're good for each other. I can make you happy. Like that kiss the other night, that meant something."

"It was a kiss on the cheek, Adam," I said, alarmed by how quickly he'd gone from a normal tone of voice to this angry whine.

"But it meant something to me, Jane," he insisted, wrapping his fingers around mine.

"I'm sorry if you got the wrong impression. I'm not the kind of person who dumps one man to be with another."

Adam's blue eyes flashed. "But that's exactly why you should leave him. He's never around. I'm here. I'm right here. If he cared, he'd never leave you alone."

Adam's words stung. And the fact that they were probably true didn't make me any happier with him for saying them. This was all wrong. It was nothing like what I'd pictured. In my efforts to get away, somehow Adam had maneuvered so that I was backed up against the counter, trapped. With a feverish glint in his eyes, he plunged his hands into my hair and pulled my mouth against his. All of my emotional channels opened wide, sending a flood of images into my head. Adam kissing me in my kitchen. Adam standing in the florist, wondering what sort of flowers I would like. Adam sitting by the phone, dialing my number, and then hanging up before it rang. Adam and me talking at the funeral. But even in these fragile, human memories, I could tell that Adam didn't really see me, just an exaggerated version of me. My smiles were sharper. My eyes shone with a vicious glint. My boobs were much bigger.

Tentatively, I flexed the invisible muscles in my mind, reaching into Adam's memory. Images raced through my head, so quickly I couldn't grab onto any of them. Like a spinner on a child's game, the muddled pictures slowed to a stop. On Adam, walking into Whitlow's Funeral Home with his mother's layered salad. He was wondering how much time he had to spend at Bob's visitation to satisfy his family's obligation to the deceased and whether he would be able to catch the final quarter of the ball game when he got home. He stopped in his tracks when he saw me standing across the room with dishes in my hands. I looked vaguely familiar and definitely hot. There was something intriguing about my smile, something sharp and slightly intimidating. He knew he'd seen me around town before, but he couldn't remember my name. In the corner of my mind where I was able to feel my own emotions, this hurt. He hadn't had any clue who I was.

In Adam's memory, he spotted some church friend of his mother's at the visitation and snagged her arm politely.

"Hi, Mrs. Morse," he said, displaying his most winning smile. Adam offered a few platitudes about the sadness of the occasion and inquired after Mrs. Morse's health, even listening and making the appropriate sympathetic noises over her sciatica, before he finally looked in my direction and asked, "That girl over there, holding the coffee cups? Who is that?"

Mrs. Morse, who was a bridge friend of my grand-mother's and therefore had heard a detailed account of every stupid thing I had ever done, made a sour face. "That's Jane Jameson, Sherry's girl. I can't believe she had the nerve to show her face here. And that Ruthie is letting her mix with decent people." Mrs. Morse sniffed. "Some women just have no sense when it comes to their grandchildren."

"Why do you say that?" Adam asked.

"She's a . . ." Mrs. Morse looked around to see who might be listening and lowered her voice to a stage whis-per. "Vampire. Let herself get turned a few months ago."

Adam's eyes zipped back across the room to my face. Jameson—that name sounded familiar to him. He thought maybe he'd gone to school with a Jenny Jame-son, a pretty blond cheerleader who was a few years ahead of him. She'd had a sister named Jane. Come to think of it, he thought, I looked a little like that klutzy egghead girl who used to stare at him in math class. God, that girl used to annoy him, always had her hand up, sometimes before the teacher asked a question. But I sure looked good now, and I was a vampire, which was even better. He'd always wondered how far he could get with a vampire, without being bitten. And if I did bite, all the better.

He crossed the room while I had my back turned and deliberately bumped into me. In his mind, I saw my embarrassed smile flash, white and gleaming. "A-Adam, hi!" I stuttered.

Inside his head, he cringed at the sound of my voice. That much he remembered. I was definitely the know-it-all band geek. And I remembered him, as most of his former classmates did, even if he couldn't recall half of their names. That could definitely work to his advantage—

I broke away from him before I could hear any more. What was worse than the direct memories were the subconscious desires I felt filtering through his brain. Adam wanted to be my pet. Well, not my pet, necessarily, but any vampire's pet. He wanted the blood play, the dangerous, possibly injurious sex, the whole dominant female package. He could live his normal life every day but explore his darker compulsions at night. He wanted what I could give him.

I felt vaguely nauseated, glaring up at Adam as he grinned expectantly. I'd focused so much energy on this man. I'd thought of him almost constantly for years, never really getting over my infatuation with him, even as an adult. And he couldn't even remember my name.

This was one of those defining life moments where you feel as if you're standing on the edge of a slippery cliff with barbells tied around your neck. I could do this. I could be a Marianne. I could be impetuous and adventurous, live in the moment. I had wanted Adam for years. And I could have him, even for a short while. I could throw myself headlong into a fling without thinking of the future or how it would affect the people around me. I could think about me for once. And it wouldn't be completely superficial. A part of me still hoped for something as human and seminormal as a relationship with Adam. Maybe we could make it work . . .

And then the Elinor part of my brain kicked in. I would lose Gabriel. I would lose his friendship, his compassion, our conversations, everything I loved about spending time with him. Everything I'd built with him in the last few months would be gone. I would be trading someone who had saved a total stranger for someone who didn't care enough to remember the name of a girl he'd known since kindergarten. Adam was only interested in me now that I was dangerous. And he was kind of a tool.

Besides, Marianne ended up with Colonel Brandon, the handsome older guy with the mysterious background. And I already had one of those waiting for me. If I lost him, it would be because Gabriel left me, not because I ruined it all for my own personal Willoughby.

"You faked it," I said, laughing bitterly. "You pretended to remember me at the funeral. All you knew was that I looked like that 'annoying band geek' who used to sit behind you in math. You had no idea who I was. You didn't care enough to remember my name."

"Yeah, but then I got to know you again," Adam protested. "And I'm so glad I did, because otherwise, I might have missed out on us."

"There is no us," I said, peeling his fingers from my arm with just a tiny bit more force than necessary. "There's me, and there's you. And you are about to leave."

"Jane?"

Dick's voice sounded to my left, from the back of the

shop. He was glaring darkly at Adam, who hadn't even noticed that someone else had entered the room.

"It's fine," I said quietly. Dick stepped back into the office, to be near Andrea. But he was watching over us. I didn't have to be psychic to see the protective anger he felt toward Adam.

"Is this some sort of punishment?" Adam demanded, flexing his bruised fingers. "Because I didn't notice you when we were kids? Well, I'm sorry. I'm sorry I didn't see you. But things are different now. You're different now, special. I see you. I don't see anything but you. It's crazy. I can't stop thinking about you."

"I was something special back then, Adam," I told him sternly, shoving him back.

"Look, Jane, I'm sorry. We can make this work."

Adam advanced on me, his intent to kiss me again burning in his eyes. In the best persuasion voice I had ever used, I growled as he scrambled back toward me. "Adam, stop!"

Dutifully, he froze in his tracks. And I had no idea what to tell him. It seemed to go against all of my instincts to send him away, but I didn't want him anywhere near me anymore. I couldn't be terribly angry with him. He didn't want me. As much as that hurt, it wasn't the crime of the century. Adam didn't want me. He didn't know who I was. He wanted some image of me, some imagined persona that had nothing to do with me and everything to do with Adam wanting to buck against the hometown-boy role in which he'd been cast. Well, his self-image issues were not my problem.

I led him, biddable as a sacrificial lamb, to the door. I took his shoulders in my hands and forced him to meet my gaze. "I want you to forget about me. Forget about me being a vampire. Forget about you being fascinated with vampires and the whole dark-side-of-the-tracks thing. You should find someone more like you. I want you to find a nice, normal girl, a girl you really like. Not just because she's sexy but because you genuinely enjoy her company. Get married, have lots of babies, and be happy."

Denial flickered across Adam's features. His eyes clenched closed, then sprang open. He shook his head slightly. In a distracted, addled tone, he said, "I have to go."

"I know." I nodded and opened the door for him. With my wounded pride, I couldn't help but feel that it was better than he deserved, telling him to find someone he was compatible with. Part of me regretted not commanding him to stand on the corner of Main Street, naked, singing "I'm a Little Teapot."

"I have to go," he repeated. He hesitated as he walked toward the door.

"Yeah," I said, patting his shoulder, and he stumbled out.

I watched Adam stagger down the sidewalk to his SUV, struggle to pull his keys out of his pocket, and drive away. And I bid good-bye to my last mortal wish.

18

There is no information available on the inner workings of a were bachelor fete. It is assumed that the theory of mutually assured destruction prevents discussion by the participants.

—*Mating Rituals and Love Customs of the Were*

By Adam standards, Gabriel was downright charming, even when you took the blood drinking and tree-related killing into account. Now well aware of how good I really had it, I launched myself at him when he knocked on my door that night.

And he promptly untangled himself from my arms and set me on my feet.

Crap.

"Jane, is there anything you'd like to tell me?"

Gabriel had that "You've disappointed me" look on his face, which put me in an immediate confessional mode. "I forgot to tell my grandmother that she's marrying a ghoul."

Gabriel shot me a withering glare. "Jane."

"Fine, fine, I didn't forget. I just haven't found a way

to do it yet. I've had a lot of other stuff on my mind. Mr. Wainwright's funeral, the shop—"

"Let me rephrase. Would you like to tell me why Dick called me to recommend that I track down an Adam Morrow and, quote, 'put a boot up his ass' because of something he did at the shop?" he demanded, fangs fully extended, eyes flashing silver. "Or why you positively reek of another man?"

"I'm sensing an uncalled-for tone," I warned him.

"What do I have to do to make my feelings clear to you, Jane?" he thundered. "Are you deliberately trying to drive me insane? Am I going to have to follow you around town, staking my claim against your many admirers?"

"Which question do you want me to answer first?" I asked.

"I would like to know what your plans are for Mr. Morrow," he spat. "You said yourself that you had fantasies about him when you were young."

"Schoolgirl fantasies," I corrected him. "I said 'schoolgirl fantasies,' emphasis on the schoolgirl. I haven't been a schoolgirl in several years."

Gabriel's voice softened, responding to my quiet, cool tone. "He was the first boy you ever loved, even if it wasn't reciprocated."

"Thank you for putting it that way, very sensitive." I glared at him.

"And maybe some part of you is encouraging his attentions," he said, "whether it's to fulfill those fantasies or to avenge the rejected gawky girl you once were."

I stood gazing at him in shocked silence.

"You said you were gawky. Those were your words, not mine." Gabriel said, sounding slightly panicked when faced with my angry expression.

And suddenly, I was exhausted. All of the confidence in our relationship that I'd felt before just evaporated. Was this ever going to end? Couldn't I just have a normal, calm conversation with my boyfriend? Would he ever stop using that disappointed-father voice on me? I took a deep breath, trying to keep my voice as calm and even as possible. "I thought we'd settled this. I don't want to be with anyone else, Gabriel. I only want you. Adam made an overture, and I let him know that I didn't want anything to do with him."

Without a word, he turned on his heel and stormed toward the door. I used my superhuman speed to step around him and throw myself across the doorway. "No, no. No. Just leave it alone. Trust that I took care of it. Take a leap of faith that I managed to handle a situation on my own without completely screwing it up. Besides, if anyone should be asking the pointed questions around here, it's me. You're the one disappearing every time I turn around, not answering your phone, not staying where you say you're going to be."

Oh. That was one of those things I didn't plan on saying out loud.

Gabriel's mouth was set in a tight line as his face turned an ashy gray. "Don't stray from the point, Jane."

But the door was open. And damn it, I needed answers. Even Elinor has her limits. So I took a deep breath and chose my words carefully. "Gabriel, please tell me the truth. Where have you been going the last few months? Who's Jeanine?"

"This isn't something I can talk about right now."

"Then when?" I asked. "Why can't you tell me? Why don't you call me when you're out of town? What's the big secret?"

"There is no big secret, Jane."

"Look, when we started this, you were cryptic, but you didn't lie to me."

"I'm not lying!" he growled.

I threw up my hands. "Fine, editing the full truth to spare my feelings. The point is, you're keeping things from me. I don't want to be this girl, OK? I hate that I've gone here. I'm just trying to figure out why the person who says he loves me is lying to me."

"Don't," he said, clasping my shoulders. "Trust me, it's not as bad as whatever scenario you've come up with."

"Then just tell me what's going on so I can stop worrying about it!"

"I—I can't," he said finally.

"Damn it, Gabriel!" I shouted, stamping my foot. Unfortunately, the impact of my shoe on the floorboards shook a heavy porcelain vase from its shelf overhead, bringing it crashing down on Gabriel's head.

Well, everyone has a little bit of Marianne in them.

"That was an accident," I assured him, dodging just before he stomped down on the floorboards and sent a cuckoo clock crashing down on my head. "Ow!"

I shoved him hard, sending him sprawling into the

living room and over the couch. He popped up and used his inhuman speed to jump across the room and throw me to the floor. I kicked down, crushing his toes with my heel. He yowled, hopping on one foot and toppling over next to me. I rolled over him, pulling at his shirt as I called him filthy, unrepeatable names.

He caught my wrists, rolling and pinning me to the floor. He panted and broke into a wide grin. I gasped, slapping at his shoulders. I pulled my shirt back into place and struggled to untangle myself from his legs. "You're turned on right now, aren't you?"

"No!" he insisted, looking all offended and righteous for a moment, until his poker face broke and he was forced to say, "Yes, yes, I am."

I threw my head back and growled, shaking various bric-a-brac with the sound of my frustration.

Gabriel looked only slightly ashamed. "I can't help it. You know I love it when you're all spluttery and defensive and aggressive."

"This is sick. Gabriel, we can't keep doing this. We cannot resolve all of our problems with violent, dirty sex."

Gabriel groaned, leaning his forehead against my shoulder. "Oh, we're not going to go through this again, are we? Violent and dirty works for us, Jane."

"Well, it's not a healthy way to work things out. We need to learn to use our words. I'll start us off. Who the hell is Jeanine?"

"It's not what you think, Jane, I promise you. When the time is right, I'll explain everything—"

Zeb burst through the door, his head swathed in white

gauze. He looked as if he'd just escaped from a scene in *One Flew over the Cuckoo's Nest.*

I moaned and made use of several words. Obscene words, but at least I was using some.

Zeb was clearly disturbed by the sight of the two of us all wrapped up in each other, but he didn't take a hint to turn around and leave. "Hey, Jolene wanted me to drop these bridal-party itineraries off, so you'll be sure to be aware of your duties every minute of our wedding day."

"Zeb, this isn't a good time," I told him.

Gabriel seemed grateful for an interruption, but he didn't bother getting up or pulling his shirt back on. "Can we talk about the headgear?" He nodded to the gauze, which I now noticed was spotted with blood around his left ear.

"Everything's fine," he assured me as Gabriel and I disengaged and got to our feet. "It was just an accident."

"Zeb, you're wearing a sling around your head," I said, inspecting the dandy bandaging work and earning a slap on the hand from the testy groom. "You just got out of the eye patch!"

He sighed. "I was fishing with Jolene's family, and uncle Burt cast back—"

"You got a hook in the ear?" I cringed. "Oh, gross! Was the worm still on it?"

Zeb made a face. "No, but thanks for the silver lining. And news flash: the emergency room uses Super Glue instead of stitches now."

"He knew you were standing right behind him, and he cast back anyway?"

"Yeah, in fact, before he did it, he leaned over to Luke

and said, 'Watch this,'" Zeb muttered. "I'm getting pretty sick of this crap. Jolene's not doing anything about it. I'm starting to wonder . . . well, I just wish they would stop going for my head."

"Out of all of this, that's what you find disturbing?"

Zeb rolled his eyes at me. "No, I find it disturbing that Timothy Dalton ranks highest on your 'Which James Bond Would You Do?' list."

"*The Living Daylights* is highly underrated." I sulked when Gabriel gave me a surprised look.

"I don't know if I can do this," Zeb said. "I don't know if I can put up with her family. It's never going to stop, and she's never going to want to move away from them. I just don't get why she wants to stay close to them."

He looked up at me, and a film of unshed tears seemed to be obscuring his normally clear brown eyes. "Jane, isn't there anything you want to tell me?"

"I'm sort of out of my element here, Zeb." I looked up to Gabriel. "Will you please talk to him? Have some sort of man-to-man exchange?"

Gabriel cleared his throat and placed a fatherly hand on Zeb's shoulder. "Loving family members do not aim for each other's soft tissues."

I made my angry-girlfriend face at him. He sighed and dug deeper into the wisdom well. "Zeb, you're dealing with a lot of dominant alpha-male personalities here. You're going to have to do something to show them that you're not a beta. You have to establish dominance. The next time the cousins are gathered, walk up to the biggest, strongest one and stare him right in the eye. And tell him to go fetch something for you. Use those exact words. 'Fetch me a soda' or 'Fetch me that chair.' And if he hesitates, keep staring at him until he folds . . . or he'll beat you severely. Either way, it will improve the pack's respect for you."

"I thought that was what you were supposed to do the first day you go to prison," I muttered.

"Jolene loves you," Gabriel said. "No matter what happens with her family, you just have to focus on that." He glanced up at me. "And remember that if she does things that don't make any sense to you, she might be trying to do what's best for you both."

I narrowed my eyes at him. He shrugged.

Zeb was placated with more generic relationship advice and the promise that Gabriel would serve as his personal vampire bodyguard during the wedding festivities. We finally shoved him out the door, and I turned on Gabriel.

"I'm not done with you," I told him.

He gave an easy grin. "Well, that's nice to hear."

I glared at him, and it was if he suddenly remembered that we were in the middle of a disagreement when Zeb burst in. "Oh."

I threaded my fingers through his and locked eyes with him. "Do you want to be in a relationship with me?"

"I love you, Jane. More than I've loved anyone, I love you."

I smiled at the warm feeling that spread through my chest at those words. It was like having a heartbeat again. "Then don't keep things from me."

"Just give me a little more time," he begged. "I'll explain everything when the time is right. Just wait a little while longer."

I took a deep breath, looking deep into Gabriel's eyes. If anyone had proven his devotion to me, it was Gabriel. Even if that devotion was destructive, it had a single focus, and that was me. I held his interest even when I was just my "annoying" human self. He didn't consider my brain or personality something to overcome. He'd saved me. He'd killed for me. He'd loved me. And for all of that, I owed him a little bit of trust.

"I love you, too," I said, cupping his face in my hands. I locked eyes with him, leveling him with my gaze. "So I'll wait. I want you to tell me what's causing you so much stress. Maybe I can help. But I want you to do it in your own time. However, you should know that if that time doesn't come soon—"

He nodded. "You will threaten any number of my orifices. I understand."

"Is it orifices or orifici?" I asked.

"I'm rather shocked that you don't know," he admitted.

The countdown to the wedding was two weeks. It was a slow night in the shop, and I had just given up on sorting through any old boxes after a traumatic incident in which Dick had to kill a rather large spider for me. I swear that thing chased me onto that chair.

When Dick returned, I had put the spider's box in the alley and opened up my file of notes for what Zeb had termed "Operation Undead Gigolo."

"What are you doing?" Dick asked, peering over my shoulder. "Oh, honey, this is worse than I thought. Normal, well-adjusted girls do not spend Friday nights looking through autopsy reports."

"When have you ever known me to be well adjusted or normal?" I asked.

"I concede."

"I'm looking into the guy my grandma is marrying. He seems sketchy. He drinks pig's blood. According to this, he's dead." I showed him the death certificate. "And he's been married several times to women who don't quite make it past their first anniversary. He's not registered on any of the official undead databases, but according to the chapel that handled his burial, he went to his grave intact, so it's possible he's a vampire."

"Wouldn't it be easier just to ask him whether he's one of us?" Dick asked, looking over Wilbur's coroner's report.

"I would, but my grandma Ruthie seems to be actively avoiding me. She doesn't come to Mama's house if she knows I'm going to be there. She screens my calls. She won't let me near Wilbur, but I don't know if it's because he's trying to hide something or she's afraid of me embarrassing her. There's no legitimate address listed for this guy, and the last three homes he shared with the corpse brides have been sold. I went to his grave to see if there was anything abnormal about it. It seemed fine. I wasn't about to try to dig him up and see if the coffin was empty, because that's how horror movies start. Dick, are you even listening to me?"

"Huh," Dick said, looking over Wilbur's death report. "Sorry, no. This is weird."

"Weird ha-ha? Or weird our territory weird?"

Dick turned the paperwork to get a better look. "Well, the nurse who did the CPR on him, Jay Lemuels, I know him. He's one of us."

"Where can we find Jay?" I asked.

Dick checked the grandfather clock on the wall. "This time of night, probably Club Rainn. It's a vampire bar. Good blood, bad sound system."

Dick jangled the keys out of his pocket.

"What are you doing?" I asked.

"We're going," he told me. "The night is young, and we're immortal, and there are unanswered questions afoot. If that doesn't make a case for a couple of beers and a ridiculously high cover charge, Stretch, I don't know what does."

"The last time I went out on the town with you, I ended up a suspect in Walter's murder."

"I'll be there to keep an eye on you."

"I don't know if that will keep me out of trouble or just get me into it more efficiently."

"Come on," he said. "It's Karaoke Night."

"OK, but you have to sing one Kenny Rogers song in a falsetto," I said, poking him in the chest.

"I will sing," he said, tossing me my jacket. "But only because my version of 'The Gambler' is both inspirational and erotic."

"Gross."

* * *

We climbed into Dick's beat-up transportation, which smelled suspiciously of burnt rope. There were dozens of empty blood bottles on the floor and what might have been counterfeit Gap jeans. I turned back to him. "If we get pulled over, am I going to have to tell the nice policeman that I've never met you before and I have no idea how those stolen car stereos got into the trunk?"

"I make no apologies for how I make my living, so to speak," Dick said. "I am simply a businessman, a servant to supply and demand."

"As long as someone else pays for the supply, you can meet the demand."

We continued this philosophical discussion of the entrepreneurial spirit until we pulled into the parking lot of Club Rainn. From the exterior, the club was pretty nondescript, aside from not having windows or a sign. Club Rainn offered all-the-undead-can-drink for free to attract vampires, like shooting fish in a barrel. The humans were the cash cows that kept this place going. As soon as we hit the door, the overpowering smell of blood practically knocked me to my knees. Desperation, fear, arousal. The sour, stale scent of need.

It was the sort of place Chris Hansen was always exposing on *Dateline,* where sad humans offer themselves up as midnight snacks to vampires without dignity. These were basically overgrown teenagers in too much makeup, too much leather. In fact, they'd look like total doofuses if the lights were on.

The DJ played only two records, Nine Inch Nails' *The Downward Spiral* and the *Blade* soundtrack. It was in-

congruous with the decor, which was early American
bordello. Red flocked wallpaper, dark ornately carved
furniture, uncomfortably stylized red velvet couches. To
be honest, it looked like River Oaks before Aunt Jettie got
hold of it. Besides the hurricane-lamp sconces, the only
wall decorations were oil paintings of historical figures
who were supposedly vampires, from Vlad the Impaler
and Elizabeth Bathory to Mercy Brown.

"I take it Gabriel has never brought you here?" Dick
asked, taking in my horrified expression. "He probably
thinks it blasphemous or unpatriotic or one of those
terms that basically means he's a tight-ass with no sense
of humor."

"You know that you're not going to get me to play
along when you say something like that," I told him.
"You say you're interested in Andrea and I'm just a
friend. You've even been getting along—well, tolerating
Gabriel's presence. Why are you still making those comments about Gabriel?"

Dick mulled that over for a moment. "Force of habit.
What the—" Dick was interrupted as a pale, lanky man
with a shock of badly dyed black curly hair knelt before
me and kissed my sandaled feet. Unfortunately, the san-
dals were pretty old, so I can only imagine how funky
that must have been.

"Um, can I help you?" I asked, finally resorting to
kicking him slightly to get him off my foot.

He peered up at me. "You are a Lonely One, are you
not? A Night Childe?"

"I'm not exactly burning up the social scene, but I

wouldn't classify myself as lonely. It's not as if I have a bunch of cats or something."

A similarly pasty girl with stringy platinum hair and smudged kohl around her eyes joined him at my feet. Dick snickered, but covered it by taking a swig of beer. "We wish to drink at the fount of your wisdom," the blonde whispered.

"Show us the way," Floppy Black Hair intoned.

"Jason—"

Floppy Black Hair objected. "My name is Bowan Ravenswood, ancient one."

"Your name is Jason Turner, and we went to Vacation Bible School together." I pulled my foot out of his grip once again.

"Let me—"

"Remove your hand, or that will be the last time you know the touch of a woman."

His smile was feverish. "I would be happy to have you initiate me."

"Jason, go home, or I'll have my mama call your mama."

I grimaced at Dick as the pasty pair slinked away.

"Did you set that up?" I demanded. "Is that like the vampire version of the TGI Friday's wait staff singing 'Happy Birthday'?"

Dick looked completely innocent for the first time since I'd met him. "No, that was totally spontaneous."

"Your lack of guile upsets me," I said, watching as Jason approached a more receptive-looking Lonely One. I shook my head.

As another whey-faced youth approached with beseeching eyes, I held up a hand and told him "No." I took a long sip of my drink and closed my eyes.

Sensing female distress, the bartender, a tall brunet with heavily lined brown eyes and a gold ankh stud in his ear, replaced my drink with a flourish and winked at me. "So, what brings you here tonight, besides karaoke?"

Dick cleared his throat, drawing the barkeep's unsettling attention from me. "We're looking for Jay."

"He still owe you money?" the brunet asked. "I don't want any trouble, not with this crowd in here."

"Yeah, but I gave up on collecting it a while ago," Dick said. "Jay's got more sob stories than an *Oprah* episode."

"In that case, he's right behind you, warming up for his Pat Benatar medley," the bartender said, grinning at me. "Get a couple of drinks in them, and every vampire thinks he's Celine Dion."

I laughed as Dick turned and spotted a tall, towheaded vampire by the karaoke machine. Jay almost smiled, then realized who he was looking at and bolted.

"Go to the back exit," Dick said before dashing after him through the crowd. "Cut him off if he circles back."

"What is this, *Cagney and Lacey*?" I asked. "I am not Tyne Daly."

The barkeep shrugged. "Just take it outside, please."

Dick had caught up with Jay before he reached the front door, making my "circling back" unnecessary.

Jay had the face of an angel but apparently no spine. Strong chin, Roman nose, full pouting lips, the deepest blue eyes I've ever seen. And because of the parallels to Adam, I took a bit of an instant dislike to him. His eyes darted wildly as I approached. "Is this is about that cash I owe you? Because I didn't know where to find you after your trailer burned down. My phone got cut off because of a mix-up with the billing. My dog got sick. Who is she? Is this your enforcer? What's she going to do? Is she going to cut off my nose? I told you, man, not necessary. I'll get the money to you—"

"No, Jay, I kissed that money good-bye a long time ago," Dick said, looking up to me. "Jay has a fixation on someone cutting off his nose."

"To spite his face?" I chirped. Both Jay and Dick gave me blank looks. "*Nobody* gets me!"

"Jane, this handsome reprobate is Jay," he said, standing Jay up and dusting off his shoulders. "Jay, this is my friend Jane."

"Hey there, how you doing?" he said, grinning with the relief of an unexpected reprieve.

"Dick's told me all about you. Don't even try," I lied, my tone a little snottier than I usually used in an introduction. I would not be charmed by a pretty face, I swore. I would not be charmed by a pretty face.

"Just because I'm not collecting doesn't mean I won't let her kick you in the goods," Dick warned him. "She's got a lot of repressed anger."

"If it's not about the money, why are you after me?" Jay whined.

Dick nodded to me, which apparently meant I was in charge of questioning. I guess I *was* Tyne Daly.

"A few years ago, you were working at Sunnyside Retirement Village—"

"Yeah, they fired me over a few missing watches. Can you believe that?" he huffed, indignant.

"I really can't. In fact, I think it might have had a little more to do with you turning one of the patients into a vampire."

"What?" Jay cried. "Why would I do that? They were half-dead anyway."

"So you have no idea how Wilbur Goosen is still walking around?"

Jay gave me an innocent look that I'm sure many girls have lost their wallets and/or undergarments to. "Not really, no."

Dick flicked Jay's ear. "Talk to her, Jay."

"Why do you keep doing that?" I asked when Jay yowled.

Dick paused flicking. "Because it bothers him. A lot."

"OK, OK, so I turned the old guy. Nothing wrong with that," Jay insisted. "He even paid me, a thousand dollars. He was going to rat me out, man. I needed that job. Do you know how many night-nurse positions there are for men out there? Not a lot. People seem to think that we can't be trusted around the patients or something."

"I can't imagine," I commented, my voice as dry as dust.

"I didn't even give him the full dose. Just enough to make him wake up in three days. Sort of a halfsie."

"So you did turn him into a ghoul? Dang it, Jay," Dick growled. "You know we're not supposed to do that."

"What's the big deal?" Jay whined. "It's not like he would have been very strong anyway."

I flicked Jay's ear myself. "Yeah, no big deal. He's just been bumping off human wives for about fifteen years, but what's a few old ladies? I mean, you got a thousand dollars out of the deal, right?"

"What's it to you?" Jay whined. "I've heard about you. You've had your share of run-ins with the council."

"I'm going to be his step-granddaughter," I said, flicking his ear again. "Ass!"

"Ow!" Jay cried. "Stop with the ears. Look, I was supposed to get Wilbur out of the home before the coroner got there. That was part of the deal. He wasn't supposed to be declared dead or leave a paper trail. I mean, this was before the Coming Out. Nobody knew we existed. But I'd never made another vampire before. I didn't know how tired it made you. I went to my trunk to lie down, and by the time I woke up, it was already daylight, and the body had been moved. So I went to the funeral home—"

"Because you were hoping he'd been embalmed and wouldn't rise."

"How was I supposed to know his family wouldn't pay for a full funeral?" He snorted. "Cheap bastards."

"Some people." Dick shook his head piteously as we departed for his car.

"So, we're square, right?" Jay called. "I don't owe you, and you're not going to call council? Right? Dick?"

Exhausted and confused, I slumped through the front door at River Oaks and passed the living-room door only to skid to a stop and backtrack. No, the eyes don't lie. Mr. Wainwright and Aunt Jettie. Kissing.

"What the?" They jumped apart. "What is going on? Were you two making out?"

"No!" Aunt Jettie cried.

"Yes!" Mr. Wainwright admitted.

"Oh, come on. Dating Grandpa Fred wasn't enough, now you've moved on to my surrogate grandpa? Wait, what about Grandpa Fred? Does he know?"

"Yes," Aunt Jettie said, the slightest hint of color slipping into her translucent cheeks. "He was very upset about it. He and all of your other step-grandpas are refusing to speak to me. It's cut me off from almost half the dead people in town."

I glared at her. "So, you were sneaking off to be together."

"We didn't want to upset you or make you worry," Mr. Wainwright said.

"We're in love."

"Oh, yuck. I mean, I'm happy for you, but this is just a lot to absorb. We'll deal with this later, OK? After I've had some sleep. I love you guys, both of you. But for the love of all that's good and decent, make yourselves invisible or something when you do that."

19

While were clans place special emphasis on male leadership, it's important to remember to show proper respect to the packs' older women. They don't lose their teeth until well into their 90s.

—*Mating Rituals and Love Customs of the Were*

I didn't know if or how I was going to approach Grandma Ruthie with Jay's information about Wilbur. Fortunately, that decision was taken out of my hands when I woke a few nights later to find her in my living room. With Wilbur. And my parents. And my sister.

I guess I shouldn't have been surprised. No matter how many times I changed the locks, Grandma Ruthie always managed to get in. River Oaks being her ancestral home, she felt she has the right to come and go whenever she wants. I considered an electric fence, but Jettie said it would ruin the aesthetics of the property.

"What are you guys doing here?" I asked.

"Well, I thought that since you haven't been able to make it to dinner lately, we would bring dinner to you.

I'll just pop this into the oven to keep it warm." Mama clapped her hands in her excitement over "roast on the go." She does love to take her food on tour. "I wanted to give you and your sister time to talk," Mama stage-whispered as she hustled me into the kitchen. "I think she's ready to apologize to you."

"Couldn't have stopped her, huh?" I muttered to my dad.

He shook his head sadly. "I tried. I really tried."

"Why shouldn't I be able to come see my own grand-daughter?" Grandma Ruthie sniffed, stroking a china shepherdess that Jettie had loved. "Besides, I grew up in this house. The doors of River Oaks are never closed to an Early."

Aunt Jettie, who appeared behind Grandma Ruthie, rolled her eyes.

"They will be if I get that electric fence," I muttered.

Grandma's watery blue eyes narrowed at me. "What's that?"

"Nothing, Grandma," I said, forcing myself to sit without any petulant flopping.

"Well, I think it's nice to see a big family getting to-gether like this," Wilbur said, making himself comfort-able on the couch and grabbing the remote control. "Do you get the Weather Channel, Janie?"

"You are losing control of your own home, pumpkin," Aunt Jettie said.

"I know."

"Well, are you going to offer us something to drink, or do you normally let guests die of thirst?" Grandma

Ruthie demanded in a tone that had me jumping back to my feet. Man, she was good at that.

"Would you like some iced tea?" I asked.

"Sweet, please," she said.

Jettie appeared at my elbow as I emptied the tea jug. To be honest, I only kept it around for Zeb and Jolene, and I had no idea when it had been brewed. "Lace it with Ex-Lax. It will do her some good."

"Don't start," I warned her quietly. "Let's just get everybody out of here as quickly as possible."

"What was that, honey?" Mama asked as she puttered around my cabinets looking for dishes that had been washed up to her standards.

"Nothing," I said, pouring the tea into a proper glass, with lemon. No laxative enhancements. I turned to find Jenny standing behind me, arms crossed, jaw set.

"Yes?"

Jenny threw up her hands. "Well?"

"Well what?"

"Well, Mama said you had something to say to me," Jenny ground out. "She said you were ready to apologize."

I shot Mama a scathing look. "Well, that's funny, because Mama said you were ready to apologize to me."

"Why would I apologize to you?" Jenny demanded.

"I don't know, for suing me? And by the way, I don't think my lawyer would appreciate your being here right now."

"Now, girls," Mama sighed.

"I'm suing you to get what I deserve!" Jenny cried.

"Trust me, you don't want what you deserve," I shot back.

"This was obviously pointless." Jenny groaned. "Enjoy your dinner, Mama."

"No, Jenny, don't go," Mama wheedled as Jenny stomped out. "You just have to stay and talk this through."

Grandma Ruthie must have cut Jenny off at the living room, because she and Wilbur were marching my sister back into the kitchen.

"You don't have to go, Jenny. You have every right to be here," Grandma told her. "You're staying."

"Yeah, I'm sure there are way more insulting things you can say to me in my own house." I grabbed a bottle of Faux Type O out of the fridge because I knew it would bother Jenny that much more.

"It's not your home," Grandma Ruthie sniffed. "It belongs to all Earlies."

"Well, that's a handy piece of information. I'll keep you guys in mind the next time I'm writing out the property-tax check. Or the check for the new boiler. Or the next time I have to make roof repairs."

Jenny huffed, indignant. "If it's such a burden—"

"It's not a burden. I'm just tired of you and Grandma Ruthie talking as if I fell into this no-maintenance pile of clover. It takes time, hard work, and money to maintain this house. And frankly, I'm better prepared to do that than either of you."

"Because you're a vampire," Grandma asked snidely.

"Yeah, because I'm a vampire. And you know, that's the first time you've actually said the v-word. So thank you."

"I don't want to go through this business again," Grandma sighed, waving my concerns away like buzzing insects.

"I don't think we went though this business the first time," I said. "You've mostly ignored me and any mention of my being a vampire."

"You know, when I was a young woman, people stayed dead."

"Sorry. This must be a real inconvenience for you."

"Don't you sass me!" she screeched.

Wilbur wagged his finger at me. "Young lady, you need to learn some respect for your elders."

"Wilbur, I don't think you want to get involved in this," I told him.

"Let's all calm down and talk about this like rational people," Daddy said.

"Jane, Jenny, stop it. You're upsetting your father," Mama said, wringing one of my dishtowels into knots.

"Sherry, hush. Jenny and Jane have been due for this conversation for a long time. I think we need to let them have it." Daddy tried to pull Mama and Grandma out the door, toward the living room, but Grandma wouldn't budge.

"No, there are things that Jane needs to hear," Grandma Ruthie insisted. "You all have coddled her for way too long and let her get away with saying or doing whatever she wants. It's time she heard the truth about how this family feels about her letting herself get turned into a vampire. We're ashamed, Jane. We're embarrassed. What you've let yourself become reflects badly on us all."

Daddy's face flushed, and he actually raised his voice to yell, "Don't you put words into my mouth, Ruthie—"

"And Jenny was only trying to show you what you're facing when you go out among decent people." Grandma sniffed. "Decent people don't want a vampire living in their neighborhood. You're just making things harder for yourself. I really think the best thing for you to do is to deed the house over to Jenny. She can sell her house and give you some of the proceeds to start fresh."

"She's finally lost her mind," Jettie whispered. "Somebody slap her. Hell, slap her just to entertain me."

"Now, Mama, you're not making any sense!" Mama exclaimed. "You need to sit down and rest. You're not yourself right now."

"Start fresh where, exactly?" I asked Grandma Ruthie, the icy calm in my voice making the color drain from Mama's cheeks.

"A big city, like New York or San Francisco, where you'd find more of your kind," she said, patting my hand for about a millisecond before drawing back.

"In other words, a big city that's thousands of miles away from you or anyone you know," I said in the calmest tone I could manage.

"Well, yes." She preened, pleased that I was seeing things her way at last. Wilbur smiled broadly, the slightest edge of his canines peeking out over his lips, as he wrapped an arm around my grandmother. He looked so damn smug that the following just sort of slipped out:

"You know what, I wasn't going to do this. But since you brought up the whole undead-shame thing, I think you should know that your husband-to-be is not quite fully living himself."

"Jane, what are you talking about?" Mama asked.

"She's just being dramatic," Grandma Ruthie huffed. "You know how she is."

"Yes, I just make random stuff up, like, for instance, that I saw Wilbur walking out of a vampire bar at four A.M. And also I did a little research on Wilbur's special macrobiotic health shakes that you so lovingly cart around for him, the key ingredient of which is *Sus scrofa domestica*. Common domestic pig. You've been hauling around pig's blood in your precious Aigner bag."

Wilbur didn't respond. He merely stared bullet holes through me with those rheumy brown eyes. Grandma, however, turned four different shades of pissed off and seemed to be struck mute. It was too good to last.

"You may have gone too far there," Aunt Jettie murmured.

"What a horrible thing to say! Why? Why would you say that?" Grandma Ruthie cried. "You're always so sarcastic and hurtful when it comes to your step-grandfathers. So hurtful, so judgmental. You think I don't hear your little comments, but I do. Can you tell me why you don't think I deserve a little bit of happiness, a little comfort, in my last years?"

"You've been having your last years since I was in middle school!" I cried. "And I think you've had more than your share of happiness and comfort in your last years."

"Why don't you like Wilbur?" Grandma whined.

"It's not that I don't like Wilbur. I don't know him well enough to dislike him. No offense, Wilbur. But there are things in his background that don't add up, things I think you should know about before you launch yourself down the aisle again. For instance, do you know how many times he's been married?"

"Just once, to his high-school sweetheart," Grandma said, dismissing me.

"Six times," I corrected her, and nodded to her engagement ring. "You might want to ask yourself how many women have worn that tasteful solitaire over the years."

"You told me—you—you told me once!" Grandma Ruthie exclaimed, staring at Wilbur and her left hand in alternating horror.

"I don't think you can afford to throw stones here, Ruthie," Daddy said.

"John!" Mama cried.

"That's all I'm saying!" Daddy said, throwing up his arms.

"Oh, Wilbur was married once, when he was still living. See, he actually kicked the bucket in 1993. But this bachelor ghoul didn't let that keep him down."

Mama *tsk*ed. "Now, Jane, I know you're upset, but that's a very unkind thing to say."

"No, Jane, there's no reason to be nasty," Jenny said absently. She'd paled and was sitting at the kitchen table, running her fingers over the smoothed old wood. She looked as if she was going to blow some very un-Martha-like chunks on my hand-hooked rag rug.

"I mean, he's an actual ghoul. He's a half-turned vampire. He's the Splenda of vampires. I don't think he would hurt you just because of his ghoulness. I'm only saying something because of his history. I'm afraid that if you marry him, something's going to happen to you. I just don't want anything to happen to you," I said, realizing that was true as the words left my mouth.

"Really?"

"We don't always get along, Grandma, but I don't wish you actual harm."

Grandma sniffed. "Oh, Janie."

The degree of emotional openness triggered some sort of channel into Grandma Ruthie's psyche. I had brief flashes from her thoughts, like old hand-tinted photos. She was remembering me as a little girl, in a starched pink linen dress, ready to go to church. Handing her a card I'd made for her birthday. And then the images turned to the time I dropped wedding ring number three down her garbage disposal. The disastrous Teeny Tea when I tripped and spilled the contents of my teacup down the front of Mrs. Neel's Sunday dress. All of the times I embarrassed her. All of the times I disappointed.

It was no wonder I'd let something like this happen to me, she was thinking. It was just the capstone to a life dedicated to embarrassing my family. If my mother had listened to her, Grandma Ruthie thought, and sent me to that reform school in New Mexico, I would have married some long-distance truck driver by now and disappeared.

"Well, everyone has problems, Jane," Grandma said, giving Wilbur a long appraising look.

"But—but—ghoul!" I sputtered.

Wilbur snorted. "Oh, and you're all so noble. Vampires walking around all more powerful than thou. As if you don't have all the same weaknesses as us halfsies. Well, I got news for you, missy. Back in my day, vampires knew their place in the world, underground. I think it's time I dished out some tough love."

"Are you serious?" I asked.

Wilbur cocked his fist like an Atlantic City pier boxer. "Time to put your money where you big, fanged mouth is, Jane."

"I'm not going to hit you," I told him. "Besides, don't you have any old-fashioned rules about not hitting girls?"

Wilbur circled me, throwing practice swings. "The way I figure it, you stopped being a girl a while ago."

"So did Grandma." I threw my hands toward my grandmother. "Besides, you can't fight me, old man. You don't have vampire strength."

"No, but I do have this," he said, pulling the handle off his cane and revealing a hidden stake.

"Wilbur!" Grandma Ruthie cried. "What on earth do you think you're doing?"

"Oh, come on, who hides a stake in their cane? What's next? Are you going to make nunchakus out of your dentures?" I yelled.

"Wilbur, don't you dare!" Grandma cried.

Wilbur flew at me, a surprisingly spry ball of geriatric

fury. I managed to grab the hand with the stake and turn so I wouldn't land on top of him as we fell to the floor. Both for the safety of his hip and my own mental well-being.

Unfortunately, Wilbur took advantage of this and rolled over me, his rank feta breath making my eyes water. I watched as yellowed, crooked fangs extended from Wilbur's canines, a long string of drool stretching between his jaws. I pressed my head back against the tiled floor to try to put as much distance between our faces as possible. Faintly, I heard my dad yelling, my mother crying, and the dull thud of my sister passing out and sliding to the floor.

"This is my family now, Jane," Wilbur hissed, his wiry peppercorn eyebrows furrowing as he tried to force the stake from my hand. "And in my family, we don't tolerate sassy mouths."

"Get off of me, you crazy . . . old . . . man!" I grunted. It took all of the strength in my legs to kick up and launch him into the refrigerator. Wilbur landed in a heap, his neck making a sickening crunch as his head skidded across the tile.

"Wilbur!" Grandma screamed. "Jane! What did you do?"

I hauled myself to my feet, cracking my own vertebrae back into place as my family stared in horror at Wilbur's lifeless body. Their silent shock was palpable. Mama was sobbing quietly as she frantically tried to revive an unconscious Jenny. Daddy moved toward Wilbur, then stumbled back on his rear when Wilbur's eyes sprang open.

"That was entirely unnecessary, young lady," Wilbur snarled, rolling to his knees and cracking his neck as the bones healed. Mama cried out and wobbled against the table legs. Wilbur pushed to his feet and sneered at me. "You have no respect for your elders."

"I guess the respectful thing would be just standing there and letting you stake me in my own kitchen." I tossed the offending wooden dagger into the garbage. "And by the way, one word, two syllables: Altoid."

"Why, you little—" Wilbur growled. "I won't stand here and be insulted like this. Ruthie, I'll call you soon."

"No, Wilbur, don't go!" Grandma Ruthie cried as Wilbur stomped out the back door. She turned on me, lip on full tremble. "Jane, I want you to go apologize to Wilbur right now."

"What? No!"

Grandma stomped her little foot and pointed me toward the door. "That man is going to be your grandpa, Jane. You need to make nice."

I stared at Grandma. "Are you kidding me? I tell you that he might be the Half-Moon Hollow equivalent to Bluebeard, he attacks me with a stake, and you still want to marry him?"

Grandma pressed her lips together. "You know, Jane, if you weren't so picky, it might be you standing at the altar."

"Now, let's not say something we regret later," said Mama, who was slowly recovering from Wilbur's abrupt departure. Jenny, while conscious, still looked a little green around the gills.

With a sniff in my direction, Grandma Ruthie grabbed her raincoat. "I will not set foot in this house again until you apologize to Wilbur and to me, Jane Enid Jameson."

As the door slammed behind her, I yelled, "Can I get that in writing?"

Jenny stood on wobbly legs and hobbled to the table, where she carefully slipped her tote bag onto her shoulder. "This is too much for me. I'll call you later, Mama."

"Wait, Jenny. I'm sorry. I'm really sorry. I hate this. I hate feeling this way, not being able to talk to you about anything. Look, there's been enough emotional . . . stuff for one evening. Why don't you just sit down and, you know, return to a normal color, and we'll—" I stopped as I jostled the bag on Jenny's arm and heard a clanking noise. "What the? What do you have in here, Jen?" I laughed as Jenny's eyes grew wide. She clutched at the bag, setting off a series of jangling and clanking.

"What the hell do you have in here, Jenny?" I demanded, pulling at the bag.

"None of your business!" Jenny yelled. "It's for a class I'm taking."

I jerked the bag away from her and looked inside to find a set of porcelain baby cups engraved with our great-grandmother's initials, a heavy silver pie plate, a brush-and-comb set carved from ivory, and several pieces of lace tatted sometime in the late 1900s. These items had been kept carefully displayed in rooms all over the house. The brush-and-comb set was taken from my own dresser. I stared up at my sister, my chest tight and cold at the shock of her betrayal. "You're stealing from me? You went into my room and *stole* from me? Do you have any idea—I mean, I *expect* Grandma Ruthie to steal from me, but you? I never thought you'd actually sink that low."

"I-it's not stealing," Jenny stammered. "I'm just taking a few things that have sentimental value for me. Some of them should be mine, anyway. Grandma Ruthie says—"

"Grandma Ruthie doesn't live here. She doesn't have any say over what leaves this house and what doesn't. We just talked about this, Jenny!"

"I deserve part of my family heritage!" Jenny yelled. "You couldn't possibly appreciate all that you have. And you don't have children to pass it on to."

"Oh, for goodness sake. You're right, I can't pass it along to my children. But guess what? I'm never going to die, which means I will always be around to take care of those precious antiques you're so enamored of. It also means your kids will never inherit them. And if anything ever happens to me, I'm leaving everything to Zeb!"

"You *wouldn't*!" Jenny gasped.

"Oh, yes, I would." I laughed. "And Zeb never uses coasters."

Jenny screeched, "Mama!"

"Now, girls—"

"Stop calling us girls, Mama. We're grown women, and we have real, court-documented problems," I said. "Will you just suck it up and pick a side, already? Tell Jenny that it's wrong to steal from me."

"You're the one who won't share!" Jenny yelled, punching my arm.

"Oh, please." I slapped her shoulder and sent her skidding into the table.

"I will treat you like grown women when you act like grown women," Mama said, her voice edging toward hysteria. "And I will not pick a side, because you're both being ridiculous. Now, either kiss and make up or get out of my kitchen."

"It's actually my kitchen," I reminded her before turning on Jenny. "You, however, should feel free to get out. You're not welcome here anymore."

Mama squeezed my shoulder. "Now, Jane—"

"What?" I demanded. "She's lucky I'm not calling the cops on her skinny ass."

"Oh, go ahead and try it." Jenny pulled her now-empty bag onto her shoulder. "I'm sure the cops will be sympathetic to some deadbeat bloodsucker. They'd probably hand me the keys to the house."

"Jenny," Mama whispered, shocked at the use of an undead slur.

"Oh, stop it, Mama. stop protecting her. Why can't we all just say it? Jane's a filthy, disgusting vampire. She let herself get bitten. If I'd done that, you'd never speak to me again, but because it's Jane, it's OK. We all just have to accept it, act like it's normal. But it's not normal!"

"What kind of glue have you been sniffing?" I demanded. "What do you mean, accept it? When have you ever—"

"Shut up, Jane!" Jenny barked. "I don't ever want to speak to you again. I don't want you near my boys. I don't want you coming to my house. If I see you out on the street, I'm going to pretend I don't know you."

Even as the words stung, I set my jaw and shoved open the back door. "Well, you should have had plenty of practice at that by now."

Jenny stomped out to her sedan and fumbled with the keys.

"Here, you forgot this!" I yelled. With red-tinged vision, I hefted the silver pie plate off the table and slung it at the rear window of her car. She shrieked as the glass exploded, shattering with a satisfying symphony of crackles. "It's all yours!"

I slammed the kitchen door, wincing as the silver burns smoked on my hands. At my parents' horrified expressions, I felt slightly ashamed. I made a halfhearted wave toward the door. "She started it."

20

Like all couples, were couples will argue. Unfortunately for the males, female weres are much better at holding out for an apology, which leads to groveling.

—*Mating Rituals and Love Customs of the Were*

After so many tours of bridesmaid duty, I didn't feel I needed to attend wedding rehearsals anymore. I was so, so wrong.

Zeb and Jolene were marrying in a clearing a respectable distance away from the house but very near the barn. With fairy lights strung in the trees and luminaries in the nearby pond, the night took on a sort of cozy *Lord of the Rings* quality . . . or maybe it was *Lord of the Flies*.

The bride's side was eager to get through the rehearsal as it put them one step closer to eating. The groom's side was sparse. Mama Ginger had apparently told most of her relatives that the wedding was canceled after Jolene was committed to a hospital for the criminally insane.

The first surprise of the evening was Dick's arrival with Andrea on his arm. She looked cool and composed in her floaty dawn-colored sundress, not giving any hint of being held hostage or blackmailed. I could only assume that Dick had finally charmed her into submission. Of course, Dick was still Dick. He wore a vintage "fake tuxedo imprinted on a T-shirt" shirt. But he seemed ecstatically happy as he seated Andrea on the groom's side and took his place with the gathering bridal party.

I winked at him. "It's good to know that occasionally, love—or relentless, unremitting courtship bordering on harassment—will win out. I take it she's coming to the wedding, too?"

"I think she's waiting to see how it goes. She said she'd let me know after the dinner," Dick said. Gabriel snickered, making Dick consider his words. "You know, it sounds sad when I say it out loud like that."

"So, it's like an audition date. It's Shakespearean, sacrificing yourself on the altar of dignity," I assured him.

"I've been with hundr—" He shot a speculative look at me. "Well, a lot of women. I like women."

"Obviously," Gabriel muttered.

"I like them. I like the way they dress, the way they smell, the sound of their voices, their laughter. But if a woman doesn't like me, I'm fine with that. Plenty of fish in the sea," he said. "I don't know why this one woman's not liking me has made me crazy."

"I think it's nice," I said. "I just wish I was gorgeous with a rare blood type. Then I could make men my bitch puppets."

"I'm no one's bitch puppet," he growled.

"Yes, you are." Gabriel laughed.

He groaned, scrubbing a hand over his face. "Yeah, I am."

"I'm glad Andrea's giving you a chance. I think you're just different enough to work. Do I have to give you the 'Hurt my friend, and you will wake up with my foot lodged in your nether regions' speech?" I asked.

"No," he promised. "But I think you need to retitle some of your speeches. They're starting to sound sort of repetitive."

I stuck my tongue out at him.

"No, thanks, I'm seeing someone," he snarked.

A slightly frantic Jolene appeared and arranged us into our marching order. Zeb was calm, even happy, making Jolene laugh as he helped her work out where we would stand and how we would hold our arms. (Seriously, bouquet grip was a five-minute debate.) I hoped that his strange behavior over the last few months had been just cold feet and that now that the wedding was here, he would be the old lovable Zeb again.

Just as Uncle Creed, the oldest male in Jolene's pack, who'd been ordained through a mail-order company, was about to run through the ceremony, a rust and blue minivan rolled up to the main house in a cloud of dust.

An "uh-oh" line formed between Jolene's brows. "Um, I don't know who that is."

"That's Eula with the cake!" Mama Ginger trilled.

Between her family's open hostility toward Zeb and Mama Ginger's finding fault with everything from the nautical decorations to the fact that the outdoor wedding site had a dirt floor, Jolene's last nerve was frayed. I squeezed her shoulder, told her I would take the delivery, and negotiated the yard as best I could in three-inch heels. Smoke rolled out in a choking cloud as Eula opened the back of the van.

"Where do you want this?" she asked, without bothering to remove the Marlboro Light dangling from her lip.

"Oh . . . no." Jolene's cake was an exercise in "yikes." The icing gleamed greasily, actually oozing essence of Crisco through the cardboard fruit crate Eula was using to cart it around. Jolene had planned to have twisted fondant ropes around the bottom of each tier, which looked like a toddler's Play-Doh craft. Instead of the subtle hints of navy and ice blue, everything was an electric Cookie Monster shade that must have required most of the bottle of food coloring.

The tiers were assembled at a forty-degree angle. And the whole thing reeked of cigarette smoke. Jolene crossed the yard and was at my side in a blink. "What's wrong?"

"You're going to want to—" I waved toward the van. Jolene's jaw dropped as she took in the sight of the cake. "Yeah."

I made a quick exit, because my support as best maid only went so far.

"What's going on?" Zeb asked as he watched Jolene try to absorb the sight of her wedding cake. Mimi followed Jolene's high-pitched cries to the van, where she had a similar reaction to the cake.

"She may be a few minutes," I told Zeb.

Zeb watched as Jolene, Mimi, and Eula had a very loud "discussion." "Should I go . . ."

"Jane, honey, why don't you just stand in for her?" Mama Ginger suggested, to Zeb's horror.

"Mama, I don't think that's—"

"You can't do that!" Uncle Creed cried.

"We can't have the rehearsal without the bride," I insisted.

"No, don't be silly," Mama Ginger warbled, pushing me into the spot next to Zeb. "There, that looks so much better anyway! Just like I always said, you and Jane are like two peas in a pod."

Zeb's brow furrowed. He was wearing his "trying to remember something" expression, or possibly his "I smell something funny" expression. Either way, the way he was looking at me was disquieting. His eyes were unfocused as he stared at me, dazed. "I can't marry Jolene."

Mama Ginger gave a victorious squeal as I spluttered, "S-say what now?"

Zeb clasped my hands in his, despite my repeated attempts to yank them loose. "I can't marry Jolene. I can't live a lie, Jane. I can't be with anybody but you."

A symphony of gasps and angry growls rippled through the bride's family. My knees turned to jelly. The wedding party was silent and aghast, besides Gabriel's shocked "Beg pardon?"

"No no no no no no. You and I have never felt that way about each other," I said in my slow and deliberate voice. I turned to Gabriel as Zeb kissed the back of my hand. Dick stared at us, slackjawed, unsure whether to laugh or, well, laugh. I asked, "Is it some sort of thrall or whammy? Please tell me it's a whammy."

Zeb wrapped his arms around me, looking into my eyes with a level of tenderness only seen when politicians are publicly apologizing to their wives. "I'm sorry I let this go so far, Jane. Jolene's a nice girl, but I wanted to get back at you for spending so much time with Gabriel, for not loving me back. We have such a long history together, Janie. Friendship and companionship, that's what's going to keep us happy for the rest of our lives. It's always been you, Janie. You were always the girl I've wanted to spend my life with. You were always the girl I wanted waiting for me at the end of the aisle."

This was all starting to sound horribly familiar. Mama Ginger "awwwed" and demanded that Floyd get up and use the disposable camera to record this beautiful moment. Jolene, who had left the Great Cake Debate to investigate why the groom was snuggling up to another woman, cried, "Zeb, honey, what the hell are you doing?"

Lonnie got to his feet and glared at Zeb with a predator's eye. "What's going on here?"

Zeb looked pained, panicked, at the sight of his bride-to-be. He pressed his lips together, then blurted, "I can't do this, Jolene. I can't. I don't want to hurt you, but I can't be with you. I can't go through with this wedding."

Jolene chuckled, looking to me to say that this was all joke. I shook my head, bewildered. "Zeb, this isn't funny."

"It's not a joke. Jolene, I can't marry you. This whole thing, it's wrong."

"What are you talking about?" Jolene demanded. "I love you!"

Sweat broke out on Zeb's forehead as he vomited out the words: "I don't love you."

Jolene let loose a strangled cry as she sank into a chair near her father. If looks could kill, Zeb would be hogtied at Lonnie's feet with an apple stuffed in his mouth. Mimi wrapped her arms around the distressed bride and murmured soothing sounds into her neck. Behind them, a wall of indignant, insulted werewolf relatives rose to their feet, glowering at Zeb and me with curled lips and bared teeth.

"You're doing the right thing, Zeb," Mama Ginger cooed. "I've told you from the beginning, this whole wedding has been a mistake."

Mimi turned on Mama Ginger and snarled. But Mama Ginger was too wrapped up in her triumph to notice.

"Let's get out of here, Jane." Zeb took my hand and tried to pull me away. Gabriel's hands clamped around my shoulders as I yanked away.

Gabriel's voice was low and stripped of the barest hint of kindness. "Leave now, Zeb. I don't think we can protect you if you say much more."

"I'm not sure if I want to," Dick muttered. "Even I have standards."

Backing toward his car, Zeb sent Jolene a last sorrowful look. "I'm sorry."

Mama Ginger and the rest of the Lavelles were packed up and peeling away from the farm in seconds. Jolene soaked her mother's shoulder with hoarse, body-wracking sobs. I glared at the girl cousins, who were snickering behind their hands, and wrapped an arm around the bride. "I don't know what to say."

From behind us, I could hear Uncle Luke demanding, "Well, what does she expect?"

"Luke," Jolene's father growled.

"No, no, I've held my tongue long enough," Luke said. "It's not right, the daughter of our alpha mating outside the pack, marrying herself to some filthy two-foot-walking human. And now he's done exactly what we all said he would do."

"Hey, no one talks about my friend that way!" I cried. "He's being a bit of a jerk right now, but he's still my friend."

"If you were a man, I'd slap you until you were spitting those fangs out the left side of your mouth," Luke snarled.

"If you were a man, I'd slap you right back—hey!" I stepped out of the way when he did try to backhand me.

Without preamble, furry bodies flew at me from all sides. Several of Jolene's aunts and cousins, wolfed out, leaped onto their uncle's back. It had nothing to do with me personally. Attacking a guest on pack property was another clan shame. (I needed to start keeping a list.) Their response brought out several uncles and cousins who secretly agreed with Luke's position and the cousins who were just itching for a good fight. I ducked around a tractor when I saw Lucy, one of the bridesmaid cousins who was still in human form, grab a bottle of Boone's Farm and clobber Vance over the head.

"Is this normal?" I yelled to Gabriel over the din.

"It's not abnormal," he said. "Mind your head."

I dipped just in time to miss the shattering plastic bomb of Aunt Vonnie's cherished punch bowl. Vonnie, on seeing this, howled with rage, wolfed out, and went after the unfortunate uncle who had tossed it. Gabriel and I crawled under a table, where Dick had already dragged Andrea to relative safety.

"What do we do?" I asked. "Call the cops? Get a bunch of rolled-up newspapers?"

Gabriel covered me against the shrapnel from a thrown hurricane lamp. "Do you really think introducing police to the mix will improve the situation?"

"Good point," I said, ducking the flying tissue-paper bells.

"I say we wait it out," he said, handing me a little flask.

"What if Jolene gets a black eye for her wedding photos?" Andrea asked in a slightly addled voice.

"I think when the groom walks out of the wedding rehearsal, the last thing the bride has to worry about is pretty pictures," Dick said.

"Wow," Andrea marveled as Jolene hefted a tractor tire over her head and launched it at her uncle Tom.

"Well, she's pretty worked up," I said. "And she's got all that werewolf strength. I just can't believe Zeb did this. This isn't him. He loves Jolene. He doesn't have the kind of heart that just stops loving."

Gabriel nodded. "It's different now, stronger. It's as if his thoughts are . . . filtered. Some of them are not his own. Have you noticed?"

"I try not to look into my friends' heads. You tend to find out things that upset you."

"I told you we'd have an unforgettable evening," Dick said, elbowing Andrea.

"Yes. I think I won't be able to forget this, no matter how much medication I'm prescribed." Andrea winced as she downed a glass of room-temperature "Fuzzy Navel"–flavored wine.

"Five bucks says Papa McClaine takes Vance out with a farm implement of some type," Dick offered in an effort to lighten the mood.

"Ten says he uses his bare fangs," Gabriel countered.

I separated their shaking hands. "Uh-uh, you two are just now talking again. No betting. Besides, shouldn't we go after Zeb?"

After the dust (and potato salad) had been cleared, Jolene was left sitting on a broken picnic table in an empty clearing. And she was naked again. That could not be sanitary.

"Oh, honey." I clutched her close to me (after I'd wrapped her in a stray tablecloth).

"I don't understand what happened." Jolene sniffled. "Everythin' was so perfect."

"Do you think Zeb could be usin' drugs?" I asked.

Jolene stared at me. "OK, it's not exactly within the realm of his character, but I would guess 'hard-core crack smoker' way before 'idiot who dumped the love of his life at the altar.'"

"You think I'm the love of his life?"

"Of course I do. Who else would it be? It sure the hell isn't me. What do you think made Zeb . . . just what the heck happened?"

"Zeb hasn't been right in months. It's little things. But I never thought—I never thought he would do somethin' like this."

"You know all that stuff Zeb was saying, that was just crazy talk, right? Zeb doesn't really love me. It was as if he had some sort of dissociative episode or started channeling Mama Ginger or something. Maybe he just got cold feet."

"The Zeb I love would not have cold feet. He was excited about getting married. How could someone just change like that? Maybe I should have married my cousin Vance, like Uncle Luke said." Jolene paled. "I've got to call everythin' off. I'm goin' to have to call two hundred of my relatives and tell them the weddin's off. And all that food! And the little mints. And the iceberg! What am I goin' to do with a thirty-foot Styrofoam iceberg?"

"What were you going to do with it after the wedding?" I asked. She glared at me through her tears. "Look, let's just hold off on canceling anything. All of the food, the drinks, everything will keep for two days, right? You just sit tight for the rest of the weekend. Don't make any decisions or announcements. Give me two days. If by Sunday I do not have a willing and groveling groom kneeling at your feet, then I will *help* you sink that dang Styrofoam iceberg."

Jolene chewed her lip.

"He loves you, Jolene. He's never loved anybody in his whole life the way he loves you."

"Two days," she agreed. "Now I just have to keep my family from killin' him."

"That would help, yes."

21

One who objects at a werewolf wedding risks serious injuries.

—*Mating Rituals and Love Customs of the Were*

After talking a half-dozen very angry werewolf males out of hunting down my best friend like a rabid raccoon, I drove to the Lavelles' house and sat out in the driveway. I had to talk to Mama Ginger. Emboldened by her meddling success, she would be impossible to deal with. I would be lucky if I didn't end up shot with a tranquilizer dart and carted off to a Vegas wedding chapel.

I found her sitting on her sun porch, on an old musty couch, chewing her nails. Mama Ginger never chewed her nails. She said the hands were the front window of a girl's "shop," and you couldn't attract a man with a messy front window. "Mama Ginger?"

She turned, and I saw actual tear tracks on her cheek. She seemed so small and deflated, with her clean, bare face and her hair tucked into a ponytail. "Oh, Janie, are you here to see Zeb?"

"No, actually, Mama Ginger, I'm here to see you."

"Well, whatever for? Honey, my boy already said everything he needed to say." She sniffed and gave me a weary smile. "You two need to talk all this over, get your heads together. We have a wedding to plan."

"No, Mama Ginger, we need to talk about why Zeb said those things in the first place. Things that sounded an awful lot like the things you've been saying. I don't know what you did to Zeb to make him do that, but you need to tell me. Because whatever you did ruined Zeb's and Jolene's lives."

"That's not true!" Mama Ginger cried, her voice cracking. I grabbed her chin and forced her to meet my gaze. I didn't want to have to use the persuasion voice on her, but I would. Finally, tears welled at the corners of her eyes, and she whispered, "Zeb's curled up in bed, practically in a damn coma. He refuses to say a word."

"His brain's probably gone into shock, Mama Ginger. You can't mess around with someone's subconscious, make them do something that is fundamentally opposed to their heart's desire, and not expect there to be side effects."

She wailed, "It wasn't supposed to be like this. He wasn't supposed to be so—a mother knows when her child is hurting, Jane. And he's just so miserable. And I did that."

In the years I'd known her, Mama Ginger had never expressed remorse. A change in heart this dramatic must have been killing her. I found small comfort in that.

"I never meant any harm," she whimpered. "I was just trying to make sure Zeb was happy."

"But he was happy, with Jolene. She made him very happy. And you can fix this. You just have to tell me what you did to make Zeb say all those things."

"But he wants you, Jane. You heard him. He wants to be with you."

"No, he doesn't. I know that you want him to want me. We both know what he really wants."

"But I've spent so much time—"

"You've spent a lot of time and energy trying to fulfill the vision you had of our future. But the future you want, marriage and babies, it's not possible. I can't have babies, Mama Ginger. I'm a vampire."

Blanching a lovely shade of ecru, Mama Ginger gasped and clapped a hand over her throat. "But you're so, so—"

"Normal? Yes, but I'm also a bloodsucking creature of the night."

"I can't believe this. You're just saying this to keep me from wanting you to marry Zeb!" she cried, stumbling back and tripping over a lawn chair.

"Well, you're not wrong, but it's still true." I reached for her hand to help her up. "I'm a vampire. I have been for almost a year now. And you didn't notice, because you tend not to pay attention when people evolve or change. Zeb and I are no longer the six-year-olds who played house. I'm not dangerous. Not to Zeb and not to you. But the bright side is that while I can never, ever bear you grandchildren, Jolene can have all the kids she and Zeb want. In fact, there's every chance that they're going to have a huge family."

"Grandbabies?" She sighed.

"Yeah, grandbabies—beautiful, strong, most likely very athletic grandbabies. But first we have to fix Zeb so he can apologize to Jolene, profusely, and they can get married."

Mama Ginger sighed, twisting a Kleenex into complex tornado shapes. "I took Zeb to Madame Zelda and told him it was for his headaches. It was stress relief, I told him. Madame Zelda could use hypnosis and suggestive imagery to put him in a better state of mind. Every time he told Jolene he was coming over here to do chores, I was taking him to Zelda. She's spent weeks planting thoughts in his head. Bad stuff about Jolene. Good stuff about you. I made her tell him that you were the only girl he could possibly marry, that you were the only one who could make him happy. That he should be more aggressive with you and let you know how he feels. Zelda fixed it so every time Zeb heard you say the word 'wedding,' he would do something to hurt Jolene's feelings or make a pass at you. And he wouldn't remember doing it later."

In my head, I ran over the conversations that had preceded Zeb's bizarre behavior. In all of them, we'd been talking about the wedding in some capacity. Considering that we'd been planning Zeb's wedding, that was natural, inevitable. Mama Ginger had set out a minefield for us. "What makes you think you have the right to do this stuff, Mama Ginger? Do you have any idea how crazy this is?"

"I just wanted everyone to be happy!" she yelled. "We weren't even sure it was working because Zeb was being so resistant. But he kept coming back. Zelda fixed it so he wouldn't remember anything except the thoughts she put in the back of his brain. We just couldn't get him to dump her."

"Because in his heart and his head, he loves Jolene," I told her. "He was rude to her a few times, said some really hurtful things. He slapped me on the butt in front of my vampire boyfriend, which put him in serious peril— oh, yeah, Gabriel and Dick are vampires, too. But Jolene loves him so much, she forgave him for all of that. So you had to do something bigger."

Mama Ginger blushed and wiped the mascara streaks from her cheeks. "Zelda fixed it so as soon as he heard someone say 'peas in a pod,' he would tell Jolene he didn't want to marry her. He'd repeat all the things that we'd been planting in his head."

"Well, if there's a trigger keyword, there has to be a release keyword, right? What is it?"

Mama Ginger flushed. "She didn't tell me. I only paid half up front. She wouldn't give me the release word until I paid the rest." I stared at her. She shrugged. "I wanted to make sure it worked."

"Well, pay her the rest!"

"I tried. Earlier tonight, I called her and told her I wanted to call it off, that my son was miserable and she had to take everything back. I may have used some words she didn't like."

"Such as?"

Mama Ginger sniffled. "Crackpot . . . crazy old coot . . . buck-toothed hag."

"Did you stop to think maybe it wasn't a great idea to use your special brand of phone manners on the person who has access to your son's subconscious?"

Mama Ginger was sobbing in earnest now, which meant she would be no further help.

"So I need to track down a psychic who specializes in hypnosis and mind-control techniques to try to wrestle information out of her?"

Mama Ginger nodded pitifully.

"Great."

After persuading Mama Ginger not to move Zeb or further scramble his brain, I followed her soggy directions to Madame Zelda's "parlor front" shop on Gaines Street. Madame Zelda lived in a one-story "shotgun"-style house with peeling green paint and a giant plywood hand advertising five-dollar palm readings.

I rang the doorbell, and after some audible shuffling inside, I was greeted by a little old wrinkled lady wearing a fringed purple shawl, a long Indian-print skirt, and a smoky topaz ring the size of a door knocker. Her eyes were heavily kohled. And suddenly, my weird encounter with Esther Barnes made sense.

"Hi, Ms. Barnes," I said, smiling sweetly.

"I am Madame Zelda," Esther said in a deep, obviously fake Transylvanian accent while she waved me into the parlor. Her house smelled of yesterday's fried chicken and overbrewed coffee. Her "office" looked ex-

actly how you would expect a five-dollar psychic to dec-
orate: beaded curtains, stinky candles, busy fabrics, and
creepy angel figurines. "I do not know this Ms. Barnes of
whom you speak."

She gestured for me to sit at a tiny tea table covered in
a sari, with a laughably large crystal ball in the middle.
"That's funny. You look so much like a lady who came
into the bookshop where I work. I must be mistaken."

"Indeed," she intoned. "How may I be of service?"

"Well, you've been helping a friend of mine with some
'headaches.'"

"I help many people," she said, her lips tightening so
that I could see the carmine-colored lipstick feathering
even further into the tiny lines around her mouth.

"Well, this is a special case. See, he came in, thinking
he was going to get your two-hundred-dollar six-ses-
sion stress treatment and tarot reading. And instead, he
ended up brainwashed into thinking he was in love with
someone other than his bride-to-be."

"You!" she growled, the venom in her voice killing off
the fake accent, turning her voice thin and brassy once
more. "You're that 'Jane' she just won't shut up about.
If I had to hear one more time how wonderful you are,
how many beautiful grandbabies you were going to
make, I was going to throw up. Wait, wait!" Suddenly,
she burst out laughing. Carefully wiping her lined eyes,
she hooted, "Ginger doesn't know you're a vampire,
does she?"

"Not until recently."

"Oh, that's priceless!" she cried. "All this time, she was

plottin' to get her boy away from a perfectly nice girl and hand him over to a vampire! Oh, you've made my day."

"Well, I do what I can," I said flatly as she lit a long brown cigarillo. "The thing is, Zeb's wedding was ruined because of that crap you put in his head. Having some experience in the psychic arena, I recognize that you've got some serious chops. I mean, whatever you did to me at the shop was impressive. My ears were ringing for hours." A faint flush of pride spread across her furrowed cheeks. "Now, look, Mama Ginger still owes you a hundred dollars. I'm willing to pay you five hundred so we can settle this whole thing without any hard feelings. All you have to do is hold up your end of the deal and give me the release keyword."

She pursed her lips. "No."

"What do you mean, no?"

"I wouldn't do it for any amount of money." She sniffed. "Ginger Lavelle insulted me personally and professionally. And she's a giant pain in the ass. I don't want to have anything to do with her. She deserves whatever she gets." She settled her gaze on me, and in a voice that reverberated inside my skull, she said, "Now, go away."

Fortunately, I was prepared for the psychic smacking, so while her efforts stung a little, they didn't do a lot of damage. I shook my head. She seemed stunned by my lack of reaction. "That was rude. I came to you in good faith. And Mama Ginger isn't suffering, her son is. Look, I know she's a pain in the ass. It's part of her charm. And if some insulted part of you feels the need to track her down and hypnotize her into thinking she's a chicken or a nudist or something, I will be more than willing to look the other way. Hell, I might pay you extra to do it. I'll consider it a wedding present for a deeply hurt daughter-in-law."

I backed her against the parlor wall and let my fangs fully extend. "I don't want to hurt you. But for my friend, I will do anything it takes to get that keyword. You might reconsider—ow!"

She had reached into a side table and pulled out a silver cross large enough to make me break out in hives. "Silly little vampire, I've seen inside you. You don't have the stomach for killing. You can't even feed on humans without torturing yourself over it. You wouldn't hurt a little old lady like me."

Wheezing and scratching the blisters forming on my arms, I spat, "Look, lady, I've got twenty-four hours to dewhammy my best friend and get him to the altar. Otherwise, he may never leave his parents' guest room again. I wouldn't overestimate the depth of my kindness. And I brought something you didn't count on."

"What's that?"

"Gloves." I slipped the black Isotoners out of my pocket and slapped the cross out of her hands. "And my big mean sire. Gabriel!"

Gabriel swept into the room, followed by a slightly less sweepy Dick.

"What's the plan?" Dick asked, rubbing his hands together and checking the room for valuables. "Carnage? Bedlam? Fisticuffs?"

Gabriel smiled solicitously and waved a hand toward Esther. Dick rolled his eyes. "Dang it."

"What?" I asked as Dick sidled up to the trembling old woman.

Gabriel snickered as he looked over the fading blisters on my arms. "Haven't you ever wondered about the nature of Dick's vampiric gift?"

"I figured it was dodging collection agents or slipping out of handcuffs."

Gabriel grinned as Dick soothingly stroked a resistant Esther's papery hands and led her to a sofa. He fetched a glass of water and cooed over her as she recovered from the "shock" of having three strange vampires in her home. "Dick can reach the heart of any woman. Through a combination of pheromones, subliminal persuasion, and old-fashioned charm, he can get anything he wants from them—money, favors, certain keywords that will help unlock your best friend's brain . . ."

"His special vampire power *is* flirty manipulation? Wait, he's not doing that to Andrea, is he? Because that's . . . icky."

"No, he rarely uses it. He hates lowering himself to it, really. So, his doing this shows you how much he likes Zeb. Using his gift doesn't seem sporting to him. And if anything, Dick adores the chase."

"I don't know if I can watch this," I said, shaking my head in disgust as Dick clasped Esther's hands against his manly chest. She was already making cow eyes at him. "Keep Dick away from my grandma."

"Now, Esther—I can call you, Esther, can't I?" Dick chuckled, giving her a saucy, intimate grin. "It seems like such a shame for you to go by any name but that of one of the most famous queens in history."

As Esther giggled coquettishly, I felt a little ill. "This is not right."

"But extremely effective," Gabriel conceded. "And you don't have the guilt of assaulting a senior citizen hanging over your conscience."

Dick stroked Esther's hands as he pleaded his case, his flashing green eyes drawing her closer across the love seat. "Esther, honey, I don't blame you for being mad at that awful Ginger Lavelle. She's a horrible woman, and I personally can't stand the sight of her, but her son is such a nice boy. He doesn't deserve this kind of hurt. Now, you've got a good heart, Esther. Anyone can see that. You don't want to break up true love, do you? Why don't you go ahead and give me the keywords?"

"I just said the exact same thing," I complained. "That's never going to—oh, come on." Gabriel smirked as Esther whispered the words "like peas and carrots" into Dick's ear.

I snorted. "What is your obsession with peas?"

She ignored me as Dick kissed both her palms and her cheeks.

"We're square, right?" I asked the nonresponsive geriatric psychic. "You're not going to come back in a year and use some secret word to make him divorce Jolene and join the Krishnas or something. Hello?"

"Aw, Esther wouldn't do that, now, would you?" Dick cooed.

"Dick, eventually, your thrall will wear out," I reminded him quietly.

"I looked over her brain. There are no other words. Esther doesn't much like to put in extra work, do you, sweetheart?" Dick kissed the top of her scarved head.

"No." Esther giggled. "I'm sorry for the misunderstanding, Jane. Will I see you again, Dick?"

"Maybe you will, maybe not." Dick smirked.

"Oh, please come by," she wheedled. "Come back and see me."

Dick merely grinned and ushered us out the door.

"Well, I learned more about you, which is always disturbing." I wrapped a purely platonic arm around him. "You are a very bad man, and I hope you're always on my side."

Zeb was not the depressive type, so it was disconcerting to see him in full Howard Hughes mode, ensconced in his mother's guest room, also known as her Precious Moments display area. The walls were lined with shelves where carefully arranged figurines stayed perfectly preserved in their plastic viewing boxes. As far as the eye could see, there were towheaded, large-pupiled children forever frozen while cavorting in adorable pastel rain slickers. Huddled under a pink chenille comforter, Zeb stared blankly at the wall.

"I don't like this place," Dick whispered after Floyd had let us into the house and flopped back into his easy chair without comment. Mama Ginger had taken to her bed. "It's like all the little eyes follow you around the room. This is a bad place."

"Well, it wasn't upsetting before, but it is now." Gabriel grimaced as he recoiled from the plush Precious Moments angel that recited the Lord's Prayer when squeezed.

"Zeb," I whispered, shaking his shoulder. "Zeb, we're here."

"Who's going to do the honors?" Dick asked. "I think unscrambling the groom's brain is a man-of-honor duty."

"But I think I should do it," Gabriel insisted. "I have the most experience sifting through human brains."

"It sounds gross when you say it like that," I told him. "And none of us is going to do this. I made a call on the way over."

We heard Floyd open the front door and grunt. Jolene stepped through the bedroom door. Ignoring the sinister surroundings, her eyes welled up at the sight of her stone-silent fiancé. She curled up against his back and stroked his shoulders, nuzzling the curve of his neck with her nose. "Zeb, honey, it's me."

Zeb's arms trembled, but his gaze stayed fixed on the wall.

"Our friends told me what happened, that what you did wasn't your fault. I love you, Zeb. And I forgive you. And I want you to snap out of it so we can have our wedding. We're like peas and carrots, Zeb. We're different, but we belong together. Did you hear me? Like peas and carrots."

Like a fairy-tale prince released from a spell, Zeb gingerly flexed his fingers and closed them around Jolene's hand. He took a deep breath and said, "I'm so sorry."

Gabriel's arm slipped around me as the pair of them sat up in bed and threw their arms around each other.

"Jolene, I'm sorry," Zeb said, his lips trembling. "It was horrible. I felt like a puppet. My lips were moving, but someone else was talking and I couldn't stop those things from coming out of my mouth. I didn't mean any of it. And afterward, I just didn't want to live without you—"

"Shhh." She chuckled, kissing his neck. "You can spend the rest of our lives making it up to me. Starting with brushing your teeth."

"Your family," he groaned. "They're going to kill me this time, aren't they?"

Jolene shook her head. "Mama and Daddy calmed them down for the most part. Vance still wants to kick your ass, but I don't think that will ever change. They are, however, pretty ticked off at your mama, so she should probably expect a cold shoulder tomorrow night at the reception."

"You still want to marry me?"

"I'd marry you right now in this bed surrounded by these creepy little dolls, if you asked me to," she said.

"Please don't ask her to," Dick begged. "I'd like to get out of here."

Zeb smiled up at us as Jolene cuddled his neck. "Thanks, guys."

I grinned. "What are the man of honor and the best maid for?"

Mama Ginger appeared in the doorway, her eyes puffy and red. Tired, timid, and contrite, she was wearing her old blue housecoat, a bundle of wet Kleenex pouched in the pocket.

Jolene got to her feet and crossed to her with deliberate steps. "It's goin' to take a long, long . . . really long time for me to totally forgive you for this. We're not goin' to have the kind of relationship the two of us would have wanted. You'll have to earn your way into being welcome at our house. But I love your son, and I'm goin' to spend the rest of my life trying to make him happy. If that means the two of us being civil to each other, that's what we're goin' to do. Got it?"

Mama Ginger nodded meekly and stepped out of Jolene's way.

Jolene blew Zeb a kiss. "I'll see you tomorrow night, honey. I'll be the one up front wearin' the white dress."

"Can I still come to the wedding?" Mama Ginger asked in a sad, humble little voice.

Zeb stood and, for the first time in his life, talked sternly to his mother. "You can come, Mama, but you're going to be nice. You're going to be sweet as pie to Jolene and her family."

"But Zeb—"

"Sweet as pie," Zeb repeated.

"But I—"

"Ginger, just shut up!" Beer in hand, Floyd stomped into the room and wagged his finger in Mama Ginger's face. "You've talked enough for the both of us over the years. And I'm going to be speaking up a little more often. You're going to be on your best behavior tomorrow. You'll tell that girl how nice her dress looks. You'll say nice things about the food, the decorations, and anything else that catches your eye. You will offer to help in any way you can, even if it means sweeping out the chicken coop. You will apologize to Jolene's family for how you've acted so far, and you will do your damnedest to make up for it over the next couple of years."

Zeb and I gaped at his father in shock. It was the most words either of us had heard him string together since he dropped a carburetor on his foot in 1989.

"Floyd Lavelle, you've never spoken to me like this in your whole life." Mama Ginger sniffled, her lip trembling. Apparently, her guilt only went so deep.

"Then it's time that I started," Floyd said. He strode out of the room after slapping Mama Ginger on the butt. "Now, everybody keep quiet. I'm trying to watch the damn game!"

Zeb grinned. "I'm going to take a shower. I'm getting married tomorrow!"

"I don't know how to take all this," Mama Ginger said, wringing a Kleenex around her fingers.

"Well, I would plan on swallowing a big slice of humble pie, Mama Ginger." I patted her arm and led Dick and Gabriel out of the room. "Maybe two."

A traditional werewolf wedding reception does not include a receiving line. They are unnecessary as 90 percent of the guest list consists of the happy couple's immediate family members.
—*Mating Rituals and Love Customs of the Were*

It was a traditional Southern wedding.

The bride was beautiful, of course. The ceremony was held outdoors under the full moon. The spring air was warm and soft. The bridesmaids were dressed like those crocheted dolls people use to disguise toilet-paper rolls.

Jolene had chosen "Nearer My God to Thee" as the processional, because she'd read that was what the band on the *Titanic* played. As I led the charge of like-dressed puffballs, I took time to look for familiar faces in the crowd.

Mama Ginger was up front, wearing a completely appropriate and demure cornflower-blue mother-of-the-groom's dress. Her slightly deflated appearance had far more to do with the fact that she'd spent most of the day tying tiny bows around the chocolate anchor favors than any lack of enthusiasm on her part. After a severe dressing down from the alpha couple, most of Jolene's family were equally meek and made a grand effort to pull together and create Jolene's dream wedding. By the time the vampire wedding-party members arrived early that evening, the air had a certain "Let's put on a show!" quality to it. Jolene's female cousins were using their werewolf agility to hang twinkle lights and hurricane lamps from precarious branches. The uncles cleared the riot debris and set up the altar. Uncle Luke, who was quite repentant, spent the afternoon attaching an outboard motor to the mysterious Styrofoam iceberg. And of course, the aunts did what they did best: cooked a feast. There was a huge spread occupying three full-length picnic tables with every kind of roast animal you could imagine, plus casseroles, grits, and congealed salads.

And in a beautiful gesture of familial unity, Raylene managed to pull together a gorgeous ice-blue four-tier wedding cake with a little fondant Jolene and Zeb atop a fake iceberg topper. And nothing on the cake looked anything like a penis. It was Raylene's cake masterpiece.

Even over the rather maudlin processional, my vampire superhearing picked up Zeb saying to Gabriel at the altar, "I feel the need to mention that, well, I love you guys. Even if you did vamp out my best friend, Gabriel, you're a really good guy. And Dick, I really appreciate you hitting on that old lady to unscramble my brain. I'm sorry I've been such a jerk lately."

Gabriel slapped Zeb on the back. "I don't have many friends, Zeb. But you're certainly the best among them."

The two men smiled at each other. A moment of silence passed.

Zeb cleared his throat. "And, uh, sorry about slapping Jane on the butt. That won't happen again."

Another silent, slightly more uncomfortable moment.

"Well, this is awkward," Dick muttered.

Zeb nodded. "Yep."

Gabriel grinned as I passed the end of the aisle and took my spot. True to his word, he was dashing in formal wear, a cutaway tux with old-fashioned four-in-hand tie. I would wonder how long he'd had it, but I think the answer would upset me.

The ceremony was short and to the point, which may have had something to do with werewolves' generally short attention span and an upcoming meal. There was no mention of "If anyone here present knows of any lawful impediment," which was in no way unintentional. There were no unity candles and, mercifully, no solos.

The happy couple marched out to "Raise the *Titanic*," which was oddly dark considering the proceedings. Zeb and Jolene boarded the iceberg while one of Jolene's teen cousins manned the tiller. They made a blessedly slow progression across the pond while Zeb stood behind Jolene, stretching out their arms and screaming, "I'm king of the world!"

"I really should have seen that coming," I told Dick as we paired up at the altar and headed down the aisle.

"I don't think anyone could have seen that coming,"

Dick told me. We were ushered straight to the reception tables as Zeb and Jolene de-berged.

Gabriel's smile could not be contained as he bent over my hand and kissed it. "You're a vision."

I narrowed my eyes at him. "Like the kind you see after a healthy dose of peyote?"

"No, you know, it sort of looks like something some of the more promiscuous girls might have worn in my day," Gabriel said.

"On what planet is that a compliment?" I demanded as Dick laughed.

After a completely unnecessary number of photos, I pulled the happy couple aside and pulled an envelope out of a pocket in my skirt. (Oh, yeah, the "Ruffles and Dreams" came with pockets.)

"I have something for you," I said. "It's not six hundred dollars' worth of pots and pans, but I think you'll like it."

"You've already done enough, Janie," Zeb assured me.

Nonetheless, I handed Jolene an envelope. She raised an eyebrow at the paper contained within. "It's a deed."

"To a piece of land about halfway between Gabriel's place and mine, in the back fifty acres. There's also a check in there to cover the construction costs of a brand-new house."

And that, combined with estimated costs of renovating and restocking the shop, would still leave me with quite a bit of money, which was disconcerting. I now felt the need actually to do something for myself but had no idea what that might be. It was like being held hostage by a retirement plan.

"That's really sweet," Zeb said. "But we just got out of a situation where we felt obligated—"

"You don't owe me anything. It's a gift."

"We would really like to make our own way," he said.

"Fine. Give me a dollar," I said.

"What?"

"Just give me a dollar," I said.

"I didn't really think of putting my wallet in these pants," he said.

Dick rolled his eyes and fished out his own wallet, an exact replica of Jules Winnfield's from *Pulp Fiction*.

"I've never seen you so eager to give away money," Gabriel told Dick.

"I want in," Dick said. "All I got them was one of those George Foreman grills."

Dick handed the bill to Zeb, who handed it over to me. In return, I handed him the envelope. "There, you have just purchased a plot of my land for one dollar."

"I can't—"

"Zeb," I said in a warning tone.

"Fine, but I can't take the check."

"Think of it as a gift certificate, a really big gift certificate," I told him. He began the protest. "Think of it as a gift certificate, or I'll kick your ass at your own wedding reception."

"I'm sorry. I can't take anything you say seriously when you're dressed like that," Zeb said.

"I think we should do what she says," Jolene whispered when I gave him the burning vampire stare of doom.

"Thanks, Jane," Zeb said, hugging me fiercely.

"I love you guys. Go, mingle," I told them after kissing Jolene's cheek.

Andrea sidled up beside me to hand me a plastic champagne flute filled with frothy pink punch. "I think it's safe. They wouldn't put meat in here, would they?"

I sipped cautiously. "It appears not. How's it going?" I asked, nodding toward Dick.

"Eh." She gave the so-so hand sign. "He's starting to pressure me, and I don't appreciate it. Why do men always want the one thing they can't have?"

"So you guys aren't . . . ?"

"What, no, we're at it like bunnies," she said, rolling her eyes. "But I won't let him drink from me."

"Dang it, I do not need those visuals in my head! And don't think about it when you're around me, I can tell. Why won't you let him drink from you?"

"Because it's too much like work," she said.

"Kind of like a masseuse who doesn't want to go home and give back rubs?" I asked.

"Yes, exactly like that *Seinfeld* episode."

"I have a limited frame of reference," I admitted as my cell phone rang from my dress pocket. The caller ID said it was my mother. Andrea was not the least bit offended when I answered it, since Dick had just approached with a tray of nibbles he'd managed to snag from the buffet line using his vampire wiles. I shook my head and giggled as I snapped open the phone. At this point, I was surprised that Dick wasn't feeding them to her.

"I just wanted to see whether you'd called your sister yet," Mama said, again dispensing with a greeting.

"No, but I have done an extensive inventory of the household contents at River Oaks and found an alarming number of items missing. The next time you're over at Jenny's, could you look for Depression glass, a silver coffee service, and some lace fans? I need to know what to put on the search warrant."

Mama sighed on the other end of the line. "You aren't really considering going to the police, are you? Jane, that would be so embarrassing to the family."

I sighed. "I'm not going to call the cops, Mama. But Jenny and Grandma should consider whatever they've taken over the years to be their inheritance. That's their share of the Early legacy. I don't want to hear anything more about it. If Jenny wants to keep the lawsuit going, she can go ahead. I can afford a much better lawyer now."

"Won't you please—"

"No, I will not," I said firmly as I stepped away from the circle of light and love and family. Because clearly, that was not the place for this conversation. Also, Mama was not aware that Zeb's wedding was that night, and I could only imagine the tear storm that would ensue if she found out she hadn't been invited. "Now, speaking of Grandma, have you heard from her in the last twenty-four hours, or should we assume that Wilbur has married and buried another wife?"

"Actually, Grandma Ruthie has canceled the wedding."

"Because of something I said?"

"Oh, no, of course not." Mama laughed. "But when you started talking about how many wives Wilbur had, it just turned her stomach. Then she realized that she'd been married almost as many times as he has."

"So, she realized her reign of matrimonial terror must end?" I asked as Gabriel approached with Solo cups full of what might have been Boone's Farm's version of champagne.

Mama snorted. "Something like that."

"Does this mean I should contact the authorities about Wilbur?" I asked. "Did he take the break-up well?"

"Oh, no, she didn't break it off with him. She says she still wants to date him," Mama said.

"Ew!" I cried. "He's a dead guy."

A hurt look flashed across Gabriel's features. I mouthed, "Not you," then pointed to the phone and added, "Wilbur."

"You're dead," Mama pointed out.

"I'm a different kind of dead. I'm a cool kind of dead. Wilbur is all graveyard smells and feeding on the bottom rung of the food chain."

"Jane, just let it go. Your grandma's a grown woman. If she wants to date a dead man, she can date a dead man."

"That's not what you said when I started dating a dead man," I grumbled.

"Well, I just want you to be nice to Wilbur when you see him at the Labor Day picnic."

"I don't have to be nice to people who try to stake me."

"Jane, it's bad enough that you aren't speaking to Jenny. Don't cause more problems with your grandmother."

"Jenny stole knickknacks from me, and I stopped

talking to her. What makes you think I'll respond any better to someone trying to stake me with a cane?"

In a maneuver that would make a NASCAR driver proud, Mama switched conversational lanes on me. "Oh, honey, I've been meaning to ask you, have you seen Adam Morrow lately? His mama was at the beauty shop today. She hasn't heard from Adam in the last day or so."

"No, I haven't seen him since he stopped by the shop the other night," I said. "He seemed . . ." Creepy. Perverse. In need of medication and negative-reinforcement therapy.

"Fine."

"Well, if you see him, tell him to call his mama," she said. "It's not right to make a mother worry like that."

"I will. Look, I've really got to go, Mama," I said as the DJ asked the crowd to clear the floor for Jolene and Zeb to have their first dance as husband and wife. I played the only excuse that I knew would get Mama off the phone. "I've got a date tonight. With Gabriel."

"Good night!" Mama squeaked, then promptly hung up.

Gabriel and I watched with interest as Zeb led his new bride onto the dance floor and the painfully familiar flute intro lilted.

"Oh, please tell me she didn't."

"What?" Gabriel asked as Celine Dion's breathy soprano warbled, "Every night in my dreams . . ."

I groaned. "Who picks 'My Heart Will Go On' for their first dance song?"

"It's a nice song."

"It's a song about people dying. Frozen people dying. Not exactly the sentiment I would want to start my married life on. Then again, why am I surprised?" I shrugged. "She has a *Titanic* chip boat."

"What would you prefer?" He snorted. " 'Hungry Like the Wolf'?"

"It would be either brilliant or brilliantly tacky," I agreed.

"She's very happy," Gabriel observed.

"Ah, don't do that," I said. "Don't make me petty."

I watched as Zeb twirled his wife across the clearing with surprising grace. Jolene was happy. She had all of the things I wanted for myself. A man whose love couldn't be questioned, or, if she could question it, she didn't. A firm handle on her special condition. Professional contentment. Parents who adored and accepted her, even if other members of the family didn't.

I would watch Jolene, learn from her. I'd ask myself, "What would Jolene do?" the way most people ask, "What would Oprah do?" Even if that meant not asking my boyfriend about the mysterious and apparently unhinged Jeanine until he was ready to talk about her. I would not look for trouble in my relationship and create problems where there was none. I would trust that Gabriel loved me. Even if it came back and bit me on the ass in a major way.

Turning to my undead date, I poked him in the side and asked, "Are you going to dance with me or what?"

"Why can't you wait to be asked?" he muttered.

"Have you met me?" I asked. "Surely you must have

figured out some of this by now. I'm contrary . . . and you love it."

He shrugged.

"So, really, which one of us is the sick one?" I asked.

"Will the best maid, the man of honor, and their escorts please join the happy couple?" the DJ asked.

"Now you have no choice," I told him.

Dick yanked Andrea onto the middle of the dance floor and offered a courtly bow. Andrea looked vaguely embarrassed but laughed as he drew her into his arms. Gabriel and I made a less dramatic entrance.

"I'm a terrible dancer," I told him.

"I don't care." He pulled me into a box step, which my vampire grace still didn't help me master. "So, I've been thinking."

I smirked. "That can be dangerous."

"You haven't quite used your triumph settlement the way you wanted to."

"Not true. Look at how happy they are." I nodded toward Jolene and Zeb.

"I know it took quite a bit of money to do that. And it will take quite a bit more money to get the shop going."

"Which is your clever way of saying that Ophelia told you exactly how much I got." I gave him a wry smile.

"I cannot comment," he said. "Because Ophelia's scarier than you are."

"Not going to argue there. But I am going to have a nice healthy nest egg. You don't have to worry about me."

"Well, we both know that's not true. The point, which

we rarely get to painlessly, is that I know that you wanted to spend some of your ill-gotten wealth on travel."

I eyed him suspiciously. "What did you do?"

"Nothing yet, but you say the word, and we will be on a plane. I'll keep my schedule open. I figured we could start in London and work our way east. I want to be with you when you see the Bibliothèque Nationale de France, harass some poor gondolier in Venice with questions. I'll even go to the Eiffel Tower if you want to be prosaic. Anywhere you want to go we'll go."

"Travel?" I asked. "For how long?"

"Until you get tired of me."

"When can we leave?" I asked.

"From here, as far as I'm concerned," he said.

"That's a little quick." I laughed. "But I would love to go. Soon. And we will go to the Eiffel Tower, thank you."

"I knew it," he said. "At heart, you're just a sentimental romantic fool."

I laughed again, watching as Jolene and Zeb circled the floor. Lord help me, I actually started misting up. "Sometimes."

"Are you crying?" he asked, lifting my chin.

"No!"

"Sentimental, romantic fool," he said again as I wiped at my eyes.

"I really hate this song," I grumbled.

He twirled me out and dipped me. "Honey, let it go."

Read on for a sneak peek of

Nice Girls Don't Live Forever

1

The worst thing you can possibly do in a relationship, vampire or otherwise, is actually telling your partner that you don't trust him. Even if it's true.

—*Love Bites: A Female Vampire's Guide to Less Destructive Relationships*

M y life didn't begin until I died.

Prefiring, prevampire Jane worked Saturdays and holidays and any other days that no one else on the library staff wanted to work. I had never done anything for myself. I'd never traveled. And now, I was my own boss. I'd had the opportunity to kiss foreign soil. Actually, it was the tile in Heathrow Airport's Sunproof Lounge. I think it embarrassed my sire/boyfriend, Gabriel Nightengale, and the pickpockets were able to peg me as a tourist right away. But I was really, really happy to be off that plane.

I have claustrophobia issues.

I'd never had a healthy adult relationship as a live girl. Then again, I'd just abandoned my 150-year-old boyfriend in a hotel room in Brussels, so maybe this one didn't count, either.

I'm pretty sure it was Brussels. We'd made quite a few stops since London.

My round-the-world romantic getaway with Gabriel turned sour early on, right after we checked into our first hotel in London. There was a note waiting for Gabriel at the front desk, fancy linen paper addressed in spidery black ink. Whatever it said, it put him in a very foul mood. The minute we'd settled into the exceedingly posh room, he put his flowy black coat back on, said he had to make some phone calls, and disappeared for most of the night. I and my newly purchased trunkload of lacy underthings took this very personally.

You know how after you've hung around a person for a while, you can tell when he's *trying* to have a good time? Well, it's just frightening in Gabriel. He was like a Carson-Wagonlit agent on crack, manically planning all-night excursions to museums, the opera, beer gardens, fancy, intimidating parties with his fancy, intimidating friends—anything that would keep us out of the hotel room from dusk 'til dawn. Gabriel's credit-card company put a fraud watch on his accounts as we switched hotels on a whim, two or three times per city. Each time we checked in, a creamy linen envelope was waiting for him at the front desk. And each time, his eyes got just a little more Manson-ish. Charles or Marilyn, take your pick.

His cell phone rang incessantly, and every time it did, he either let it go to voice mail or whispered, "Business," and took the call outside. I tried to ignore the warning signs. I tried to give Gabriel the benefit of the doubt, but a girl can only bury her head so deep in the sand. He had told me months before that he was having issues he couldn't tell me about. There were frequent business trips where I couldn't reach him by phone. And I'd found out that on several occasions, he'd lied about where he'd been. He'd assured me that it wasn't another woman, despite the fact that the name Jeanine had popped up on his cell phone on several occasions. Never had I wished so much that my stupid, inconsistent mind-reading powers worked on my sire. And even though I still had (raging, screaming) doubts, I chose to believe him. But now, I was starting to feel like one of those women at whom people yell "How stupid can you be?" when they inevitably appear on *Dr. Phil*.

I suppose one should expect a certain amount of drama in a relationship that started with one party dying in a muddy ditch off a dark country road. I don't like talking about the night I was turned. Every young vampire eventually gets drunk with buddies and shares war stories about his or her transformation. I do not partake in such revelries. Why?

The short version is this: I was (unfairly, unceremoniously) fired from the library and replaced by my supervisor's barely literate firebug stepdaughter. But instead of getting a severance check, I got just enough of a gift certificate to get rip-snorting drunk at Shenanigans. I met Gabriel, and flirtation ensued. I sobered enough to drive, but because of unfortunate circumstances, my ancient car, Big Bertha, died halfway home. I was spotted walking down the road by the town drunk, Bud McElray, who mistook me for a deer and shot me. I was left in the ditch to die, only to be found and turned by Gabriel.

You don't become a vampire just by being bitten. Otherwise, the world would be overrun with bloodsuckers. To make a childe, a vampire will feed on a victim until he or she reaches the point of death. The vampire must be careful as drinking too much can leave the initiate unconscious and unable to drink the blood that will change him. I know, it sounds gross. But when faced with death by gunshot wound, it's a tempting offer. The process takes a lot out of a vampire sire and is said to be the closest the undead can come to childbirth. It's why a vampire will only turn a handful of "children" in his or her lifetime.

So, yes, Gabriel is both my sire and my boyfriend, which can cause some complications in our relationship. It was his job to lead me through the transition to vampirism, but since I rarely listened to him, that didn't work out so well. And confrontations between the two of us tended to get sort of violent . . . and naked.

Instead of indulging in accusations of infidelity and undead Sid-and-Nancy–style hotel theatrics, I bit my tongue. Hell, I bit a hole through my tongue. Fortunately, I have vampire healing, so it grew right back. But then we checked into the Mandarin Oriental Hotel in Munich, and a linen envelope was waiting. The look on Gabriel's face made a bellboy cry.

Our itinerary became even more packed. I was frequently left alone with Gabriel's strange friends as he held urgent "business meetings." I occasionally woke up and couldn't figure out where I was. And when Gabriel was in the shower one night, I happened to peek into the wastebasket, where he'd left the torn remnants of his latest note. I saw words like, "bloodmate" and "love you."

I swear, it wasn't my fault that the basket tipped over

and those little bits of paper somehow managed to perfectly reassemble in their original order.

OK, fine, I abused my jigsaw puzzle skills. But if Gabriel didn't want me reading the note, he probably should have burned it. My vision tinged red as I made out phrases like, "Remember what we are to each other." "Remember what we have." "The woman you're with can't satisfy you like I do."

Excuse me? Remember what we *are*? Satisfy you like I *do*? As in the presence tense? As in Gabriel had recently been satisfied by this woman? I fell on my knees, stunned by an explosion of pain in my chest. If my heart beat, I would have sworn I'd blown an aorta. He'd promised. He'd sworn that he was faithful to me. And, like an idiot, I'd believed him.

The phone rang. With numbed fingers, I knocked the phone off its cradle and heard the voice of my best friend, Zeb. I launched into a paranoid diatribe on cheating boyfriends and rude people who don't embrace deodorant. I ignored all attempts on his part to make me think like a normal person or believe that all of this could be a very complicated coincidence.

"Whose side are you on?" I hissed, listening for the sound of Gabriel's shower running. I swiped the little bits of paper back into the wastebasket.

"Um, logic and reason?" Zeb suggested. "And as much as I enjoy paying twelve dollars a minute to listen to you rant hysterically, I called to let you know there was a burglary at the shop last night."

After my masterful string of profanity, Zeb explained that renovations at the bookstore were progressing nicely.

The expansion into the adult-video store next door had gone faster than expected, thanks to a central wall that collapsed on its own. But two nights before, someone had thrown a brick through the front window and ransacked the stock. Oddly enough, some of the more valuable items, figurines and crystals and ceremonial items, had been ignored in favor of tearing through boxes of books. Books were thrown aside, their spines cracked and damaged, Zeb's descriptions of which were enough to make me produce distressed sounds in several different languages.

Zeb said in a soothing voice, "Fortunately, they didn't know how valuable some of the books were, because they didn't take anything."

"What kind of underachieving burglars don't take anything?" I asked, grasping at any excuse not to think about the nauseating ripple of pain shredding through my body. I could do this. I could get through this. I just had to focus on what Zeb was saying.

"I don't know. Mr. Wainwright was out on the town with your aunt Jettie, so he was confused and was searching for his recommended daily allowance of visual stimuli," Zeb said as I pulled my suitcase out of the closet. "Dick thinks it was someone looking for something specific but who couldn't understand your weird shelving system."

"Yeah, alphabetical order is revolutionary." I snorted. "So, how much damage are we talking about here?"

"Not much. Other than the window being broken and the books being tossed around, nothing. Which, to me, says the thieves were over thirty. No angry teenager could pass up the chance to mess up newly painted walls and a shiny new espresso machine."

"Look, I'm coming home on the next flight," I said, randomly tossing clothes into my bag.

"What? No, Jane, there's no reason to do that. Dick and Andrea can take care of everything. Andrea's almost as anal-retentive as you are. She's doing a great job."

"I'm coming home, Zeb," I repeated.

"Jane, don't turn this into a—you're hanging up on me now, aren't you? Dang it, Jane!" he cried as I snapped the phone back into the cradle.

Gabriel emerged from the bathroom, his hips swathed in a huge white towel. His eyes tracked from my packed bag to the phone. "Who were you talking to?"

My head snapped up and it took everything in me not to throw the nightstand across the room at him. I wanted to scream at him, to strike at him until he hurt as much as I did. But I couldn't. I was numb. Empty. I took a few deep breaths, unlocked my jaws, and concentrated on keeping my tone even, unaffected.

"There's been a break-in at the shop. I need to go home and take care of it," I said, clicking the suitcase shut. "If you could send the rest of my stuff home later, I'd appreciate it."

I looked up, hoping to see some sign of response from Gabriel, something to show that he wanted me to stay. But he seemed relieved. "Well, if you have to go, you have to go. It's probably better this way."

And then he helped me pack. What the hell? It was like being slapped with indifference. He honestly did not care whether I was there or not. I could have just announced that I was going to take a flying leap off the roof, and he would nod obligingly. Of course, a flying leap off the roof wouldn't injure me, but it was hurtful all the same.

"Well, OK, then," I muttered, throwing my coat on. "I'll see you when you get home. After you've finished your business."

"I'll see you soon," he promised as gave me a sterile peck on the forehead. It was a sad, dismissive, and fatherly sort of kiss. "This is really for the best. I think we can both agree this trip hasn't quite worked out as we'd hoped. I'll call you."

As the door literally hit me in the butt on my way out, I was similarly struck by the realization that Gabriel had just used classic brush-off platitudes on me. Did he just break up with me and not even have the decency to tell me? Somewhere between numb and well and truly pissed, I carted my luggage to the front desk.

You know those French movies, where a weary lover climbs into a taxi wearing an oversized shawl and Jackie O sunglasses, and as Paris slowly fades away as she's driven to the airport, they might show a single dramatic tear sliding down her cheek? Yes, the image is dramatic and glamorous, but living it just plain sucks.

If one is undead and hell-bent on travel, I must suggest Virgin Airlines' Vamp Air. Trust Richard Branson to find a niche market involving carefully shaded windows and a selection of blood constantly warmed to exactly 98.6 degrees. Plus, few parents are willing to bring crying babies onto a plane full of vampires. I dragged my sunscreened, jet-lagged carcass through the Nashville International baggage claim at four A.M.

to find Zeb waiting for me, holding a sign that said, "Undead Tourism Bureau."

I propped my sunglasses on top of my head and smirked. "What were you going to do if someone else fit the bill?"

"What'd you bring me? What'd you bring me?" he asked, hopping up and down.

"Tiny liquor bottles from the mini-bar," I said, holding up my suitcase proudly and thumping it into his chest.

"Sadly, that's the same thing my uncle Ron gave me for Christmas." He took my sad little carry-on bag onto his shoulder.

"I wrapped them in hotel towels from four different countries," I added.

He grinned. "Excellent."

I actually had gotten him and Jolene fancy 500-thread-count sheets and some very expensive snacks from Harrods. The hotel towels were for me.

Zeb started the car and paid the exorbitant parking fee. "So, tell me everything. Where did you go? What did you see?"

"Went to some parties, met strange and snotty people. Saw some great museums and restaurants, but being in France and not being able to eat anything is downright masochistic. Oh, we saw *Carmen* performed in Vienna. Did you know the whole first song is about cigarette smoke?"

"I didn't know that," Zeb admitted. "But I'm surprised *you* didn't know that."

"Oh, ha-ha. So where's your lovely wife?" I asked as we pulled onto the interstate. "What's she doing letting you take off for Nashville after midnight? Doesn't she know you get lost?"

Zeb grimaced.

"What?" I asked. I knew things between Jolene and Zeb had been tense lately. They were trying to build a home on the land I'd given them as a wedding present. The house was slow to finish because Jolene's family was pressuring them to move back onto the McClaine family compound. Werewolves are notoriously territorial, and Jolene was the first McClaine to live "off-site" since they'd settled in the Hollow 200 years before. The family owned multiple businesses in the Hollow, including several construction firms. And what they didn't own they could influence with scary male-werewolf dominance. So, to say that it was difficult to get contractors to get contractors to show up, risking pissing off Jolene's kin, much less finish their work, was an understatement.

To top it off, the brand-newish trailer they'd been offered as an incentive to live on McClaine land had mysteriously been claimed by a recently divorced cousin from a neighboring county, leaving Zeb and Jolene to live in the camper recently vacated by Jolene's stoner cousin Larry. And one could only live in the close quarters of a cannabis-saturated camper for so long before one's marriage began to feel like the last half of *The Shining*.

I would say that Zeb was a saint to put up with such interference from his in-laws, but his family's no prize herd, either. Let's just say that one of the Lavelle family's favorite Christmas activities is to gather around the TV and watch their highlight reel from the "Rowdy Rural Towns" episode of *COPS*.

Oddly enough, it wasn't my thwarting Ginger Lavelle's plans to kill her son's will to wed a five-dollar hypnotist that resulted in her no longer speaking to me. To bastardize Harry Potter, I was Zeb's Secret Keeper for his honeymoon destination. Zeb told his family that he and Jolene were going to the mountain retreats of Gatlinburg, when he, in fact, took his blushing bride to Biloxi for a week of Gulf shrimp, putt-putt, and blessed silence. Their hotel information was sealed in an envelope and given to me with the instructions that it was to be opened only if someone was dead or incapacitated.

While contrite over her wacky antiwedding antics, Mama Ginger could only remain chastised for so long. Incensed that she could not locate her son after calling every hotel in Gatlinburg, Mama Ginger called me at home at seven A.M. to demand that I give her the location and phone number *right now,* because she was having chest pains and was being taken to the hospital. Used to this ploy, I refused. She then switched tactics and said that she needed the number because Zeb's father, Floyd, had dropped an automatic cigarette lighter into his lap while driving and was being treated for several third-degree burns in sensitive areas.

While that was far more plausible, I still withheld the number. And Mama Ginger announced that she would never speak to me again. I was not properly devastated by this announcement, which just made her madder. Whereas she'd long held out hope that Zeb and I would ond day wed, onnce she know about my "unfortunate condition," Mama Ginger was slightly ashamed to have wanted a vampire as an in-law. While she was less than civil to Jolene, she now preferred her daughter-in-law, because at least Jolene wasn't a vampire. Of course, Zeb hadn't yet broken the news about his new bride being a werewolf, but that was neither here nor there.

I'd promised myself that I was going to back off and stop interfering in Jolene and Zeb's relationship, but it was so much healthier than talking about my own relationship. So, I think I earned a pass just this once. "I was only gone for a few weeks. The honeymoon can't be over already."

Zeb sighed. "Marriage is a little harder than I thought it would be. Just normal stuff, you know. Things that get on each other's nerves." He began ticking off Jolene's numerous faults on his fingers. "She chews her fingernails *and* her toenails. She cannot stop herself from answering the questions from *Jeopardy* out loud, even when she knows she's wrong. She sheds. She puts ketchup on her egg rolls."

"Blasphemy." I shuddered. "And as much as it would be in my own personal interests to interfere with your marriage and reclaim your full attention, you do realize that you are married to arguably one of the most beautiful women on the planet. And you are a male kindergarten teacher who collects dolls."

"Action figures," he corrected.

"And she stuck with you, despite the fact that your mother tried to make casting changes in the bridal couple at her wedding rehearsal."

"Her family put out a bear trap for me!" he huffed.

"Well, that just means that your families cancel each other out."

He snickered, his expression softening. "She's pregnant."

My jaw actually hit the middle of my chest. "Well, that explains the egg rolls and ketchup."

My throat tightened at the thought of Zeb having a baby. This was so huge, the last step toward us really growing up and being old. I'll admit I was a little jealous. I was being left behind again. But as I'd discovered last year, when Zeb's mom dumped an infant on my doorstep in an attempt to jumpstart my biological clock, I am not cut out to nurture. And because I no longer have a pulse, I can't have children; which works out nicely.

"But this is a good thing, right?" I shook his shoulder. "I'm going to be an honorary aunt."

"It's a great thing, other than the idea of being responsible for a whole family sort of scaring the crap out of me. But we wanted to have kids right away and given how fertile her family is, we knew there was no contraception on earth that would work.

"But that's not really . . . Her mother comes over every single day. Her aunts are always bringing over food or they're putting up homemade curtains or they're moving our dishes around in the cabinets without asking. And Jolene just lets them. And the men! If they don't back off and let a contractor come out to finish the house, we're going to be raising their grandchild in a pot-soaked RV; is that what they want? I'm just frustrated and feel . . . impotent."

"Well, obviously, that's not the case. When is she due?"

"In about four months," he said.

"What? You guys were pregnant before the wedding? And you didn't tell me?"

Zeb rolled his eyes. "It's a werewolf thing. The average wolf pregnancy is only about sixty days. Werewolves sort of split the difference with five months."

"Wow. You have very little time to get ready for this baby—babies? How many kids is Jolene going to have? Is it going to be like a litter?"

Zeb looked horror-struck.

"Maybe I should drive," I suggested.

"No, let's talk about why you think Gabriel would suddenly start cheating on you. That will keep me awake."

"Let's not," I told him. "I don't want to rehash the whole thing. I just want to pretend it didn't happen."

"Because denial usually works so well for you."

"I'm going to deny that I just heard that. Should we stop by the shop?" I asked.

"Nah. We boarded up the windows. Besides, the sun's going to rise soon." He nodded to the lightening blue-gray sky on the horizon. "We'll have just enough time to get you home."

As the sky turned toward lilac, I snuggled under a blanket and dozed the last hour or so before we reached the family manse, River Oaks. More English country cottage than sprawling Georgian plantation, River Oaks is at its heart just an old family home that happened to be built before the Civil War. Despite having spent the last few weeks in buildings that were much older and far more elegant, my house had never seemed so beautiful.

I kissed Zeb's cheeks, mumbled a good night, and dashed for the door with the blanket over my head. In my room, on sheets that were weeks old and slightly musty, I lay down and, for reasons I hadn't quite processed yet, cried.